INVADER ZIM

™

VOLUME 1

Created by
JHONEN VASQUEZ

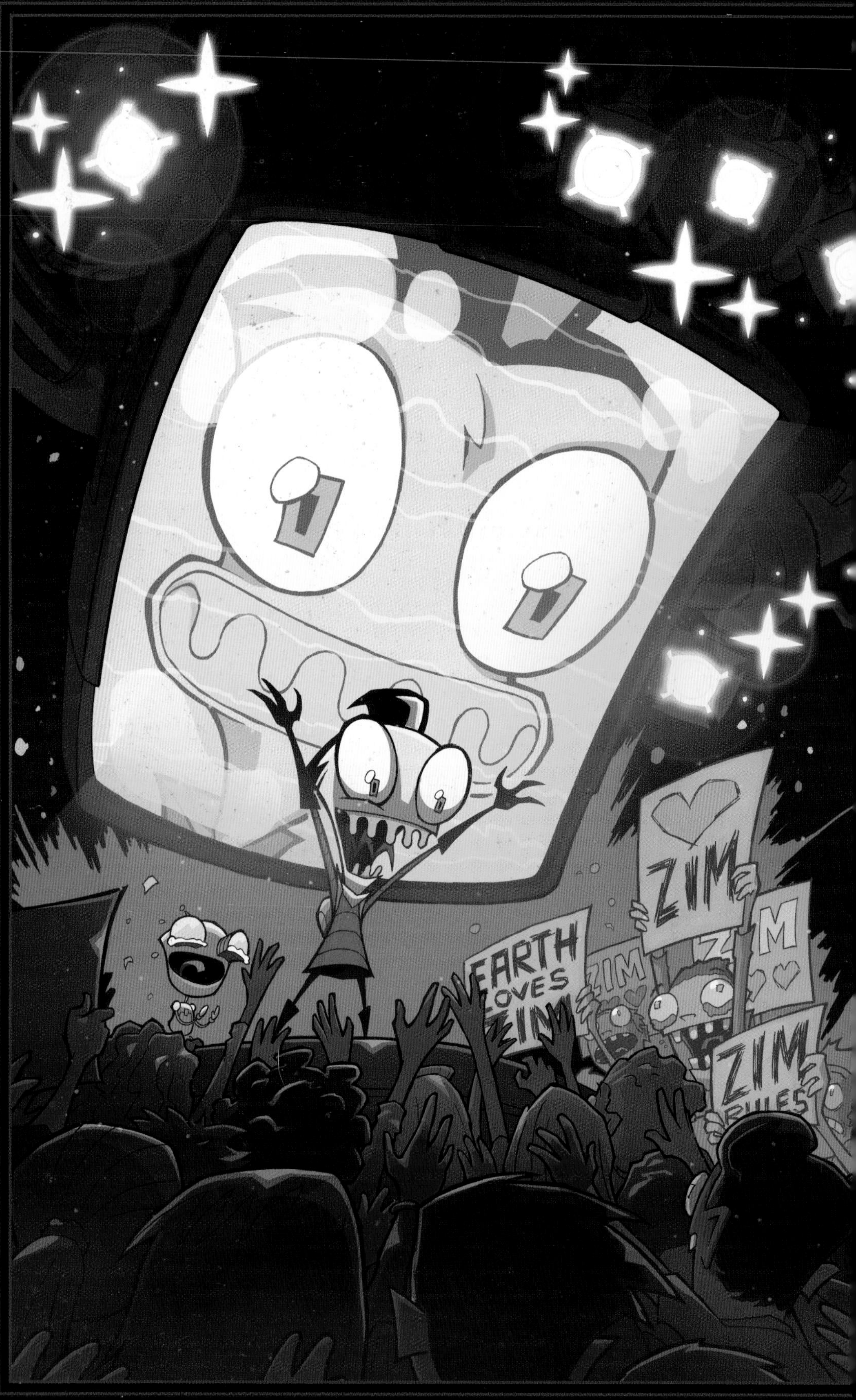
ZIM
EARTH
ZIM
ZIM

VOLUME 1

Writer, Chapter 1, 2, 5 **JHONEN VASQUEZ**

Writer, Chapter 2, 3, 4 **ERIC TRUEHEART**

Penciller **AARON ALEXOVICH**   Inker **MEGAN LAWTON**

Colorist, Chapter 1, 2 **SIMON "HUTT" TROUSSELLIER**

lorist, Chapter 3 **RIKKI SIMONS**   Colorist, Chapter 4 **MILDRED LOUIS**

Colorist, Chapter 5 **CASSIE KELLY**   Color Consultant **J. R. GOLDBERG**

Letterer **WARREN WUCINICH**

Front and back cover illustrated by **AARON ALEXOVICH** and **SIMON TROUSSELLIER**

Fried Pie variant cover illustrated by **JHONEN VASQUEZ**

Oni Press variant cover illustrated by **JHONEN VASQUEZ** and **J. R. GOLDBERG**

Hot Topic variant cover illustrated by **AARON ALEXOVICH**

Color flats **ANDERSON CARMAN, JONATHAN MULLINS,
RIKKI SIMONS, TAVISHA WOLFGARTH-SIMONS**

Control Brain **JHONEN VASQUEZ**   Designed by **KEITH WOOD**

Edited by **ROBIN HERRERA & JAMES LUCAS JONES**

AN ONI PRESS PUBLICATION

Published by Oni Press, Inc.

publisher **JOE NOZEMACK**

editor in chief **JAMES LUCAS JONES**

director of sales **CHEYENNE ALLOTT**

marketing coordinator **AMBER O'NEILL**

publicity coordinator **RACHEL REED**

director of design & production **TROY LOOK**

graphic designer **HILARY THOMPSON**

digital art technician **JARED JONES**

managing editor **ARI YARWOOD**

senior editor **CHARLIE CHU**

editor **ROBIN HERRERA**

editorial assistant **BESS PALLARES**

director of logistics **BRAD ROOKS**

office assistant **JUNG LEE**

This volume collects issues #1-5 of the
Oni Press series *Invader Zim*.

Oni Press, Inc.
1305 SE Martin Luther King Jr. Blvd.
Suite A
Portland, OR 97214
USA

onipress.com • facebook.com/onipress • twitter.com/onipress
onipress.tumblr.com • instagram.com/onipress

First edition: January 2016

ISBN 978-1-62010-293-0 • eISBN 978-1-62010-294-7
Fried Pie Exclusive ISBN: 978-1-62010-308-1
Hot Topic Exclusive ISBN: 978-1-62010-325-8

nickelodeon

Library of Congress Control Number: 2015950610

10 9 8 7 6 5 4 3 2

PRINTED IN CHINA.

PREVIOUSLY ON INVADER ZIM

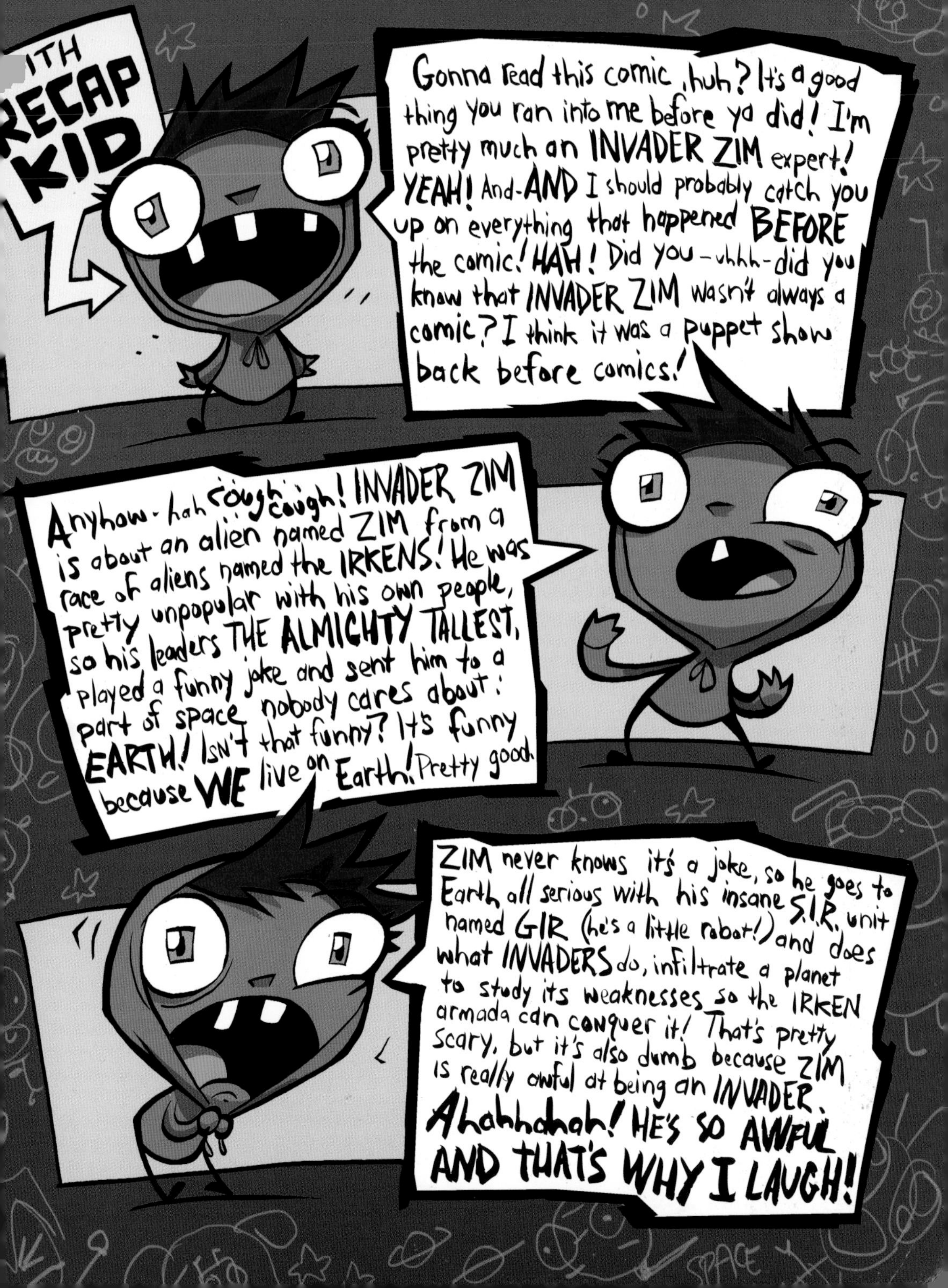

WITH RECAP KID
Gonna read this comic, huh? It's a good thing you ran into me before ya did! I'm pretty much an INVADER ZIM expert! YEAH! And-AND I should probably catch you up on everything that happened BEFORE the comic! HAH! Did you-uhhh-did you know that INVADER ZIM wasn't always a comic? I think it was a puppet show back before comics!
Anyhow-hah cough cough! INVADER ZIM is about an alien named ZIM from a race of aliens named the IRKENS! He was pretty unpopular with his own people, so his leaders THE ALMIGHTY TALLEST, played a funny joke and sent him to a part of space nobody cares about: EARTH! Isn't that funny? It's funny because WE live on Earth! Pretty good.
ZIM never knows it's a joke, so he goes to Earth all serious with his insane S.I.R. unit named GIR (he's a little robot!) and does what INVADERS do, infiltrate a planet to study its weaknesses so the IRKEN armada can conquer it! That's pretty scary, but it's also dumb because ZIM is really awful at being an INVADER. Ahahhahah! HE'S SO AWFUL AND THAT'S WHY I LAUGH!

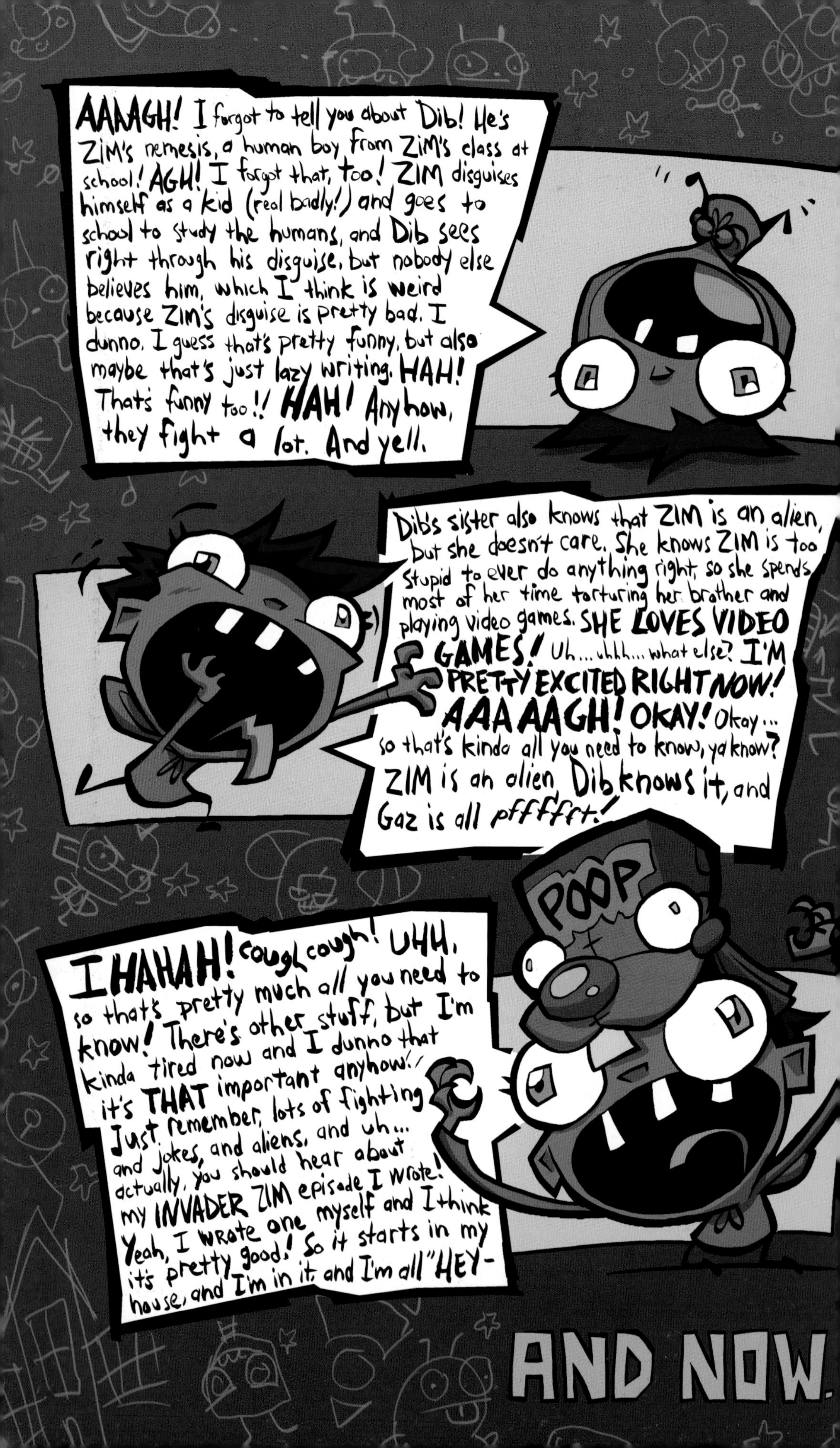
AAAAGH! I forgot to tell you about Dib! He's ZIM's nemesis, a human boy from ZIM's class at school! AGH! I forgot that, too! ZIM disguises himself as a kid (real badly!) and goes to school to study the humans, and Dib sees right through his disguise, but nobody else believes him, which I think is weird because ZIM's disguise is pretty bad. I dunno. I guess that's pretty funny, but also maybe that's just lazy writing. HAH! That's funny too!! HAH! Anyhow, they fight a lot. And yell.
Dib's sister also knows that ZIM is an alien, but she doesn't care. She knows ZIM is too stupid to ever do anything right, so she spends most of her time torturing her brother and playing video games. SHE LOVES VIDEO GAMES! Uh... uhhh... what else? I'M PRETTY EXCITED RIGHT NOW! AAAAAGH! OKAY! Okay... so that's kinda all you need to know, ya know? ZIM is an alien, Dib knows it, and Gaz is all pffffft!
POOP
IHAHAH! cough cough! UHH, so that's pretty much all you need to know! There's other stuff, but I'm kinda tired now and I dunno that it's THAT important anyhow. Just remember, lots of fighting and jokes, and aliens, and uh... actually, you should hear about my INVADER ZIM episode I wrote! Yeah, I wrote one myself and I think it's pretty good! So it starts in my house, and I'm in it, and I'm all "HEY-
AND NOW.

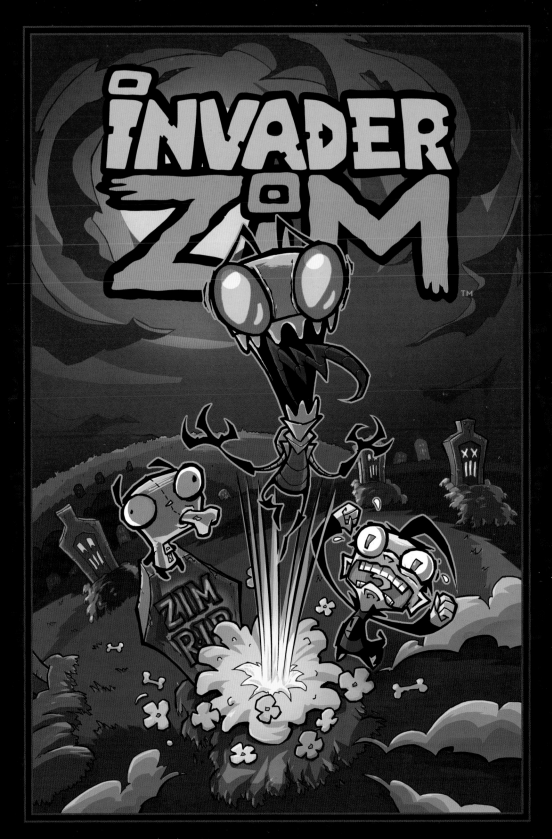

 CHAPTER: 1

illustration by **AARON ALEXOVICH** and **RIKKI SIMONS**

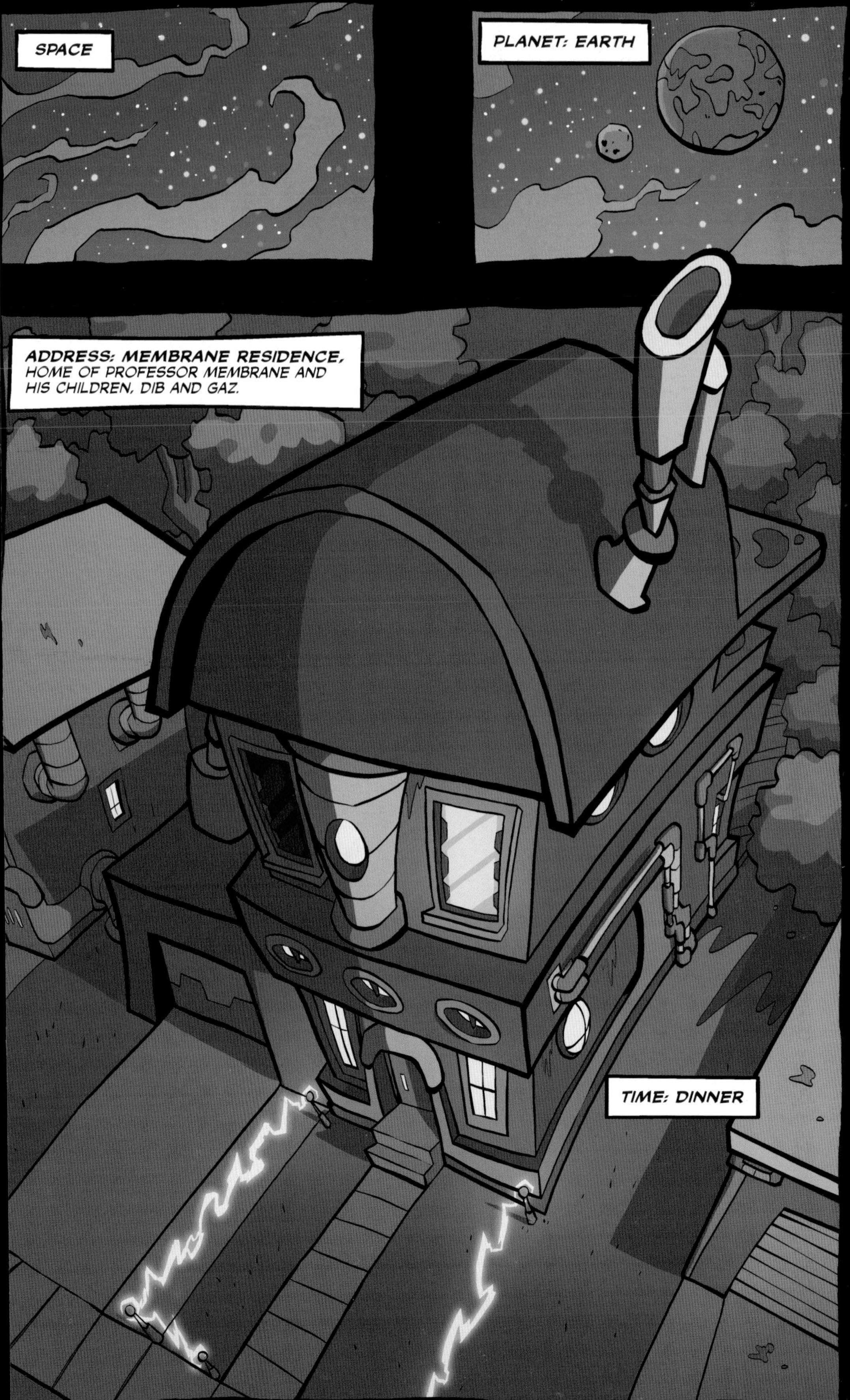
SPACE
PLANET: EARTH
ADDRESS: MEMBRANE RESIDENCE,
HOME OF PROFESSOR MEMBRANE AND
HIS CHILDREN, DIB AND GAZ.
TIME: DINNER

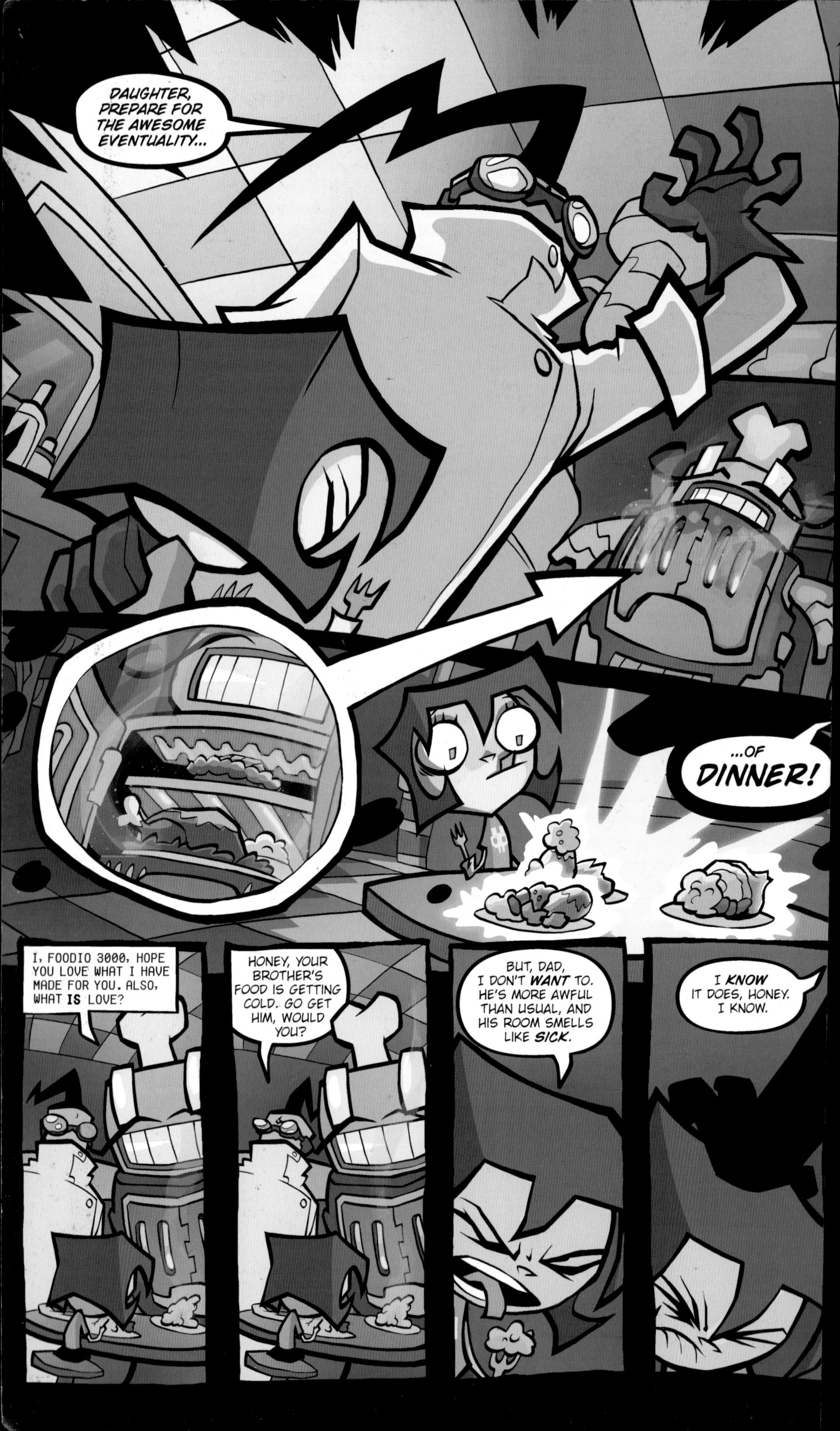
DAUGHTER, PREPARE FOR THE AWESOME EVENTUALITY...
...OF DINNER!
I, FOODIO 3000, HOPE YOU LOVE WHAT I HAVE MADE FOR YOU. ALSO, WHAT IS LOVE?
HONEY, YOUR BROTHER'S FOOD IS GETTING COLD. GO GET HIM, WOULD YOU?
BUT, DAD, I DON'T WANT TO. HE'S MORE AWFUL THAN USUAL, AND HIS ROOM SMELLS LIKE SICK.
I KNOW IT DOES, HONEY. I KNOW.

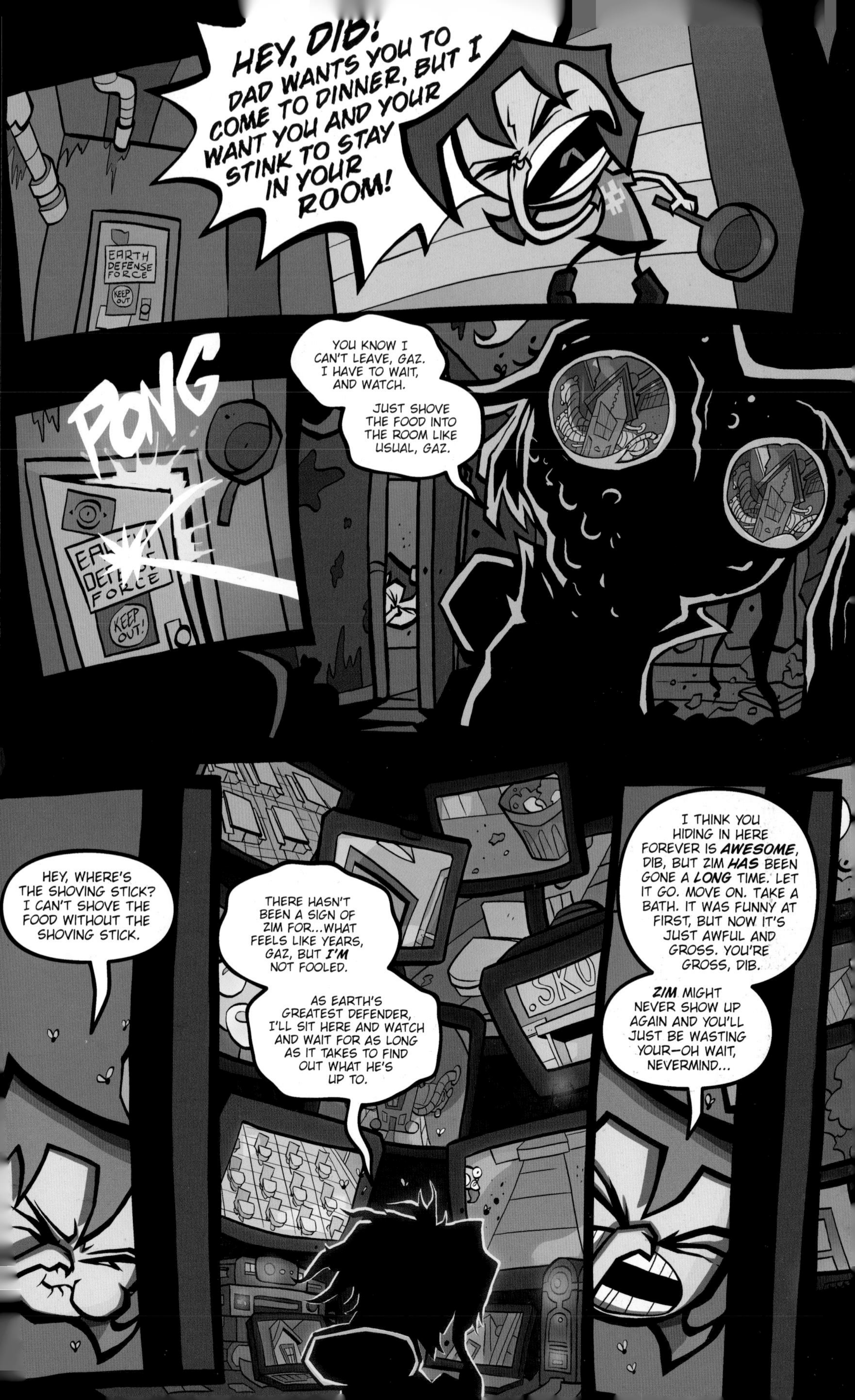
HEY, DIB! DAD WANTS YOU TO COME TO DINNER, BUT I WANT YOU AND YOUR STINK TO STAY IN YOUR ROOM!
EARTH DEFENSE FORCE
KEEP OUT
PONG
YOU KNOW I CAN'T LEAVE, GAZ. I HAVE TO WAIT, AND WATCH.
JUST SHOVE THE FOOD INTO THE ROOM LIKE USUAL, GAZ.
EARTH DEFENSE FORCE
KEEP OUT!
HEY, WHERE'S THE SHOVING STICK? I CAN'T SHOVE THE FOOD WITHOUT THE SHOVING STICK.
THERE HASN'T BEEN A SIGN OF ZIM FOR...WHAT FEELS LIKE YEARS, GAZ, BUT I'M NOT FOOLED.
AS EARTH'S GREATEST DEFENDER, I'LL SIT HERE AND WATCH AND WAIT FOR AS LONG AS IT TAKES TO FIND OUT WHAT HE'S UP TO.
I THINK YOU HIDING IN HERE FOREVER IS AWESOME, DIB, BUT ZIM HAS BEEN GONE A LONG TIME. LET IT GO. MOVE ON. TAKE A BATH. IT WAS FUNNY AT FIRST, BUT NOW IT'S JUST AWFUL AND GROSS. YOU'RE GROSS, DIB.
ZIM MIGHT NEVER SHOW UP AGAIN AND YOU'LL JUST BE WASTING YOUR—OH WAIT, NEVERMIND...

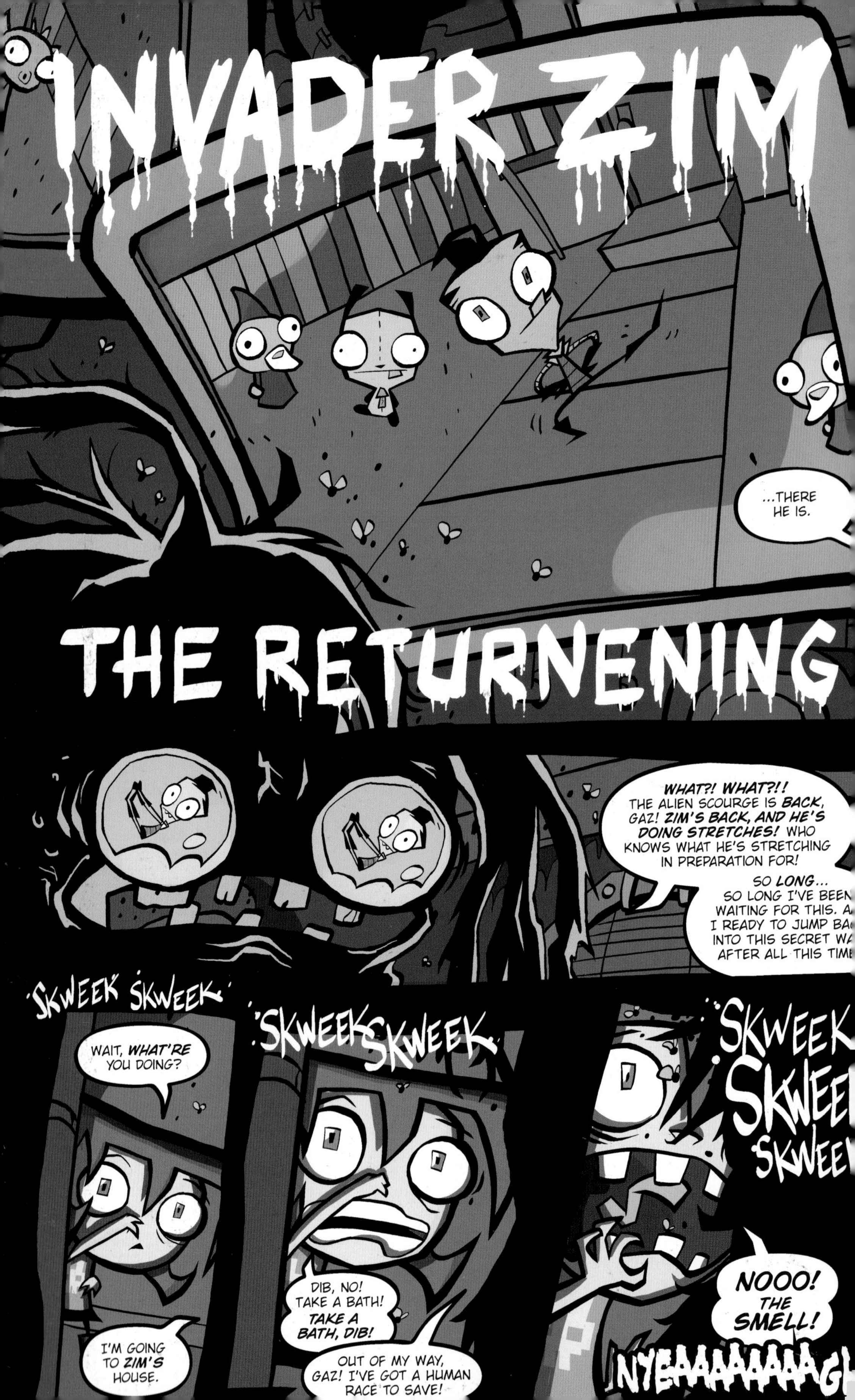
INVADER ZIM
...THERE HE IS.
THE RETURNENING
WHAT?! WHAT?!! THE ALIEN SCOURGE IS BACK, GAZ! ZIM'S BACK, AND HE'S DOING STRETCHES! WHO KNOWS WHAT HE'S STRETCHING IN PREPARATION FOR!
SO LONG... SO LONG I'VE BEEN WAITING FOR THIS. A I READY TO JUMP BA INTO THIS SECRET WA AFTER ALL THIS TIM
SKWEEK SKWEEK
WAIT, WHAT'RE YOU DOING?
I'M GOING TO ZIM'S HOUSE.
SKWEEK SKWEEK
DIB, NO! TAKE A BATH! TAKE A BATH, DIB!
OUT OF MY WAY, GAZ! I'VE GOT A HUMAN RACE TO SAVE!
SKWEEK SKWEE SKWEE
NOOO! THE SMELL!
NYEAAAAAAAGH

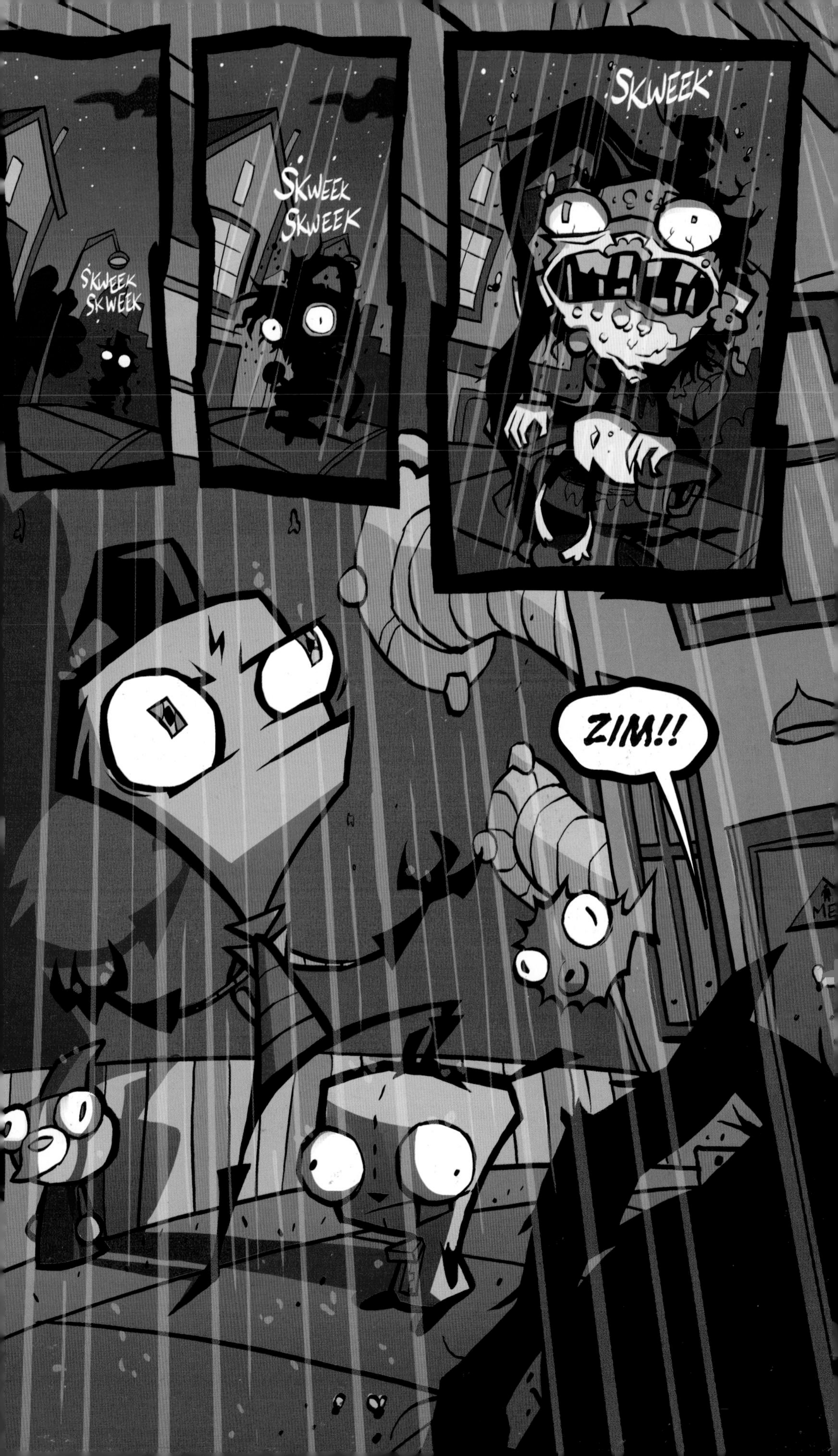
SKWEEK SKWEEK
SKWEEK SKWEEK
SKWEEK
ZIM!!

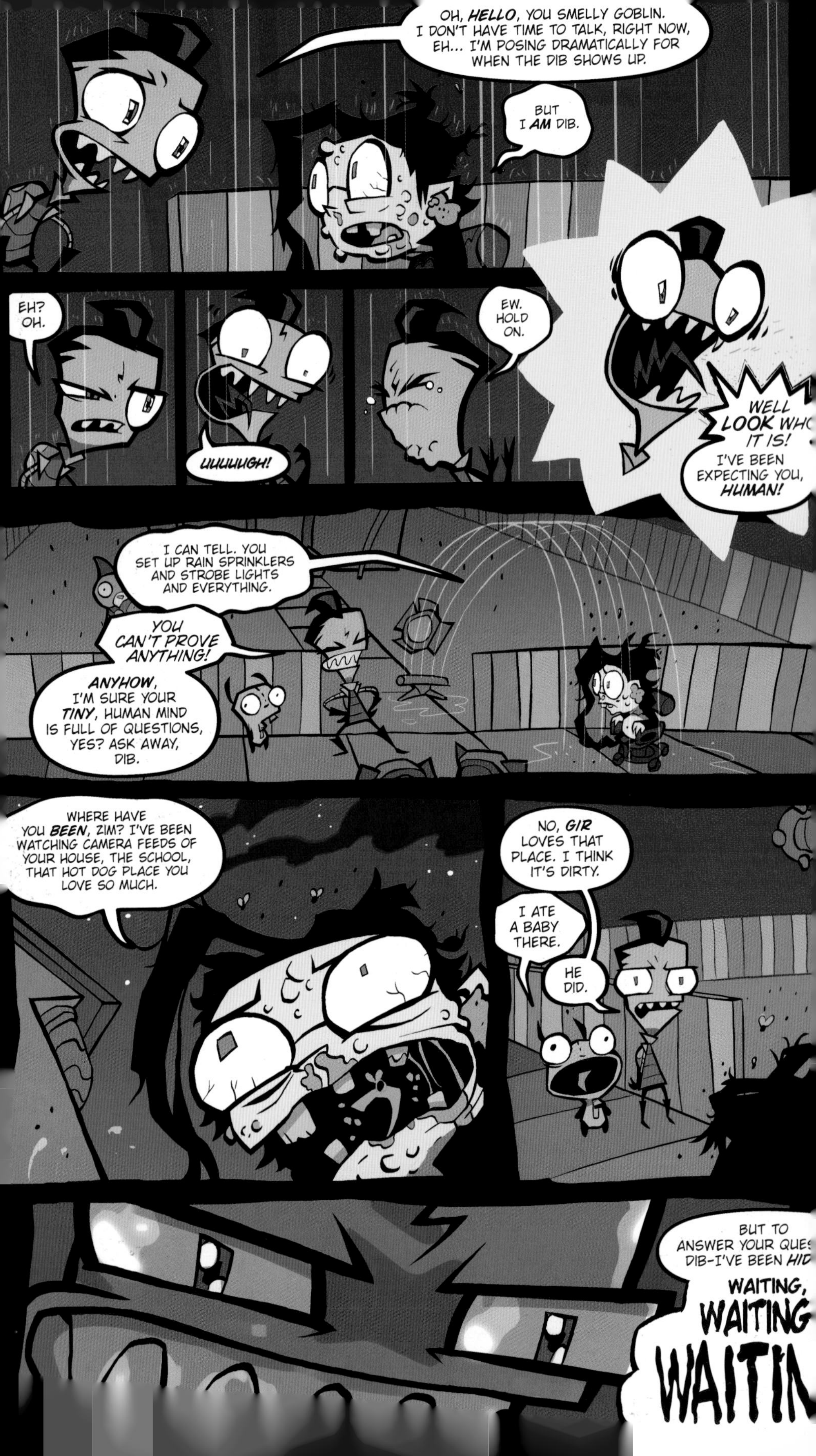

OH, HELLO, YOU SMELLY GOBLIN. I DON'T HAVE TIME TO TALK, RIGHT NOW, EH... I'M POSING DRAMATICALLY FOR WHEN THE DIB SHOWS UP.
BUT I AM DIB.
EH? OH.
UUUUUGH!
EW. HOLD ON.
WELL LOOK WHO IT IS!
I'VE BEEN EXPECTING YOU, HUMAN!
I CAN TELL. YOU SET UP RAIN SPRINKLERS AND STROBE LIGHTS AND EVERYTHING.
YOU CAN'T PROVE ANYTHING!
ANYHOW, I'M SURE YOUR TINY, HUMAN MIND IS FULL OF QUESTIONS, YES? ASK AWAY, DIB.
WHERE HAVE YOU BEEN, ZIM? I'VE BEEN WATCHING CAMERA FEEDS OF YOUR HOUSE, THE SCHOOL, THAT HOT DOG PLACE YOU LOVE SO MUCH.
NO, GIR LOVES THAT PLACE. I THINK IT'S DIRTY.
I ATE A BABY THERE.
HE DID.
BUT TO ANSWER YOUR QUES
DIB-I'VE BEEN HID
WAITING,
WAITING
WAITIN

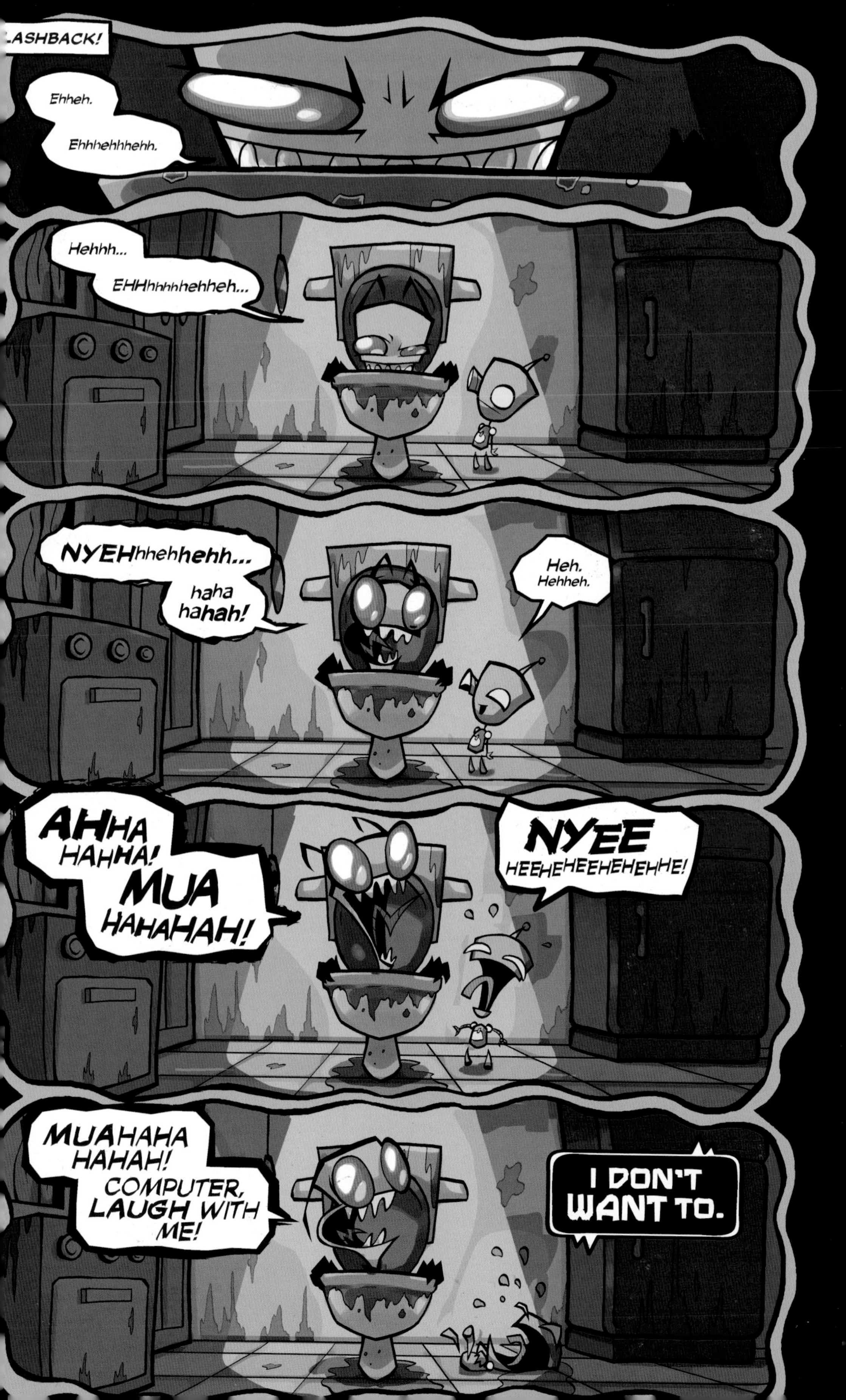

LASHBACK!
Ehhheh.
Ehhhehhhehh.
Hehhh...
EHHhhhhhehheh...
NYEHhhehhehh...
haha hahah!
Heh. Hehheh.
AHHA HAHHA! MUA HAHAHAH!
NYEE HEEHEHEEHEHEHHE!
MUAHAHA HAHAH! COMPUTER, LAUGH WITH ME!
I DON'T WANT TO.

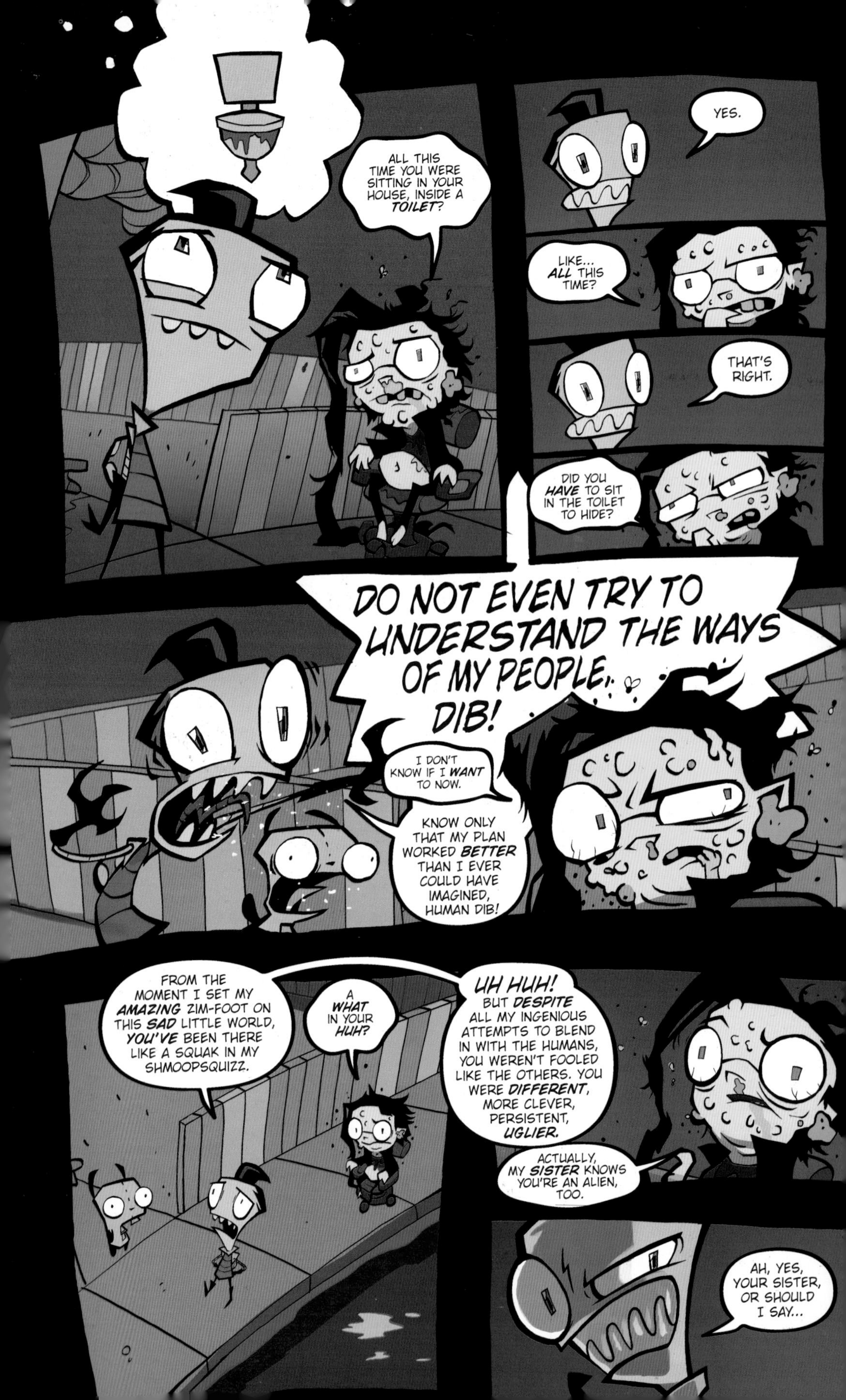
ALL THIS TIME YOU WERE SITTING IN YOUR HOUSE, INSIDE A TOILET?
YES.
LIKE... ALL THIS TIME?
THAT'S RIGHT.
DID YOU HAVE TO SIT IN THE TOILET TO HIDE?
DO NOT EVEN TRY TO UNDERSTAND THE WAYS OF MY PEOPLE.. DIB!
I DON'T KNOW IF I WANT TO NOW.
KNOW ONLY THAT MY PLAN WORKED BETTER THAN I EVER COULD HAVE IMAGINED, HUMAN DIB!
FROM THE MOMENT I SET MY AMAZING ZIM-FOOT ON THIS SAD LITTLE WORLD, YOU'VE BEEN THERE LIKE A SQUAK IN MY SHMOOPSQUIZZ.
A WHAT IN YOUR HUH?
UH HUH! BUT DESPITE ALL MY INGENIOUS ATTEMPTS TO BLEND IN WITH THE HUMANS, YOU WEREN'T FOOLED LIKE THE OTHERS. YOU WERE DIFFERENT, MORE CLEVER, PERSISTENT, UGLIER.
ACTUALLY, MY SISTER KNOWS YOU'RE AN ALIEN, TOO.
AH, YES, YOUR SISTER, OR SHOULD I SAY...

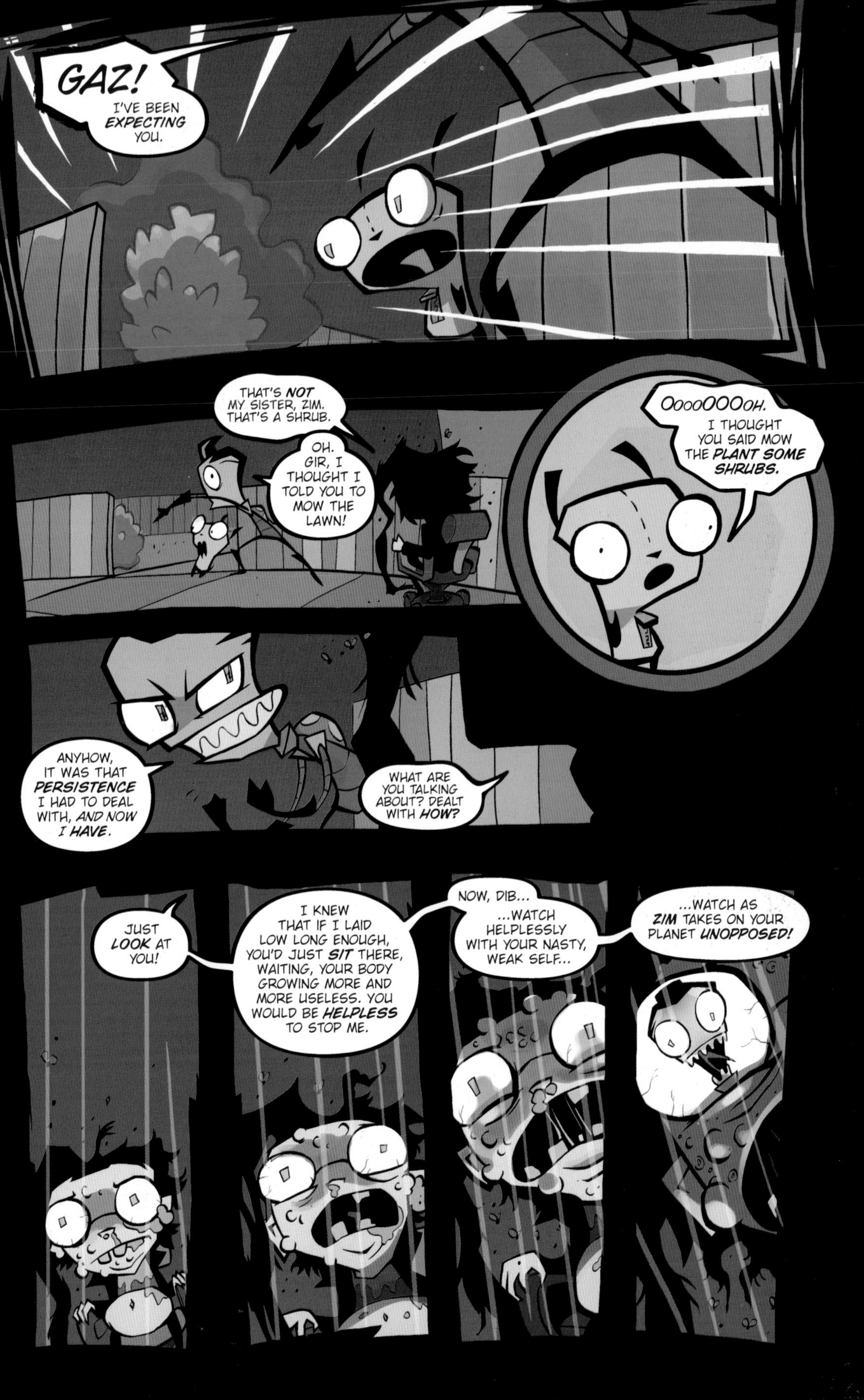
GAZ! I'VE BEEN EXPECTING YOU.
THAT'S NOT MY SISTER, ZIM. THAT'S A SHRUB.
OH. GIR, I THOUGHT I TOLD YOU TO MOW THE LAWN!
OooOOOOOH. I THOUGHT YOU SAID MOW THE PLANT SOME SHRUBS.
ANYHOW, IT WAS THAT PERSISTENCE I HAD TO DEAL WITH, AND NOW I HAVE.
WHAT ARE YOU TALKING ABOUT? DEALT WITH HOW?
JUST LOOK AT YOU!
I KNEW THAT IF I LAID LOW LONG ENOUGH, YOU'D JUST SIT THERE, WAITING, YOUR BODY GROWING MORE AND MORE USELESS. YOU WOULD BE HELPLESS TO STOP ME.
NOW, DIB...
...WATCH HELPLESSLY WITH YOUR NASTY, WEAK SELF...
...WATCH AS ZIM TAKES ON YOUR PLANET UNOPPOSED!

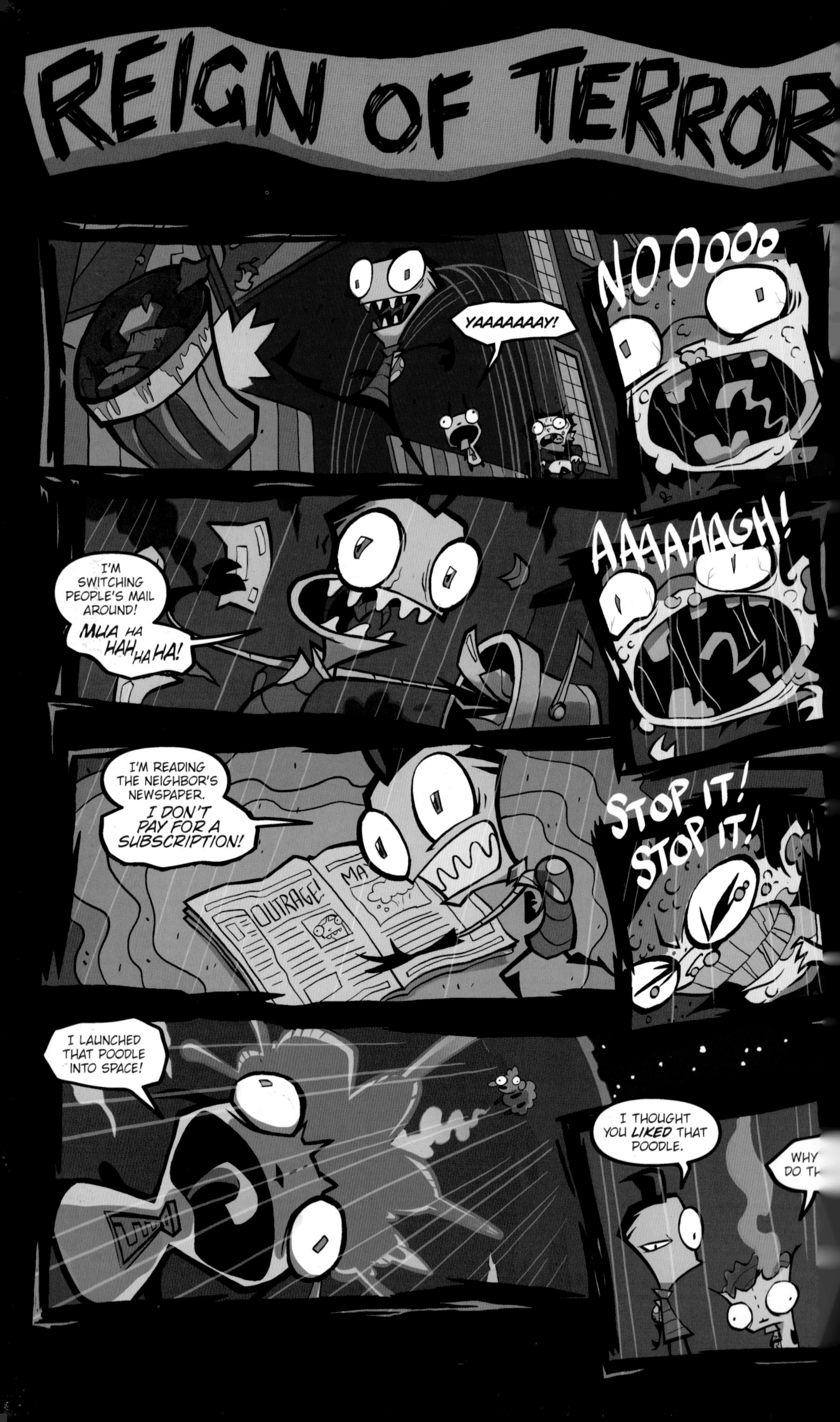

REIGN OF TERROR
YAAAAAAAY!
NOOOOOO
I'M SWITCHING PEOPLE'S MAIL AROUND! MUA HA HAH HA HA!
AAAAAAGH!
I'M READING THE NEIGHBOR'S NEWSPAPER. I DON'T PAY FOR A SUBSCRIPTION!
OUTRAGE!
STOP IT! STOP IT!
I LAUNCHED THAT POODLE INTO SPACE!
I THOUGHT YOU LIKED THAT POODLE.

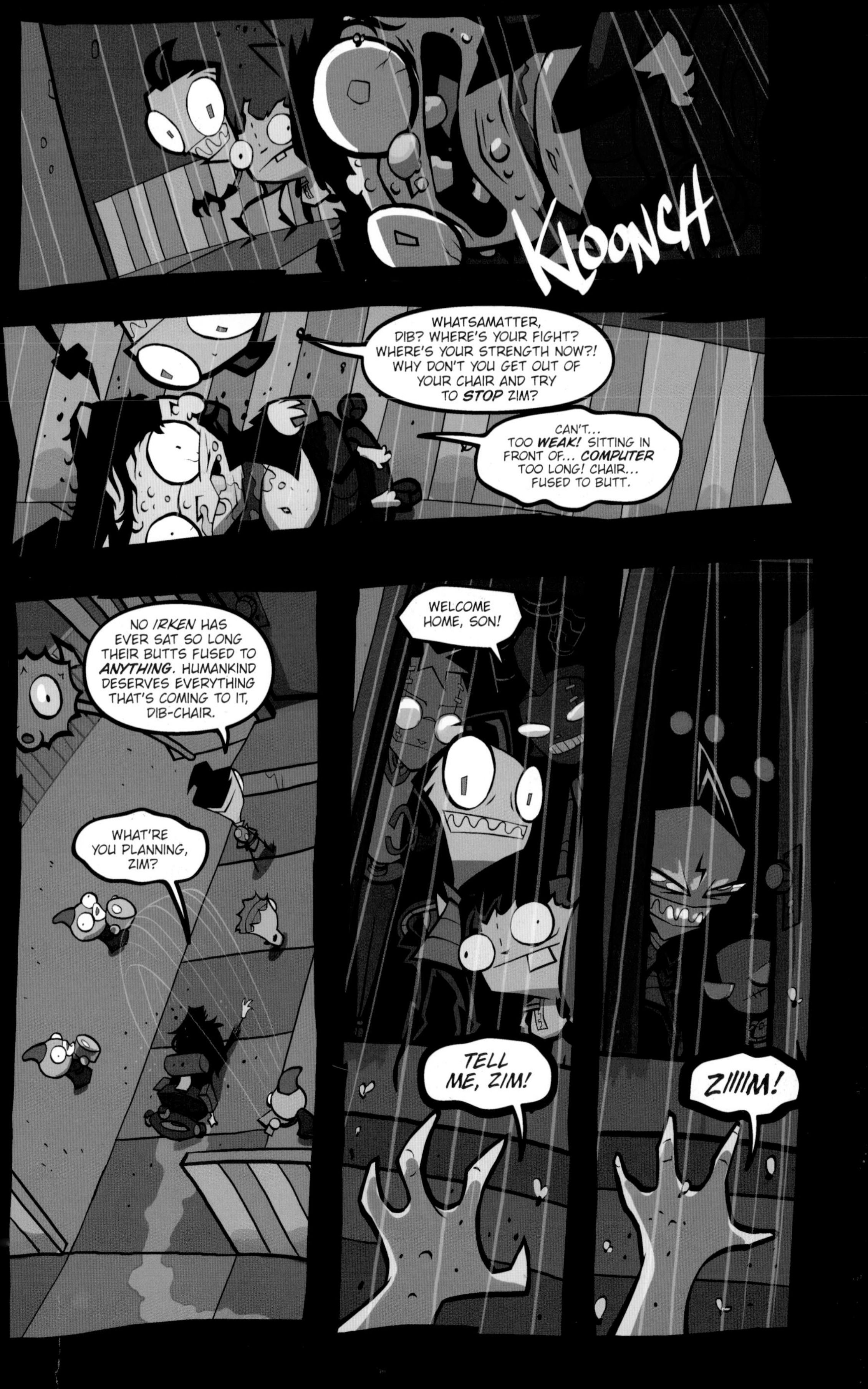
KLOONCH
WHATSAMATTER, DIB? WHERE'S YOUR FIGHT? WHERE'S YOUR STRENGTH NOW?! WHY DON'T YOU GET OUT OF YOUR CHAIR AND TRY TO STOP ZIM?
CAN'T... TOO WEAK! SITTING IN FRONT OF... COMPUTER TOO LONG! CHAIR... FUSED TO BUTT.
NO IRKEN HAS EVER SAT SO LONG THEIR BUTTS FUSED TO ANYTHING. HUMANKIND DESERVES EVERYTHING THAT'S COMING TO IT, DIB-CHAIR.
WHAT'RE YOU PLANNING, ZIM?
WELCOME HOME, SON!
TELL ME, ZIM!
ZIIIIM!

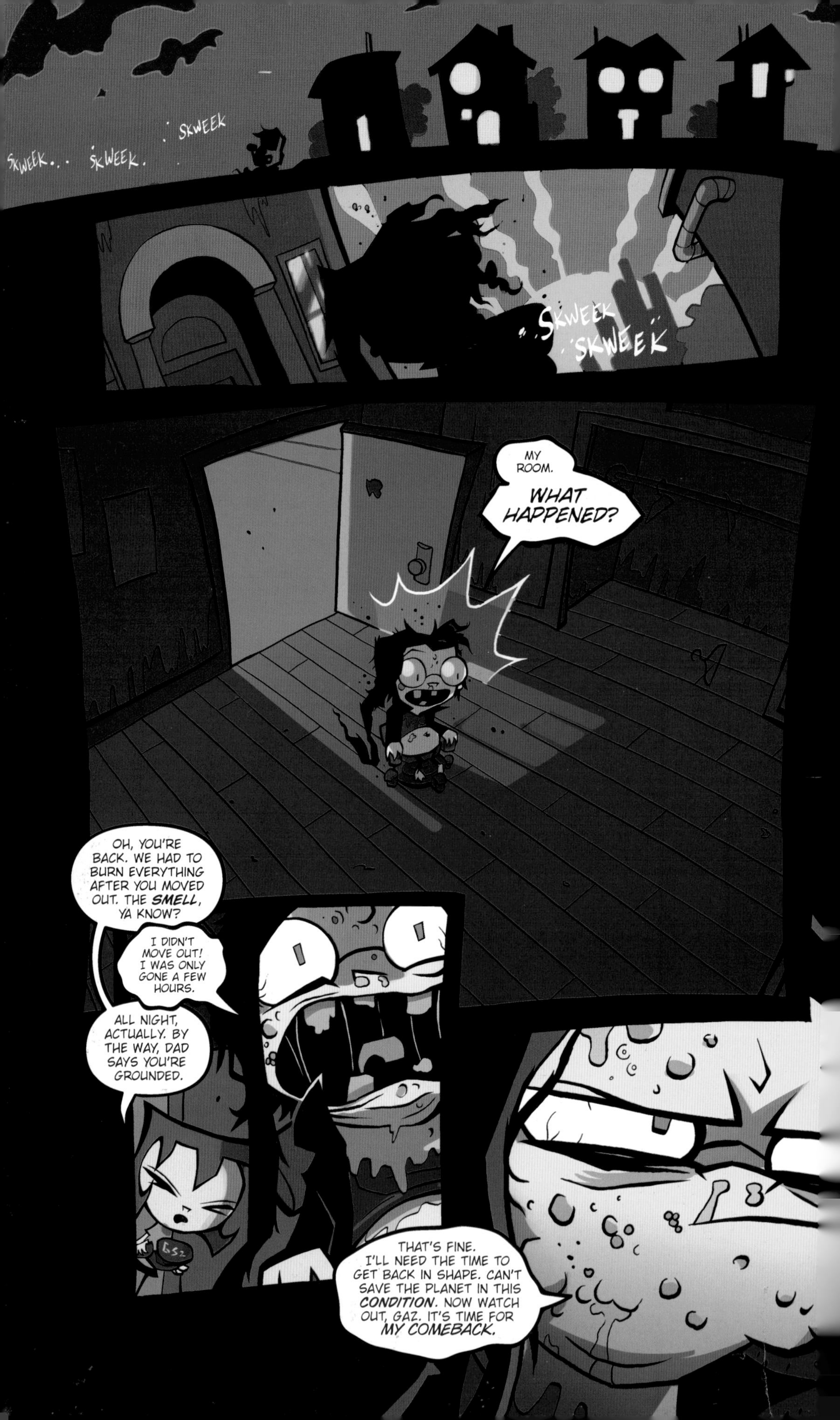
SKWEEK... SKWEEK. . SKWEEK
SKWEEK SKWEEK
MY ROOM. WHAT HAPPENED?
OH, YOU'RE BACK. WE HAD TO BURN EVERYTHING AFTER YOU MOVED OUT. THE SMELL, YA KNOW?
I DIDN'T MOVE OUT! I WAS ONLY GONE A FEW HOURS.
ALL NIGHT, ACTUALLY. BY THE WAY, DAD SAYS YOU'RE GROUNDED.
THAT'S FINE. I'LL NEED THE TIME TO GET BACK IN SHAPE. CAN'T SAVE THE PLANET IN THIS CONDITION. NOW WATCH OUT, GAZ. IT'S TIME FOR MY COMEBACK.

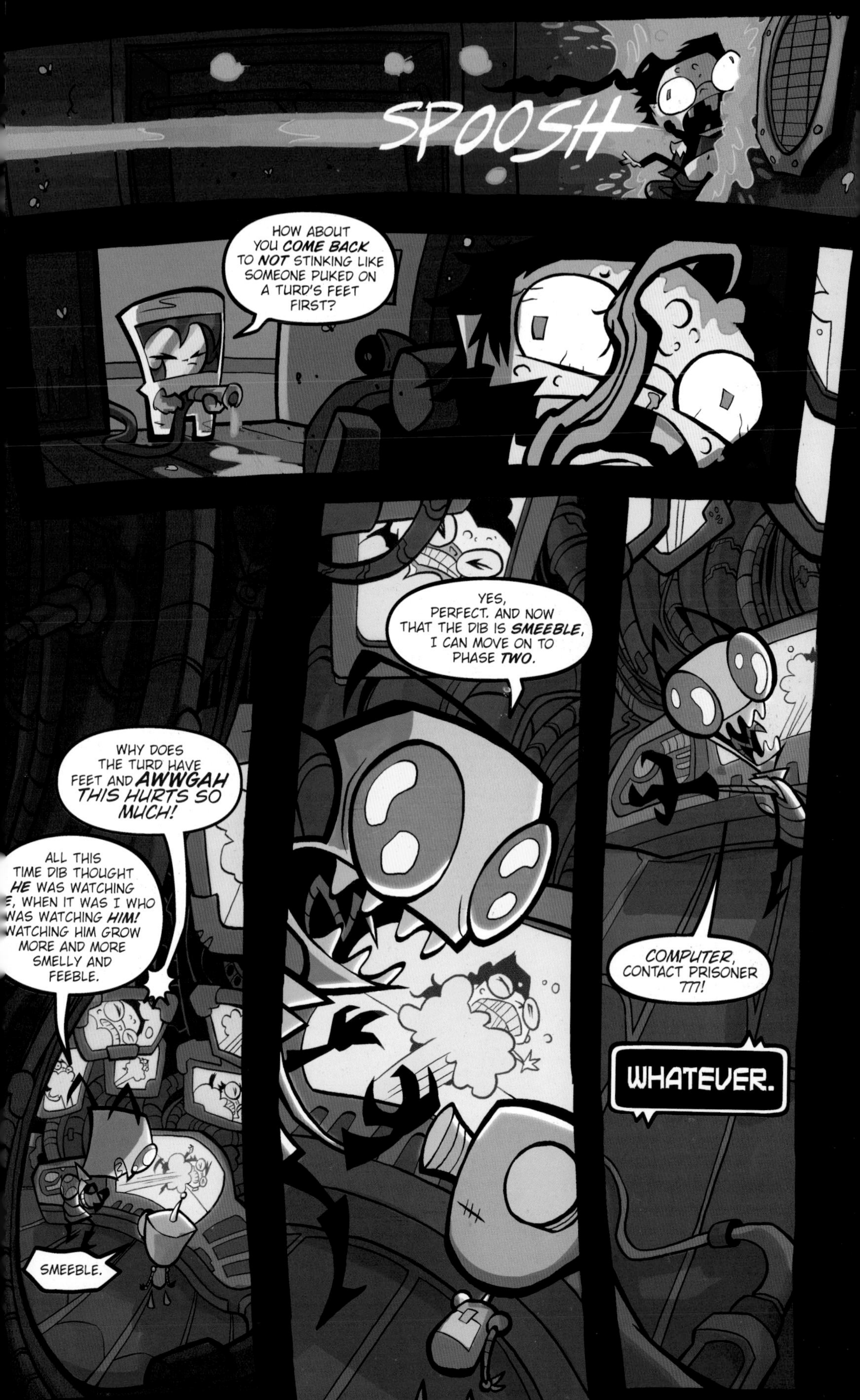
SPOOSH
HOW ABOUT YOU COME BACK TO NOT STINKING LIKE SOMEONE PUKED ON A TURD'S FEET FIRST?
YES, PERFECT. AND NOW THAT THE DIB IS SMEEBLE, I CAN MOVE ON TO PHASE TWO.
WHY DOES THE TURD HAVE FEET AND AWWGAH THIS HURTS SO MUCH!
ALL THIS TIME DIB THOUGHT HE WAS WATCHING E, WHEN IT WAS I WHO WAS WATCHING HIM! WATCHING HIM GROW MORE AND MORE SMELLY AND FEEBLE.
SMEEBLE.
COMPUTER, CONTACT PRISONER 777!
WHATEVER.

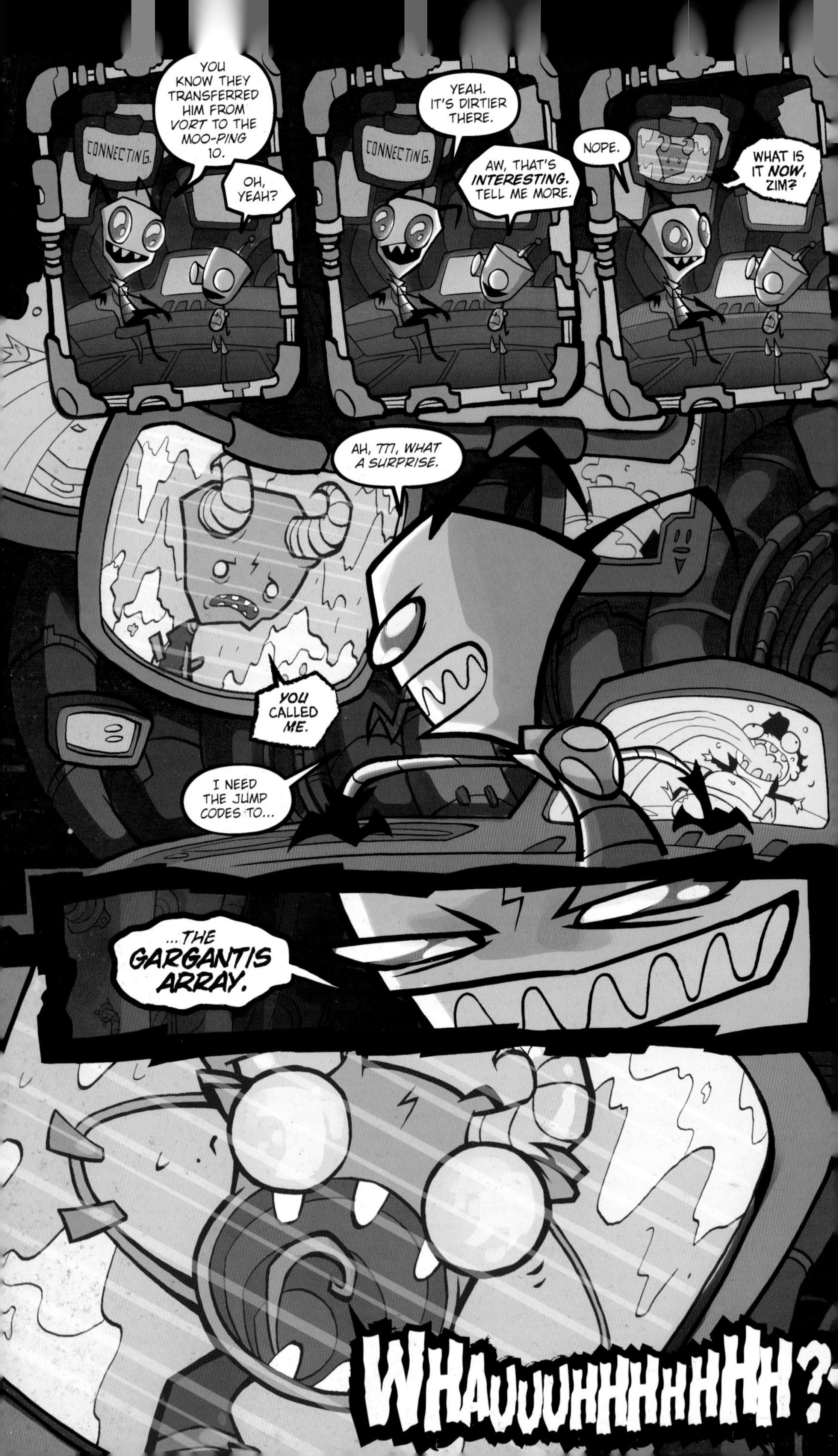
CONNECTING.
YOU KNOW THEY TRANSFERRED HIM FROM VORT TO THE MOO-PING 10.
OH, YEAH?
CONNECTING.
YEAH. IT'S DIRTIER THERE.
AW, THAT'S INTERESTING. TELL ME MORE.
NOPE.
WHAT IS IT NOW, ZIM?
AH, TTT, WHAT A SURPRISE.
YOU CALLED ME.
I NEED THE JUMP CODES TO...
...THE GARGANTIS ARRAY.
WHAUUUHHHHHHH?

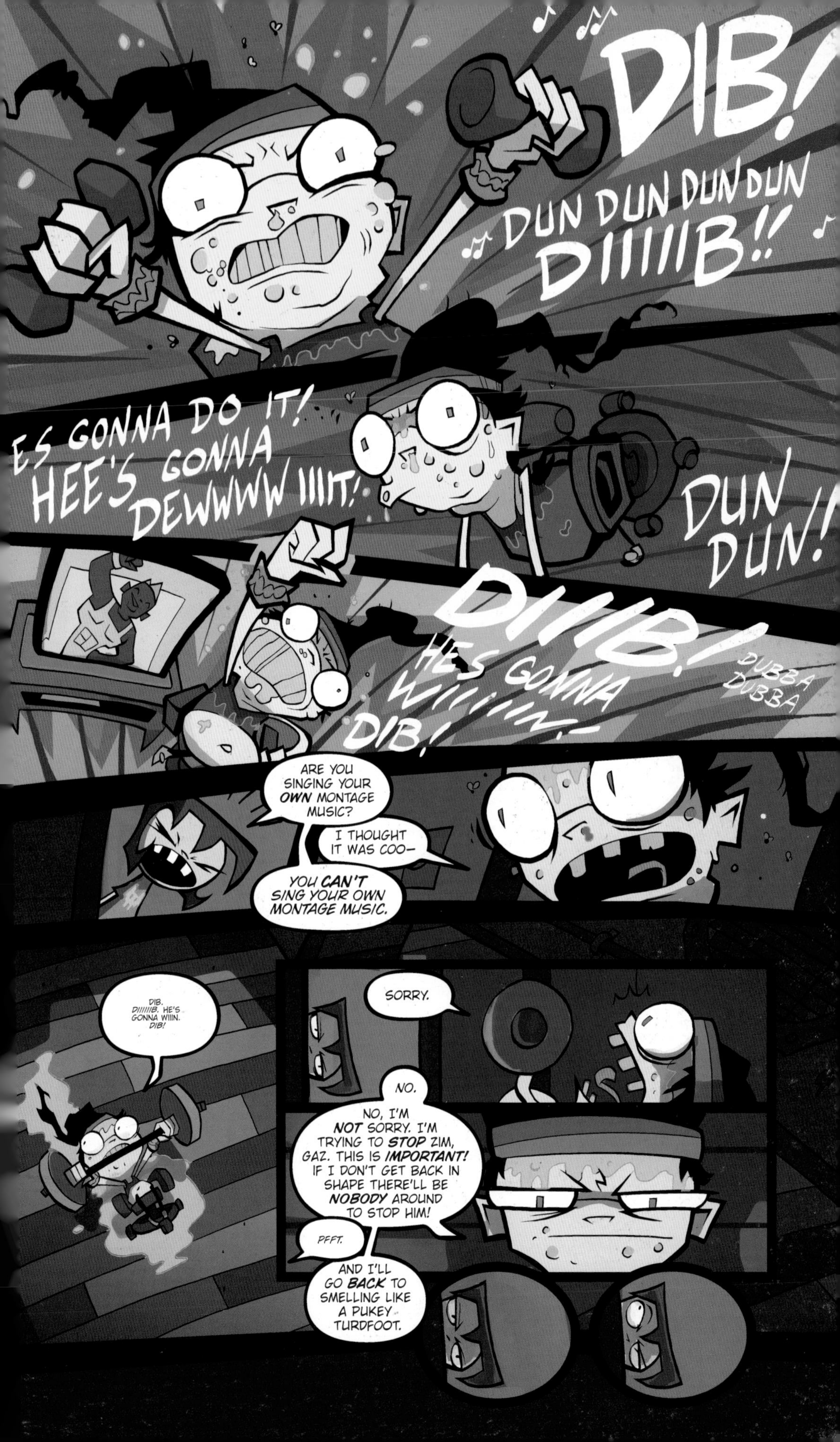
DIB!
DUN DUN DUN DUN
DIIIIIB!!
ES GONNA DO IT!
HEE'S GONNA DEWWWW IIIIT!
DUN DUN!
DIIIB!
HE'S GONNA WIIIIN-
DIB!
DUBBA DUBBA
ARE YOU SINGING YOUR OWN MONTAGE MUSIC?
I THOUGHT IT WAS COO—
YOU CAN'T SING YOUR OWN MONTAGE MUSIC.
DIB. DIIIIIIB. HE'S GONNA WIIIN. DIB!
SORRY.
NO.
NO, I'M NOT SORRY. I'M TRYING TO STOP ZIM, GAZ. THIS IS IMPORTANT! IF I DON'T GET BACK IN SHAPE THERE'LL BE NOBODY AROUND TO STOP HIM!
PFFT.
AND I'LL GO BACK TO SMELLING LIKE A PUKEY TURDFOOT.

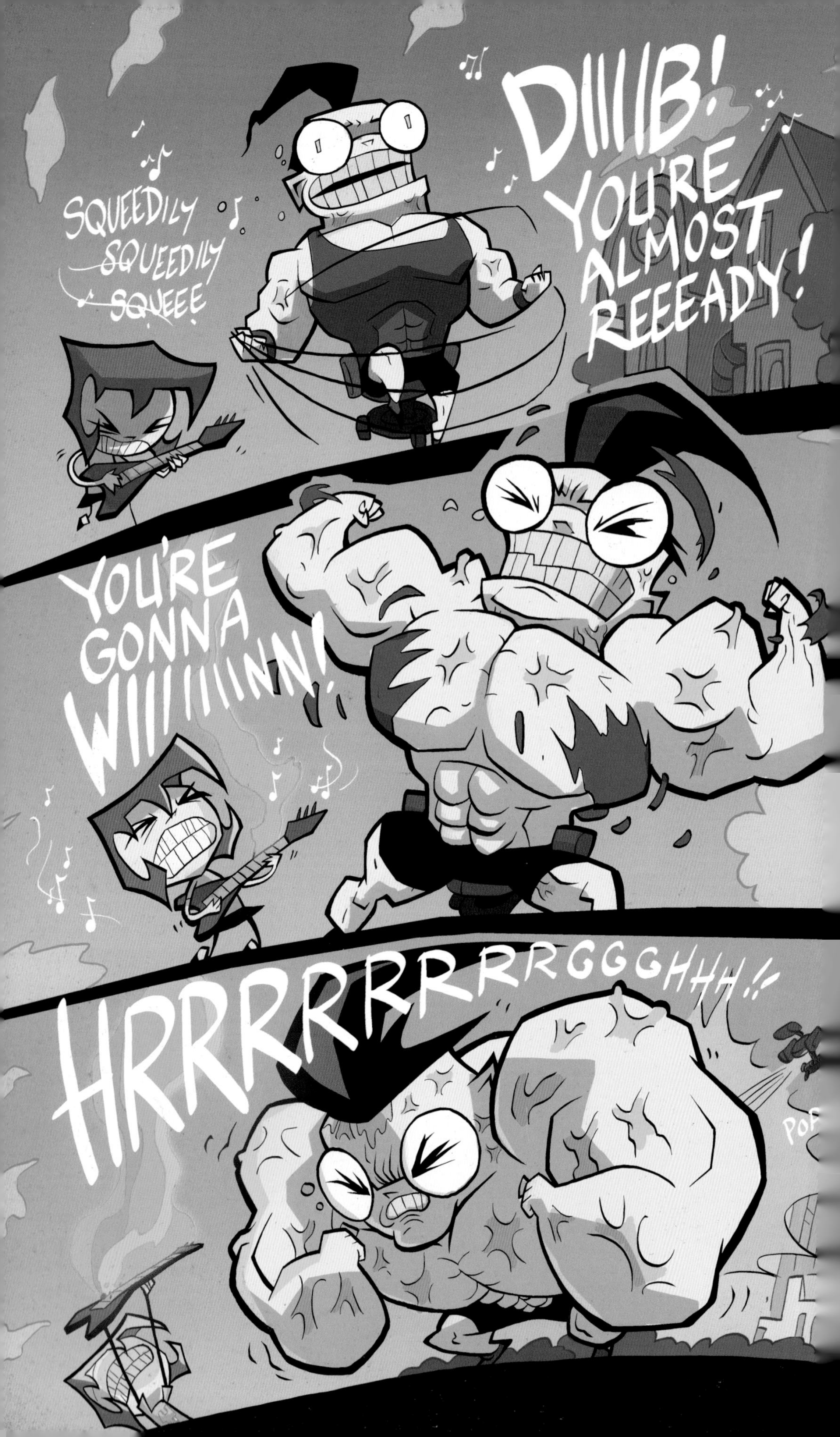
SQUEEDILY SQUEEDILY SQUEEE
DIIIIB! YOU'RE ALMOST REEEADY!
YOU'RE GONNA WIIIIIIINN!
HRRRRRRRRGGGHHH!!
POP

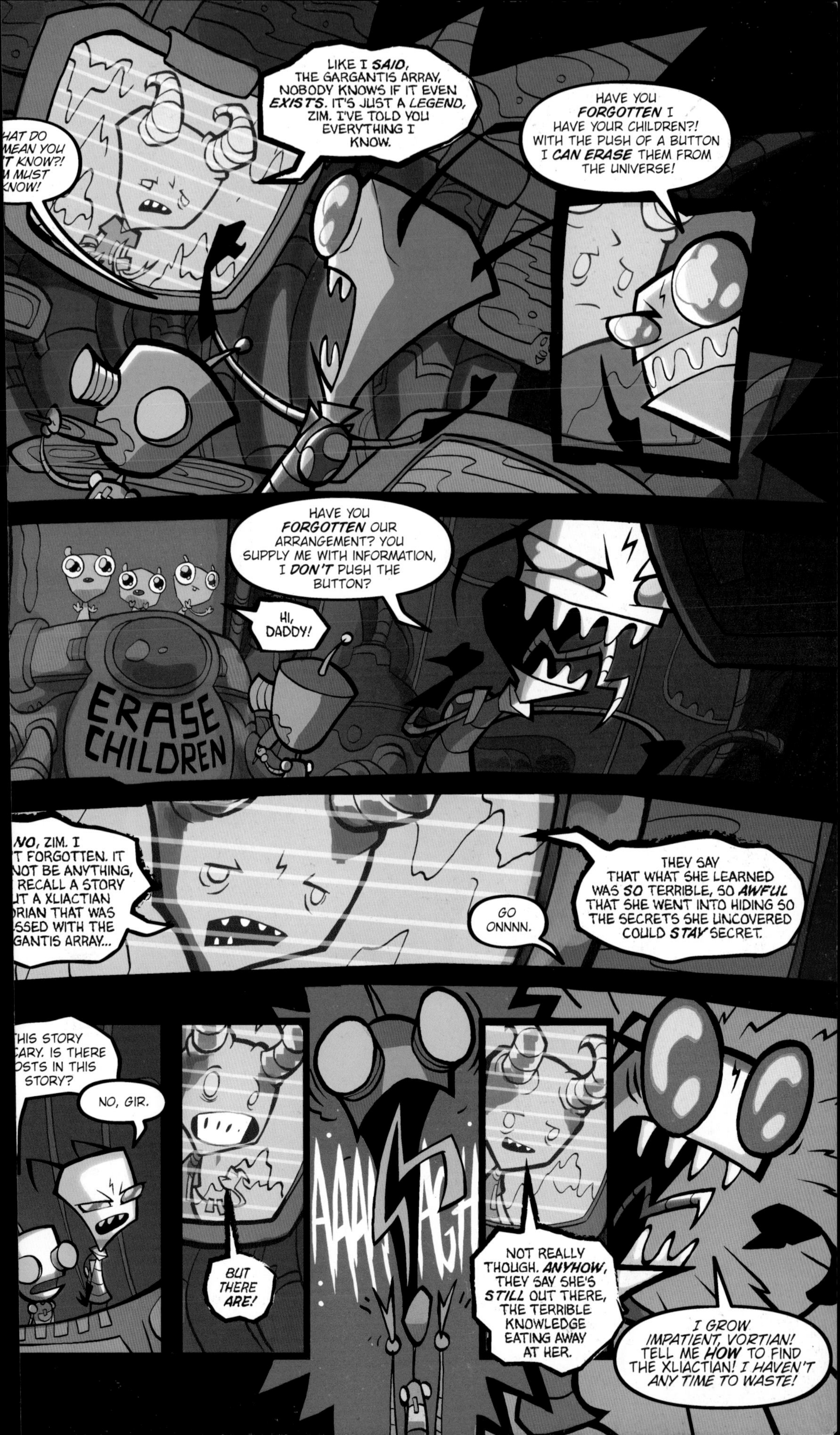

HAT DO
MEAN YOU
T KNOW?!
M MUST
KNOW!
LIKE I SAID, THE GARGANTIS ARRAY, NOBODY KNOWS IF IT EVEN EXISTS. IT'S JUST A LEGEND, ZIM. I'VE TOLD YOU EVERYTHING I KNOW.
HAVE YOU FORGOTTEN I HAVE YOUR CHILDREN?! WITH THE PUSH OF A BUTTON I CAN ERASE THEM FROM THE UNIVERSE!
HAVE YOU FORGOTTEN OUR ARRANGEMENT? YOU SUPPLY ME WITH INFORMATION, I DON'T PUSH THE BUTTON?
HI, DADDY!
ERASE CHILDREN
NO, ZIM. I
T FORGOTTEN. IT
NOT BE ANYTHING,
RECALL A STORY
UT A XLIACTIAN
ORIAN THAT WAS
SSED WITH THE
GANTIS ARRAY...
GO ONNNN.
THEY SAY THAT WHAT SHE LEARNED WAS SO TERRIBLE, SO AWFUL THAT SHE WENT INTO HIDING SO THE SECRETS SHE UNCOVERED COULD STAY SECRET.
THIS STORY
CARY. IS THERE
OSTS IN THIS
STORY?
NO, GIR.
BUT THERE ARE!
AAAAGH
NOT REALLY THOUGH. ANYHOW, THEY SAY SHE'S STILL OUT THERE, THE TERRIBLE KNOWLEDGE EATING AWAY AT HER.
I GROW IMPATIENT, VORTIAN! TELL ME HOW TO FIND THE XLIACTIAN! I HAVEN'T ANY TIME TO WASTE!

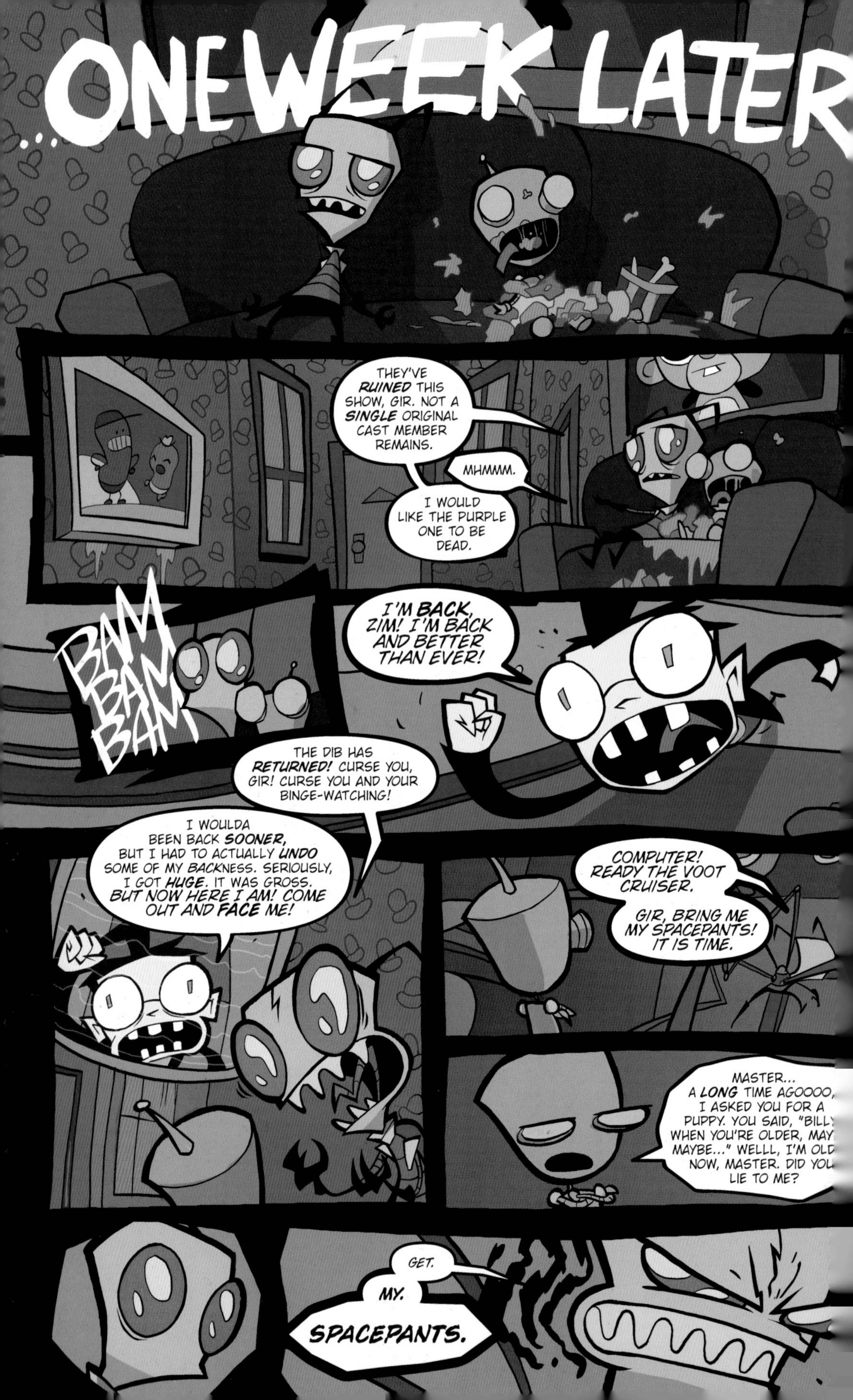
...ONE WEEK LATER
THEY'VE RUINED THIS SHOW, GIR. NOT A SINGLE ORIGINAL CAST MEMBER REMAINS.
MHMMM.
I WOULD LIKE THE PURPLE ONE TO BE DEAD.
BAM BAM BAM
I'M BACK, ZIM! I'M BACK AND BETTER THAN EVER!
THE DIB HAS RETURNED! CURSE YOU, GIR! CURSE YOU AND YOUR BINGE-WATCHING!
I WOULDA BEEN BACK SOONER, BUT I HAD TO ACTUALLY UNDO SOME OF MY BACKNESS. SERIOUSLY, I GOT HUGE. IT WAS GROSS. BUT NOW HERE I AM! COME OUT AND FACE ME!
COMPUTER! READY THE VOOT CRUISER.
GIR, BRING ME MY SPACEPANTS! IT IS TIME.
GET.
MY.
SPACEPANTS.

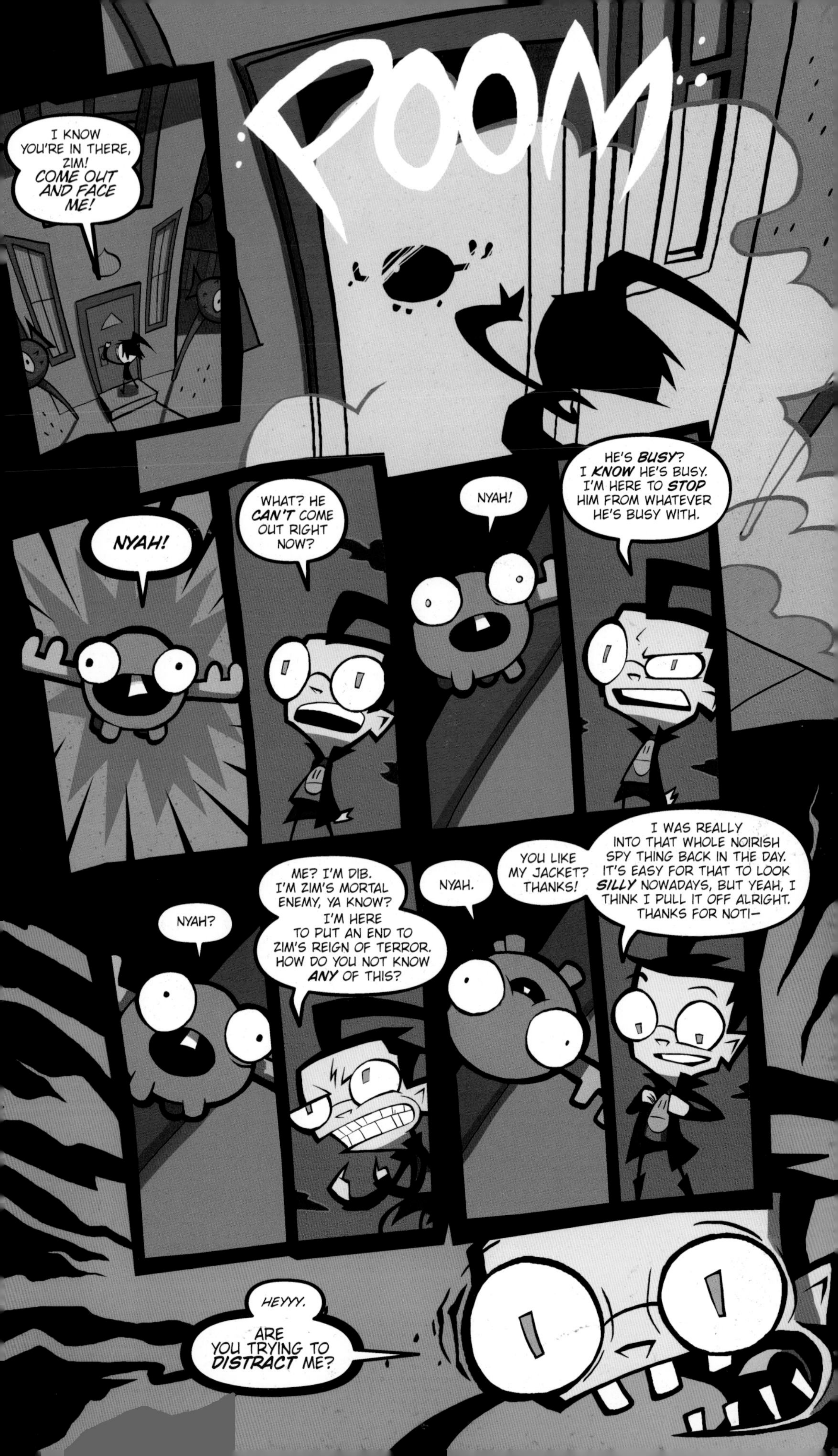
POOM
I KNOW YOU'RE IN THERE, ZIM! COME OUT AND FACE ME!
NYAH!
WHAT? HE CAN'T COME OUT RIGHT NOW?
NYAH!
HE'S BUSY? I KNOW HE'S BUSY. I'M HERE TO STOP HIM FROM WHATEVER HE'S BUSY WITH.
NYAH?
ME? I'M DIB. I'M ZIM'S MORTAL ENEMY, YA KNOW? I'M HERE TO PUT AN END TO ZIM'S REIGN OF TERROR. HOW DO YOU NOT KNOW ANY OF THIS?
NYAH.
YOU LIKE MY JACKET? THANKS!
I WAS REALLY INTO THAT WHOLE NOIRISH SPY THING BACK IN THE DAY. IT'S EASY FOR THAT TO LOOK SILLY NOWADAYS, BUT YEAH, I THINK I PULL IT OFF ALRIGHT. THANKS FOR NOTI—
HEYYY.
ARE YOU TRYING TO DISTRACT ME?

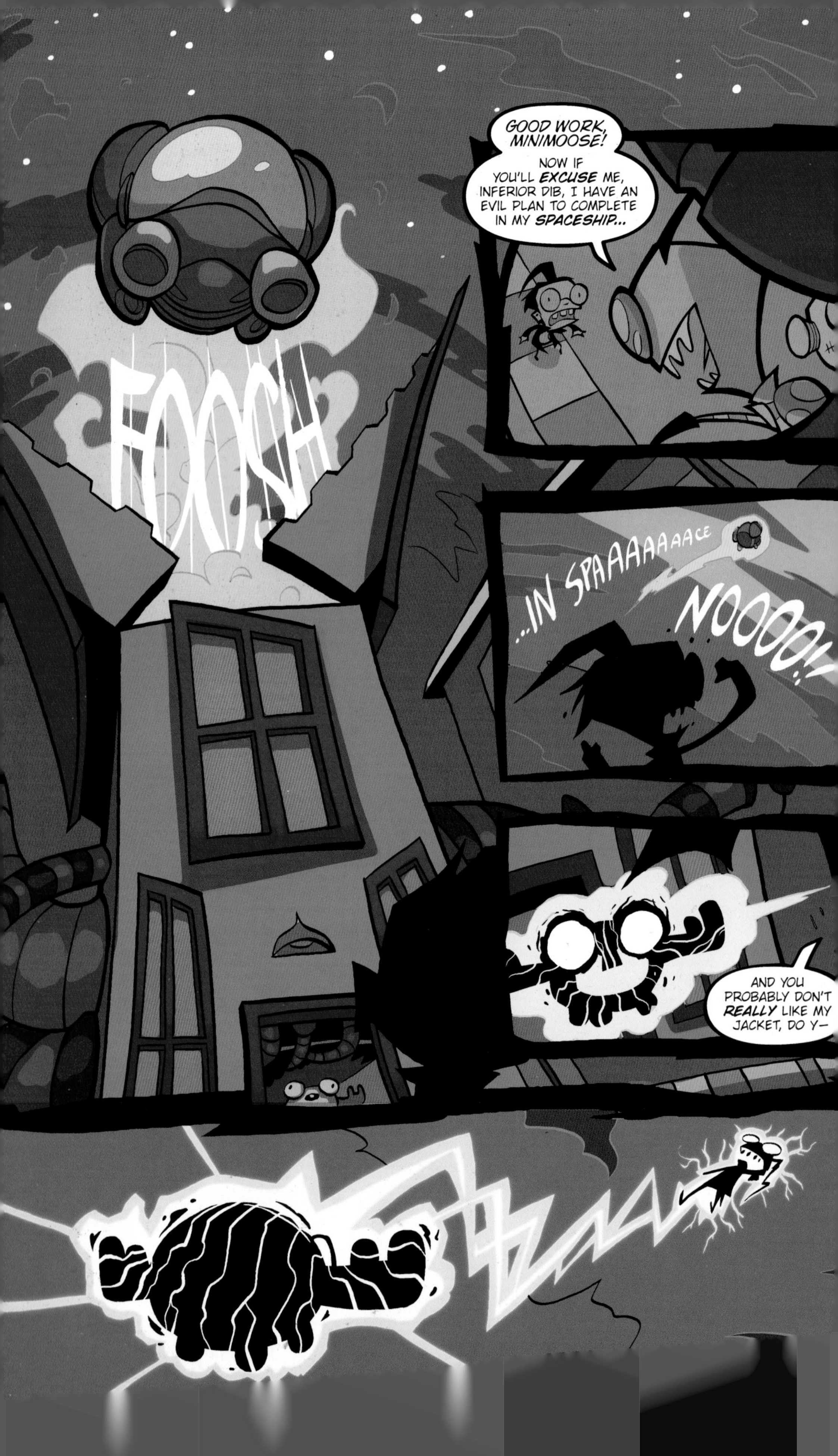
FOOSH
GOOD WORK, MINIMOOSE!
NOW IF YOU'LL EXCUSE ME, INFERIOR DIB, I HAVE AN EVIL PLAN TO COMPLETE IN MY SPACESHIP...
...IN SPAAAAAAACE
NOOOO!!
AND YOU PROBABLY DON'T REALLY LIKE MY JACKET, DO Y—

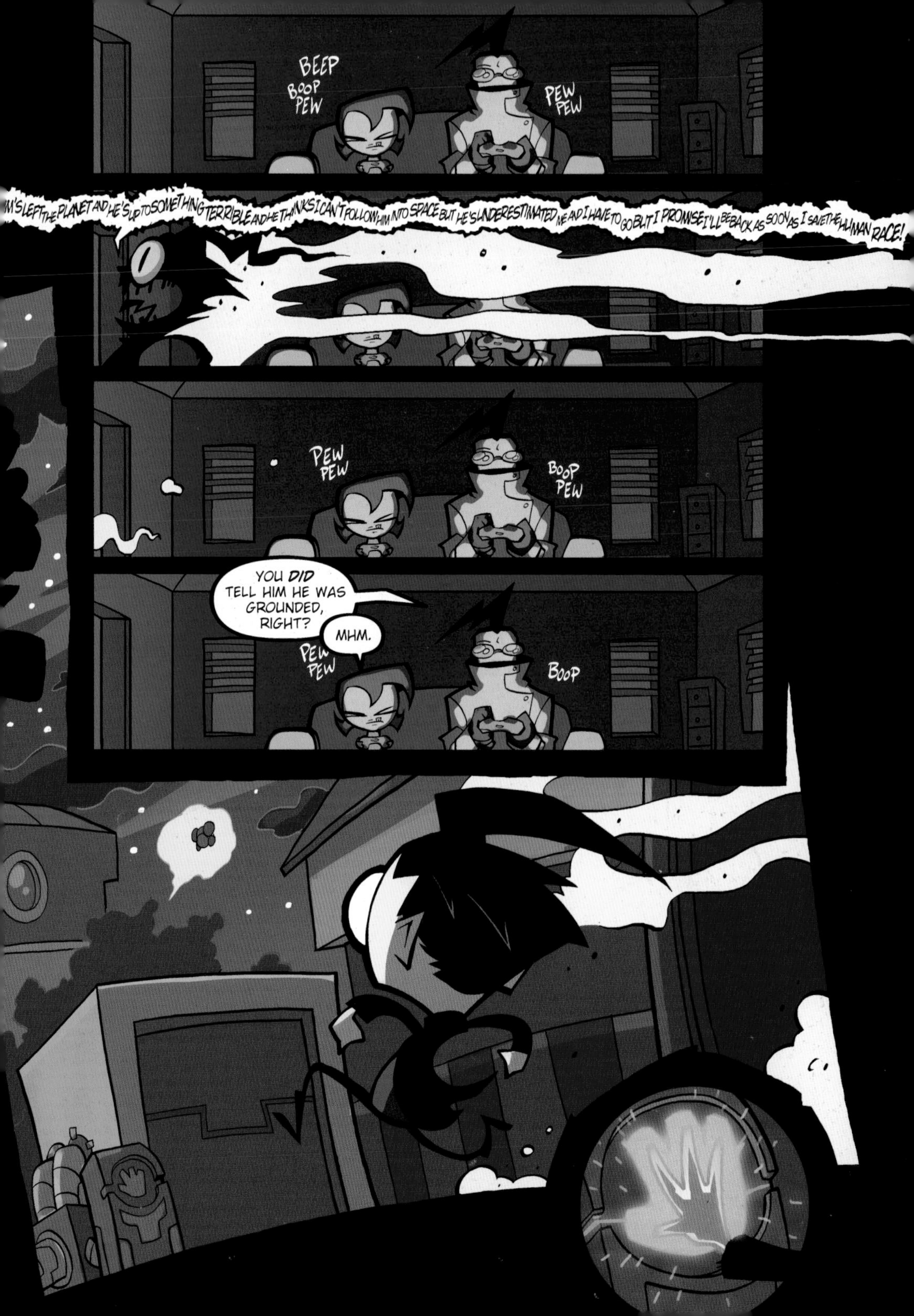
BEEP
BOOP
PEW
PEW
PEW
M'S LEFT THE PLANET AND HE'S UP TO SOMETHING TERRIBLE AND HE THINKS I CAN'T FOLLOW HIM INTO SPACE BUT HE'S UNDERESTIMATED ME AND I HAVE TO GO BUT I PROMISE I'LL BE BACK AS SOON AS I SAVE THE HUMAN RACE!
PEW
PEW
BOOP
PEW
YOU DID TELL HIM HE WAS GROUNDED, RIGHT?
MHM.
PEW
PEW
BOOP

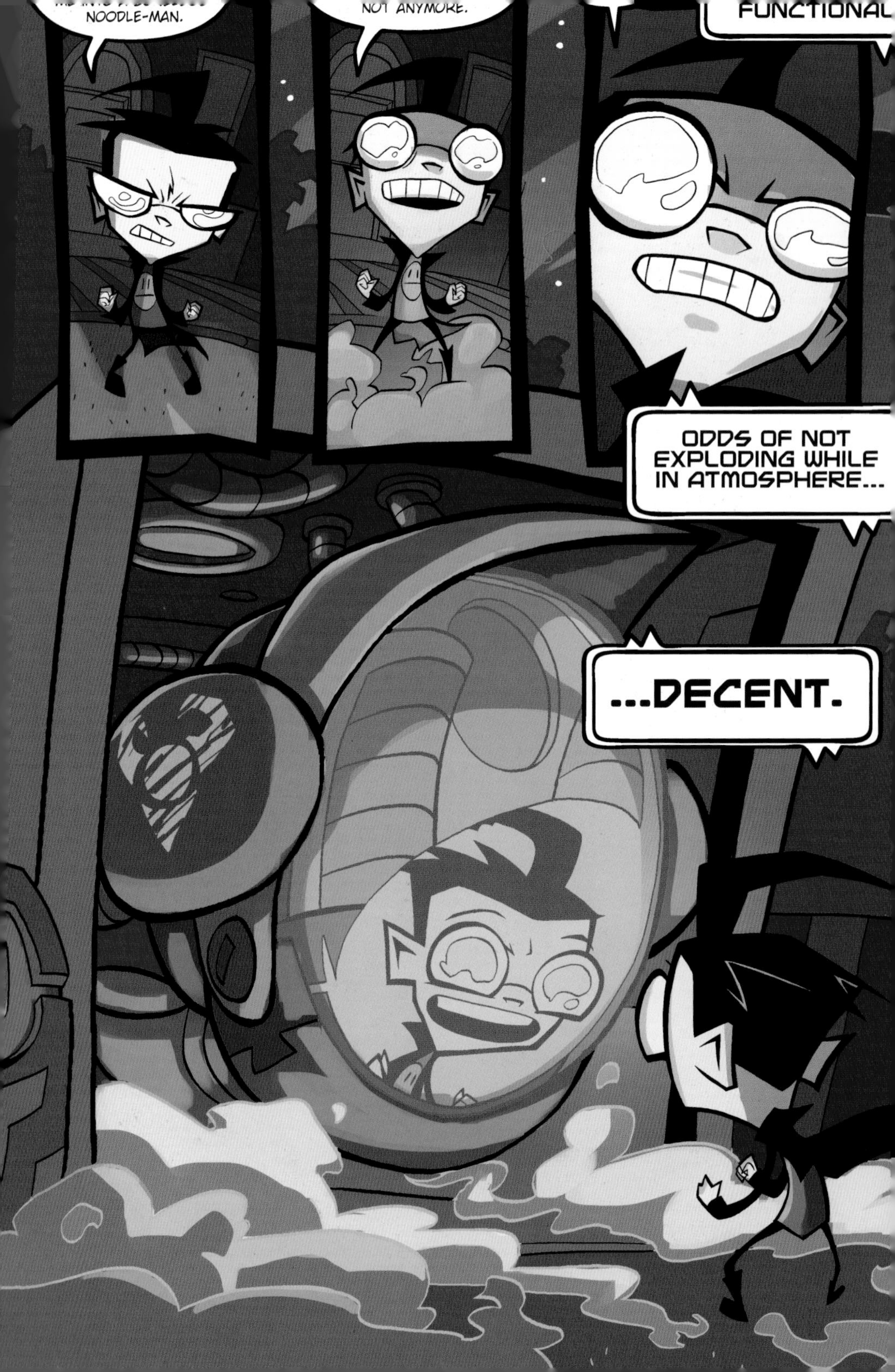

NOODLE-MAN.
NOT ANYMORE.
FUNCTIONAL
ODDS OF NOT EXPLODING WHILE IN ATMOSPHERE...
...DECENT.

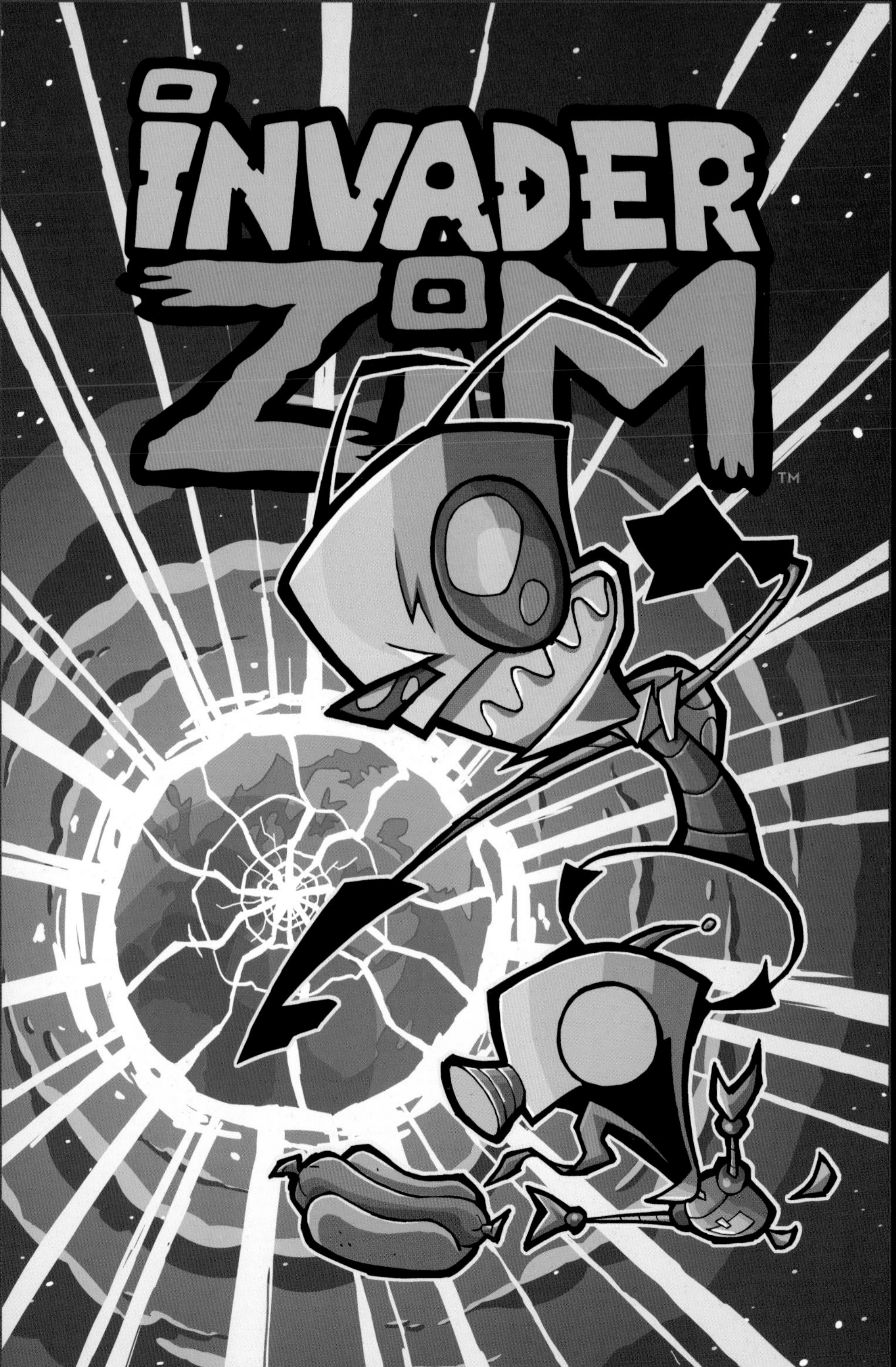

INVADER ZIM™

CHAPTER: 2

illustration by AARON ALEXOVICH and J.R. GOLDBERG

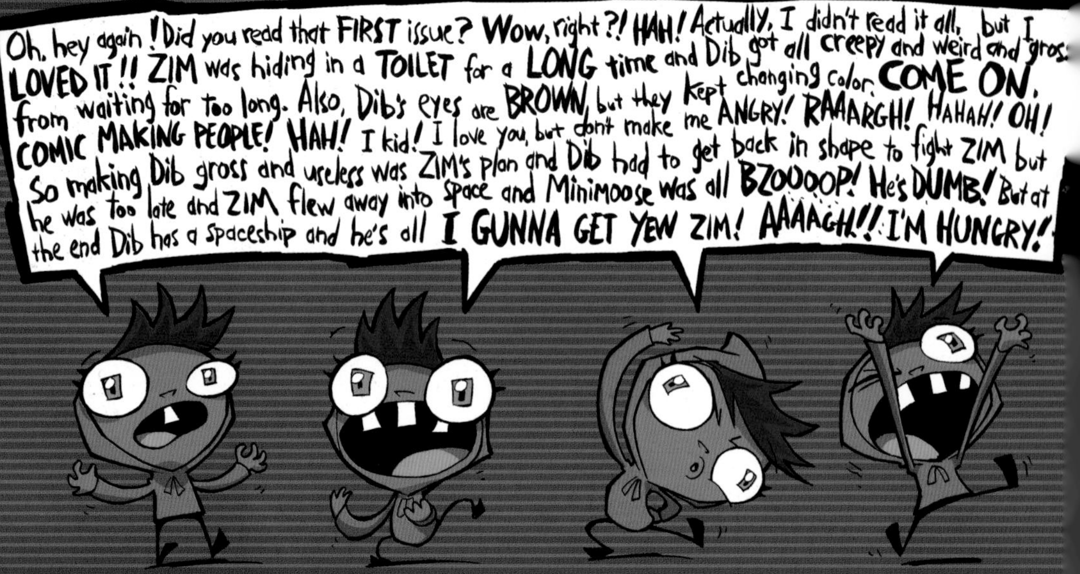
Oh, hey again! Did you read that FIRST issue? Wow, right?! HAH! Actually, I didn't read it all, but I LOVED IT!! ZIM was hiding in a TOILET for a LONG time and Dib got all creepy and weird and gros from waiting for too long. Also, Dib's eyes are BROWN, but they kept changing color. COME ON, COMIC MAKING PEOPLE! HAH! I kid! I love you, but don't make me ANGRY! RAAARGH! HAHAH! OH! So making Dib gross and useless was ZIM's plan and Dib had to get back in shape to fight ZIM but he was too late and ZIM flew away into space and Minimoose was all BZOOOOP! He's DUMB! But at the end Dib has a spaceship and he's all I GUNNA GET YEW ZIM! AAAAGH!! I'M HUNGRY!

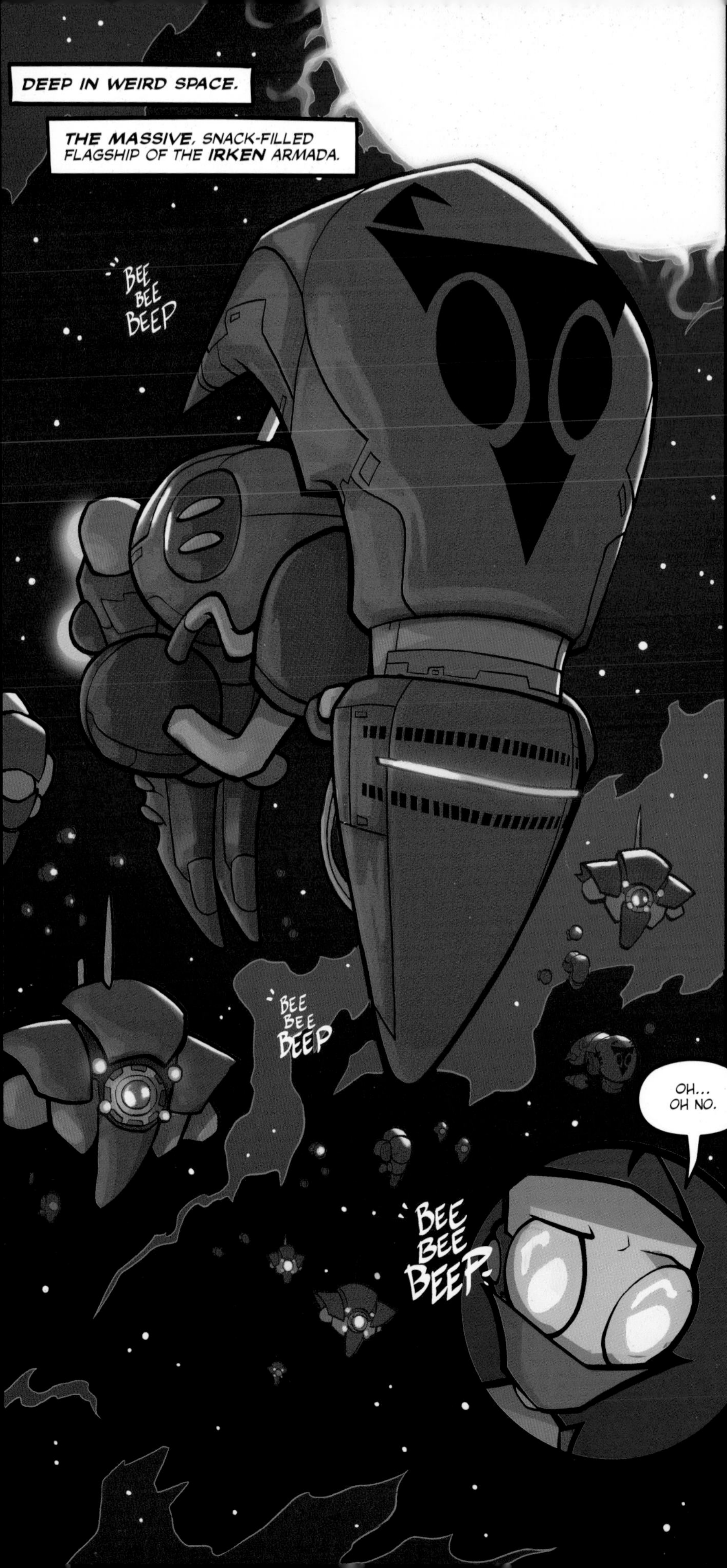
DEEP IN WEIRD SPACE.
THE MASSIVE, SNACK-FILLED FLAGSHIP OF THE IRKEN ARMADA.
BEE BEE BEEP
BEE BEE BEEP
BEE BEE BEEP
OH... OH NO.

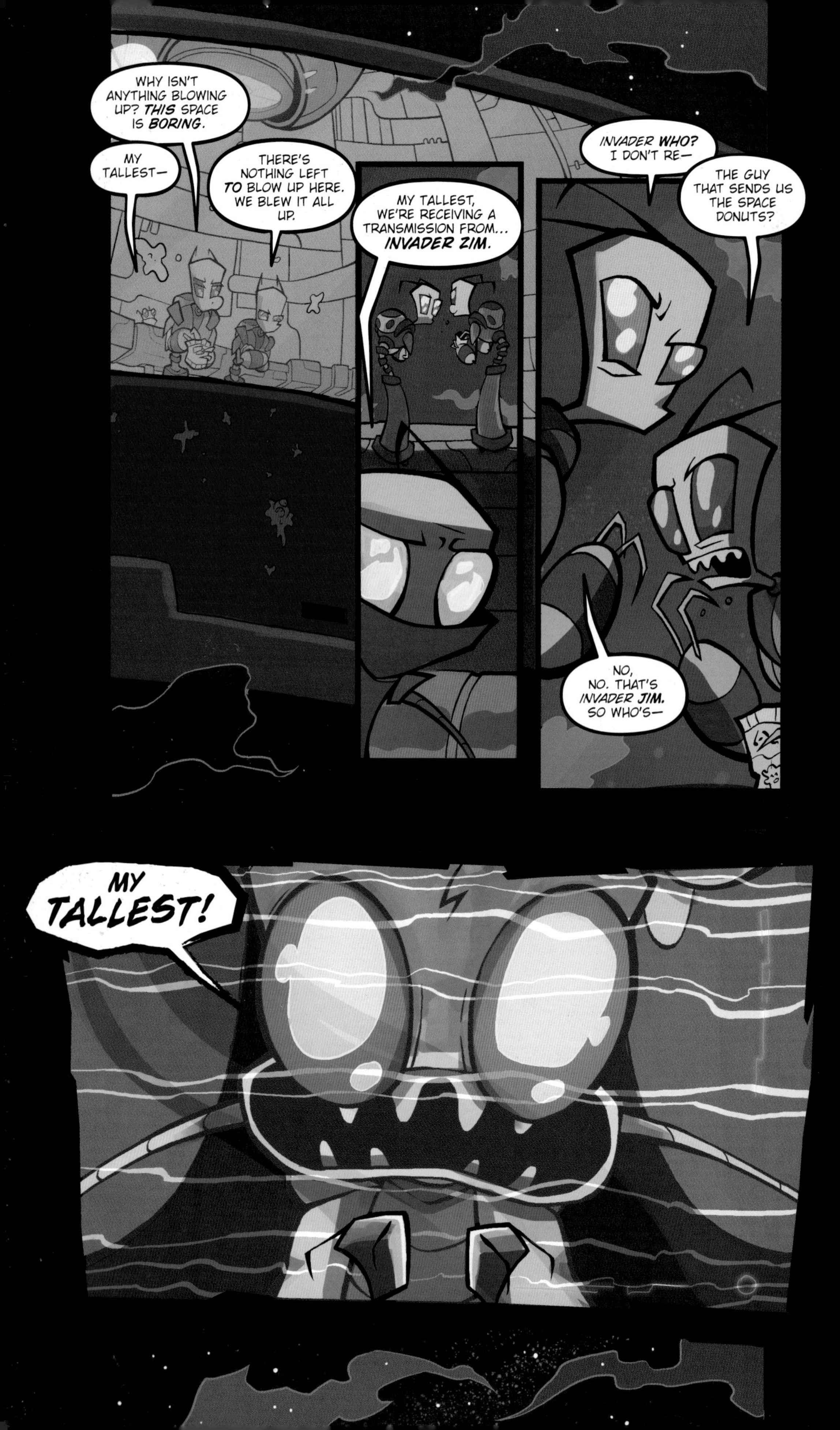
WHY ISN'T ANYTHING BLOWING UP? THIS SPACE IS BORING.
MY TALLEST—
THERE'S NOTHING LEFT TO BLOW UP HERE. WE BLEW IT ALL UP.
MY TALLEST, WE'RE RECEIVING A TRANSMISSION FROM... INVADER ZIM.
INVADER WHO? I DON'T RE—
THE GUY THAT SENDS US THE SPACE DONUTS?
NO, NO. THAT'S INVADER JIM. SO WHO'S—
MY TALLEST!

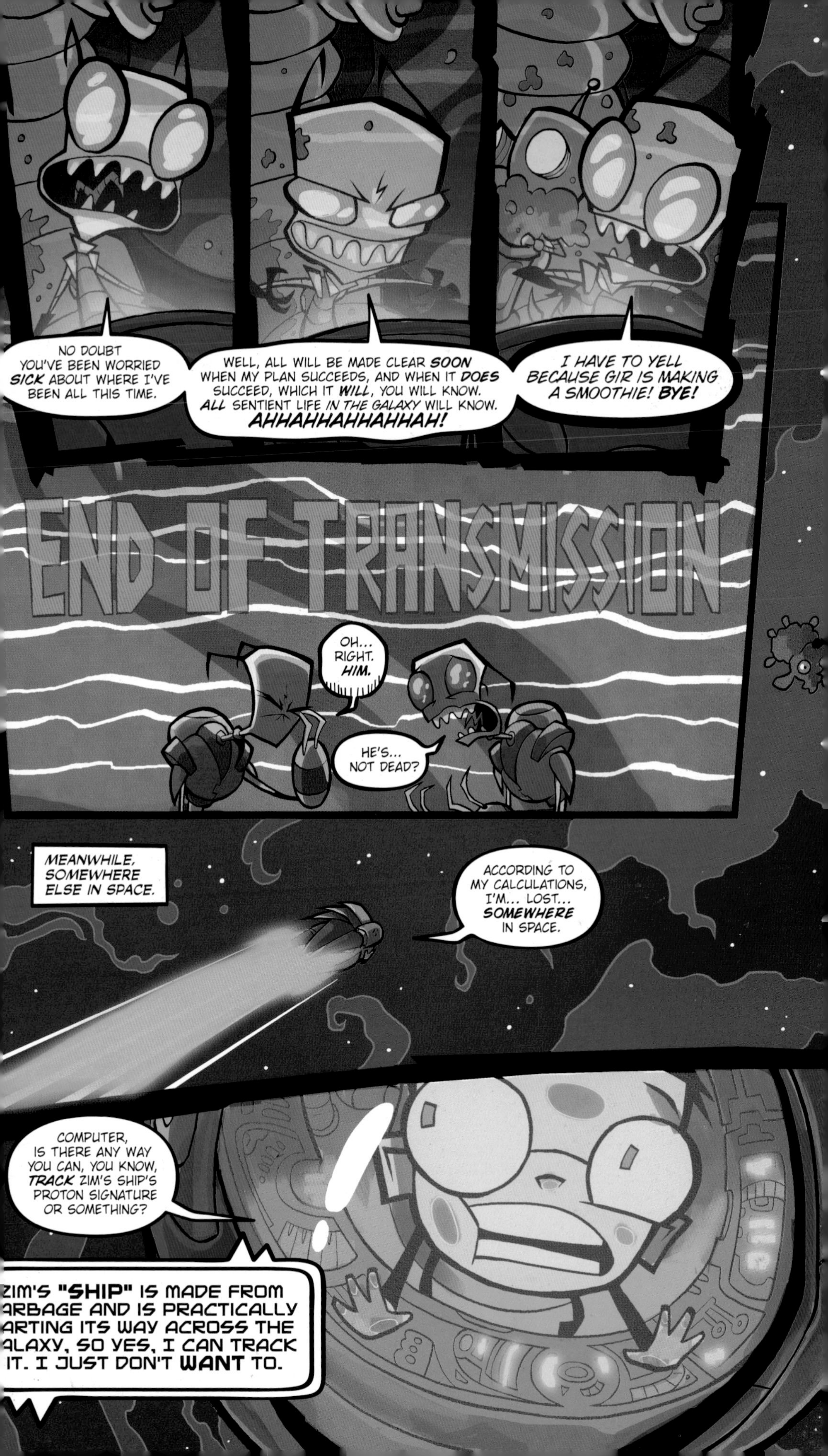
NO DOUBT YOU'VE BEEN WORRIED SICK ABOUT WHERE I'VE BEEN ALL THIS TIME.
WELL, ALL WILL BE MADE CLEAR SOON WHEN MY PLAN SUCCEEDS, AND WHEN IT DOES SUCCEED, WHICH IT WILL, YOU WILL KNOW. ALL SENTIENT LIFE IN THE GALAXY WILL KNOW. AHHAHHAHHAHHAH!
I HAVE TO YELL BECAUSE GIR IS MAKING A SMOOTHIE! BYE!
END OF TRANSMISSION
OH... RIGHT. HIM.
HE'S... NOT DEAD?
MEANWHILE, SOMEWHERE ELSE IN SPACE.
ACCORDING TO MY CALCULATIONS, I'M... LOST... SOMEWHERE IN SPACE.
COMPUTER, IS THERE ANY WAY YOU CAN, YOU KNOW, TRACK ZIM'S SHIP'S PROTON SIGNATURE OR SOMETHING?
ZIM'S "SHIP" IS MADE FROM ARBAGE AND IS PRACTICALLY ARTING ITS WAY ACROSS THE ALAXY, SO YES, I CAN TRACK IT. I JUST DON'T WANT TO.

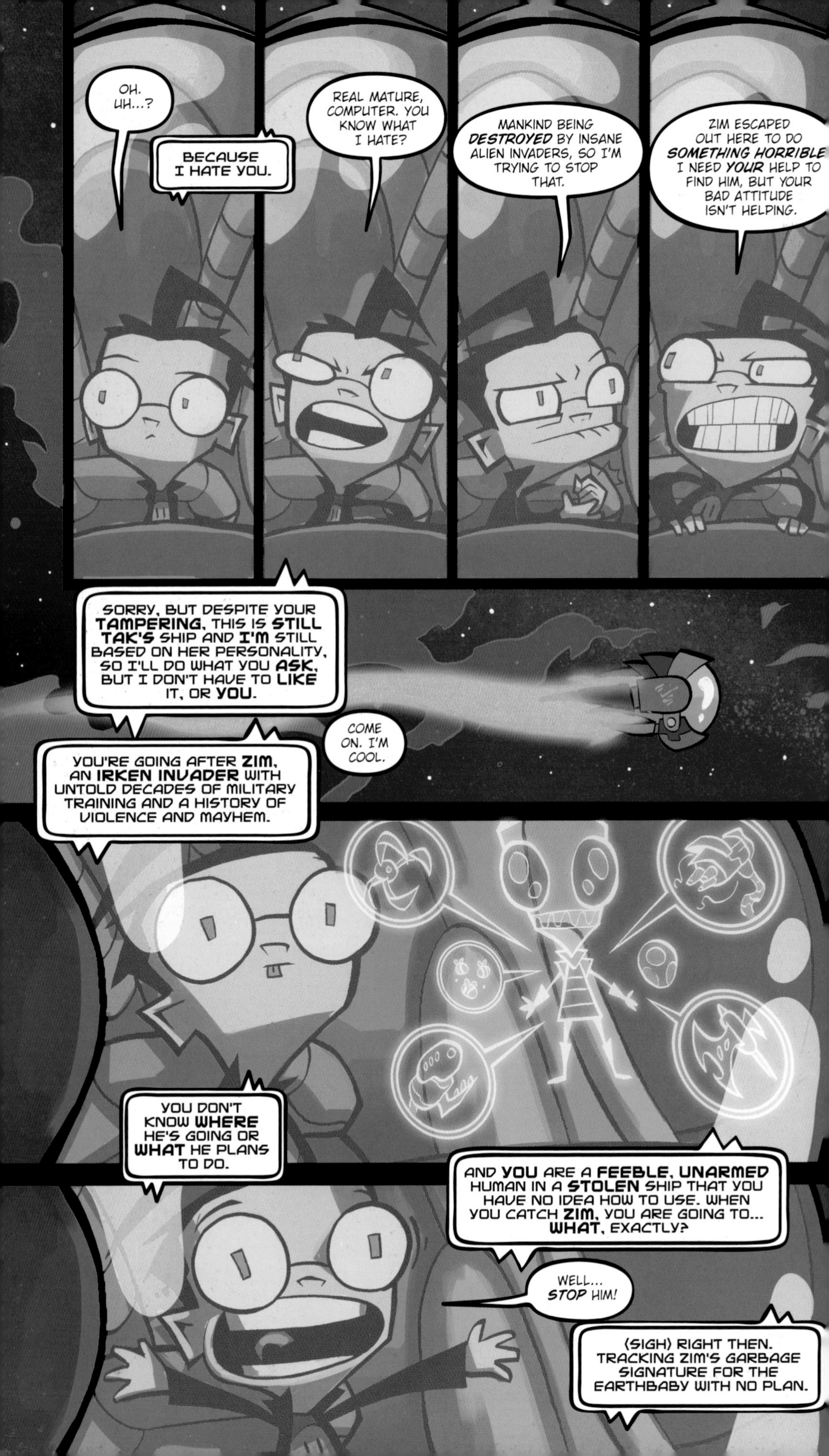
OH. UH...?
BECAUSE I HATE YOU.
REAL MATURE, COMPUTER. YOU KNOW WHAT I HATE?
MANKIND BEING DESTROYED BY INSANE ALIEN INVADERS, SO I'M TRYING TO STOP THAT.
ZIM ESCAPED OUT HERE TO DO SOMETHING HORRIBLE. I NEED YOUR HELP TO FIND HIM, BUT YOUR BAD ATTITUDE ISN'T HELPING.
SORRY, BUT DESPITE YOUR TAMPERING, THIS IS STILL TAK'S SHIP AND I'M STILL BASED ON HER PERSONALITY, SO I'LL DO WHAT YOU ASK, BUT I DON'T HAVE TO LIKE IT, OR YOU.
COME ON. I'M COOL.
YOU'RE GOING AFTER ZIM, AN IRKEN INVADER WITH UNTOLD DECADES OF MILITARY TRAINING AND A HISTORY OF VIOLENCE AND MAYHEM.
YOU DON'T KNOW WHERE HE'S GOING OR WHAT HE PLANS TO DO.
AND YOU ARE A FEEBLE, UNARMED HUMAN IN A STOLEN SHIP THAT YOU HAVE NO IDEA HOW TO USE. WHEN YOU CATCH ZIM, YOU ARE GOING TO... WHAT, EXACTLY?
WELL... STOP HIM!
(SIGH) RIGHT THEN. TRACKING ZIM'S GARBAGE SIGNATURE FOR THE EARTHBABY WITH NO PLAN.

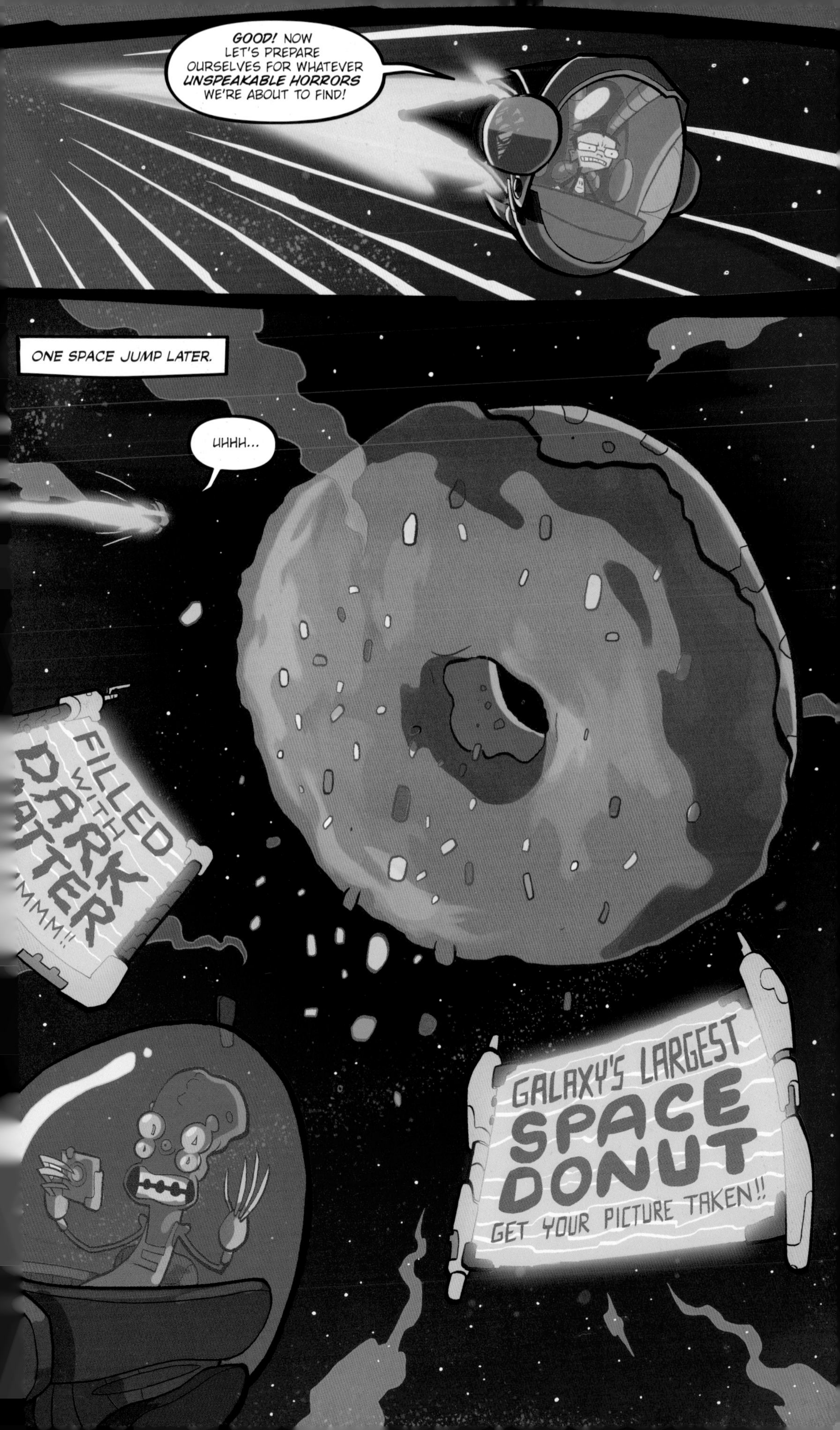
GOOD! NOW LET'S PREPARE OURSELVES FOR WHATEVER UNSPEAKABLE HORRORS WE'RE ABOUT TO FIND!
ONE SPACE JUMP LATER.
UHHH...
FILLED WITH DARK
GALAXY'S LARGEST SPACE DONUT
GET YOUR PICTURE TAKEN!!

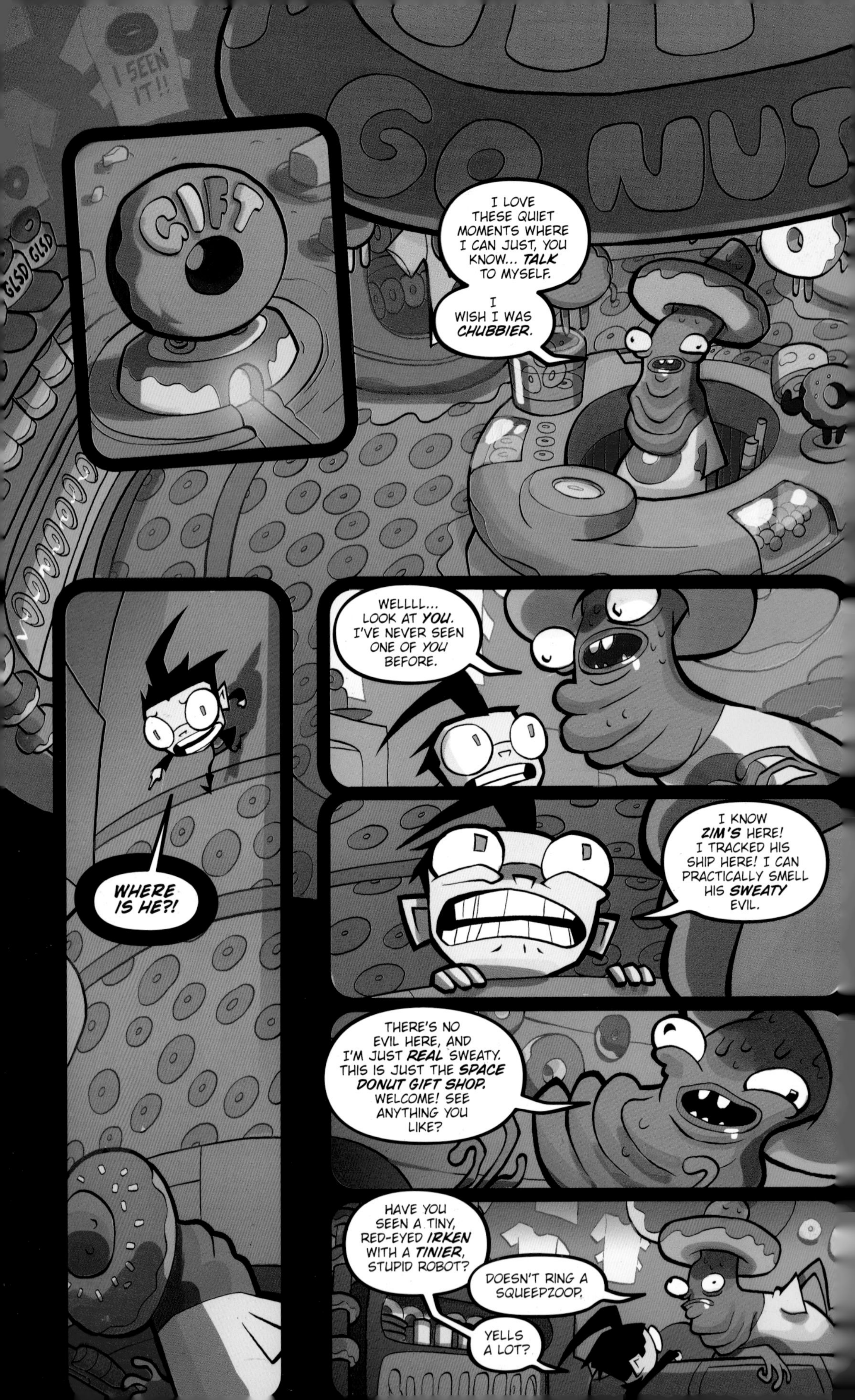

I SEEN IT!!
GO NUTS
GIFT
GLSD GLSD
I LOVE THESE QUIET MOMENTS WHERE I CAN JUST, YOU KNOW... TALK TO MYSELF.
I WISH I WAS CHUBBIER.
WHERE IS HE?!
WELLLL... LOOK AT YOU. I'VE NEVER SEEN ONE OF YOU BEFORE.
I KNOW ZIM'S HERE! I TRACKED HIS SHIP HERE! I CAN PRACTICALLY SMELL HIS SWEATY EVIL.
THERE'S NO EVIL HERE, AND I'M JUST REAL SWEATY. THIS IS JUST THE SPACE DONUT GIFT SHOP. WELCOME! SEE ANYTHING YOU LIKE?
HAVE YOU SEEN A TINY, RED-EYED IRKEN WITH A TINIER, STUPID ROBOT?
DOESN'T RING A SQUEEPZOOP.
YELLS A LOT?

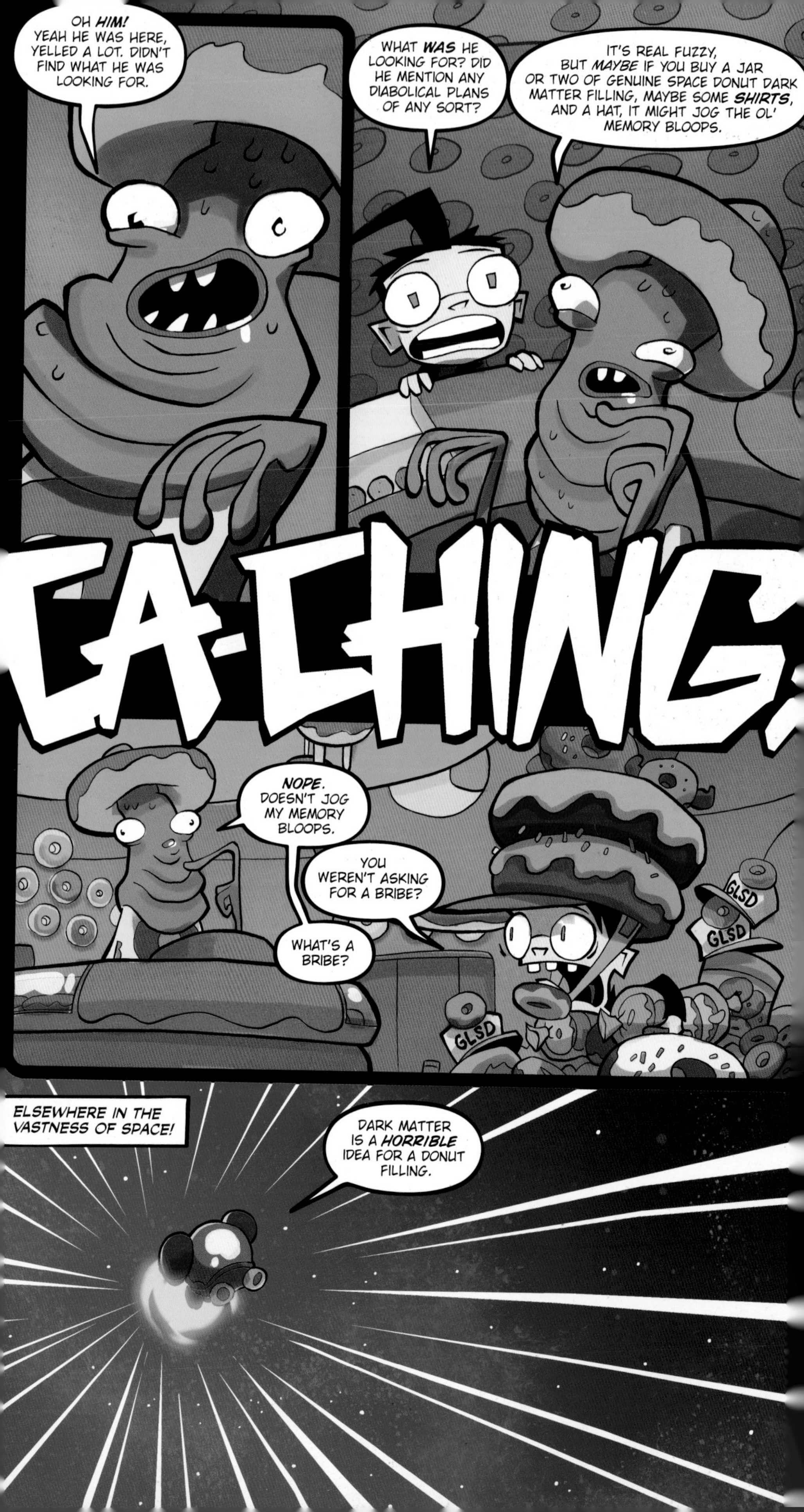

OH *HIM!* YEAH HE WAS HERE, YELLED A LOT. DIDN'T FIND WHAT HE WAS LOOKING FOR.
WHAT *WAS* HE LOOKING FOR? DID HE MENTION ANY DIABOLICAL PLANS OF ANY SORT?
IT'S REAL FUZZY, BUT *MAYBE* IF YOU BUY A JAR OR TWO OF GENUINE SPACE DONUT DARK MATTER FILLING, MAYBE SOME *SHIRTS*, AND A HAT, IT MIGHT JOG THE OL' MEMORY BLOOPS.
KA-CHING!
NOPE. DOESN'T JOG MY MEMORY BLOOPS.
YOU WEREN'T ASKING FOR A BRIBE?
WHAT'S A BRIBE?
GLSD
GLSD
GLSD
GLSD
ELSEWHERE IN THE VASTNESS OF SPACE!
DARK MATTER IS A *HORRIBLE* IDEA FOR A DONUT FILLING.

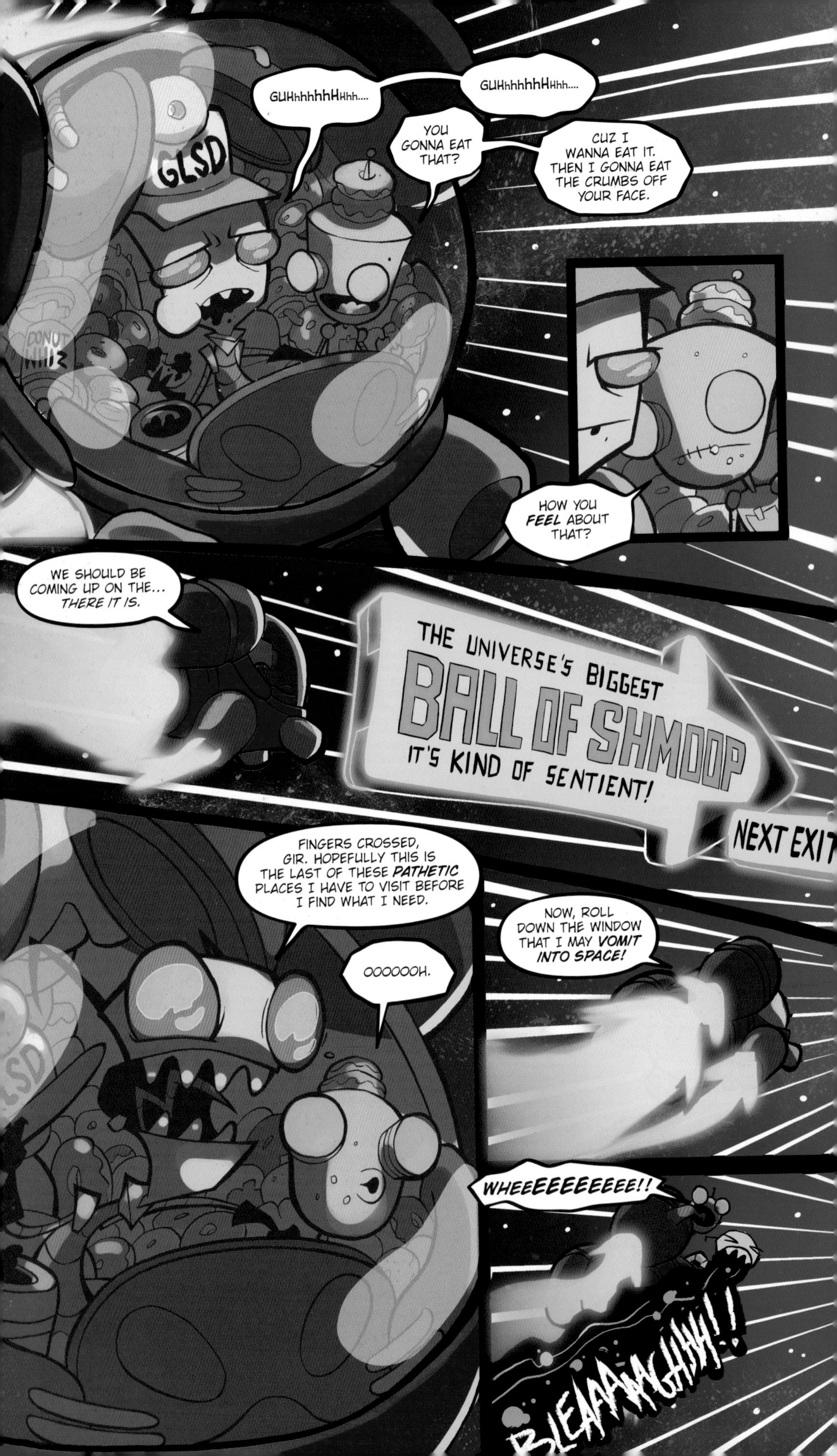

GUHhhhhhHHhh....
GUHhhhhhHHhh....
YOU GONNA EAT THAT?
CUZ I WANNA EAT IT. THEN I GONNA EAT THE CRUMBS OFF YOUR FACE.
GLSD
HOW YOU FEEL ABOUT THAT?
WE SHOULD BE COMING UP ON THE... THERE IT IS.
THE UNIVERSE'S BIGGEST
BALL OF SHMOOP
IT'S KIND OF SENTIENT!
NEXT EXIT
FINGERS CROSSED, GIR. HOPEFULLY THIS IS THE LAST OF THESE PATHETIC PLACES I HAVE TO VISIT BEFORE I FIND WHAT I NEED.
OOOOOOH.
NOW, ROLL DOWN THE WINDOW THAT I MAY VOMIT INTO SPACE!
WHEEEEEEEEEE!!
BLEAAAAGHHH!!

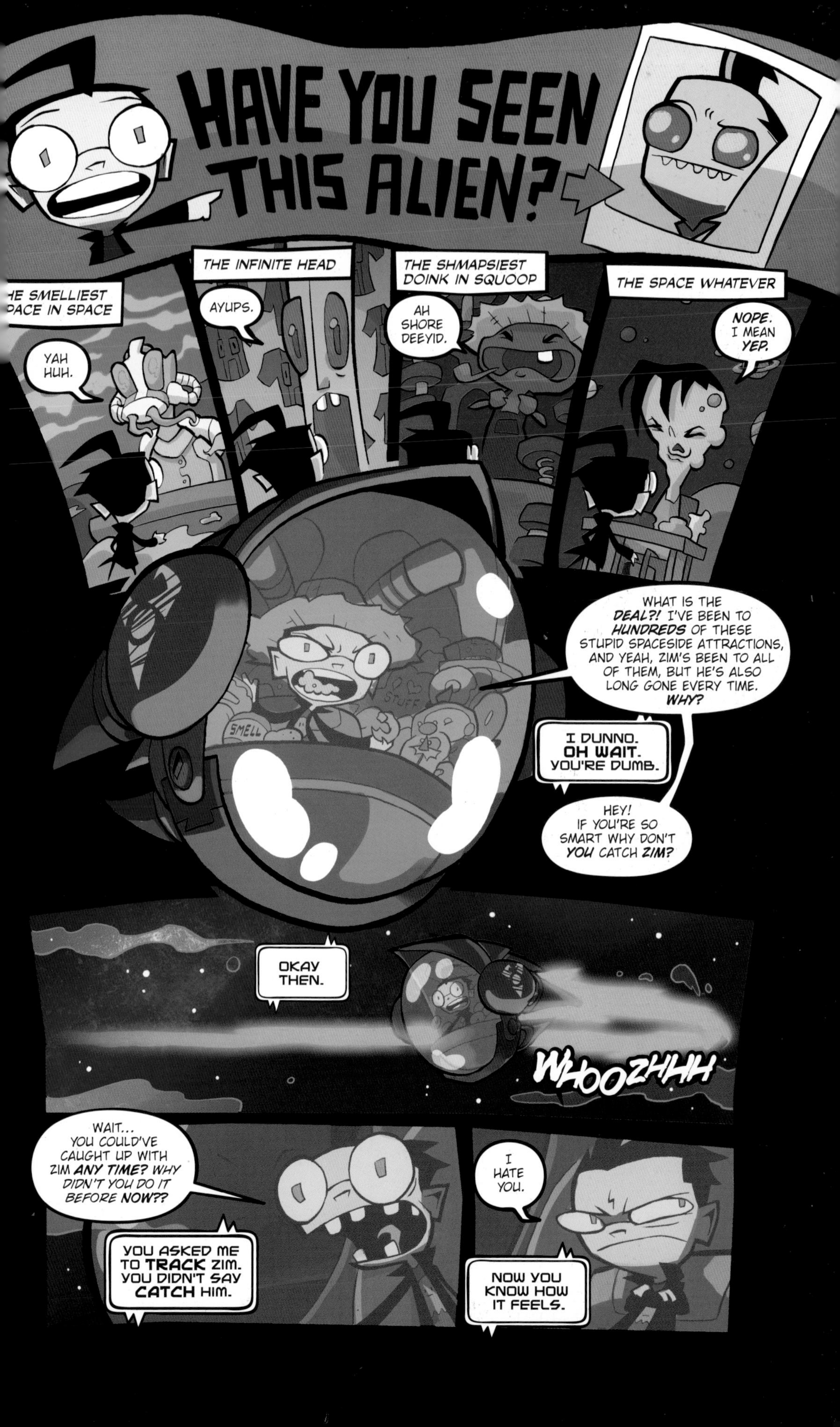
HAVE YOU SEEN THIS ALIEN?
THE SMELLIEST SPACE IN SPACE
YAH HUH.
THE INFINITE HEAD
AYUPS.
THE SHMAPSIEST DOINK IN SQUOOP
AH SHORE DEEYID.
THE SPACE WHATEVER
NOPE. I MEAN YEP.
WHAT IS THE DEAL?! I'VE BEEN TO HUNDREDS OF THESE STUPID SPACESIDE ATTRACTIONS, AND YEAH, ZIM'S BEEN TO ALL OF THEM, BUT HE'S ALSO LONG GONE EVERY TIME. WHY?
STUFF
SMELL
I DUNNO. OH WAIT. YOU'RE DUMB.
HEY! IF YOU'RE SO SMART WHY DON'T YOU CATCH ZIM?
OKAY THEN.
WHOOZHHH
WAIT... YOU COULD'VE CAUGHT UP WITH ZIM ANY TIME? WHY DIDN'T YOU DO IT BEFORE NOW??
YOU ASKED ME TO TRACK ZIM. YOU DIDN'T SAY CATCH HIM.
I HATE YOU.
NOW YOU KNOW HOW IT FEELS.

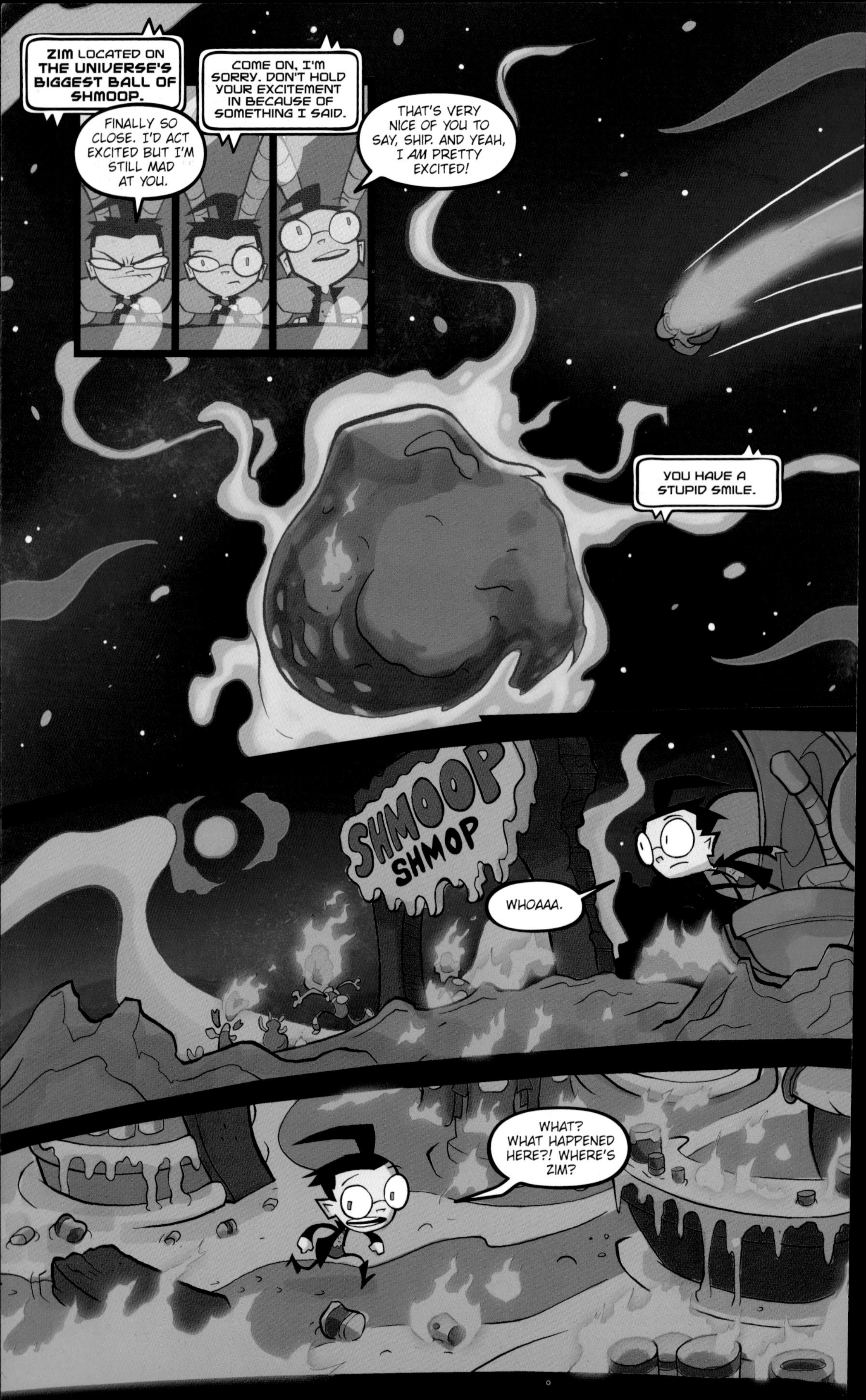
ZIM LOCATED ON THE UNIVERSE'S BIGGEST BALL OF SHMOOP.
FINALLY SO CLOSE. I'D ACT EXCITED BUT I'M STILL MAD AT YOU.
COME ON, I'M SORRY. DON'T HOLD YOUR EXCITEMENT IN BECAUSE OF SOMETHING I SAID.
THAT'S VERY NICE OF YOU TO SAY, SHIP. AND YEAH, I *AM* PRETTY EXCITED!
YOU HAVE A STUPID SMILE.
SHMOOP SHMOP
WHOAAA.
WHAT? WHAT HAPPENED HERE?! WHERE'S ZIM?

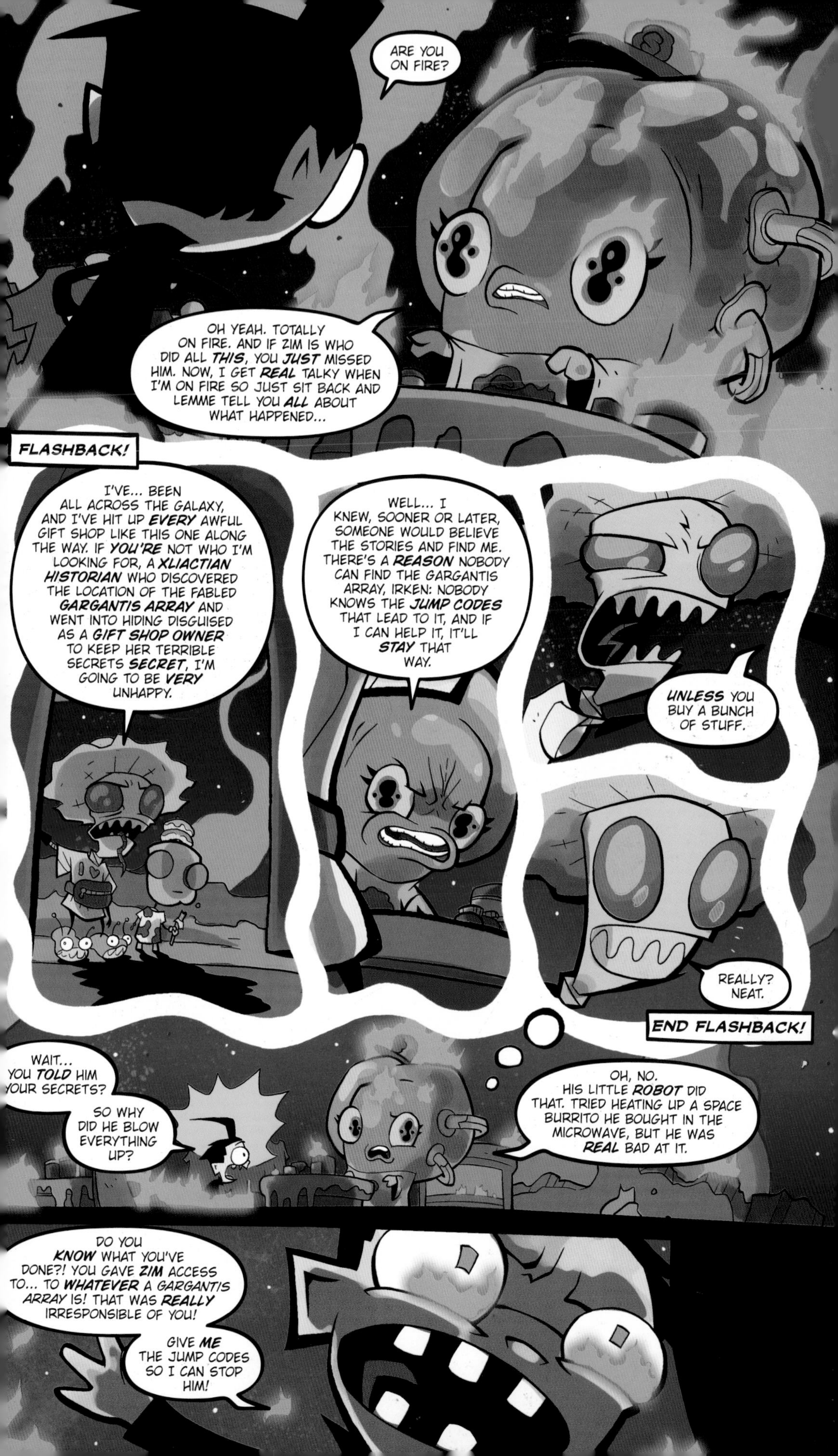

ARE YOU ON FIRE?
OH YEAH. TOTALLY ON FIRE. AND IF ZIM IS WHO DID ALL THIS, YOU JUST MISSED HIM. NOW, I GET REAL TALKY WHEN I'M ON FIRE SO JUST SIT BACK AND LEMME TELL YOU ALL ABOUT WHAT HAPPENED...
FLASHBACK!
I'VE... BEEN ALL ACROSS THE GALAXY, AND I'VE HIT UP EVERY AWFUL GIFT SHOP LIKE THIS ONE ALONG THE WAY. IF YOU'RE NOT WHO I'M LOOKING FOR, A XLIACTIAN HISTORIAN WHO DISCOVERED THE LOCATION OF THE FABLED GARGANTIS ARRAY AND WENT INTO HIDING DISGUISED AS A GIFT SHOP OWNER TO KEEP HER TERRIBLE SECRETS SECRET, I'M GOING TO BE VERY UNHAPPY.
WELL... I KNEW, SOONER OR LATER, SOMEONE WOULD BELIEVE THE STORIES AND FIND ME. THERE'S A REASON NOBODY CAN FIND THE GARGANTIS ARRAY, IRKEN: NOBODY KNOWS THE JUMP CODES THAT LEAD TO IT, AND IF I CAN HELP IT, IT'LL STAY THAT WAY.
UNLESS YOU BUY A BUNCH OF STUFF.
REALLY? NEAT.
END FLASHBACK!
WAIT... YOU TOLD HIM YOUR SECRETS?
SO WHY DID HE BLOW EVERYTHING UP?
OH, NO. HIS LITTLE ROBOT DID THAT. TRIED HEATING UP A SPACE BURRITO HE BOUGHT IN THE MICROWAVE, BUT HE WAS REAL BAD AT IT.
DO YOU KNOW WHAT YOU'VE DONE?! YOU GAVE ZIM ACCESS TO... TO WHATEVER A GARGANTIS ARRAY IS! THAT WAS REALLY IRRESPONSIBLE OF YOU!
GIVE ME THE JUMP CODES SO I CAN STOP HIM!

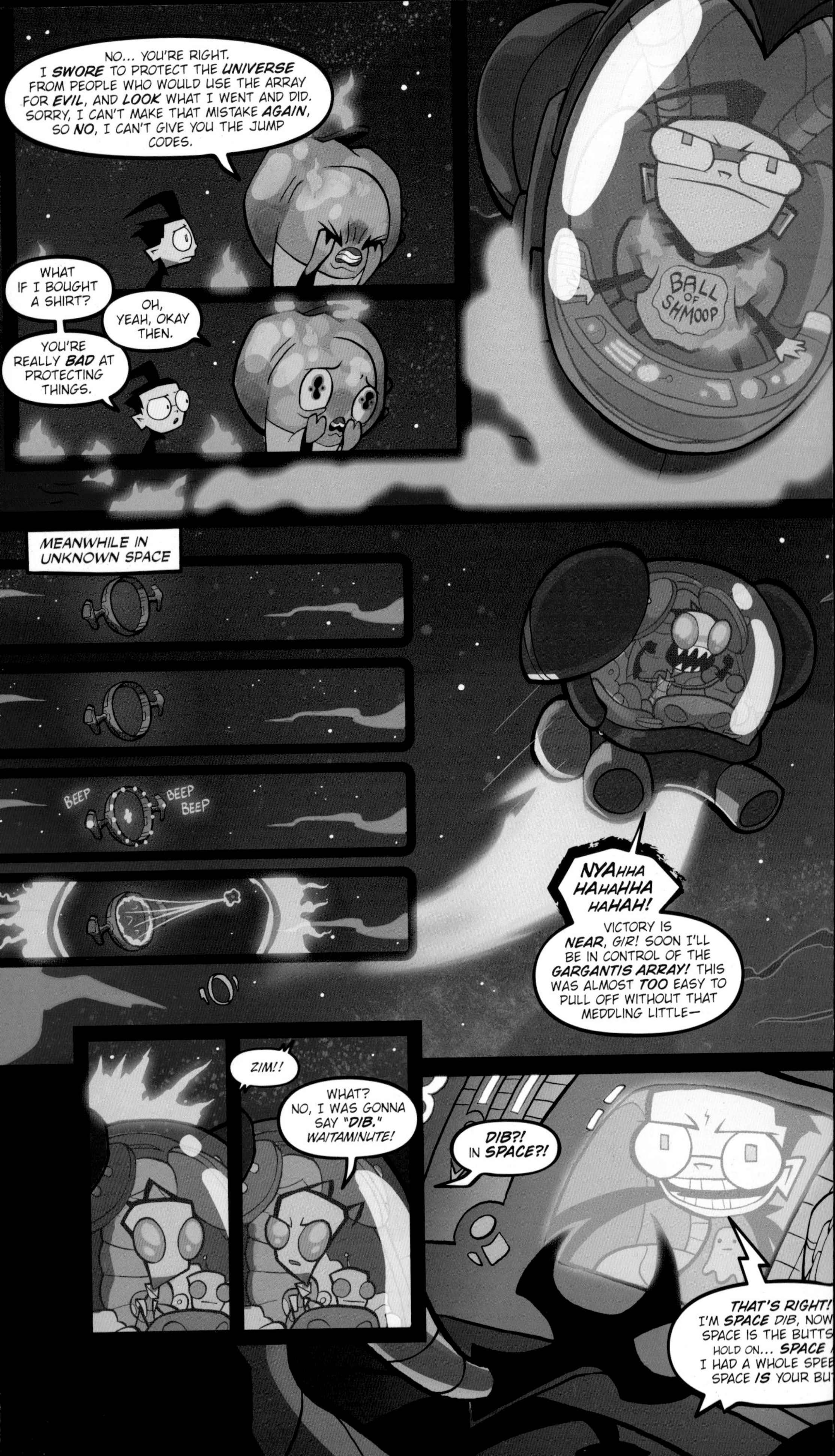

NO... YOU'RE RIGHT. I SWORE TO PROTECT THE UNIVERSE FROM PEOPLE WHO WOULD USE THE ARRAY FOR EVIL, AND LOOK WHAT I WENT AND DID. SORRY, I CAN'T MAKE THAT MISTAKE AGAIN, SO NO, I CAN'T GIVE YOU THE JUMP CODES.
WHAT IF I BOUGHT A SHIRT?
OH, YEAH, OKAY THEN.
YOU'RE REALLY BAD AT PROTECTING THINGS.
BALL OF SHMOOP
MEANWHILE IN UNKNOWN SPACE
BEEP
BEEP BEEP
NYAHHA HAHAHHA HAHAH! VICTORY IS NEAR, GIR! SOON I'LL BE IN CONTROL OF THE GARGANTIS ARRAY! THIS WAS ALMOST TOO EASY TO PULL OFF WITHOUT THAT MEDDLING LITTLE—
ZIM!!
WHAT? NO, I WAS GONNA SAY "DIB." WAITAMINUTE!
DIB?! IN SPACE?!
THAT'S RIGHT! I'M SPACE DIB, NOW SPACE IS THE BUTTS HOLD ON... SPACE I HAD A WHOLE SPEE SPACE IS YOUR BU

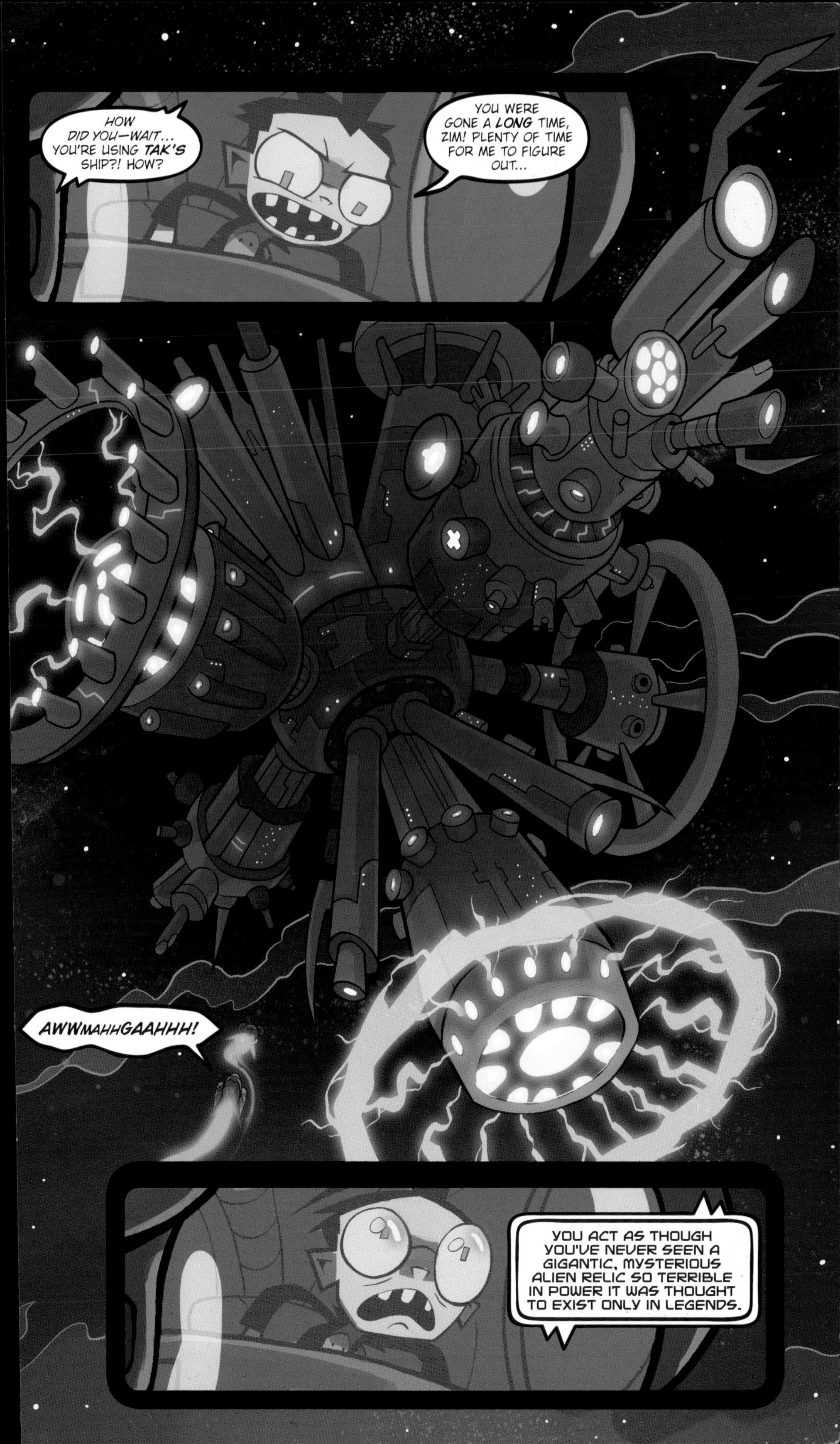
HOW DID YOU—WAIT... YOU'RE USING TAK'S SHIP?! HOW?
YOU WERE GONE A LONG TIME, ZIM! PLENTY OF TIME FOR ME TO FIGURE OUT...
AWWMAHHGAAHHH!
YOU ACT AS THOUGH YOU'VE NEVER SEEN A GIGANTIC, MYSTERIOUS ALIEN RELIC SO TERRIBLE IN POWER IT WAS THOUGHT TO EXIST ONLY IN LEGENDS.

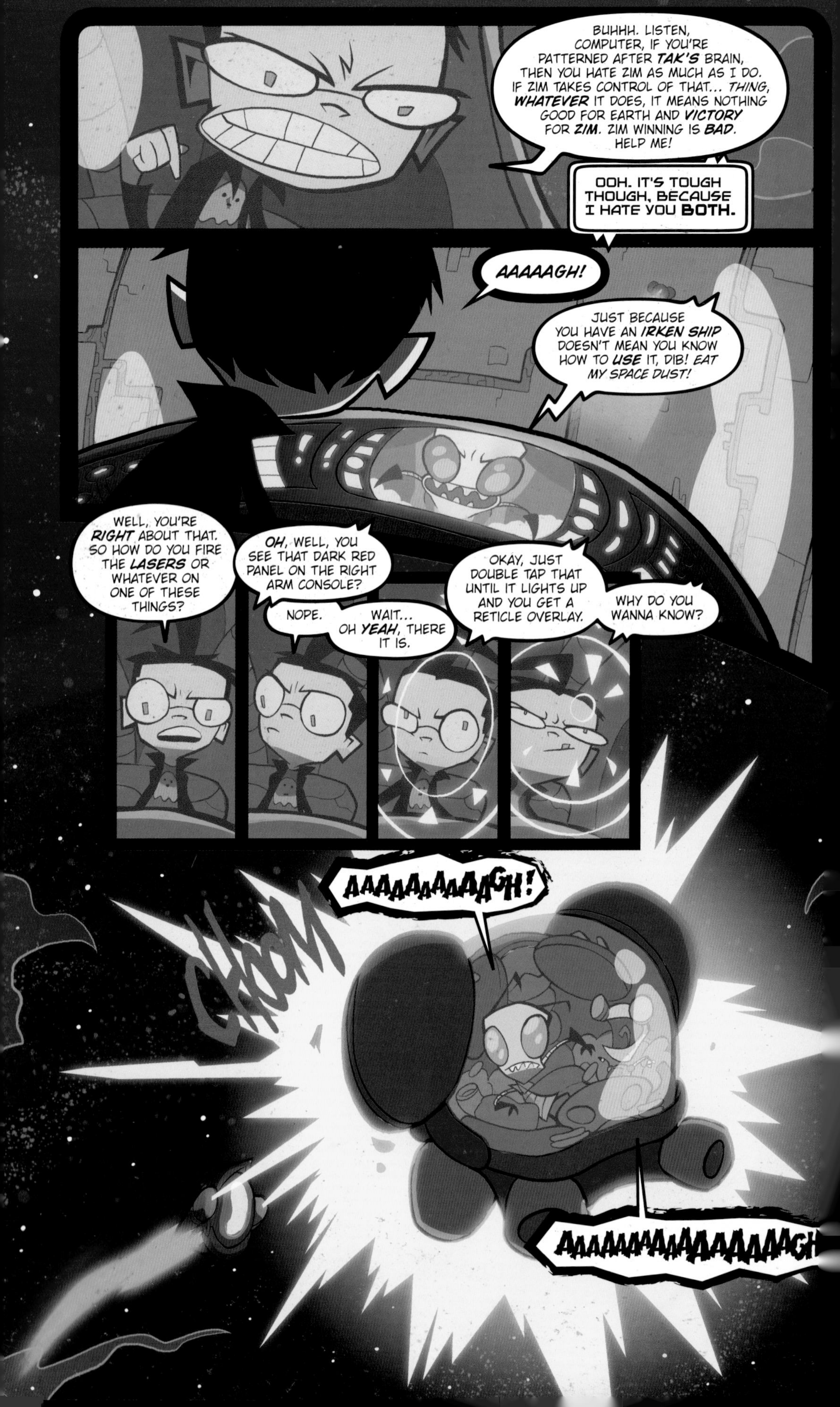
BUHHH. LISTEN, COMPUTER, IF YOU'RE PATTERNED AFTER TAK'S BRAIN, THEN YOU HATE ZIM AS MUCH AS I DO. IF ZIM TAKES CONTROL OF THAT... THING, WHATEVER IT DOES, IT MEANS NOTHING GOOD FOR EARTH AND VICTORY FOR ZIM. ZIM WINNING IS BAD. HELP ME!
OOH. IT'S TOUGH THOUGH, BECAUSE I HATE YOU BOTH.
AAAAAGH!
JUST BECAUSE YOU HAVE AN IRKEN SHIP DOESN'T MEAN YOU KNOW HOW TO USE IT, DIB! EAT MY SPACE DUST!
WELL, YOU'RE RIGHT ABOUT THAT. SO HOW DO YOU FIRE THE LASERS OR WHATEVER ON ONE OF THESE THINGS?
OH, WELL, YOU SEE THAT DARK RED PANEL ON THE RIGHT ARM CONSOLE?
NOPE.
WAIT... OH YEAH, THERE IT IS.
OKAY, JUST DOUBLE TAP THAT UNTIL IT LIGHTS UP AND YOU GET A RETICLE OVERLAY.
WHY DO YOU WANNA KNOW?
AAAAAAAAAAGH!
CHOOM
AAAAAAAAAAAAAAAAGH

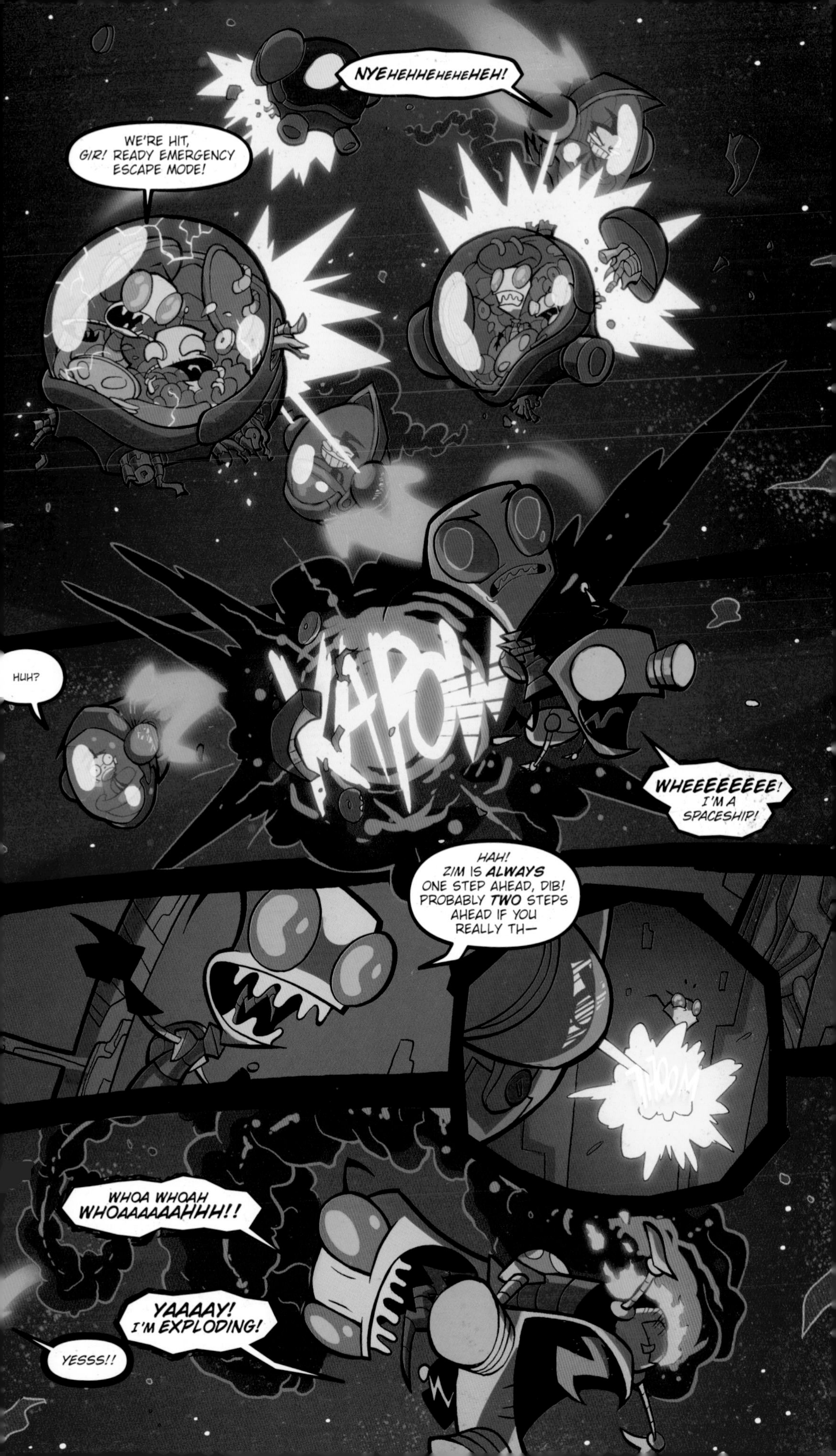
NYEHEHHEHEHEHEH!
WE'RE HIT, GIR! READY EMERGENCY ESCAPE MODE!
HUH?
KAPOW
WHEEEEEEEE! I'M A SPACESHIP!
HAH! ZIM IS ALWAYS ONE STEP AHEAD, DIB! PROBABLY TWO STEPS AHEAD IF YOU REALLY TH—
THOOM
WHOA WHOAH WHOAAAAAAHHH!!
YAAAAY! I'M EXPLODING!
YESSS!!

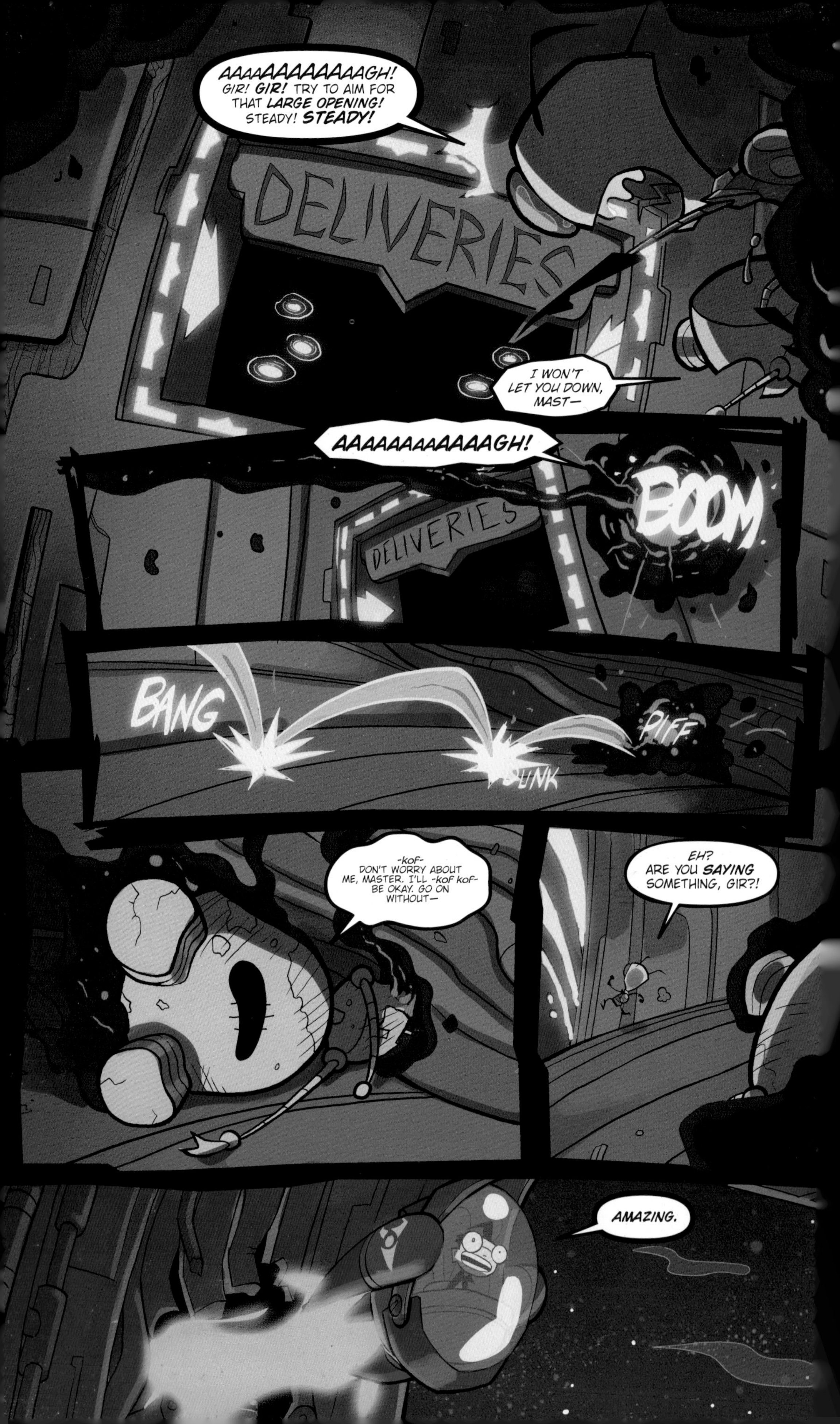
AAAAAAAAAAAAAGH! GIR! GIR! TRY TO AIM FOR THAT LARGE OPENING! STEADY! STEADY!
DELIVERIES
I WON'T LET YOU DOWN, MAST—
AAAAAAAAAAAAAGH!
DELIVERIES
BOOM
BANG
BUNK
PIFF
-kof- DON'T WORRY ABOUT ME, MASTER. I'LL -kof kof- BE OKAY. GO ON WITHOUT—
EH? ARE YOU SAYING SOMETHING, GIR?!
AMAZING.

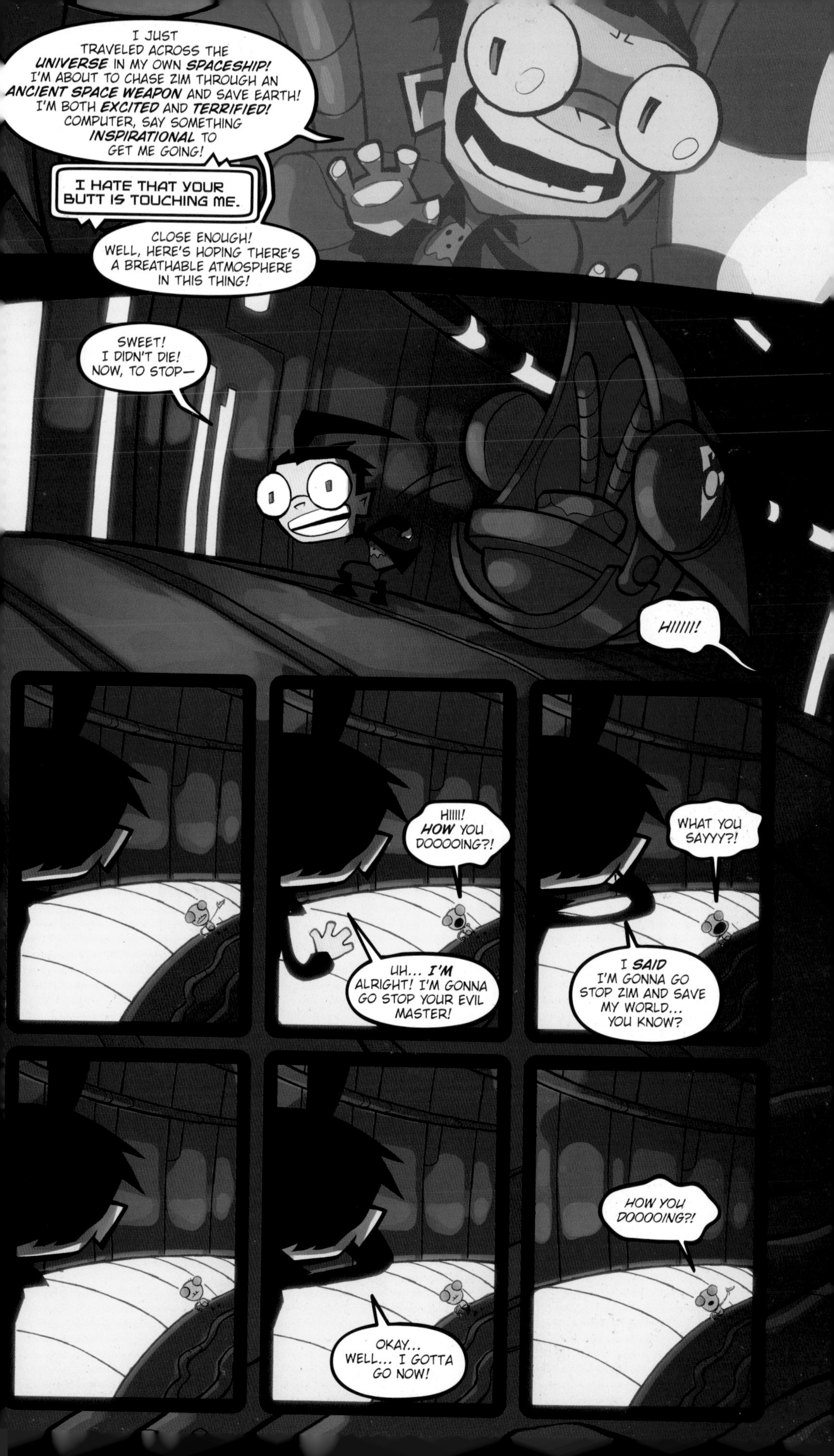
I JUST TRAVELED ACROSS THE UNIVERSE IN MY OWN SPACESHIP! I'M ABOUT TO CHASE ZIM THROUGH AN ANCIENT SPACE WEAPON AND SAVE EARTH! I'M BOTH EXCITED AND TERRIFIED! COMPUTER, SAY SOMETHING INSPIRATIONAL TO GET ME GOING!
I HATE THAT YOUR BUTT IS TOUCHING ME.
CLOSE ENOUGH! WELL, HERE'S HOPING THERE'S A BREATHABLE ATMOSPHERE IN THIS THING!
SWEET! I DIDN'T DIE! NOW, TO STOP—
HIIIII!
HIIII! HOW YOU DOOOOING?!
UH... I'M ALRIGHT! I'M GONNA GO STOP YOUR EVIL MASTER!
WHAT YOU SAYYY?!
I SAID I'M GONNA GO STOP ZIM AND SAVE MY WORLD... YOU KNOW?
OKAY... WELL... I GOTTA GO NOW!
HOW YOU DOOOOING?!

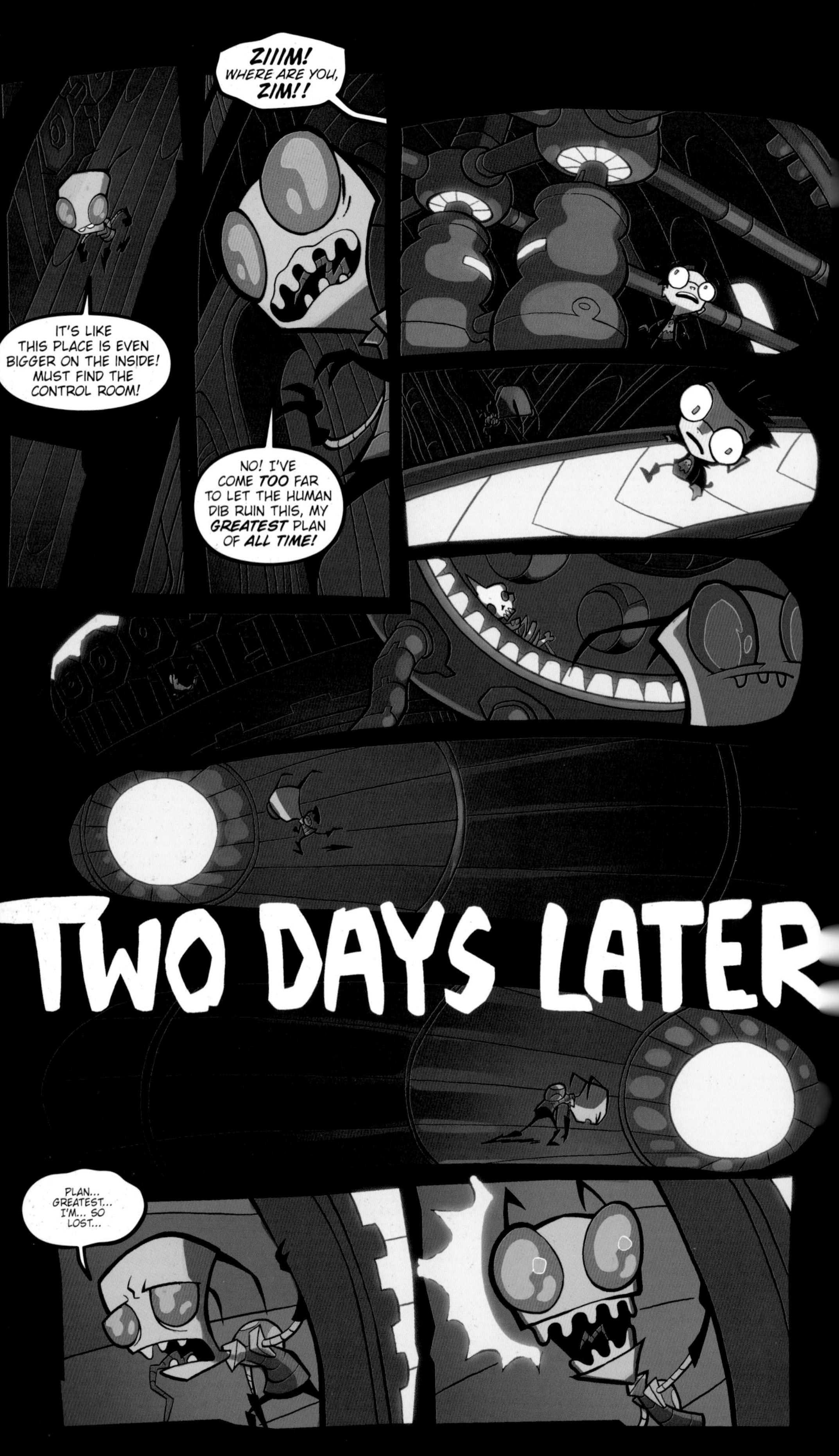
IT'S LIKE THIS PLACE IS EVEN BIGGER ON THE INSIDE! MUST FIND THE CONTROL ROOM!
ZIIIM! WHERE ARE YOU, ZIM!!
NO! I'VE COME TOO FAR TO LET THE HUMAN DIB RUIN THIS, MY GREATEST PLAN OF ALL TIME!
TWO DAYS LATER
PLAN... GREATEST... I'M... SO LOST...

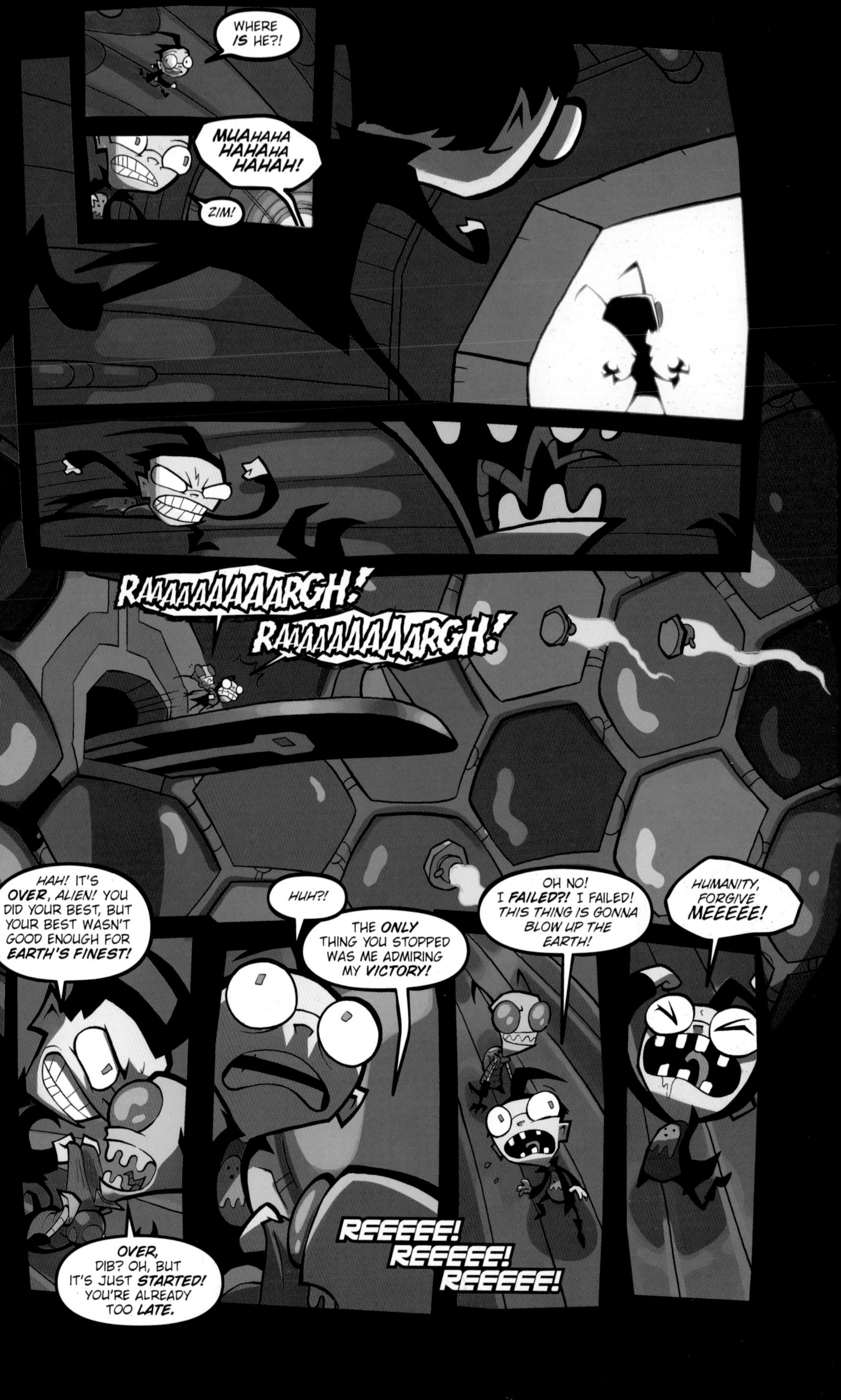

WHERE IS HE?!
MUAHAHA HAHAHA HAHAH!
ZIM!
RAAAAAAAAAARGH!
RAAAAAAAAAARGH!
HAH! IT'S OVER, ALIEN! YOU DID YOUR BEST, BUT YOUR BEST WASN'T GOOD ENOUGH FOR EARTH'S FINEST!
OVER, DIB? OH, BUT IT'S JUST STARTED! YOU'RE ALREADY TOO LATE.
HUH?!
THE ONLY THING YOU STOPPED WAS ME ADMIRING MY VICTORY!
REEEEE! REEEEE! REEEEE!
OH NO! I FAILED?! I FAILED! THIS THING IS GONNA BLOW UP THE EARTH!
HUMANITY, FORGIVE MEEEEE!

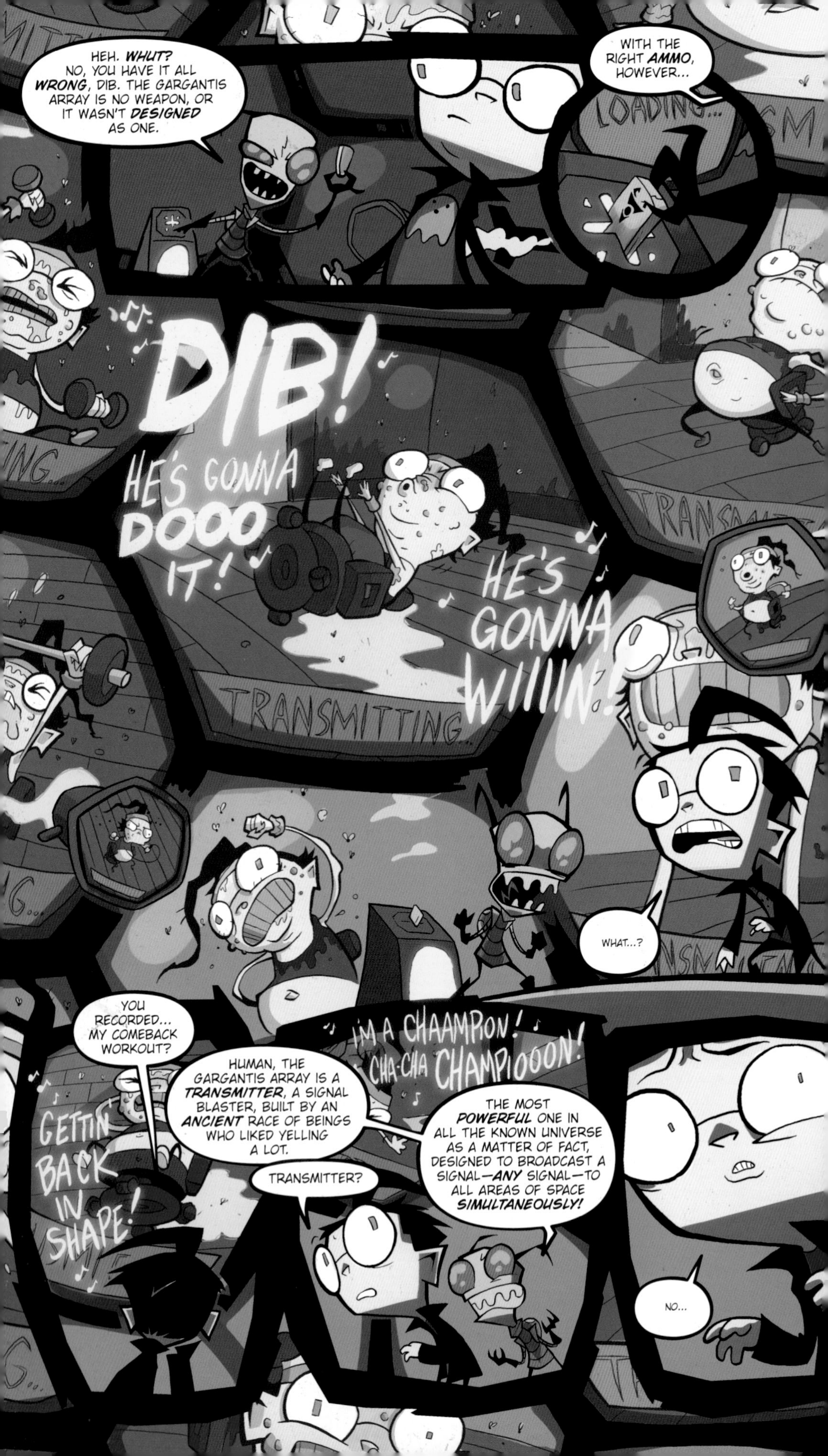
HEH. WHUT? NO, YOU HAVE IT ALL WRONG, DIB. THE GARGANTIS ARRAY IS NO WEAPON, OR IT WASN'T DESIGNED AS ONE.
WITH THE RIGHT AMMO, HOWEVER...
LOADING...
DIB!
HE'S GONNA DOOO IT!
HE'S GONNA WIIIIN!
TRANSMITTING...
WHAT...?
YOU RECORDED... MY COMEBACK WORKOUT?
I'M A CHAAMPION! CHA-CHA CHAMPIOOON!
GETTIN' BACK IN SHAPE!
HUMAN, THE GARGANTIS ARRAY IS A TRANSMITTER, A SIGNAL BLASTER, BUILT BY AN ANCIENT RACE OF BEINGS WHO LIKED YELLING A LOT.
TRANSMITTER?
THE MOST POWERFUL ONE IN ALL THE KNOWN UNIVERSE AS A MATTER OF FACT, DESIGNED TO BROADCAST A SIGNAL—ANY SIGNAL—TO ALL AREAS OF SPACE SIMULTANEOUSLY!
NO...

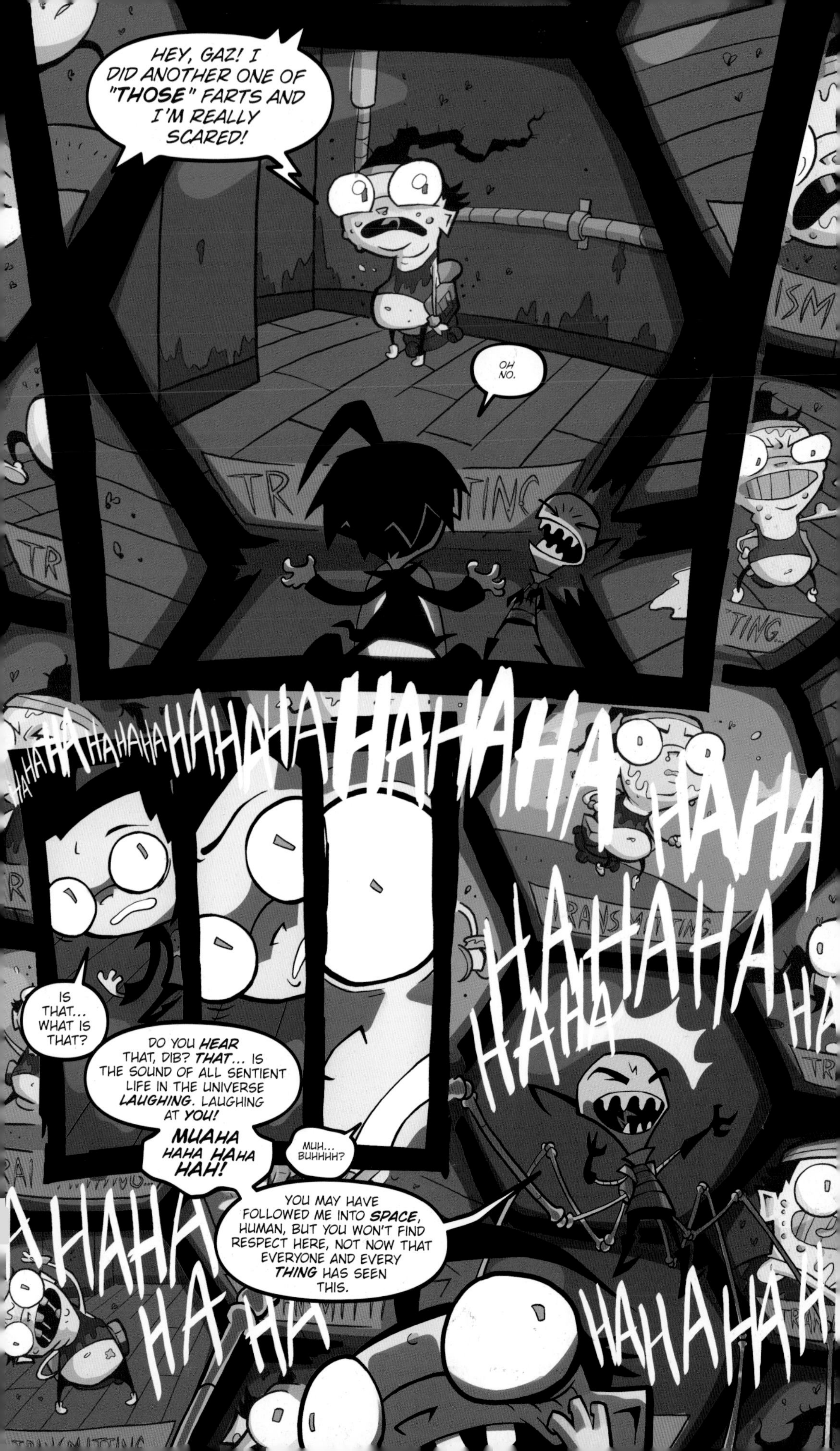
HEY, GAZ! I DID ANOTHER ONE OF "THOSE" FARTS AND I'M REALLY SCARED!
OH NO.
HAHAHAHAHAHAHAHAHAHAHAHAHAHA
IS THAT... WHAT IS THAT?
DO YOU HEAR THAT, DIB? THAT... IS THE SOUND OF ALL SENTIENT LIFE IN THE UNIVERSE LAUGHING. LAUGHING AT YOU! MUAHA HAHA HAHA HAH!
MUH... BUHHHH?
YOU MAY HAVE FOLLOWED ME INTO SPACE, HUMAN, BUT YOU WON'T FIND RESPECT HERE, NOT NOW THAT EVERYONE AND EVERY THING HAS SEEN THIS.
HAHAHA HA HA
HAHAHAH

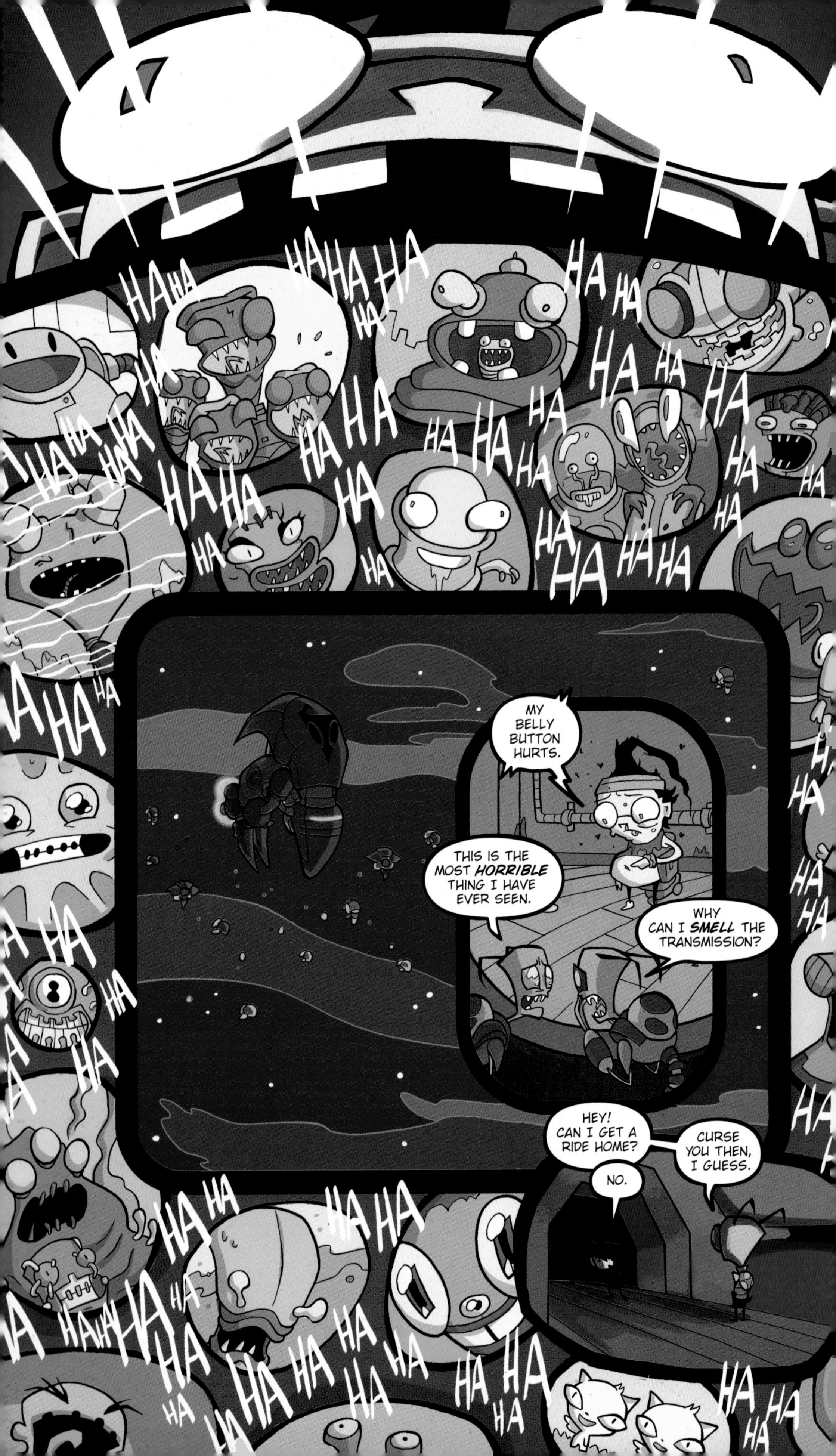

HA HA HA HA HA HA
MY BELLY BUTTON HURTS.
THIS IS THE MOST HORRIBLE THING I HAVE EVER SEEN.
WHY CAN I SMELL THE TRANSMISSION?
HEY! CAN I GET A RIDE HOME?
NO.
CURSE YOU THEN, I GUESS.
HA HA HA HA

THE END

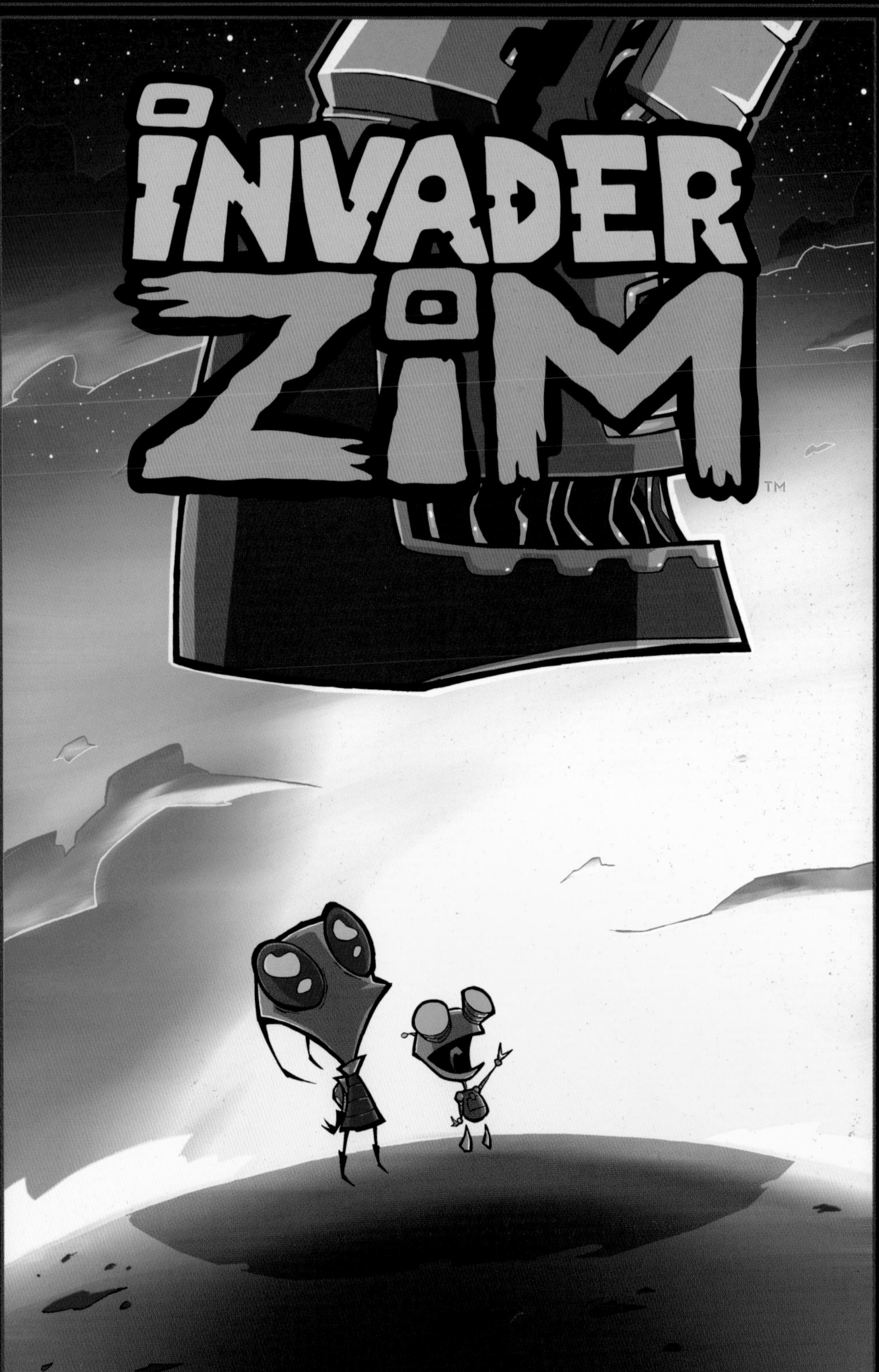
INVADER ZIM™

CHAPTER: 3

illustration by AARON ALEXOVICH and RIKKI SIMONS

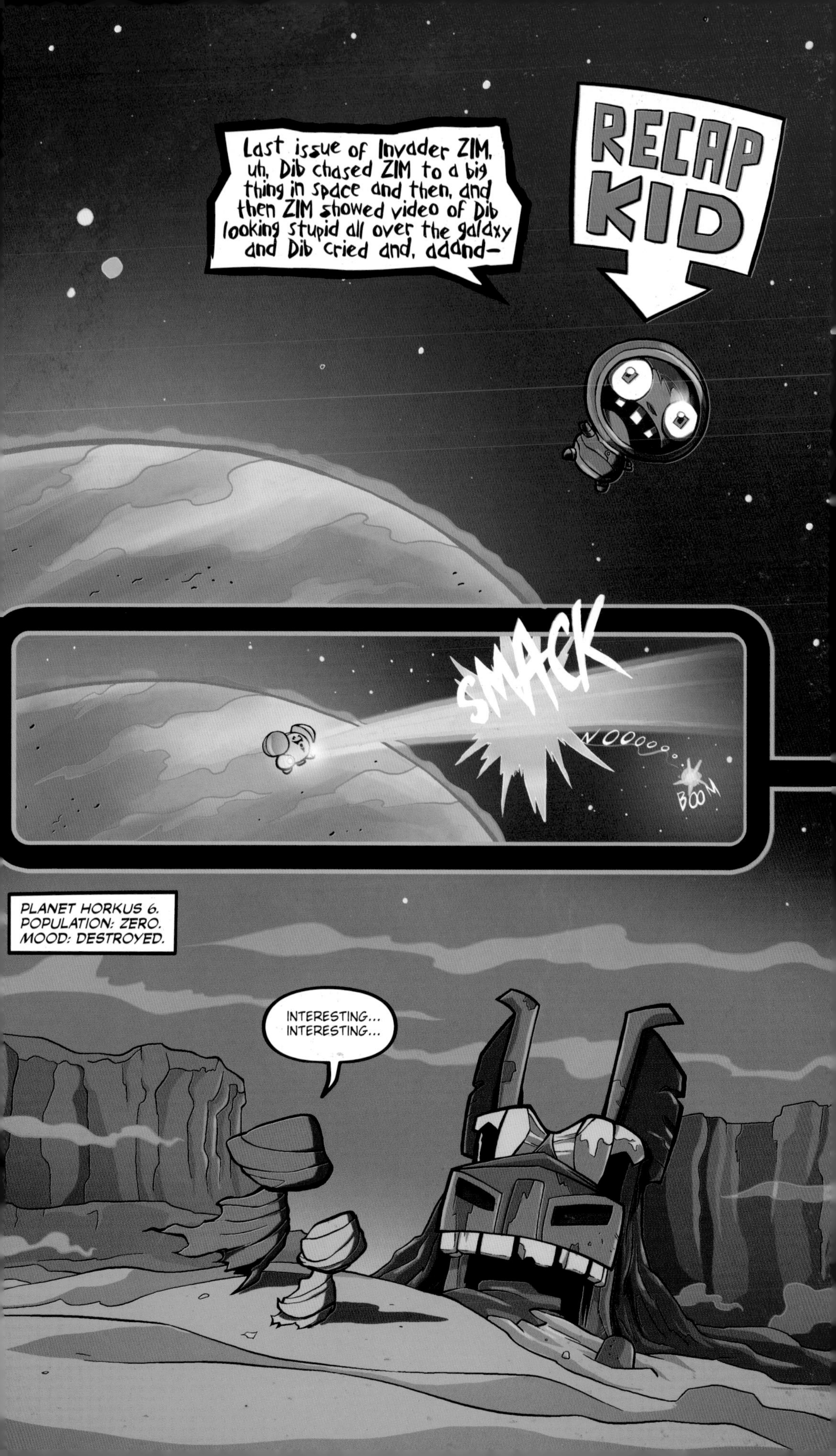
RECAP KID
Last issue of Invader ZIM, uh, Dib chased ZIM to a big thing in space and then, and then ZIM showed video of Dib looking stupid all over the galaxy and Dib cried and, aaand-
SMACK
NOOOooo...
BOOM
PLANET HORKUS 6. POPULATION: ZERO. MOOD: DESTROYED.
INTERESTING... INTERESTING...

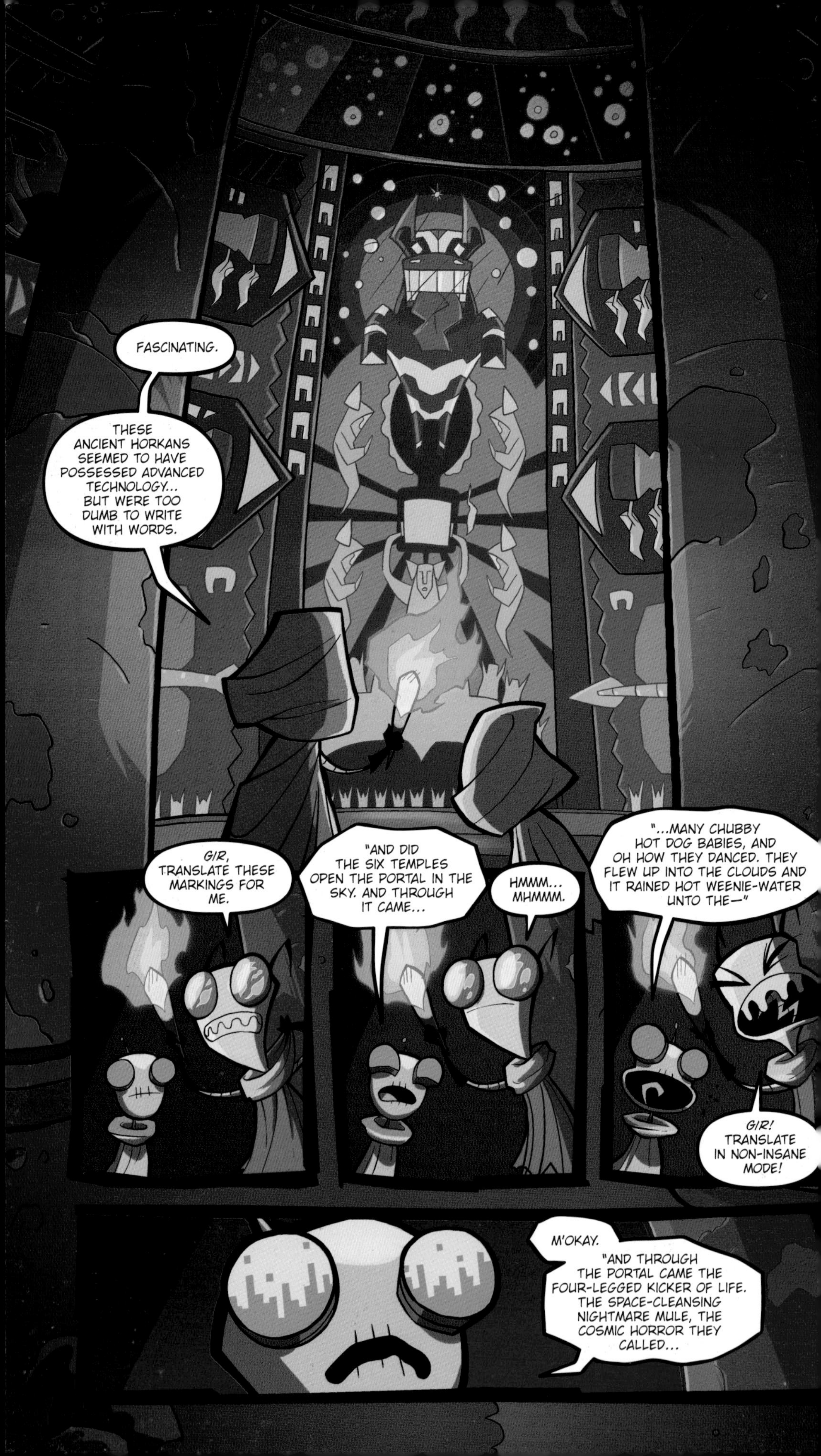

FASCINATING.
THESE ANCIENT HORKANS SEEMED TO HAVE POSSESSED ADVANCED TECHNOLOGY... BUT WERE TOO DUMB TO WRITE WITH WORDS.
GIR, TRANSLATE THESE MARKINGS FOR ME.
"AND DID THE SIX TEMPLES OPEN THE PORTAL IN THE SKY. AND THROUGH IT CAME...
HMMM... MHMMM.
"...MANY CHUBBY HOT DOG BABIES, AND OH HOW THEY DANCED. THEY FLEW UP INTO THE CLOUDS AND IT RAINED HOT WEENIE-WATER UNTO THE—"
GIR! TRANSLATE IN NON-INSANE MODE!
M'OKAY.
"AND THROUGH THE PORTAL CAME THE FOUR-LEGGED KICKER OF LIFE. THE SPACE-CLEANSING NIGHTMARE MULE, THE COSMIC HORROR THEY CALLED...

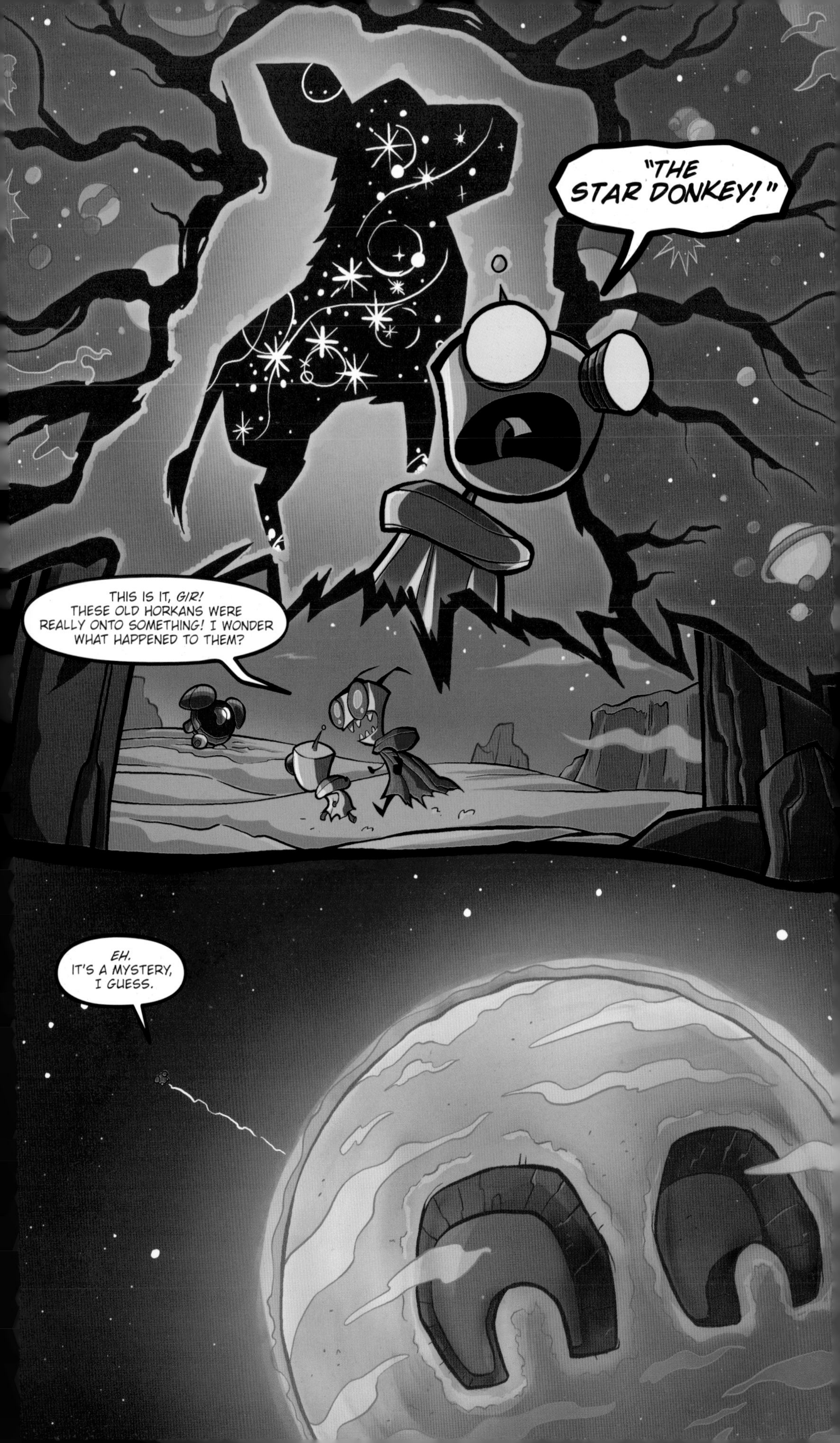
"THE STAR DONKEY!"
THIS IS IT, *GIR!* THESE OLD HORKANS WERE REALLY ONTO SOMETHING! I WONDER WHAT HAPPENED TO THEM?
EH. IT'S A MYSTERY, I GUESS.

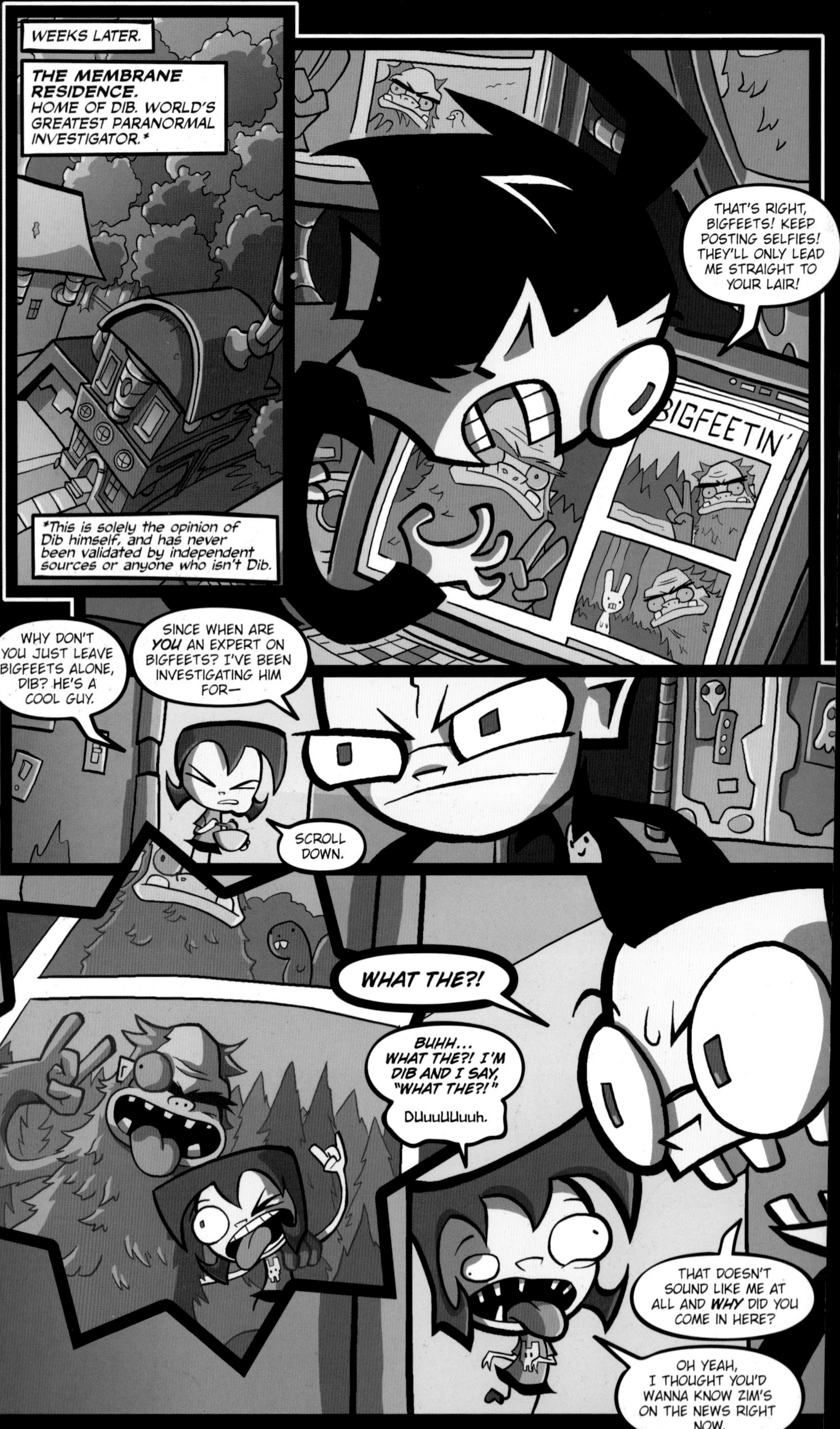
WEEKS LATER.
THE MEMBRANE RESIDENCE. HOME OF DIB. WORLD'S GREATEST PARANORMAL INVESTIGATOR.*
*This is solely the opinion of Dib himself, and has never been validated by independent sources or anyone who isn't Dib.
THAT'S RIGHT, BIGFEETS! KEEP POSTING SELFIES! THEY'LL ONLY LEAD ME STRAIGHT TO YOUR LAIR!
BIGFEETIN'
WHY DON'T YOU JUST LEAVE BIGFEETS ALONE, DIB? HE'S A COOL GUY.
SINCE WHEN ARE YOU AN EXPERT ON BIGFEETS? I'VE BEEN INVESTIGATING HIM FOR—
SCROLL DOWN.
WHAT THE?!
BUHH... WHAT THE?! I'M DIB AND I SAY, "WHAT THE?!"
DUuuUUuuh.
THAT DOESN'T SOUND LIKE ME AT ALL AND WHY DID YOU COME IN HERE?
OH YEAH, I THOUGHT YOU'D WANNA KNOW ZIM'S ON THE NEWS RIGHT NOW.

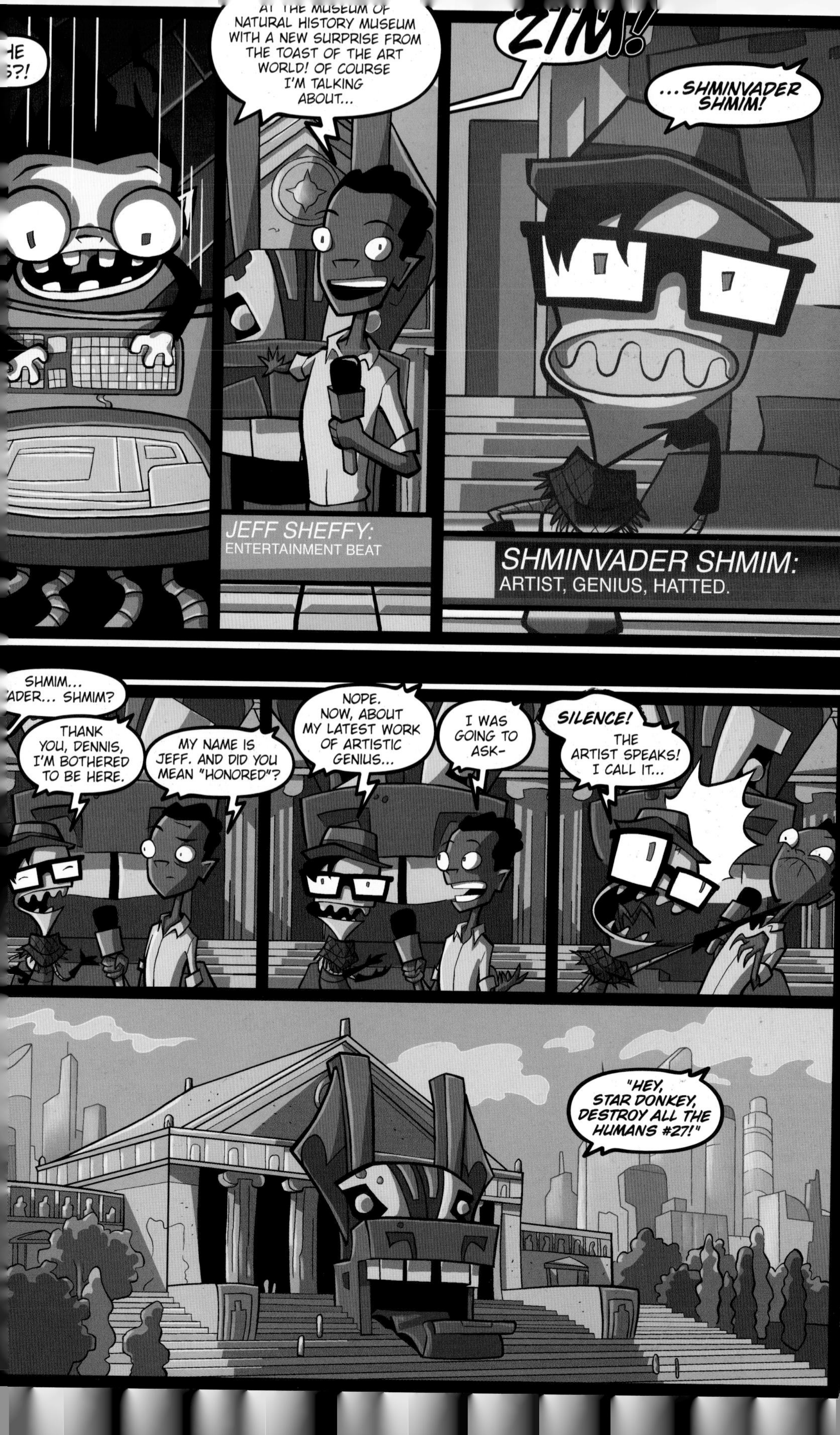

HE
S?!
AT THE MUSEUM OF NATURAL HISTORY MUSEUM WITH A NEW SURPRISE FROM THE TOAST OF THE ART WORLD! OF COURSE I'M TALKING ABOUT...
ZIM!
...SHMINVADER SHMIM!
JEFF SHEFFY:
ENTERTAINMENT BEAT
SHMINVADER SHMIM:
ARTIST, GENIUS, HATTED.
SHMIM... ADER... SHMIM?
THANK YOU, DENNIS, I'M BOTHERED TO BE HERE.
MY NAME IS JEFF. AND DID YOU MEAN "HONORED"?
NOPE. NOW, ABOUT MY LATEST WORK OF ARTISTIC GENIUS...
I WAS GOING TO ASK-
SILENCE!
THE ARTIST SPEAKS! I CALL IT...
"HEY, STAR DONKEY, DESTROY ALL THE HUMANS #27!"

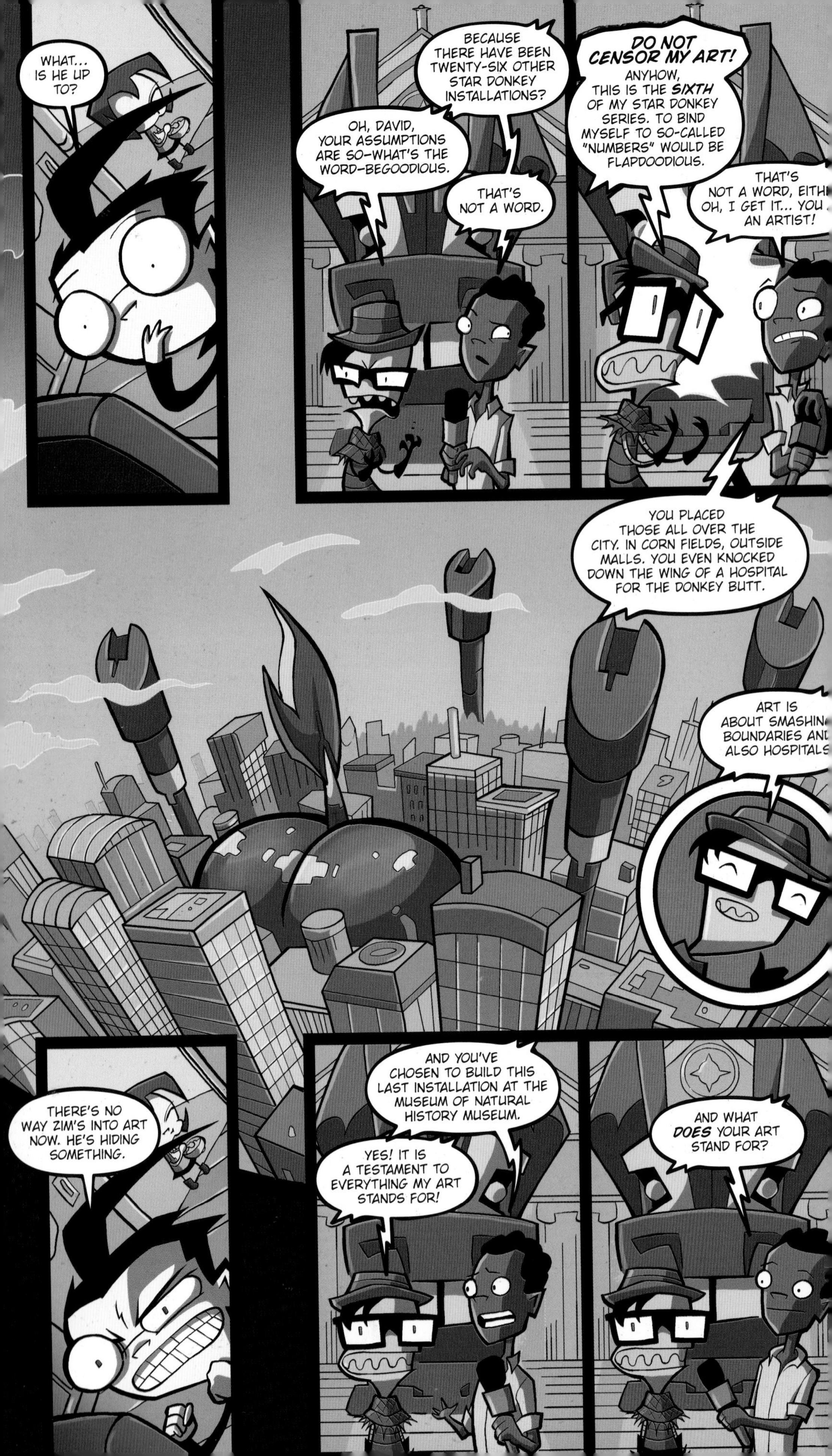

WHAT... IS HE UP TO?
BECAUSE THERE HAVE BEEN TWENTY-SIX OTHER STAR DONKEY INSTALLATIONS?
OH, DAVID, YOUR ASSUMPTIONS ARE SO–WHAT'S THE WORD–BEGOODIOUS.
THAT'S NOT A WORD.
DO NOT CENSOR MY ART! ANYHOW, THIS IS THE SIXTH OF MY STAR DONKEY SERIES. TO BIND MYSELF TO SO-CALLED "NUMBERS" WOULD BE FLAPDOODIOUS.
THAT'S NOT A WORD, EITH OH, I GET IT... YOU AN ARTIST!
YOU PLACED THOSE ALL OVER THE CITY. IN CORN FIELDS, OUTSIDE MALLS. YOU EVEN KNOCKED DOWN THE WING OF A HOSPITAL FOR THE DONKEY BUTT.
ART IS ABOUT SMASHIN BOUNDARIES AN ALSO HOSPITALS
THERE'S NO WAY ZIM'S INTO ART NOW. HE'S HIDING SOMETHING.
AND YOU'VE CHOSEN TO BUILD THIS LAST INSTALLATION AT THE MUSEUM OF NATURAL HISTORY MUSEUM.
YES! IT IS A TESTAMENT TO EVERYTHING MY ART STANDS FOR!
AND WHAT DOES YOUR ART STAND FOR?

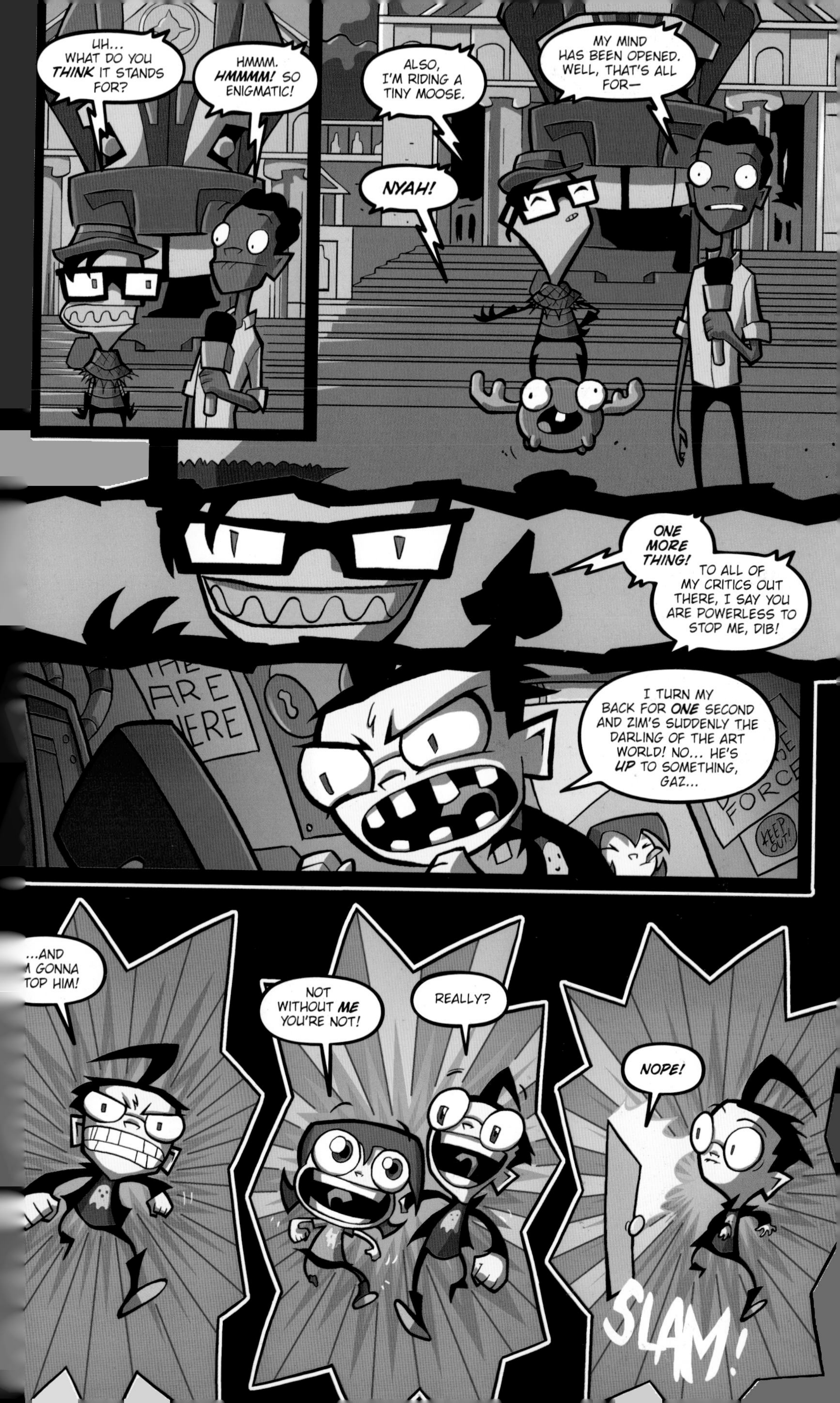

UH... WHAT DO YOU *THINK* IT STANDS FOR?
HMMM. *HMMMM!* SO ENIGMATIC!
ALSO, I'M RIDING A TINY MOOSE.
NYAH!
MY MIND HAS BEEN OPENED. WELL, THAT'S ALL FOR—
ONE MORE THING! TO ALL OF MY CRITICS OUT THERE, I SAY YOU ARE POWERLESS TO STOP ME, DIB!
I TURN MY BACK FOR *ONE* SECOND AND ZIM'S SUDDENLY THE DARLING OF THE ART WORLD! NO... HE'S *UP* TO SOMETHING, GAZ...
...AND M GONNA TOP HIM!
NOT WITHOUT *ME* YOU'RE NOT!
REALLY?
NOPE!
SLAM!

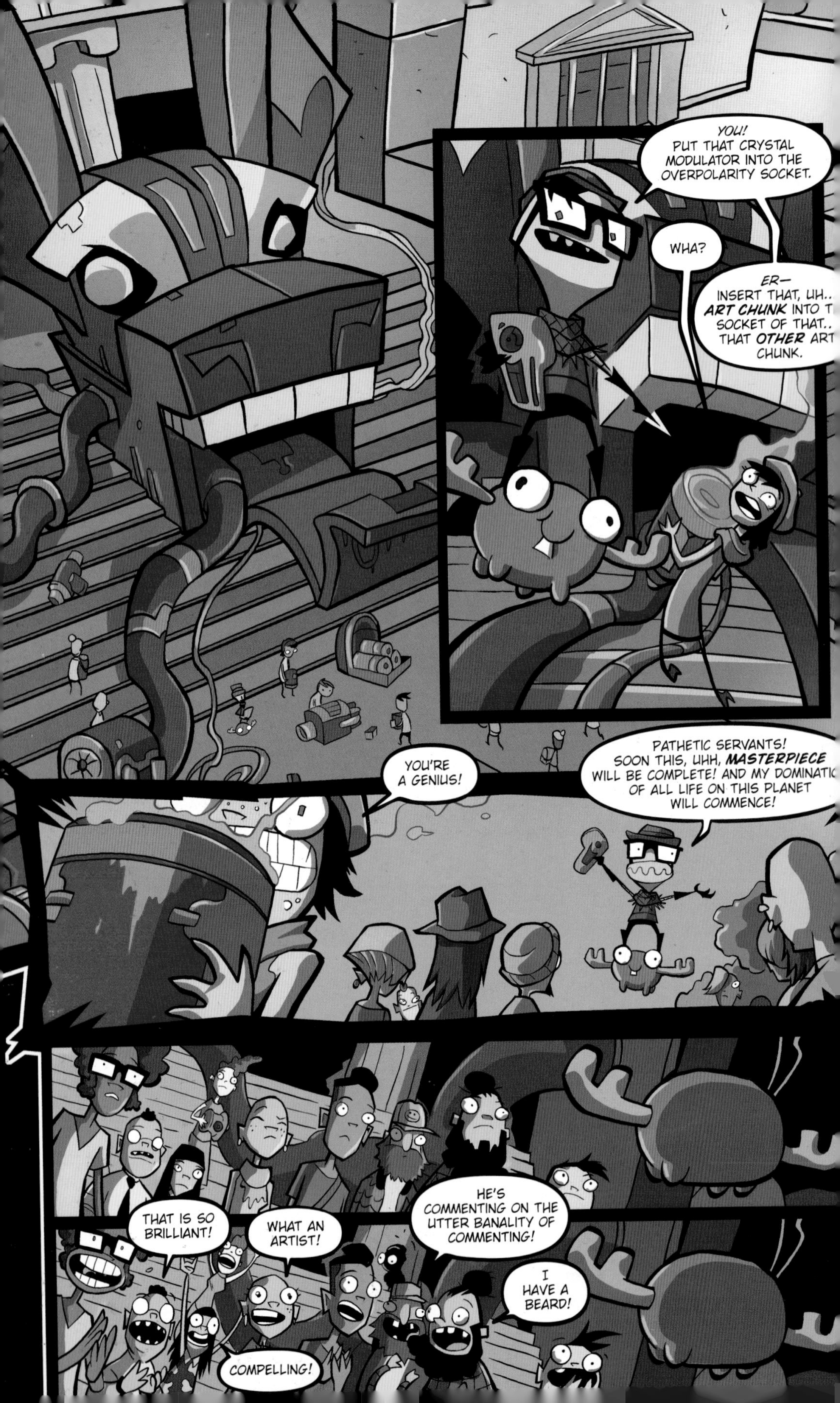

YOU! PUT THAT CRYSTAL MODULATOR INTO THE OVERPOLARITY SOCKET.
WHA?
ER— INSERT THAT, UH.. ART CHUNK INTO T SOCKET OF THAT.. THAT OTHER ART CHUNK.
YOU'RE A GENIUS!
PATHETIC SERVANTS! SOON THIS, UHH, MASTERPIECE WILL BE COMPLETE! AND MY DOMINATI OF ALL LIFE ON THIS PLANET WILL COMMENCE!
THAT IS SO BRILLIANT!
WHAT AN ARTIST!
HE'S COMMENTING ON THE UTTER BANALITY OF COMMENTING!
I HAVE A BEARD!
COMPELLING!

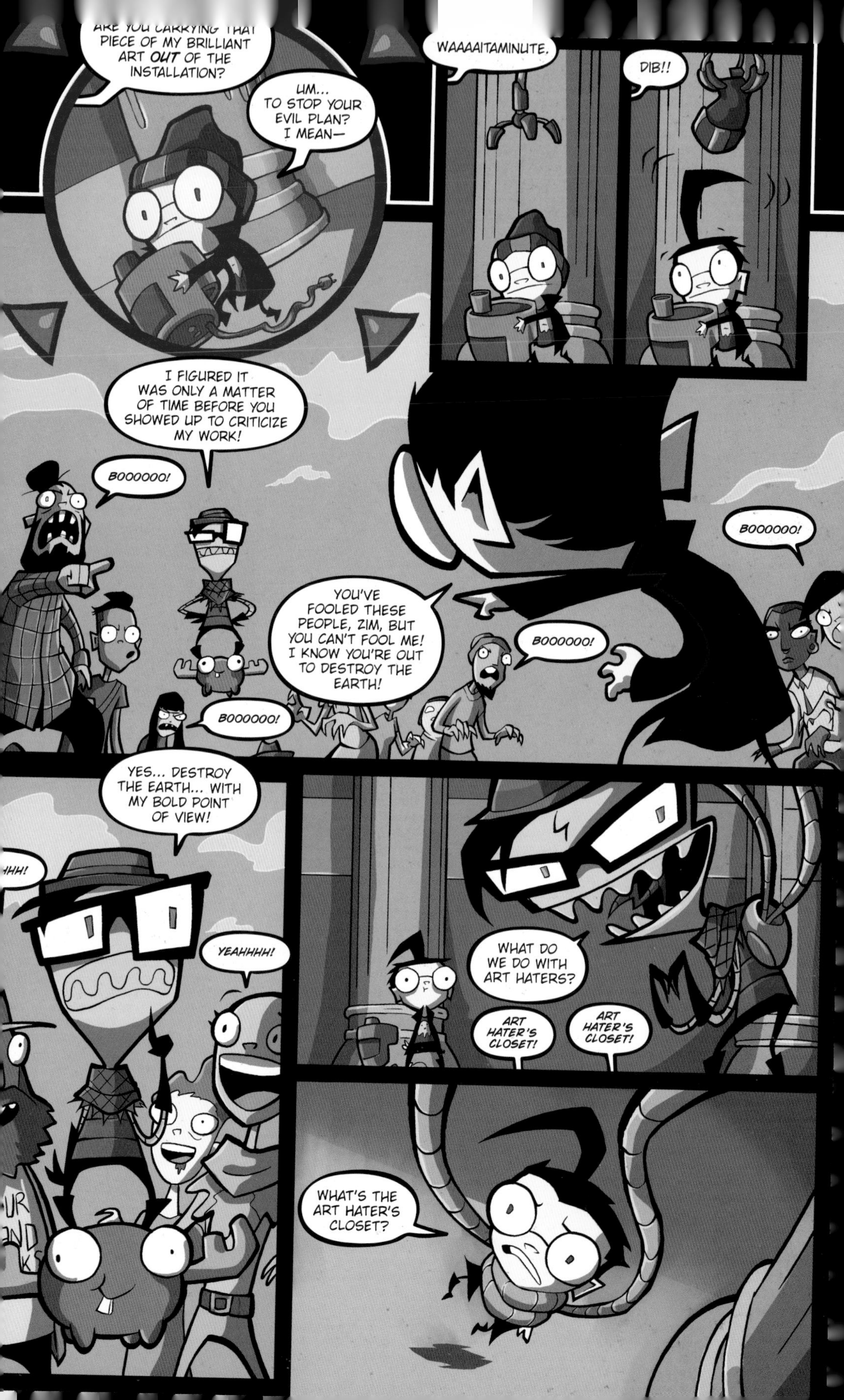

ARE YOU CARRYING THAT PIECE OF MY BRILLIANT ART OUT OF THE INSTALLATION?
UM... TO STOP YOUR EVIL PLAN? I MEAN—
WAAAAITAMINUTE.
DIB!!
I FIGURED IT WAS ONLY A MATTER OF TIME BEFORE YOU SHOWED UP TO CRITICIZE MY WORK!
BOOOOOO!
BOOOOOO!
YOU'VE FOOLED THESE PEOPLE, ZIM, BUT YOU CAN'T FOOL ME! I KNOW YOU'RE OUT TO DESTROY THE EARTH!
BOOOOOO!
BOOOOOO!
YES... DESTROY THE EARTH... WITH MY BOLD POINT OF VIEW!
HHH!
YEAHHHH!
WHAT DO WE DO WITH ART HATERS?
ART HATER'S CLOSET!
ART HATER'S CLOSET!
WHAT'S THE ART HATER'S CLOSET?

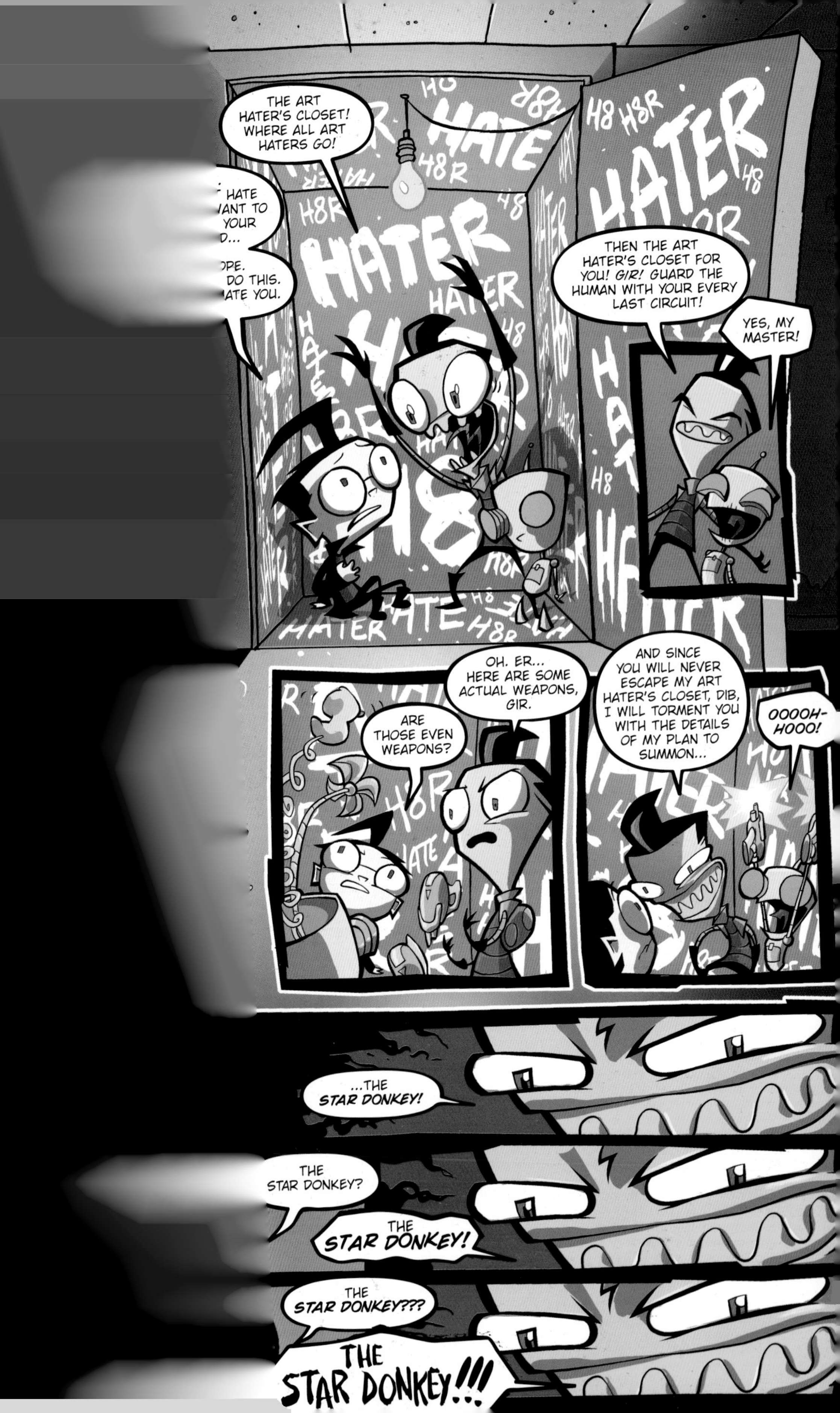

THE ART HATER'S CLOSET! WHERE ALL ART HATERS GO!
T HATE ANT TO YOUR D... OPE. DO THIS. ATE YOU.
THEN THE ART HATER'S CLOSET FOR YOU! GIR! GUARD THE HUMAN WITH YOUR EVERY LAST CIRCUIT!
YES, MY MASTER!
ARE THOSE EVEN WEAPONS?
OH. ER... HERE ARE SOME ACTUAL WEAPONS, GIR.
AND SINCE YOU WILL NEVER ESCAPE MY ART HATER'S CLOSET, DIB, I WILL TORMENT YOU WITH THE DETAILS OF MY PLAN TO SUMMON...
OOOOH-HOOO!
...THE STAR DONKEY!
THE STAR DONKEY?
THE STAR DONKEY!
THE STAR DONKEY???
THE STAR DONKEY!!!

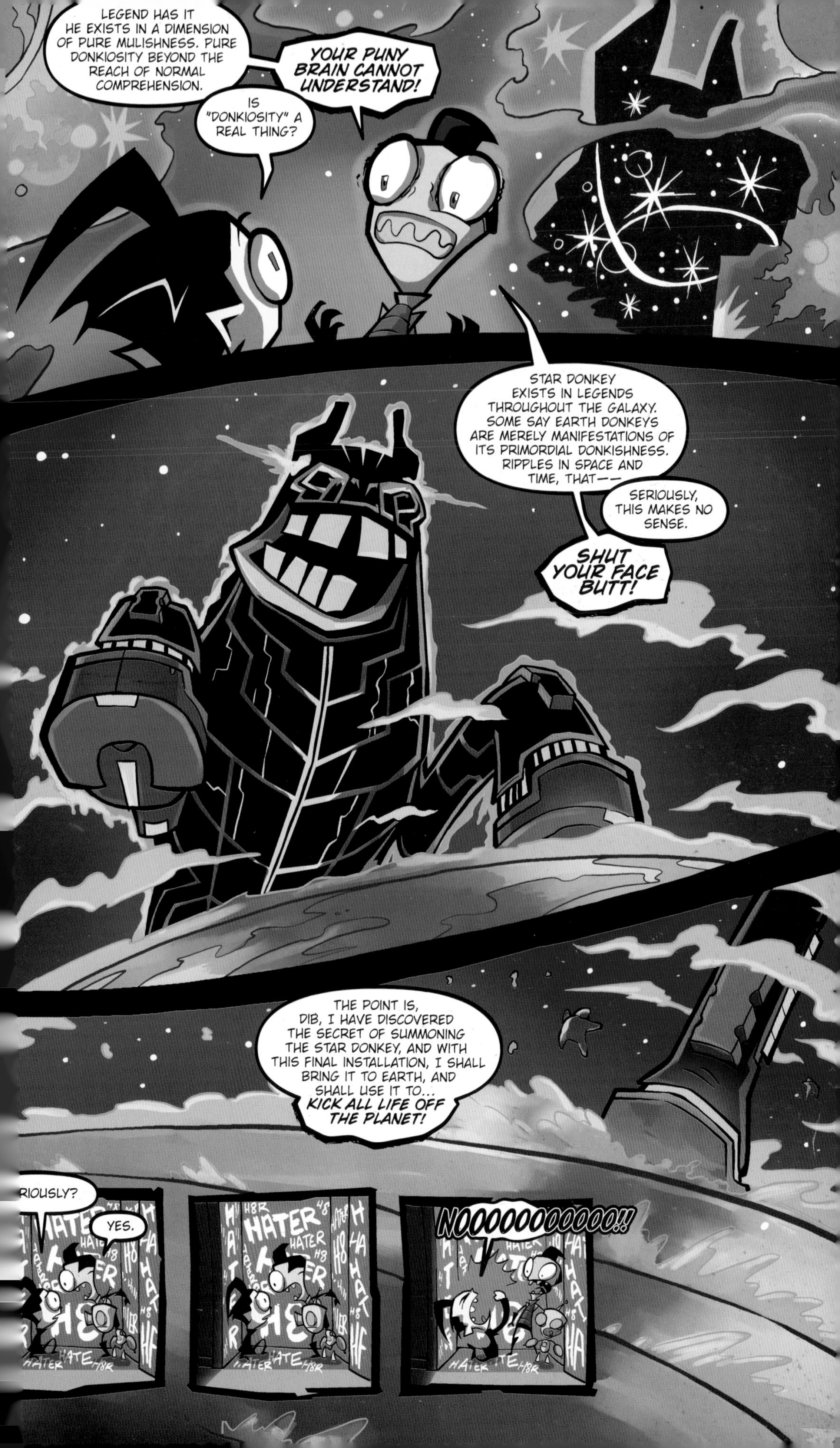
LEGEND HAS IT HE EXISTS IN A DIMENSION OF PURE MULISHNESS. PURE DONKIOSITY BEYOND THE REACH OF NORMAL COMPREHENSION.
YOUR PUNY BRAIN CANNOT UNDERSTAND!
IS "DONKIOSITY" A REAL THING?
STAR DONKEY EXISTS IN LEGENDS THROUGHOUT THE GALAXY. SOME SAY EARTH DONKEYS ARE MERELY MANIFESTATIONS OF ITS PRIMORDIAL DONKISHNESS. RIPPLES IN SPACE AND TIME, THAT——
SERIOUSLY, THIS MAKES NO SENSE.
SHUT YOUR FACE BUTT!
THE POINT IS, DIB, I HAVE DISCOVERED THE SECRET OF SUMMONING THE STAR DONKEY, AND WITH THIS FINAL INSTALLATION, I SHALL BRING IT TO EARTH, AND SHALL USE IT TO... KICK ALL LIFE OFF THE PLANET!
RIOUSLY?
YES.
NOOOOOOOOOOO!!

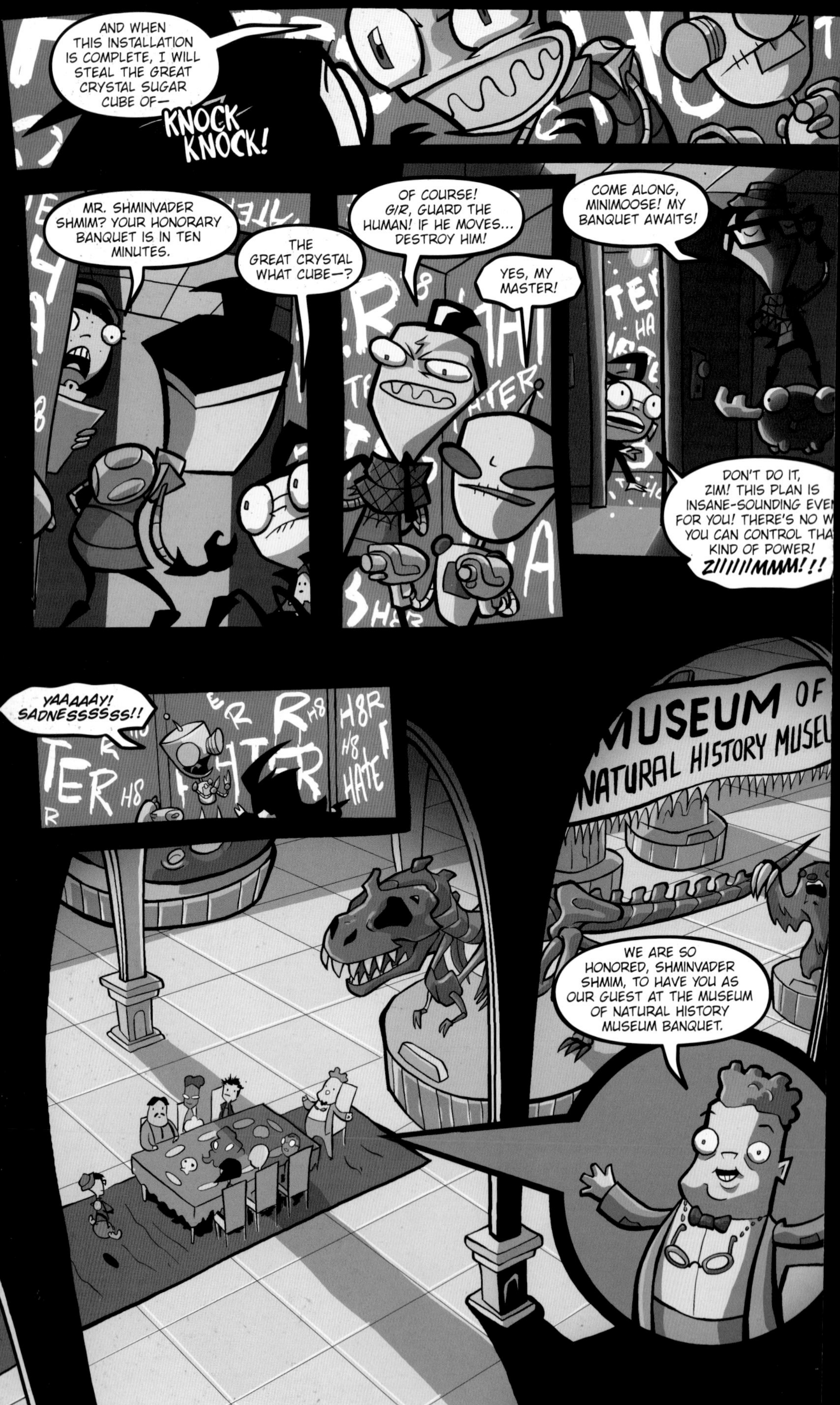
AND WHEN THIS INSTALLATION IS COMPLETE, I WILL STEAL THE GREAT CRYSTAL SUGAR CUBE OF—
KNOCK KNOCK!
MR. SHMINVADER SHMIM? YOUR HONORARY BANQUET IS IN TEN MINUTES.
THE GREAT CRYSTAL WHAT CUBE—?
OF COURSE! GIR, GUARD THE HUMAN! IF HE MOVES... DESTROY HIM!
YES, MY MASTER!
COME ALONG, MINIMOOSE! MY BANQUET AWAITS!
YAAAAAY! SADNESSSSSS!!
MUSEUM OF NATURAL HISTORY MUSEU
WE ARE SO HONORED, SHMINVADER SHMIM, TO HAVE YOU AS OUR GUEST AT THE MUSEUM OF NATURAL HISTORY MUSEUM BANQUET.

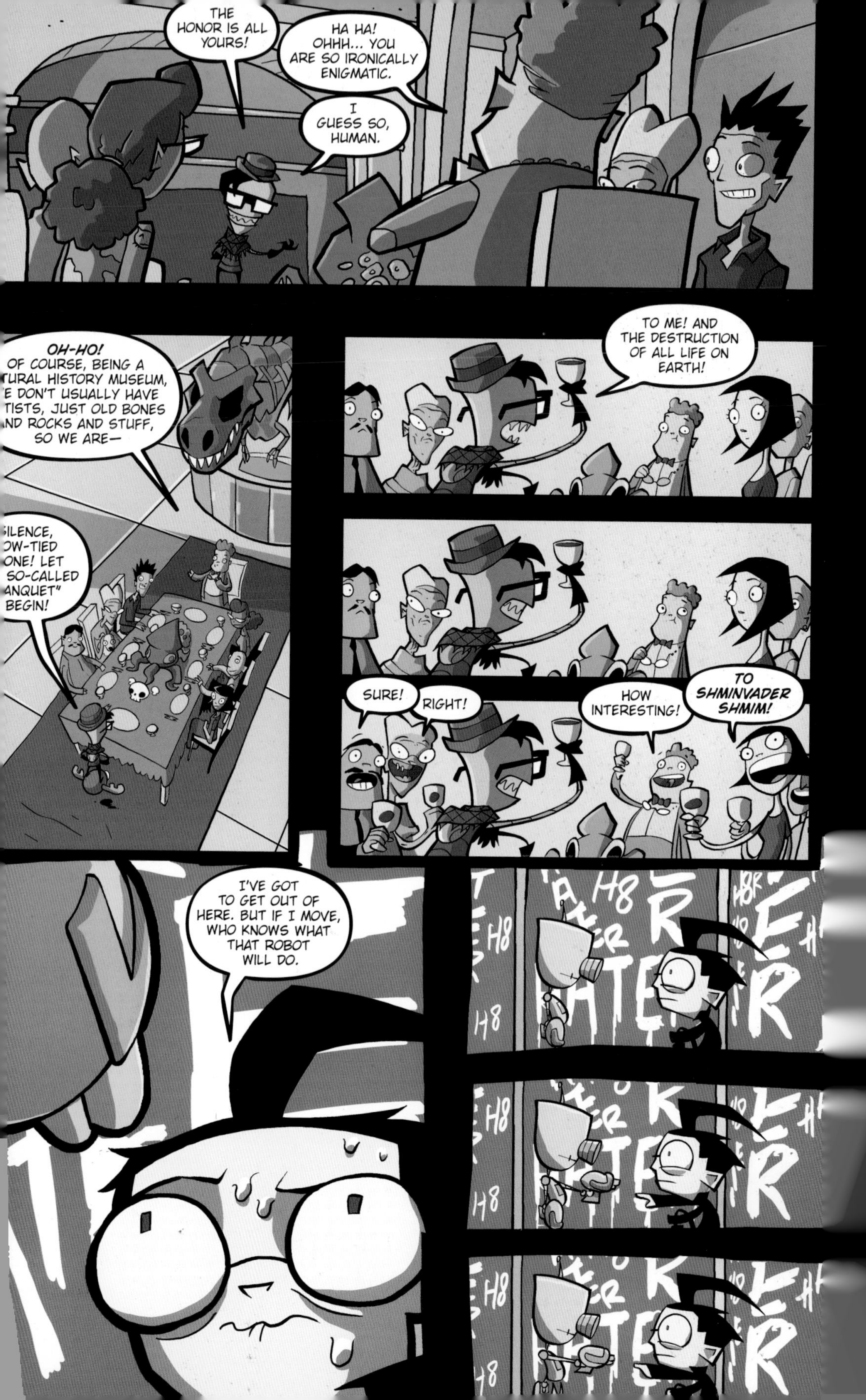
THE HONOR IS ALL YOURS!
HA HA! OHHH... YOU ARE SO IRONICALLY ENIGMATIC.
I GUESS SO, HUMAN.
OH-HO! OF COURSE, BEING A
TURAL HISTORY MUSEUM,
'E DON'T USUALLY HAVE
TISTS, JUST OLD BONES
ND ROCKS AND STUFF,
SO WE ARE—
ILENCE, OW-TIED ONE! LET SO-CALLED ANQUET" BEGIN!
TO ME! AND THE DESTRUCTION OF ALL LIFE ON EARTH!
SURE!
RIGHT!
HOW INTERESTING!
TO SHMINVADER SHMIM!
I'VE GOT TO GET OUT OF HERE. BUT IF I MOVE, WHO KNOWS WHAT THAT ROBOT WILL DO.

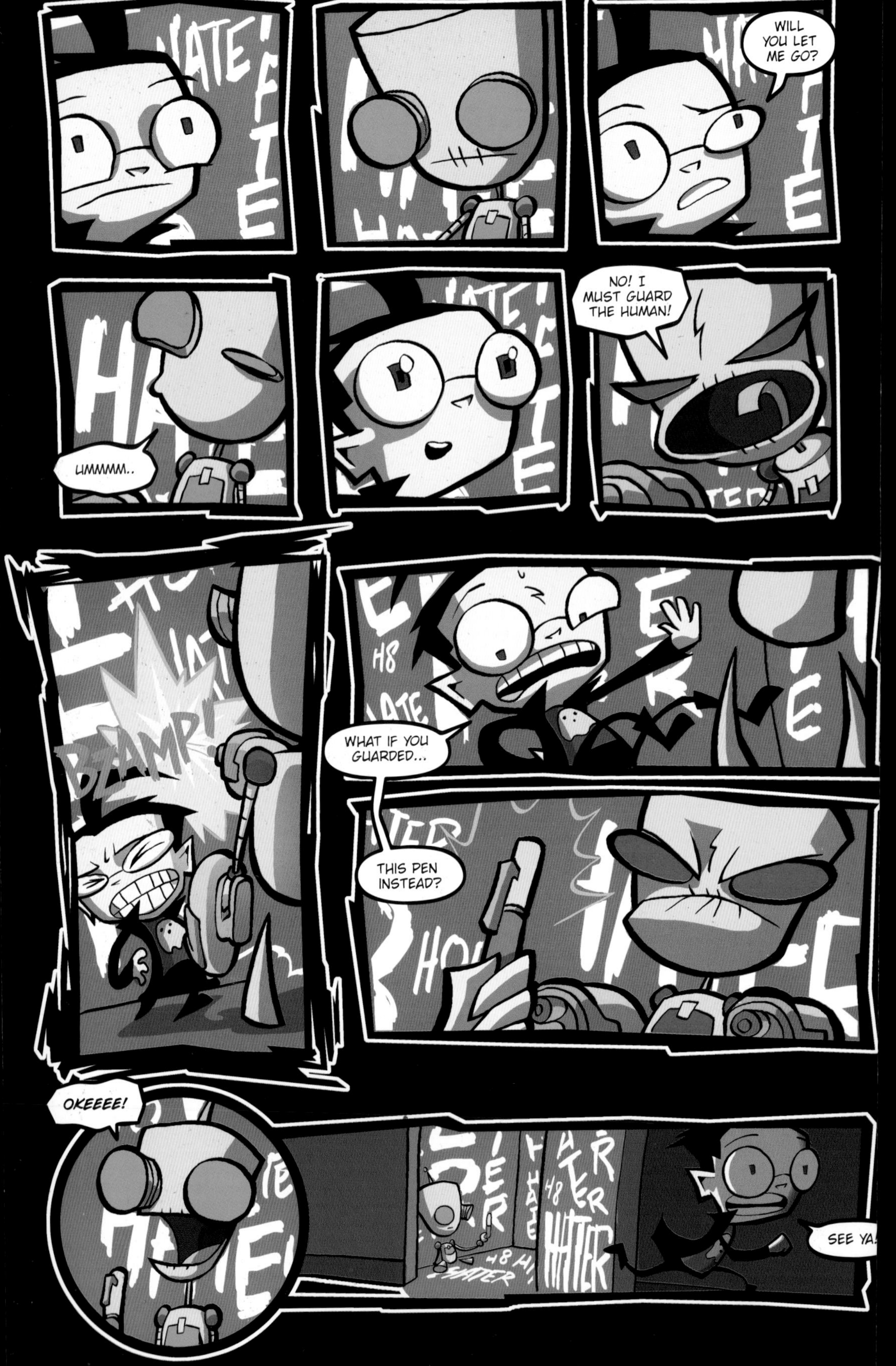

WILL YOU LET ME GO?
UMMMM..
NO! I MUST GUARD THE HUMAN!
BZAMP!
WHAT IF YOU GUARDED...
THIS PEN INSTEAD?
OKEEEE!
SEE YA!

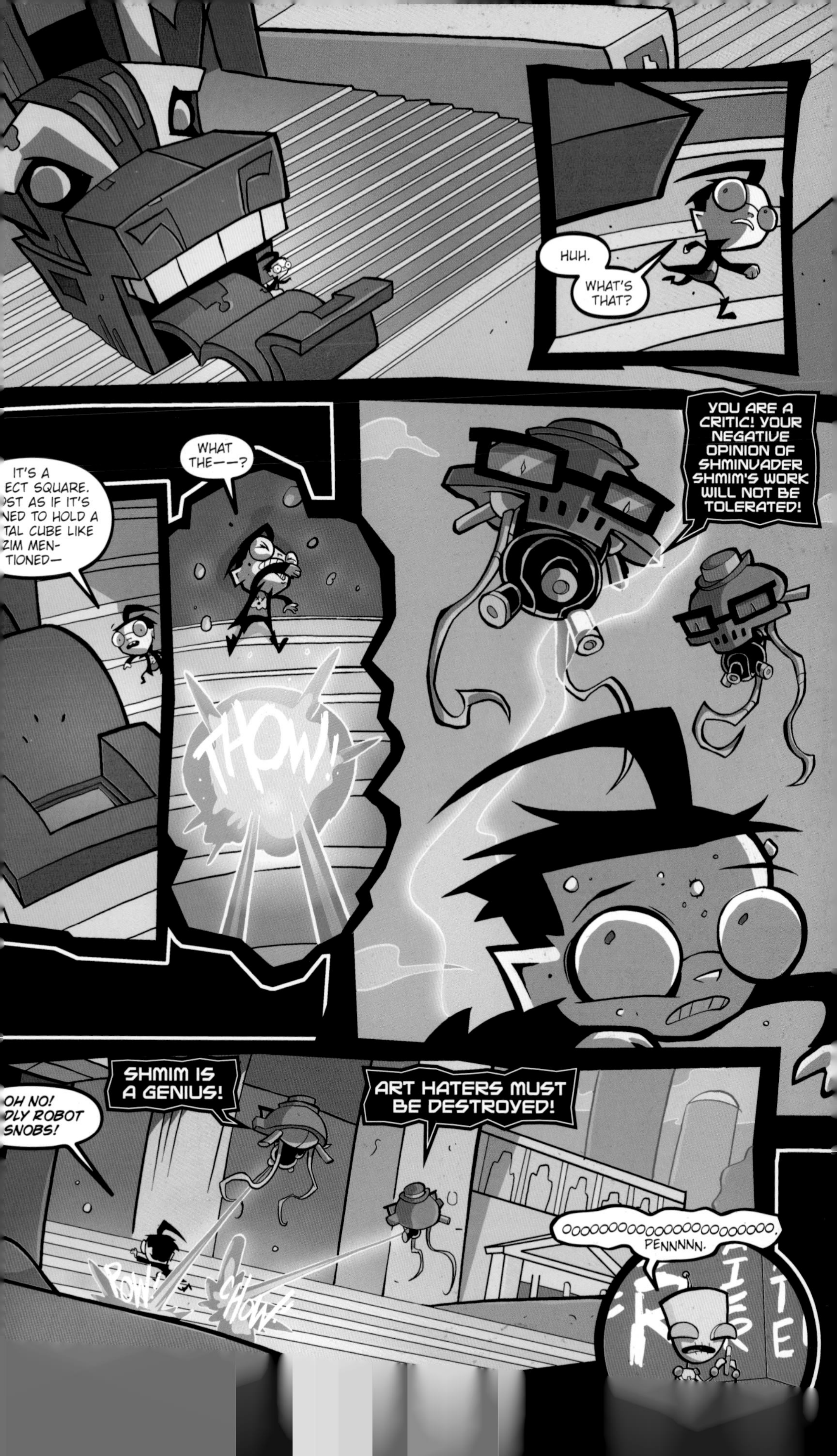

HUH.
WHAT'S THAT?
IT'S A ECT SQUARE. OST AS IF IT'S NED TO HOLD A TAL CUBE LIKE ZIM MEN-TIONED—
WHAT THE——?
THOW!
YOU ARE A CRITIC! YOUR NEGATIVE OPINION OF SHMINVADER SHMIM'S WORK WILL NOT BE TOLERATED!
OH NO! DLY ROBOT SNOBS!
SHMIM IS A GENIUS!
ART HATERS MUST BE DESTROYED!
POW!
CHOW!
OOOOOOOOOOOOOOOOOOOOOO. PENNNNN.

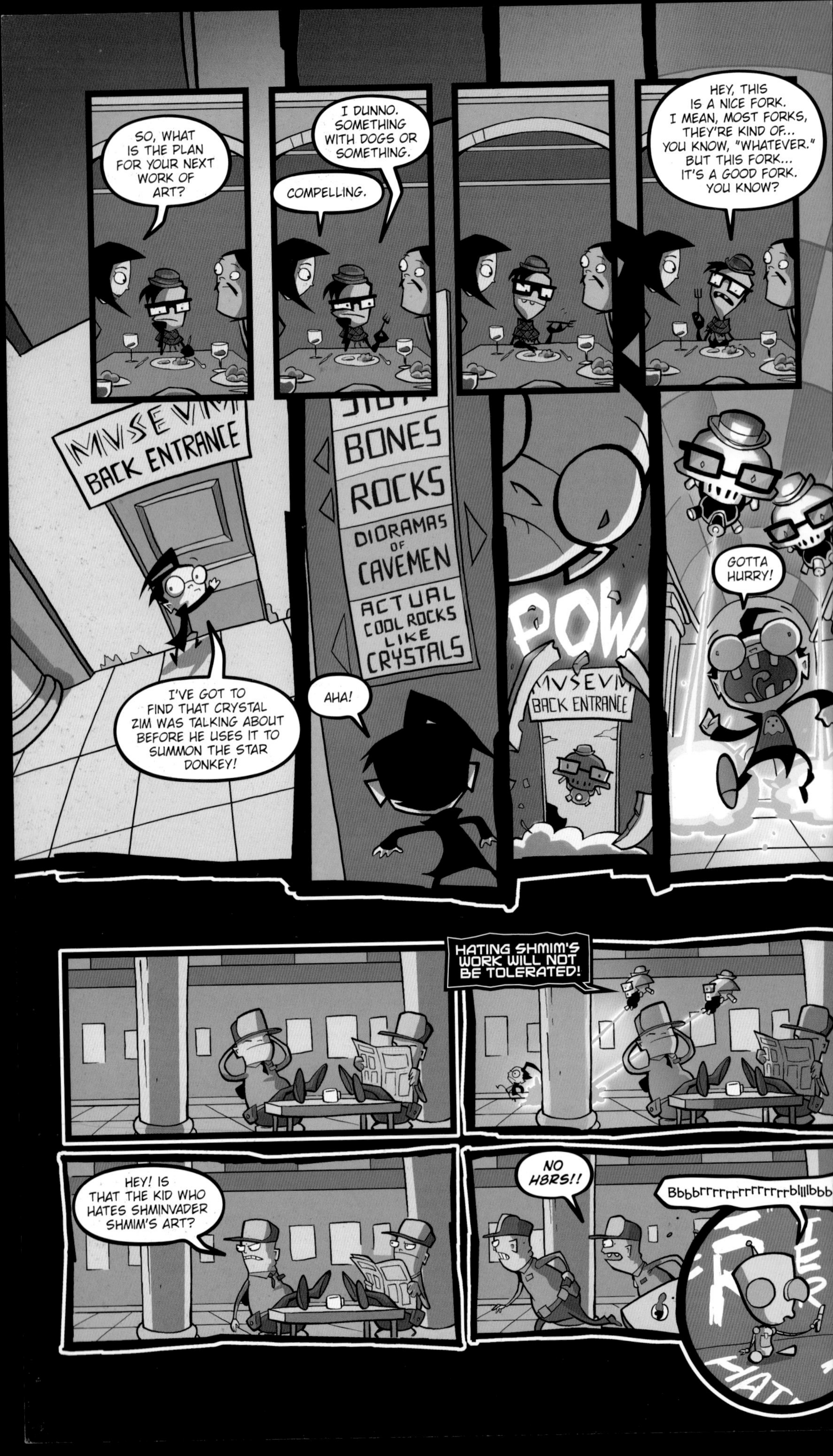
SO, WHAT IS THE PLAN FOR YOUR NEXT WORK OF ART?
I DUNNO. SOMETHING WITH DOGS OR SOMETHING.
COMPELLING.
HEY, THIS IS A NICE FORK. I MEAN, MOST FORKS, THEY'RE KIND OF... YOU KNOW, "WHATEVER." BUT THIS FORK... IT'S A GOOD FORK. YOU KNOW?
MVSEVM BACK ENTRANCE
I'VE GOT TO FIND THAT CRYSTAL ZIM WAS TALKING ABOUT BEFORE HE USES IT TO SUMMON THE STAR DONKEY!
BONES
ROCKS
DIORAMAS OF CAVEMEN
ACTUAL COOL ROCKS LIKE CRYSTALS
AHA!
POW
MVSEVM BACK ENTRANCE
GOTTA HURRY!
HATING SHMIM'S WORK WILL NOT BE TOLERATED!
HEY! IS THAT THE KID WHO HATES SHMINVADER SHMIM'S ART?
NO H8RS!!
Bbbbrrrrrrrrrrrrrblllllbbb

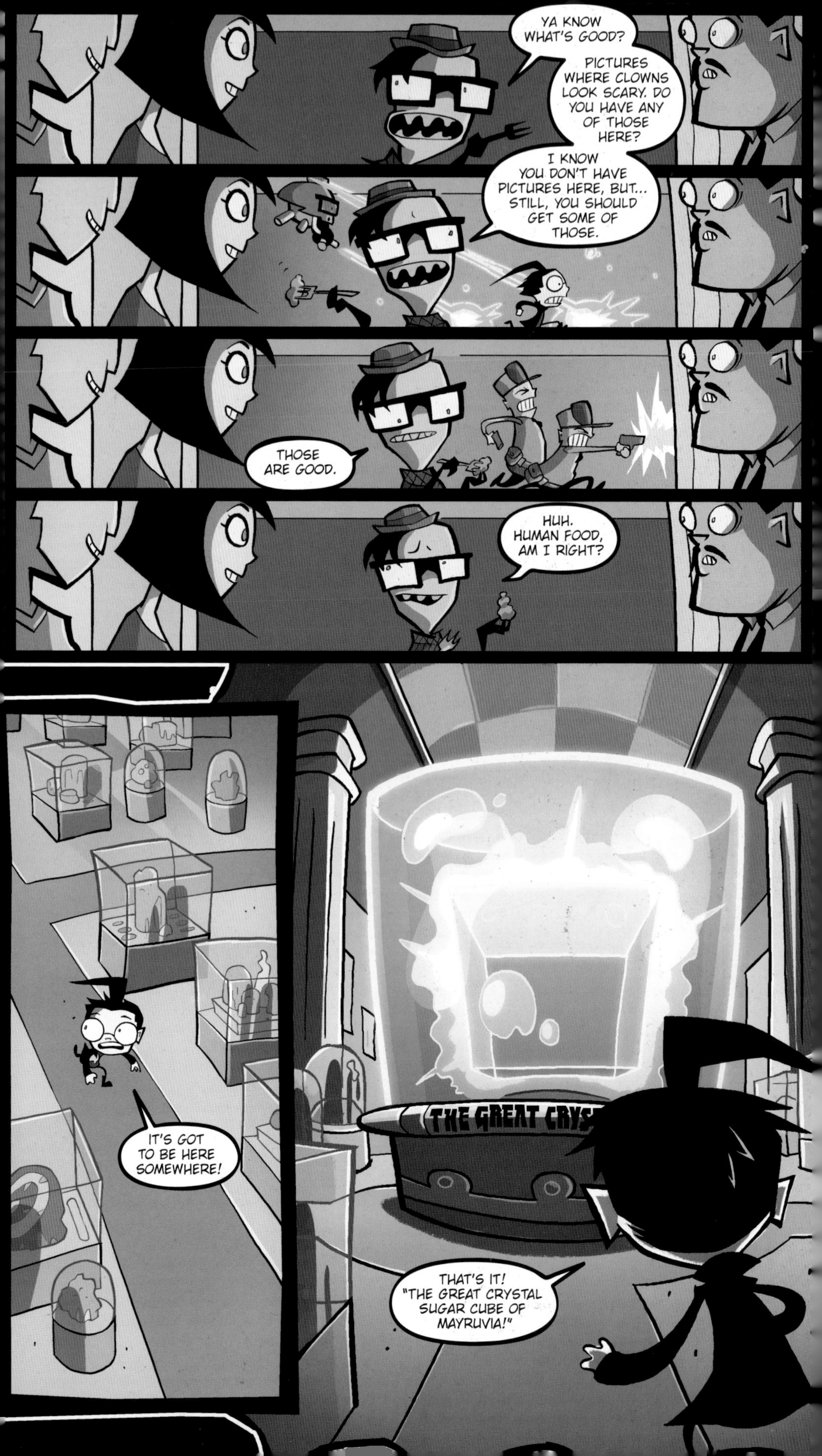
YA KNOW WHAT'S GOOD?
PICTURES WHERE CLOWNS LOOK SCARY. DO YOU HAVE ANY OF THOSE HERE?
I KNOW YOU DON'T HAVE PICTURES HERE, BUT... STILL, YOU SHOULD GET SOME OF THOSE.
THOSE ARE GOOD.
HUH. HUMAN FOOD, AM I RIGHT?
IT'S GOT TO BE HERE SOMEWHERE!
THE GREAT CRYS
THAT'S IT! "THE GREAT CRYSTAL SUGAR CUBE OF MAYRUVIA!"

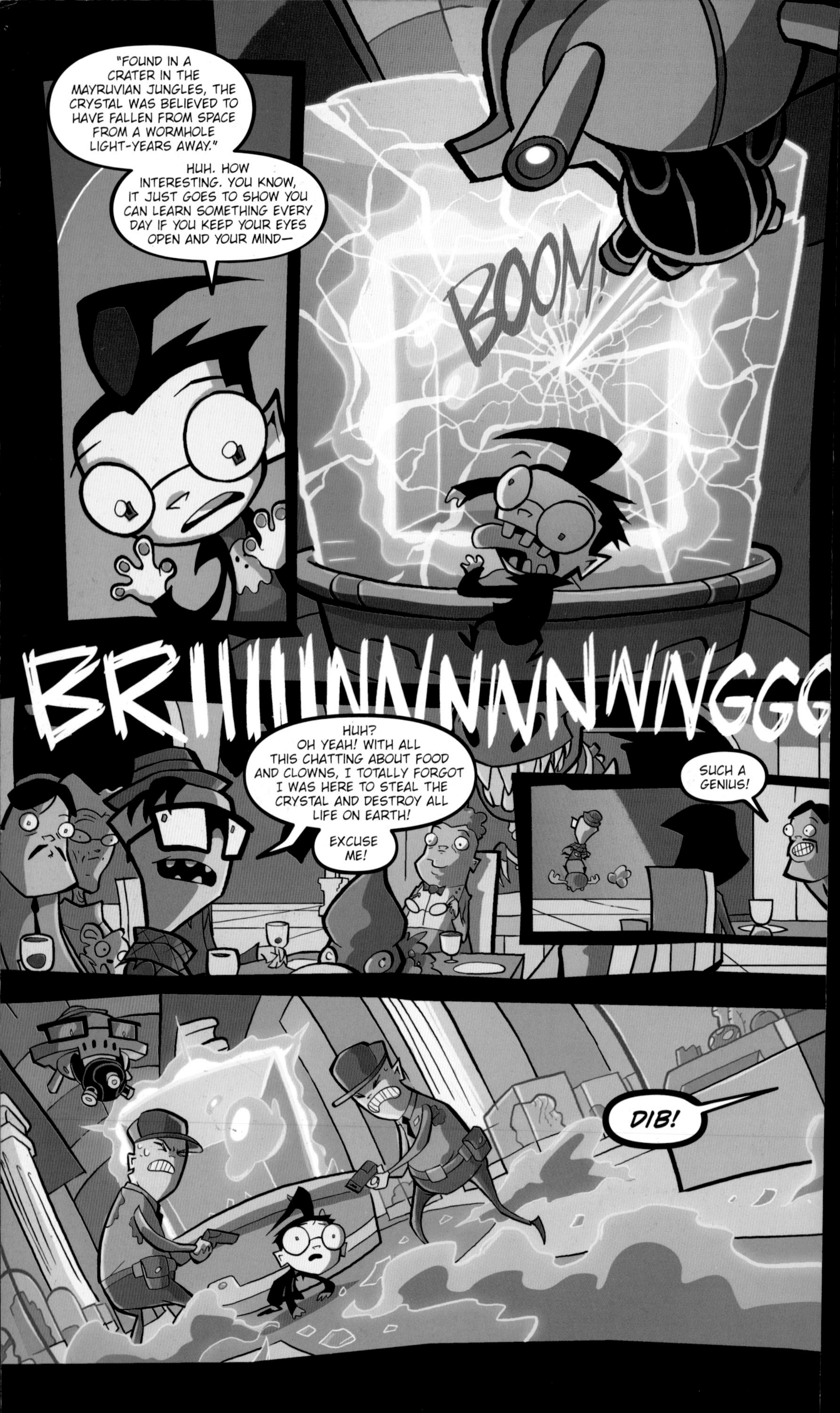
"FOUND IN A CRATER IN THE MAYRUVIAN JUNGLES, THE CRYSTAL WAS BELIEVED TO HAVE FALLEN FROM SPACE FROM A WORMHOLE LIGHT-YEARS AWAY."
HUH. HOW INTERESTING. YOU KNOW, IT JUST GOES TO SHOW YOU CAN LEARN SOMETHING EVERY DAY IF YOU KEEP YOUR EYES OPEN AND YOUR MIND—
BOOM!
BRIIIINNNNNNNGGG
HUH? OH YEAH! WITH ALL THIS CHATTING ABOUT FOOD AND CLOWNS, I TOTALLY FORGOT I WAS HERE TO STEAL THE CRYSTAL AND DESTROY ALL LIFE ON EARTH!
EXCUSE ME!
SUCH A GENIUS!
DIB!

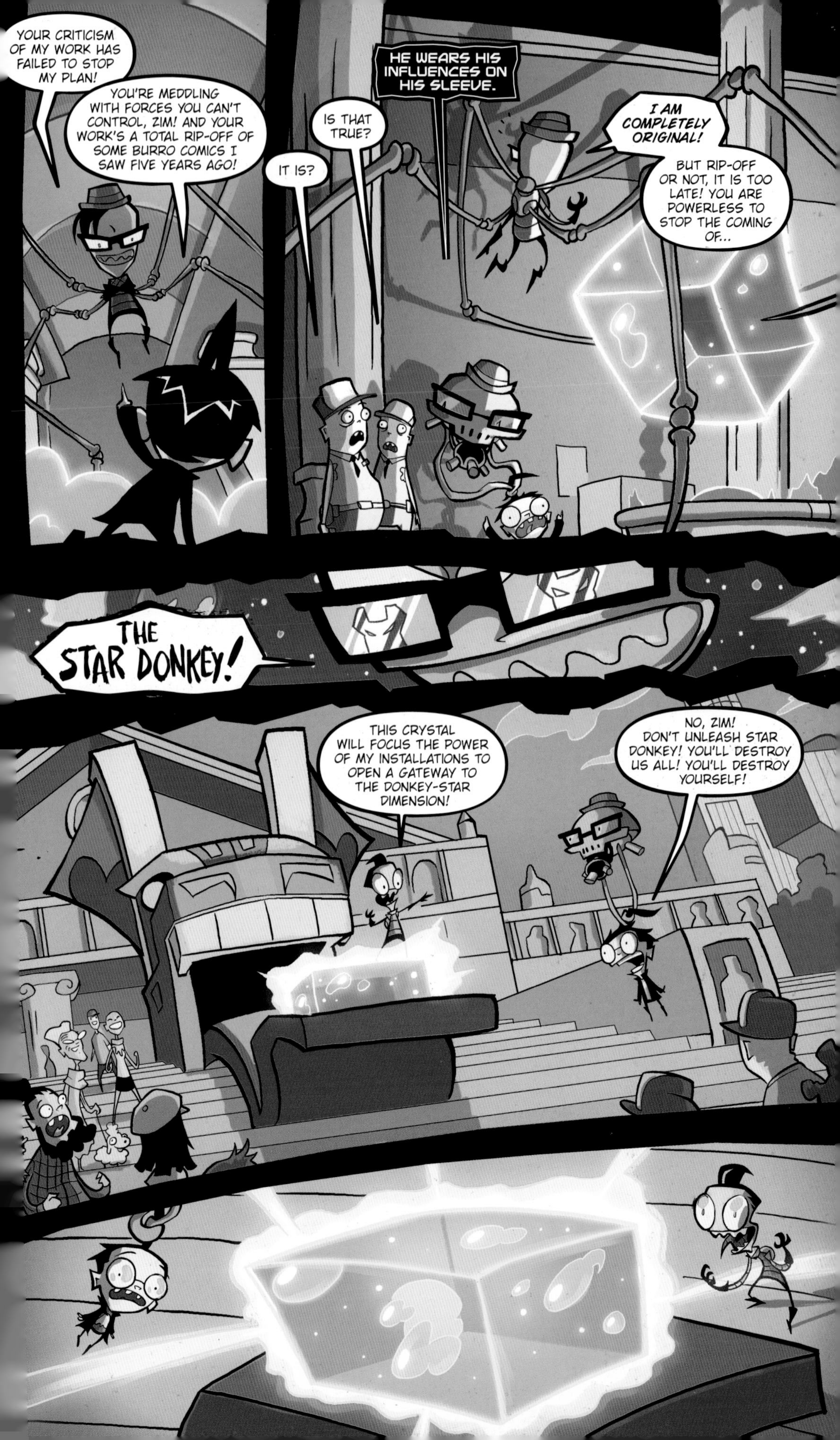

YOUR CRITICISM OF MY WORK HAS FAILED TO STOP MY PLAN!
YOU'RE MEDDLING WITH FORCES YOU CAN'T CONTROL, ZIM! AND YOUR WORK'S A TOTAL RIP-OFF OF SOME BURRO COMICS I SAW FIVE YEARS AGO!
HE WEARS HIS INFLUENCES ON HIS SLEEVE.
IS THAT TRUE?
IT IS?
I AM COMPLETELY ORIGINAL!
BUT RIP-OFF OR NOT, IT IS TOO LATE! YOU ARE POWERLESS TO STOP THE COMING OF...
THE STAR DONKEY!
THIS CRYSTAL WILL FOCUS THE POWER OF MY INSTALLATIONS TO OPEN A GATEWAY TO THE DONKEY-STAR DIMENSION!
NO, ZIM! DON'T UNLEASH STAR DONKEY! YOU'LL DESTROY US ALL! YOU'LL DESTROY YOURSELF!

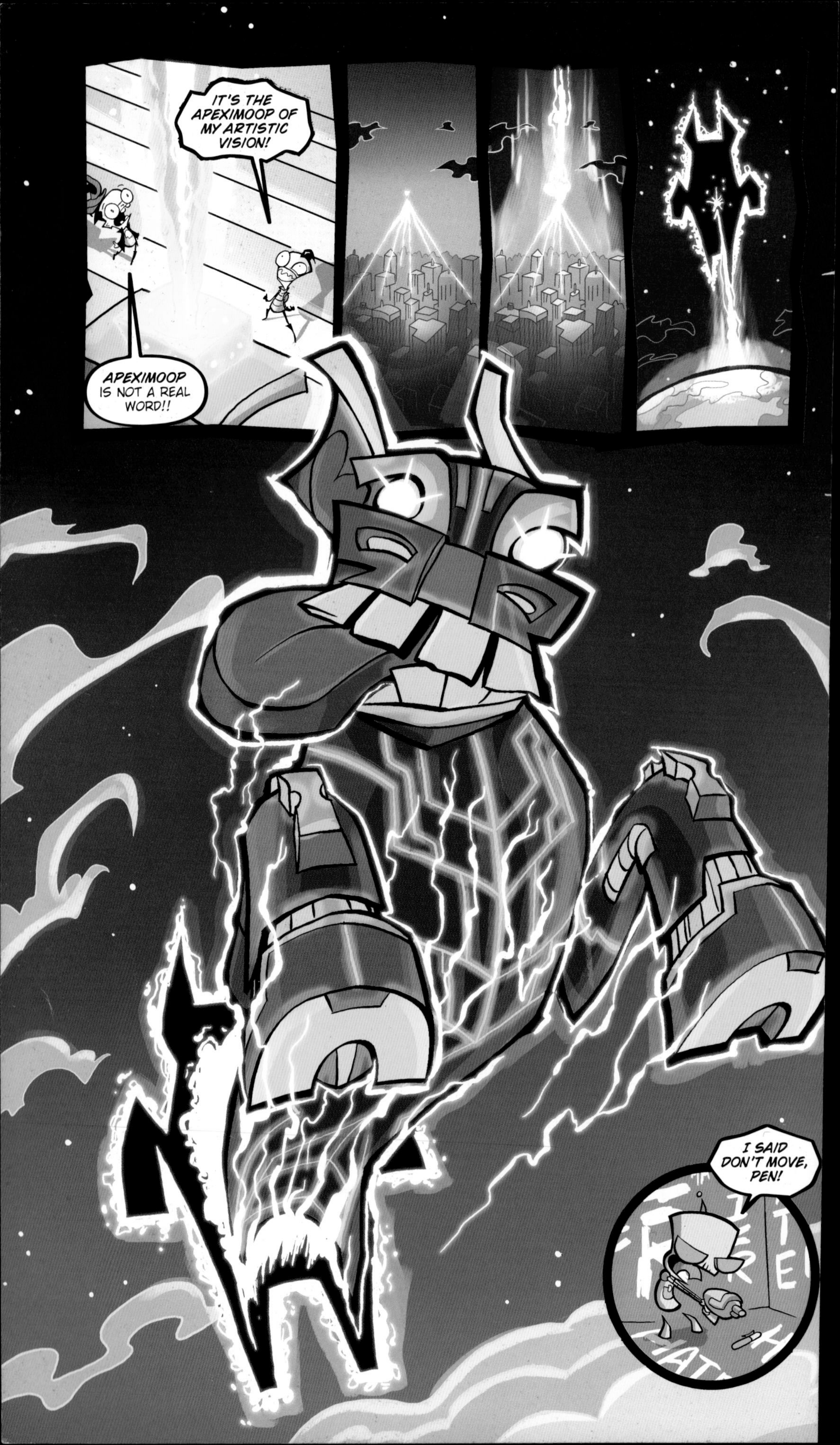
IT'S THE APEXIMOOP OF MY ARTISTIC VISION!
APEXIMOOP IS NOT A REAL WORD!!
I SAID DON'T MOVE, PEN!

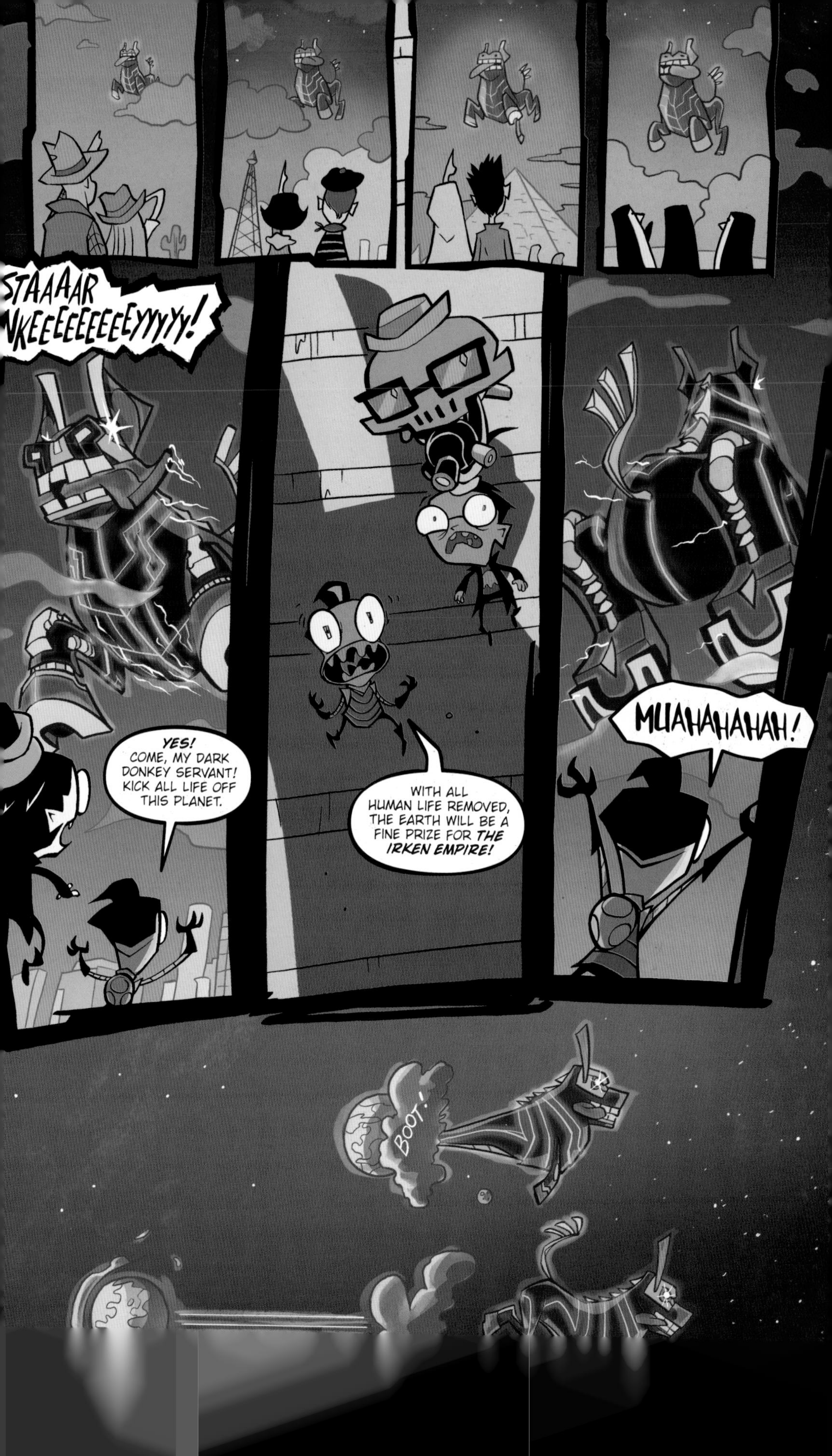

STAAAAR
NKEEEEEEEEEYYYYY!
YES! COME, MY DARK DONKEY SERVANT! KICK ALL LIFE OFF THIS PLANET.
WITH ALL HUMAN LIFE REMOVED, THE EARTH WILL BE A FINE PRIZE FOR THE IRKEN EMPIRE!
MUAHAHAHAH!
BOOT!

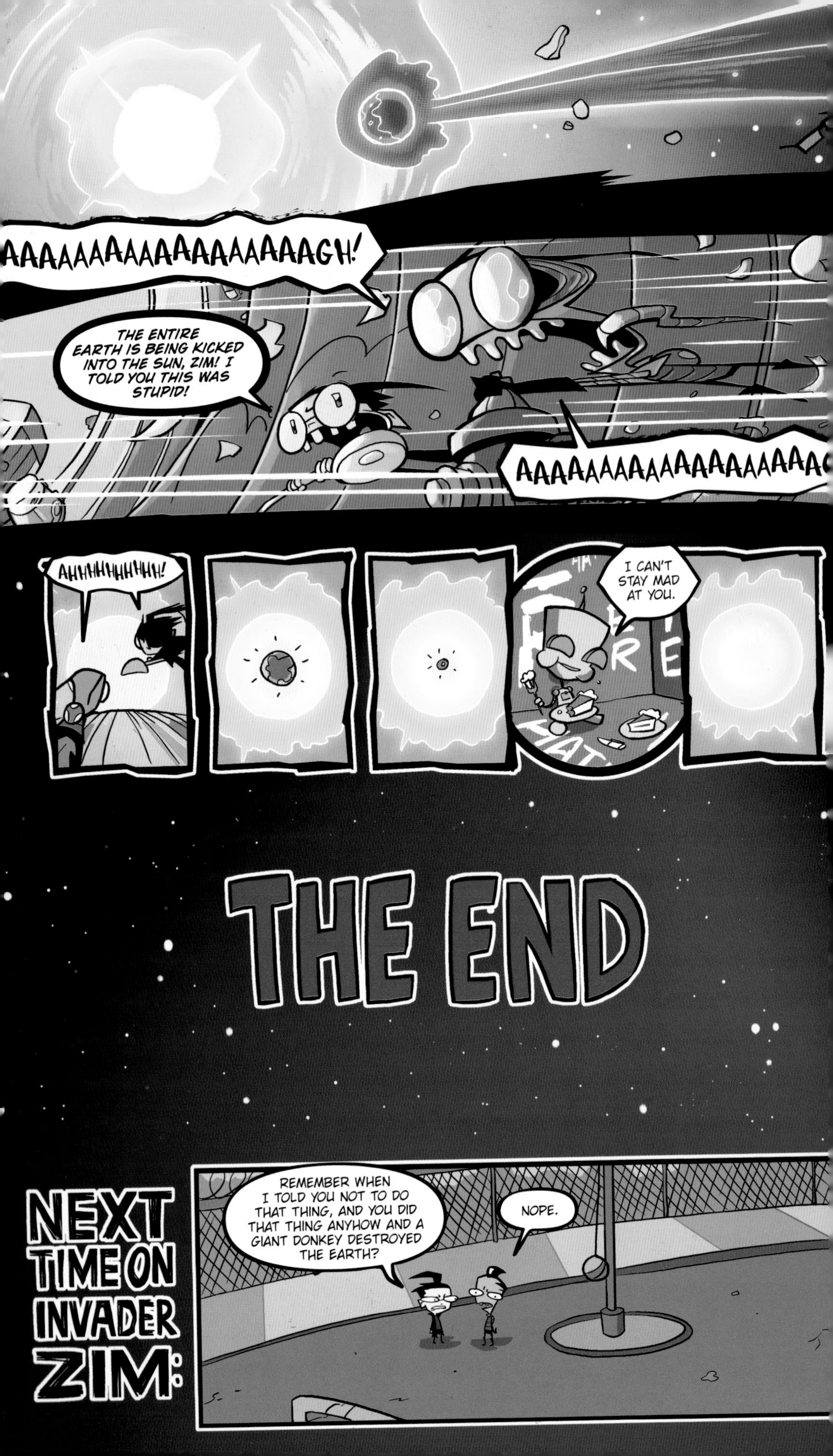

AAAAAAAAAAAAAAAAAAAGH!
THE ENTIRE EARTH IS BEING KICKED INTO THE SUN, ZIM! I TOLD YOU THIS WAS STUPID!
AAAAAAAAAAAAAAAAAAAA
AHHHHHHHHHH!
I CAN'T STAY MAD AT YOU.
THE END
NEXT TIME ON INVADER ZIM:
REMEMBER WHEN I TOLD YOU NOT TO DO THAT THING, AND YOU DID THAT THING ANYHOW AND A GIANT DONKEY DESTROYED THE EARTH?
NOPE.

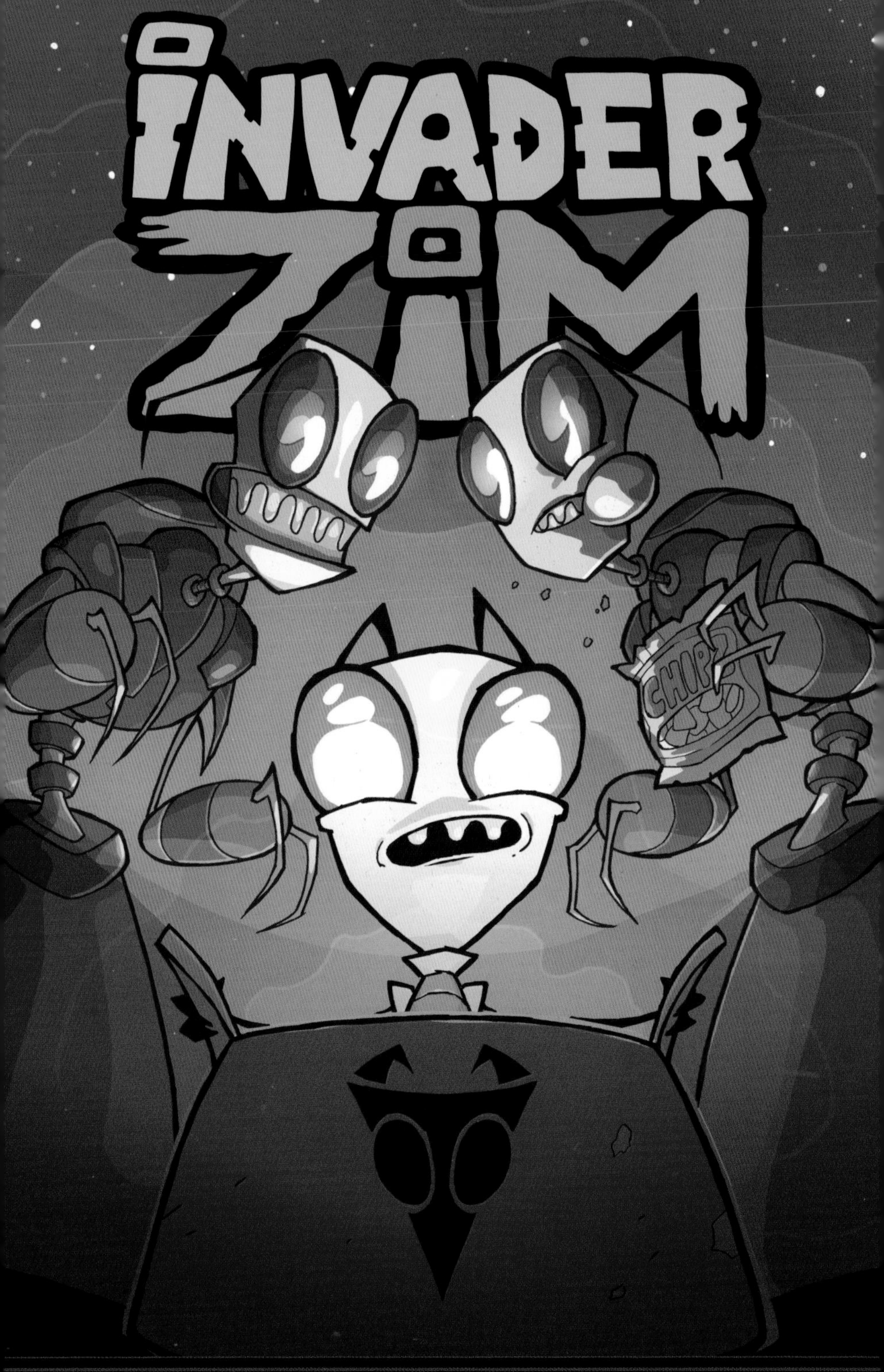
INVADER ZIM™
CHIPZ

CHAPTER: 4

illustration by AARON ALEXOVICH and RIKKI SIMONS

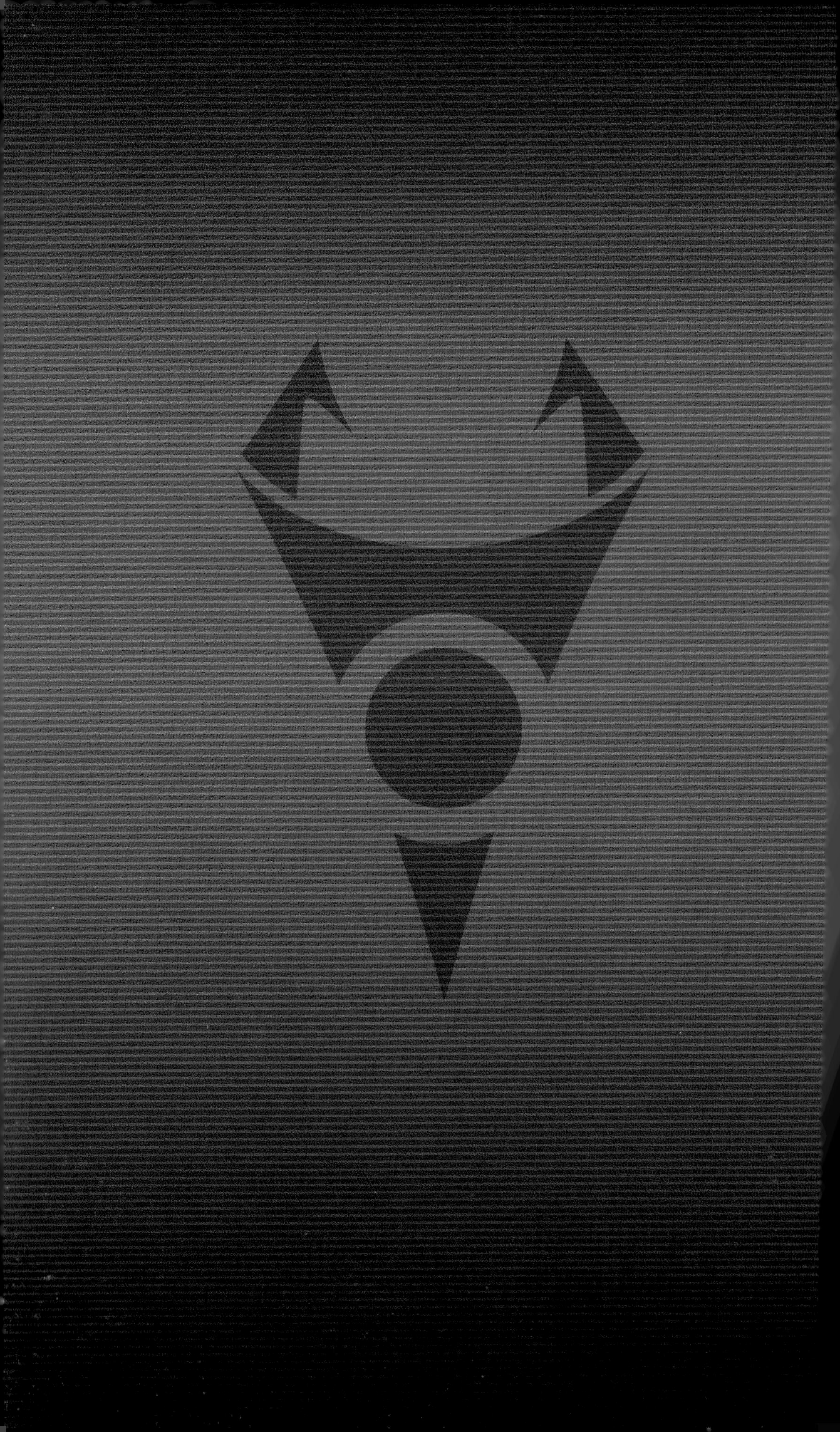

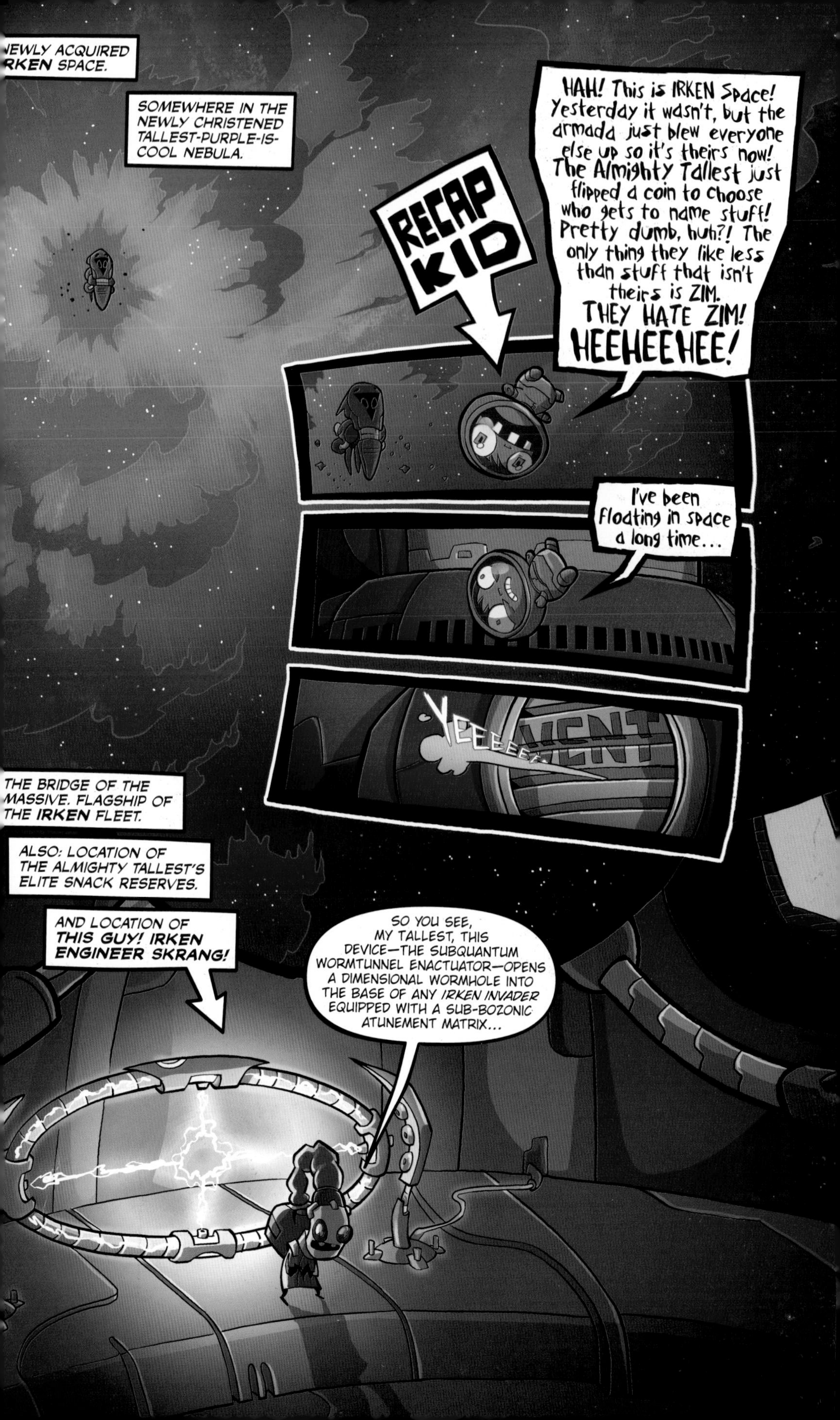

NEWLY ACQUIRED IRKEN SPACE.
SOMEWHERE IN THE NEWLY CHRISTENED TALLEST-PURPLE-IS-COOL NEBULA.
RECAP KID
HAH! This is IRKEN Space! Yesterday it wasn't, but the armada just blew everyone else up so it's theirs now! The Almighty Tallest just flipped a coin to choose who gets to name stuff! Pretty dumb, huh?! The only thing they like less than stuff that isn't theirs is ZIM. THEY HATE ZIM! HEEHEEHEE!
I've been floating in space a long time...
YEEEEEE...
VENT
THE BRIDGE OF THE MASSIVE. FLAGSHIP OF THE IRKEN FLEET.
ALSO: LOCATION OF THE ALMIGHTY TALLEST'S ELITE SNACK RESERVES.
AND LOCATION OF THIS GUY! IRKEN ENGINEER SKRANG!
SO YOU SEE, MY TALLEST, THIS DEVICE—THE SUBQUANTUM WORMTUNNEL ENACTUATOR—OPENS A DIMENSIONAL WORMHOLE INTO THE BASE OF ANY IRKEN INVADER EQUIPPED WITH A SUB-BOZONIC ATUNEMENT MATRIX...

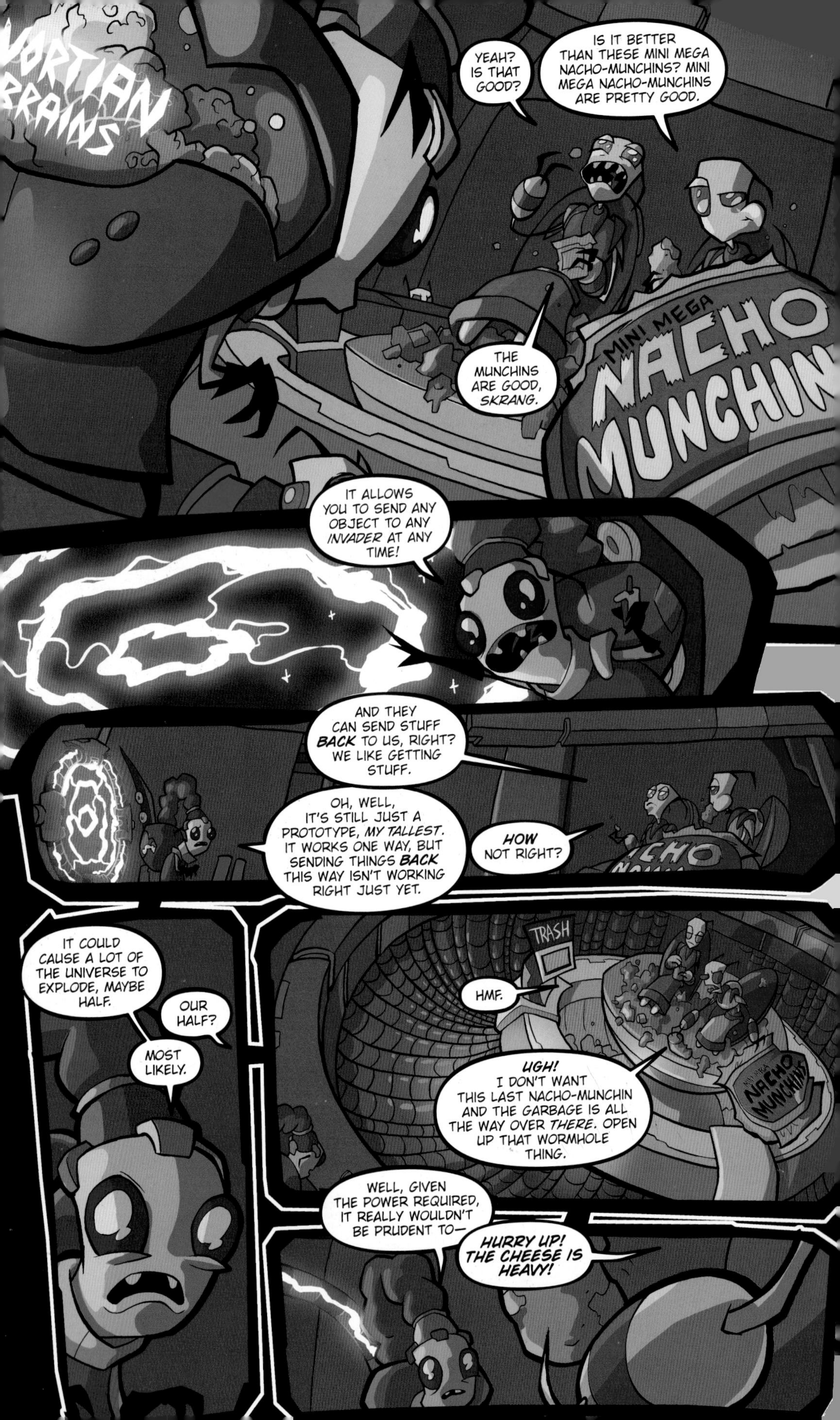
VORTIAN BRAINS
YEAH? IS THAT GOOD?
IS IT BETTER THAN THESE MINI MEGA NACHO-MUNCHINS? MINI MEGA NACHO-MUNCHINS ARE PRETTY GOOD.
THE MUNCHINS ARE GOOD, SKRANG.
MINI MEGA NACHO MUNCHIN
IT ALLOWS YOU TO SEND ANY OBJECT TO ANY INVADER AT ANY TIME!
AND THEY CAN SEND STUFF BACK TO US, RIGHT? WE LIKE GETTING STUFF.
OH, WELL, IT'S STILL JUST A PROTOTYPE, MY TALLEST. IT WORKS ONE WAY, BUT SENDING THINGS BACK THIS WAY ISN'T WORKING RIGHT JUST YET.
HOW NOT RIGHT?
IT COULD CAUSE A LOT OF THE UNIVERSE TO EXPLODE, MAYBE HALF.
OUR HALF?
MOST LIKELY.
TRASH
HMF.
UGH! I DON'T WANT THIS LAST NACHO-MUNCHIN AND THE GARBAGE IS ALL THE WAY OVER THERE. OPEN UP THAT WORMHOLE THING.
MINI MEGA NACHO MUNCHINS
WELL, GIVEN THE POWER REQUIRED, IT REALLY WOULDN'T BE PRUDENT TO—
HURRY UP! THE CHEESE IS HEAVY!

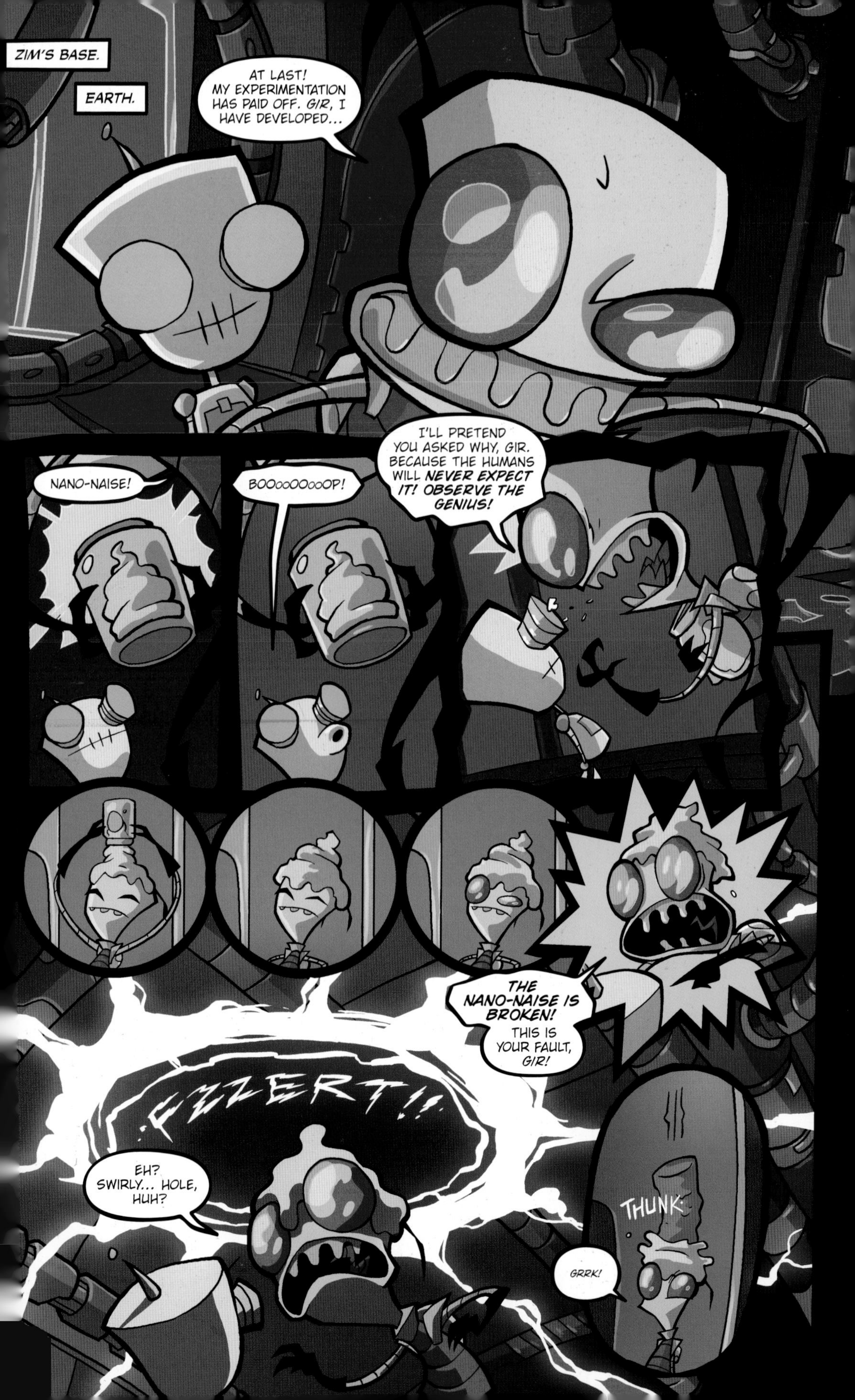
ZIM'S BASE.
EARTH.
AT LAST! MY EXPERIMENTATION HAS PAID OFF. GIR, I HAVE DEVELOPED...
NANO-NAISE!
BOOooOOooOP!
I'LL PRETEND YOU ASKED WHY, GIR. BECAUSE THE HUMANS WILL NEVER EXPECT IT! OBSERVE THE GENIUS!
THE NANO-NAISE IS BROKEN! THIS IS YOUR FAULT, GIR!
FZZERT!!
EH? SWIRLY... HOLE, HUH?
THUNK
GRRK!

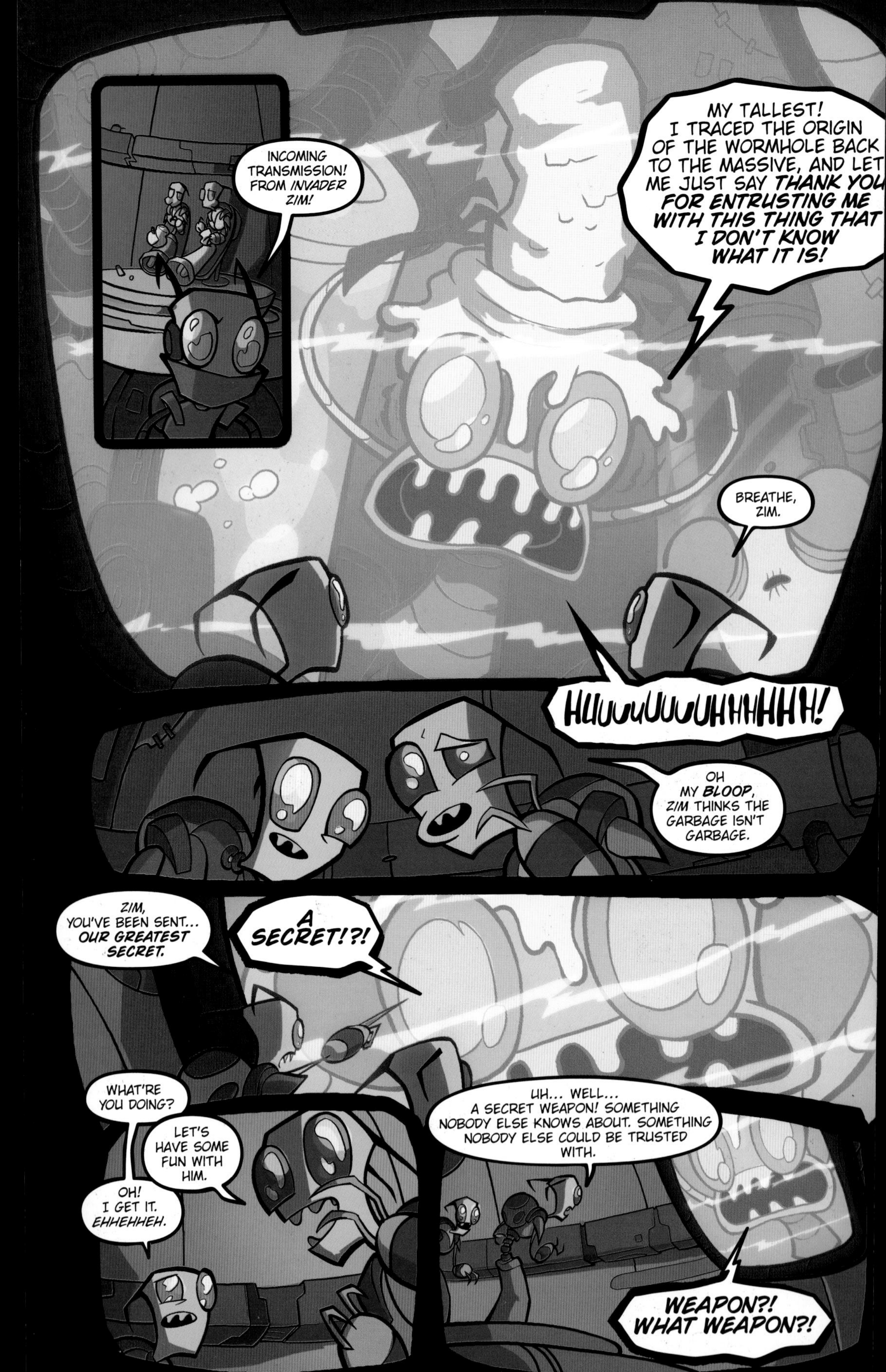
INCOMING TRANSMISSION! FROM *INVADER* ZIM!
MY TALLEST! I TRACED THE ORIGIN OF THE WORMHOLE BACK TO THE MASSIVE, AND LET ME JUST SAY ***THANK YOU FOR ENTRUSTING ME WITH THIS THING THAT I DON'T KNOW WHAT IT IS!***
BREATHE, ZIM.
HUUUUUUUUHHHHHH!
OH MY ***BLOOP***, *ZIM* THINKS THE GARBAGE ISN'T GARBAGE.
ZIM, YOU'VE BEEN SENT... ***OUR GREATEST SECRET.***
A SECRET!?!
WHAT'RE YOU DOING?
LET'S HAVE SOME FUN WITH HIM.
OH! I GET IT. *EHHEHHEH.*
UH... WELL... A SECRET WEAPON! SOMETHING NOBODY ELSE KNOWS ABOUT. SOMETHING NOBODY ELSE COULD BE TRUSTED WITH.
WEAPON?! WHAT WEAPON?!

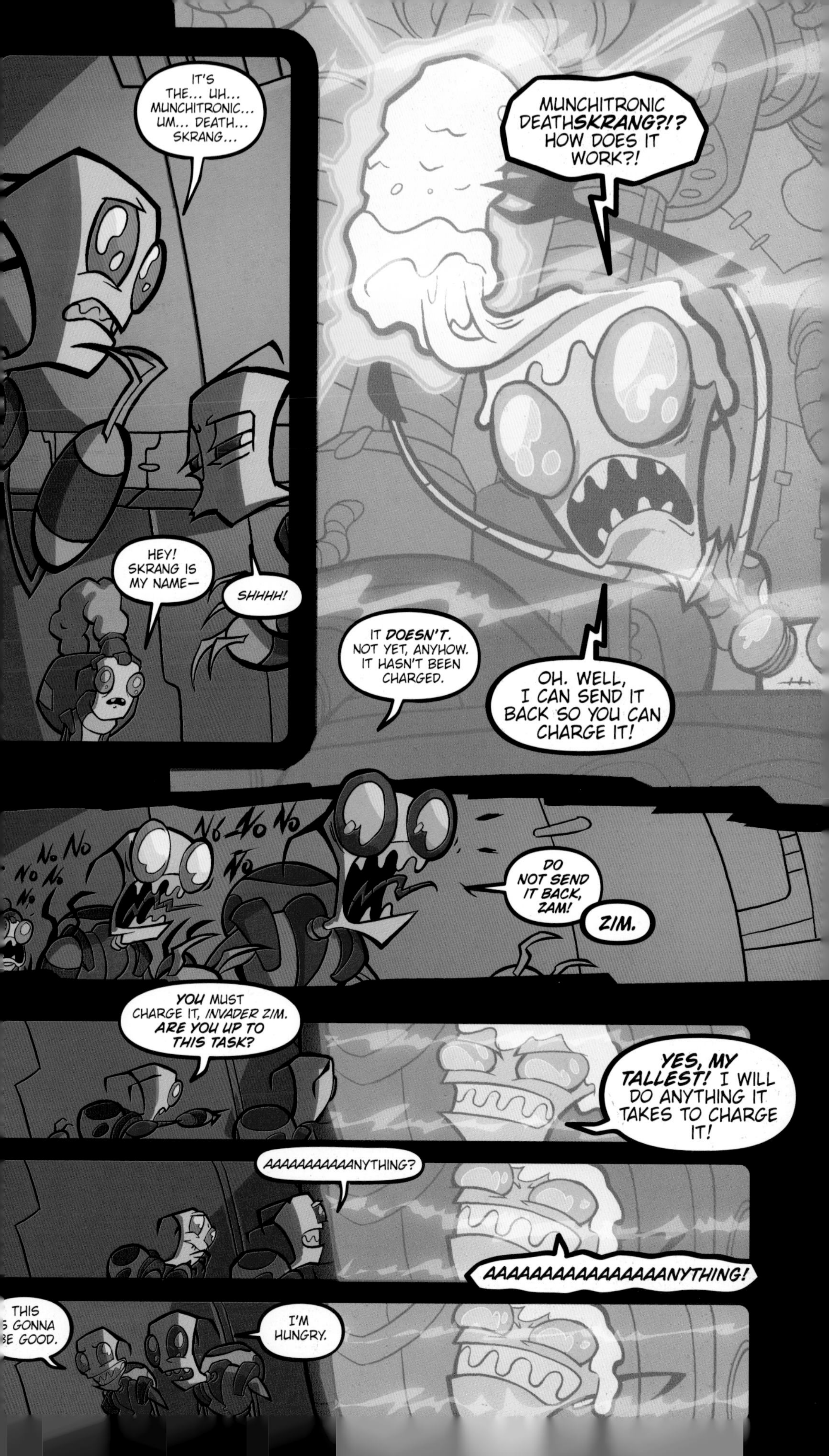

IT'S THE... UH... MUNCHITRONIC... UM... DEATH... SKRANG...
MUNCHITRONIC DEATHSKRANG?!? HOW DOES IT WORK?!
HEY! SKRANG IS MY NAME—
SHHHH!
IT DOESN'T. NOT YET, ANYHOW. IT HASN'T BEEN CHARGED.
OH. WELL, I CAN SEND IT BACK SO YOU CAN CHARGE IT!
No No No No No No No No No No
DO NOT SEND IT BACK, ZAM!
ZIM.
YOU MUST CHARGE IT, INVADER ZIM. ARE YOU UP TO THIS TASK?
YES, MY TALLEST! I WILL DO ANYTHING IT TAKES TO CHARGE IT!
AAAAAAAAAAANYTHING?
AAAAAAAAAAAAAAAANYTHING!
THIS S GONNA BE GOOD.
I'M HUNGRY.

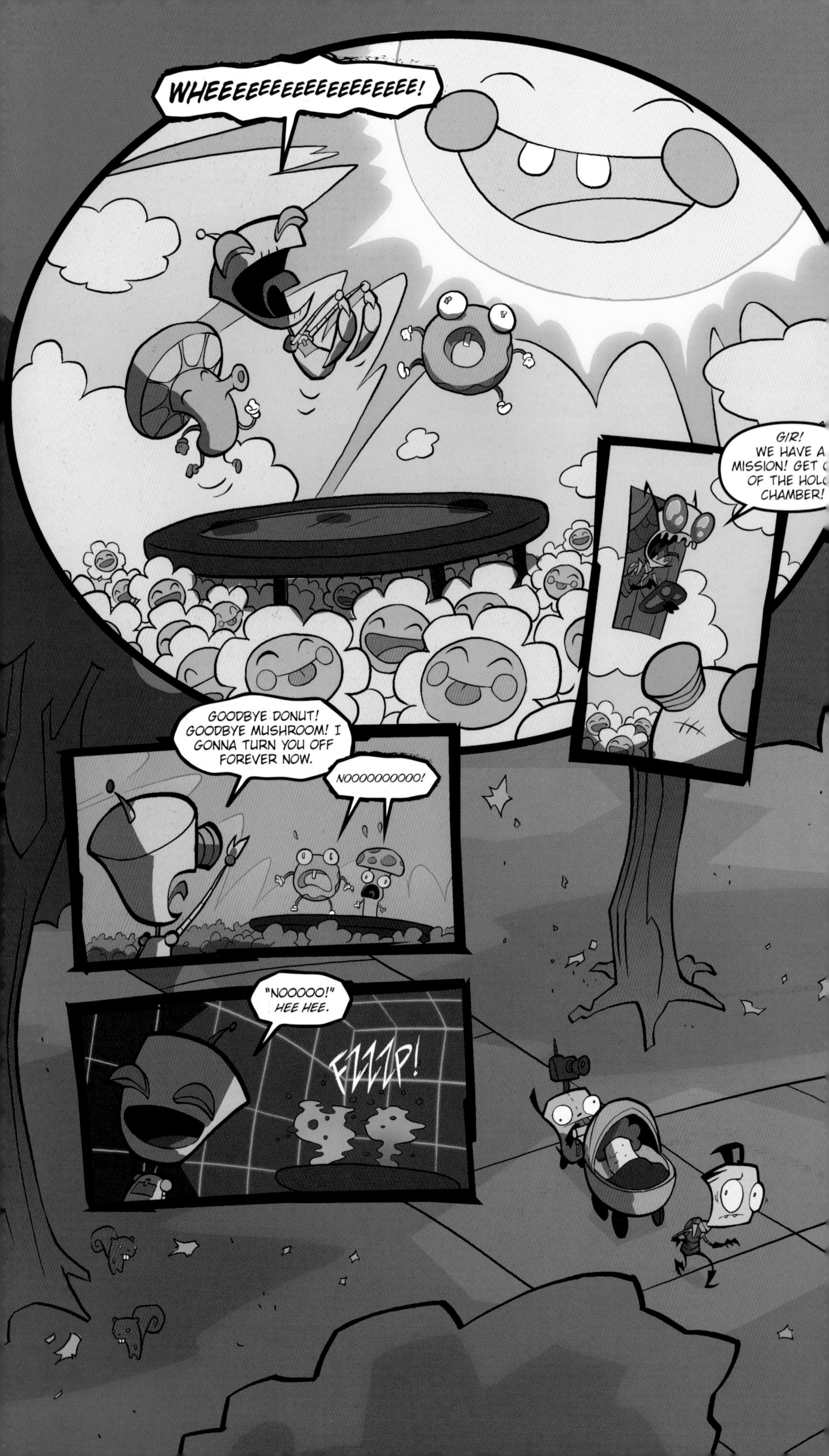
WHEEEEEEEEEEEEEEEEE!
GIR! WE HAVE A MISSION! GET OF THE HOLO CHAMBER!
GOODBYE DONUT! GOODBYE MUSHROOM! I GONNA TURN YOU OFF FOREVER NOW.
NOOOOOOOOOO!
"NOOOOO!" HEE HEE.
FZZZP!

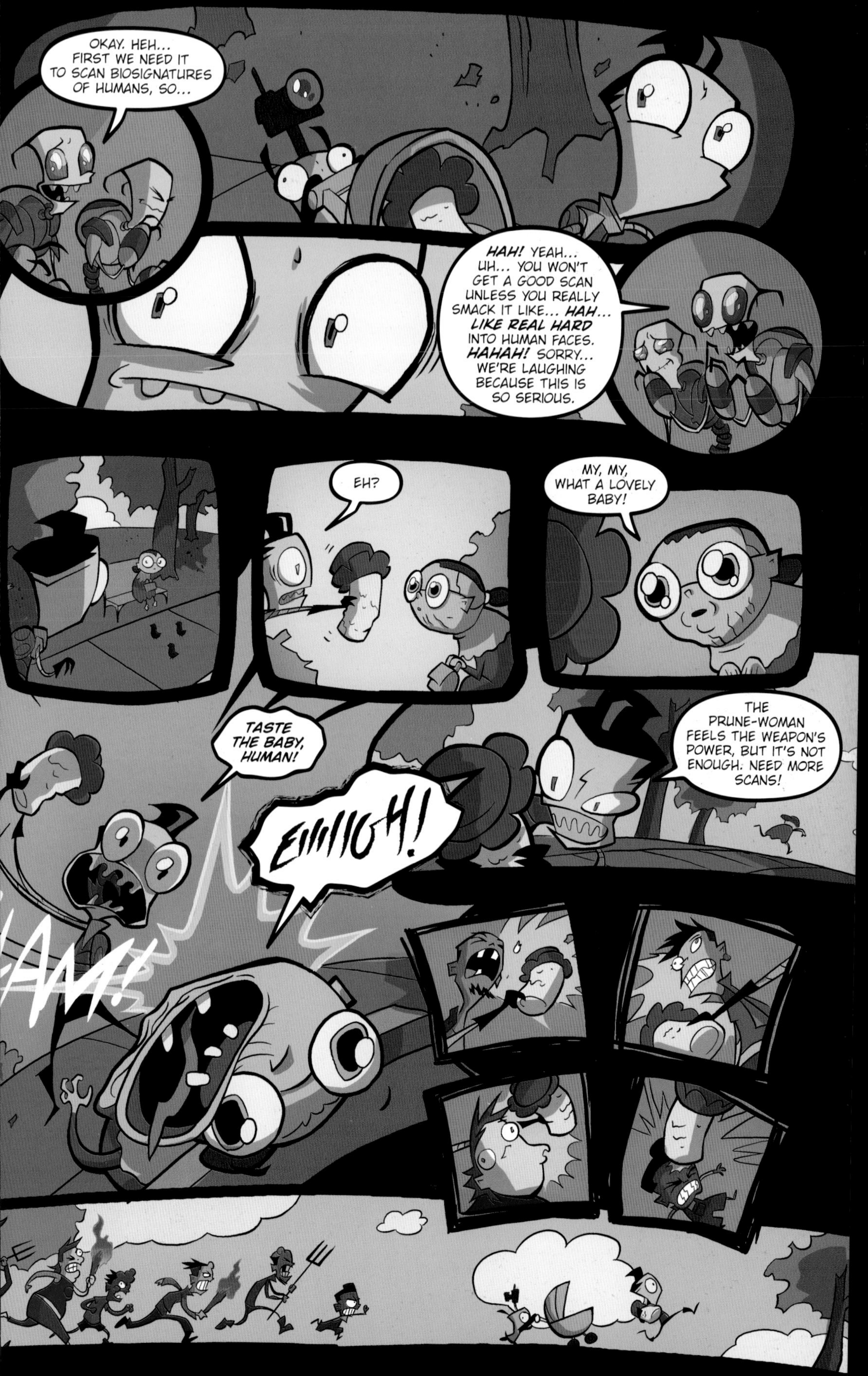
OKAY. HEH... FIRST WE NEED IT TO SCAN BIOSIGNATURES OF HUMANS, SO...
HAH! YEAH... UH... YOU WON'T GET A GOOD SCAN UNLESS YOU REALLY SMACK IT LIKE... HAH... LIKE REAL HARD INTO HUMAN FACES. HAHAH! SORRY... WE'RE LAUGHING BECAUSE THIS IS SO SERIOUS.
EH?
MY, MY, WHAT A LOVELY BABY!
TASTE THE BABY, HUMAN!
THE PRUNE-WOMAN FEELS THE WEAPON'S POWER, BUT IT'S NOT ENOUGH. NEED MORE SCANS!

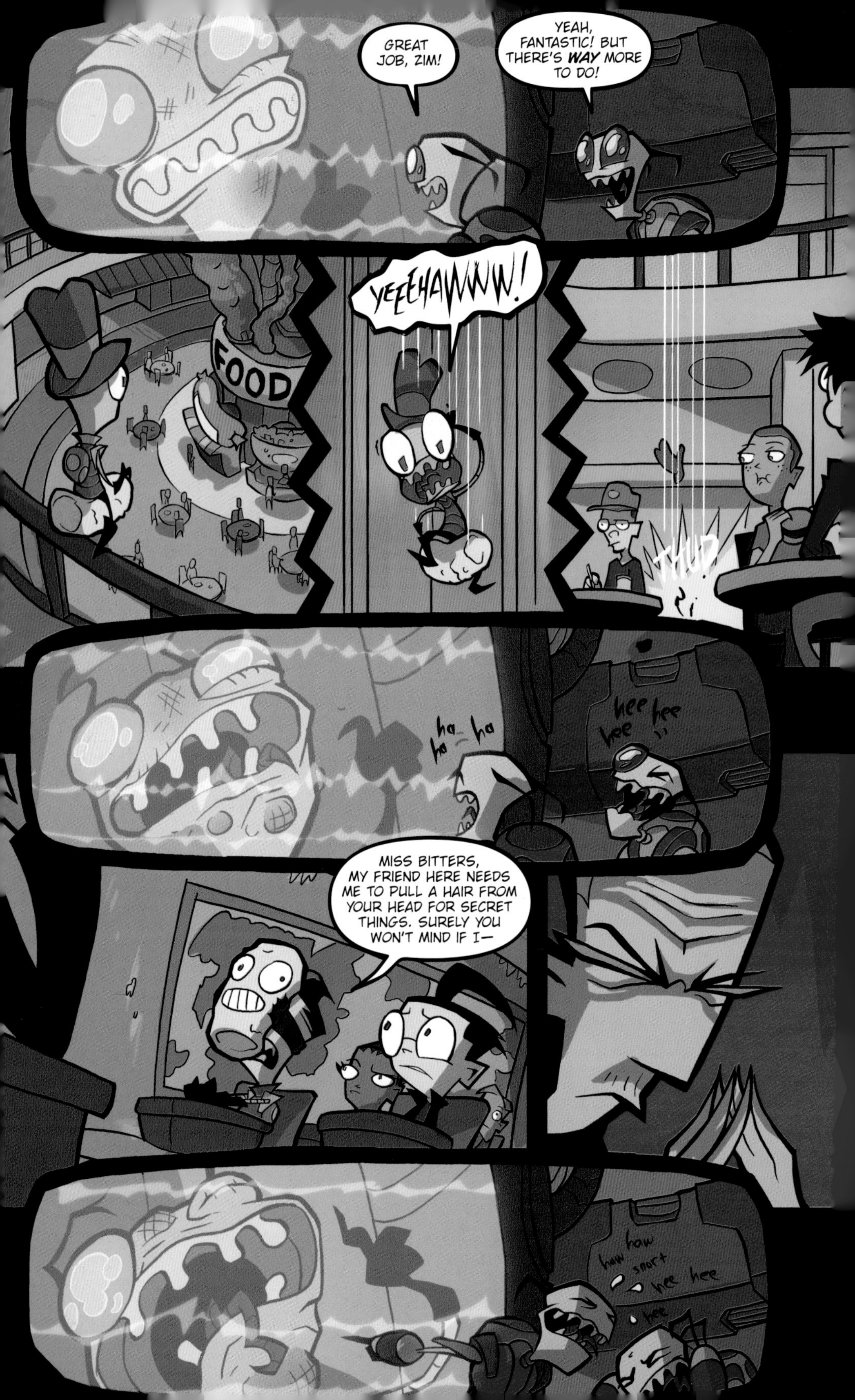
GREAT JOB, ZIM!
YEAH, FANTASTIC! BUT THERE'S **WAY** MORE TO DO!
YEEEHAWWW!
THUD!
ha ha ha
hee hee hee
MISS BITTERS, MY FRIEND HERE NEEDS ME TO PULL A HAIR FROM YOUR HEAD FOR SECRET THINGS. SURELY YOU WON'T MIND IF I—
haw haw snort hee hee
hee

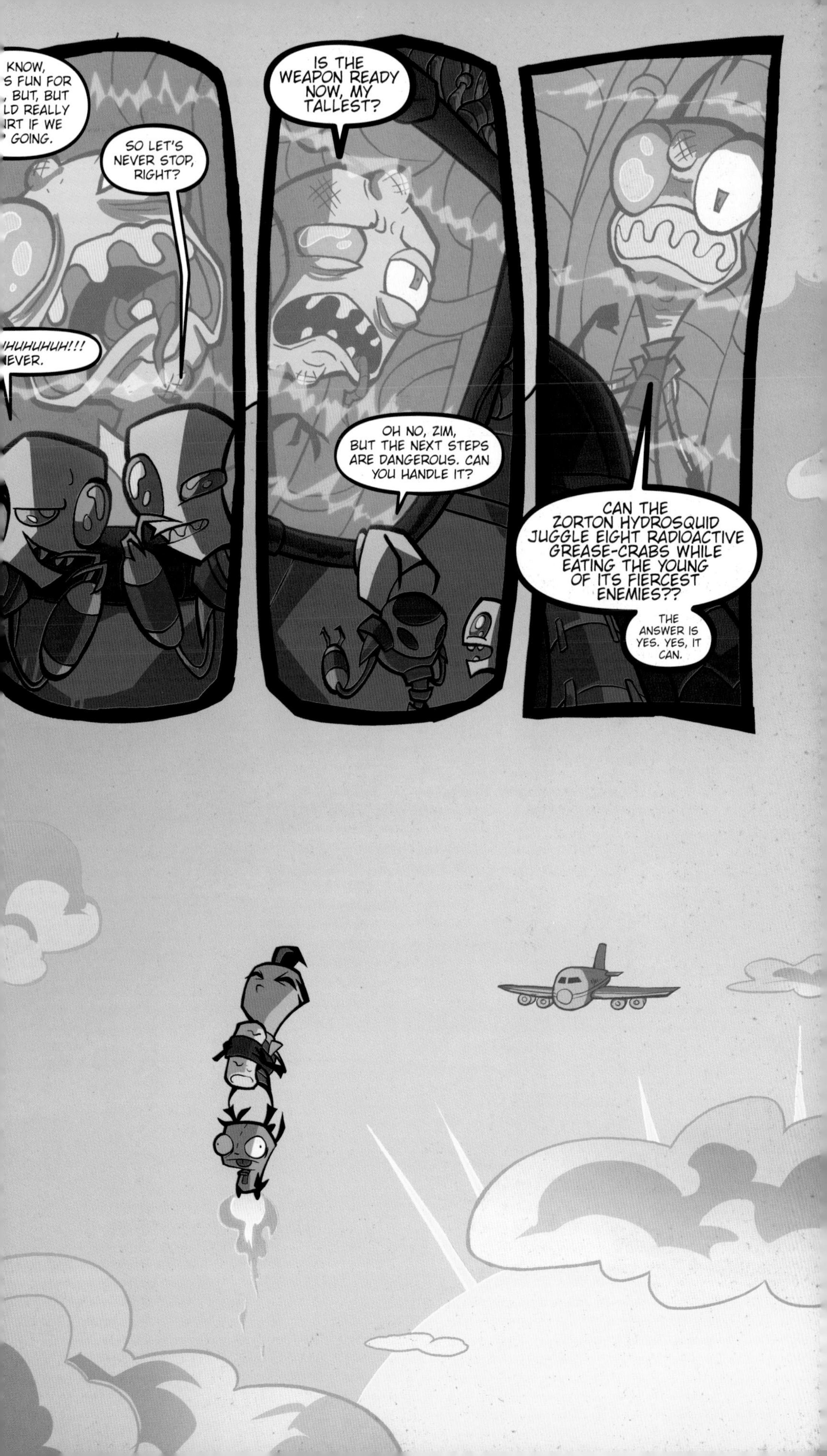
KNOW,
S FUN FOR
, BUT, BUT
LD REALLY
IRT IF WE
GOING.
SO LET'S NEVER STOP, RIGHT?
HUHUHUH!!!
NEVER.
IS THE WEAPON READY NOW, MY TALLEST?
OH NO, ZIM, BUT THE NEXT STEPS ARE DANGEROUS. CAN YOU HANDLE IT?
CAN THE ZORTON HYDROSQUID JUGGLE EIGHT RADIOACTIVE GREASE-CRABS WHILE EATING THE YOUNG OF ITS FIERCEST ENEMIES??
THE ANSWER IS YES. YES, IT CAN.

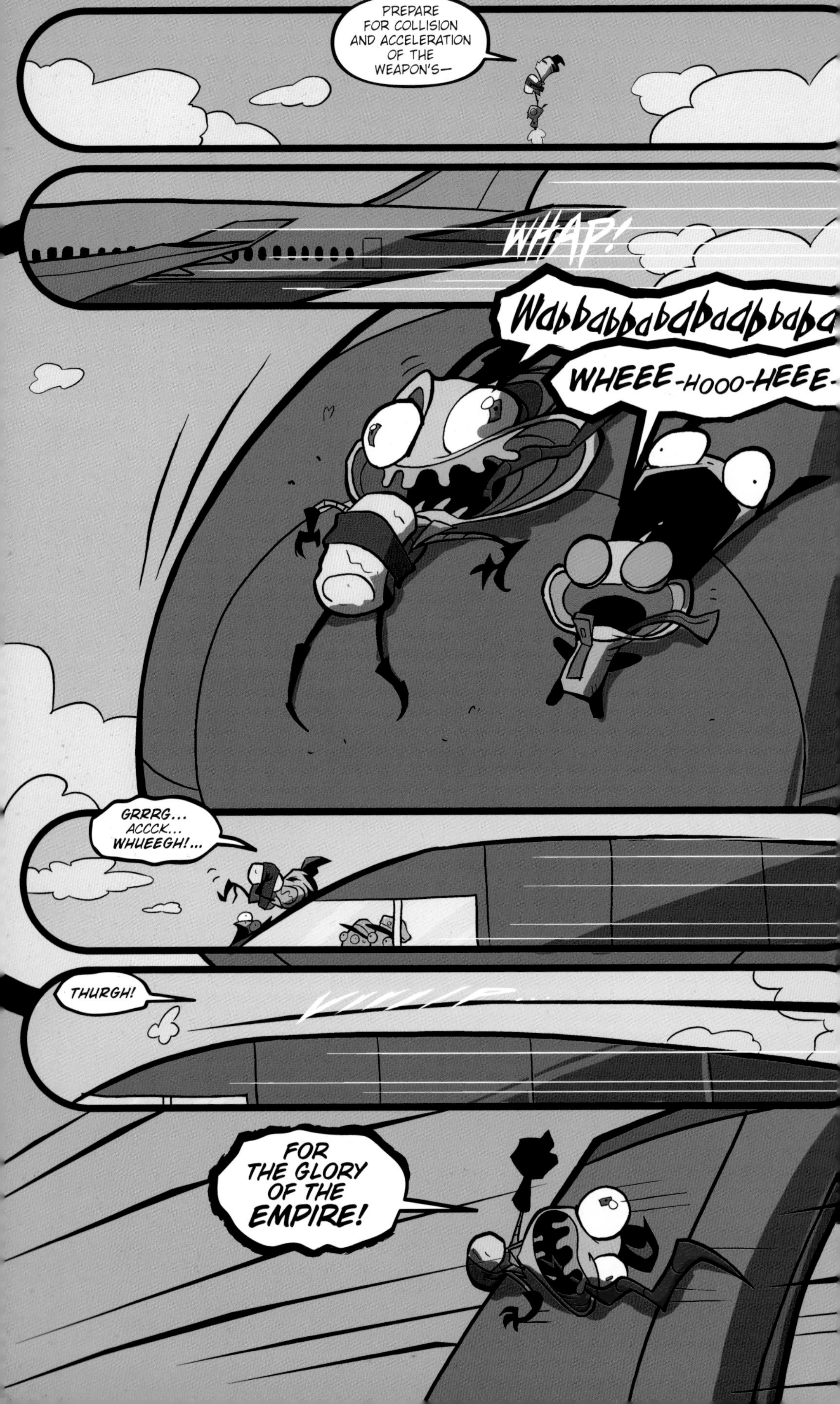
PREPARE FOR COLLISION AND ACCELERATION OF THE WEAPON'S—
WHAP!
Wabbabbababababbaba
WHEEE-HOOO-HEEE-
GRRRG... ACCCK... WHUEEGH!...
THURGH!
FOR THE GLORY OF THE EMPIRE!

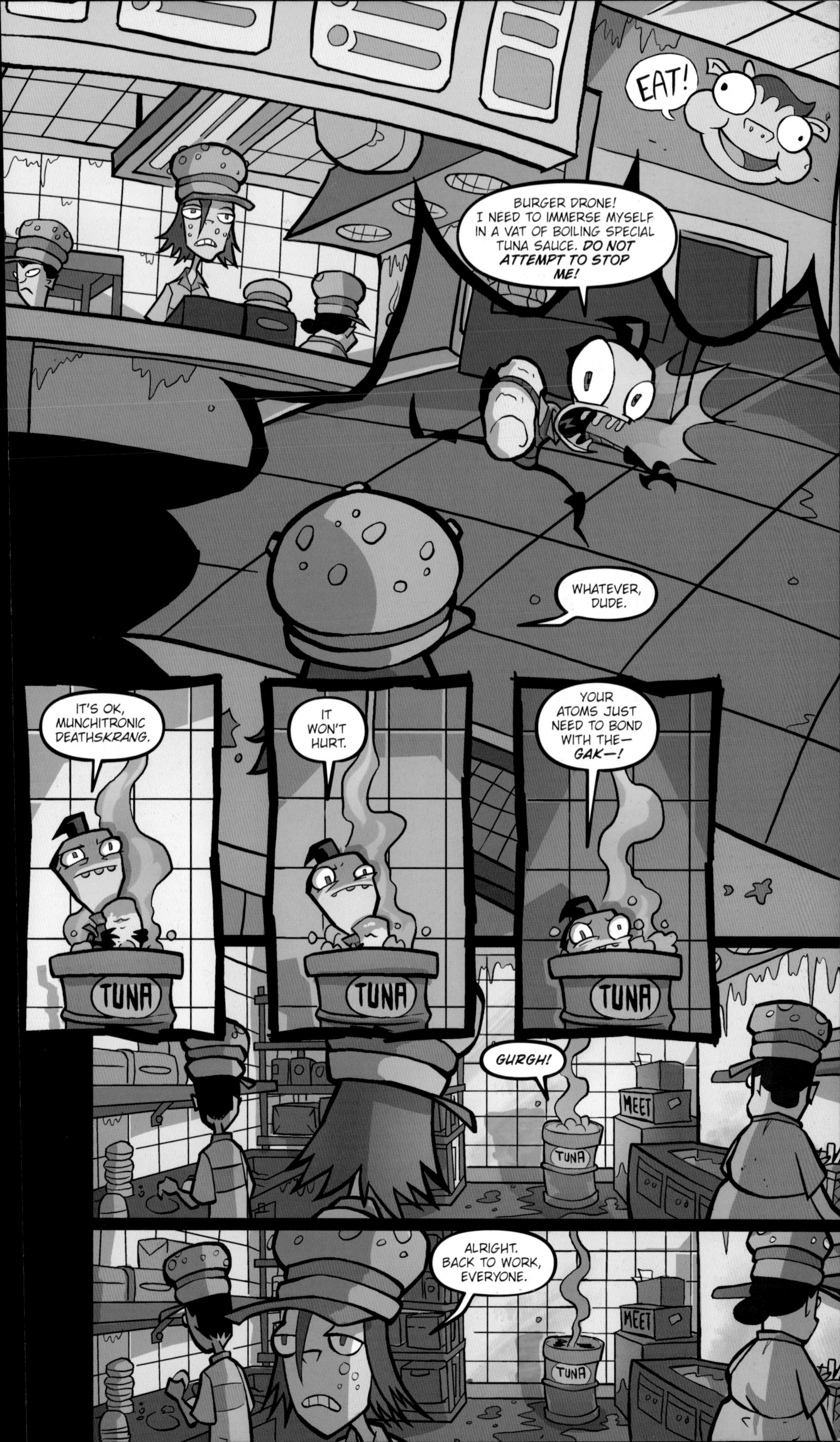
EAT!
BURGER DRONE! I NEED TO IMMERSE MYSELF IN A VAT OF BOILING SPECIAL TUNA SAUCE. DO NOT ATTEMPT TO STOP ME!
WHATEVER, DUDE.
IT'S OK, MUNCHITRONIC DEATHSKRANG.
TUNA
IT WON'T HURT.
TUNA
YOUR ATOMS JUST NEED TO BOND WITH THE—GAK—!
TUNA
GURGH!
MEET
TUNA
ALRIGHT. BACK TO WORK, EVERYONE.
MEET
TUNA

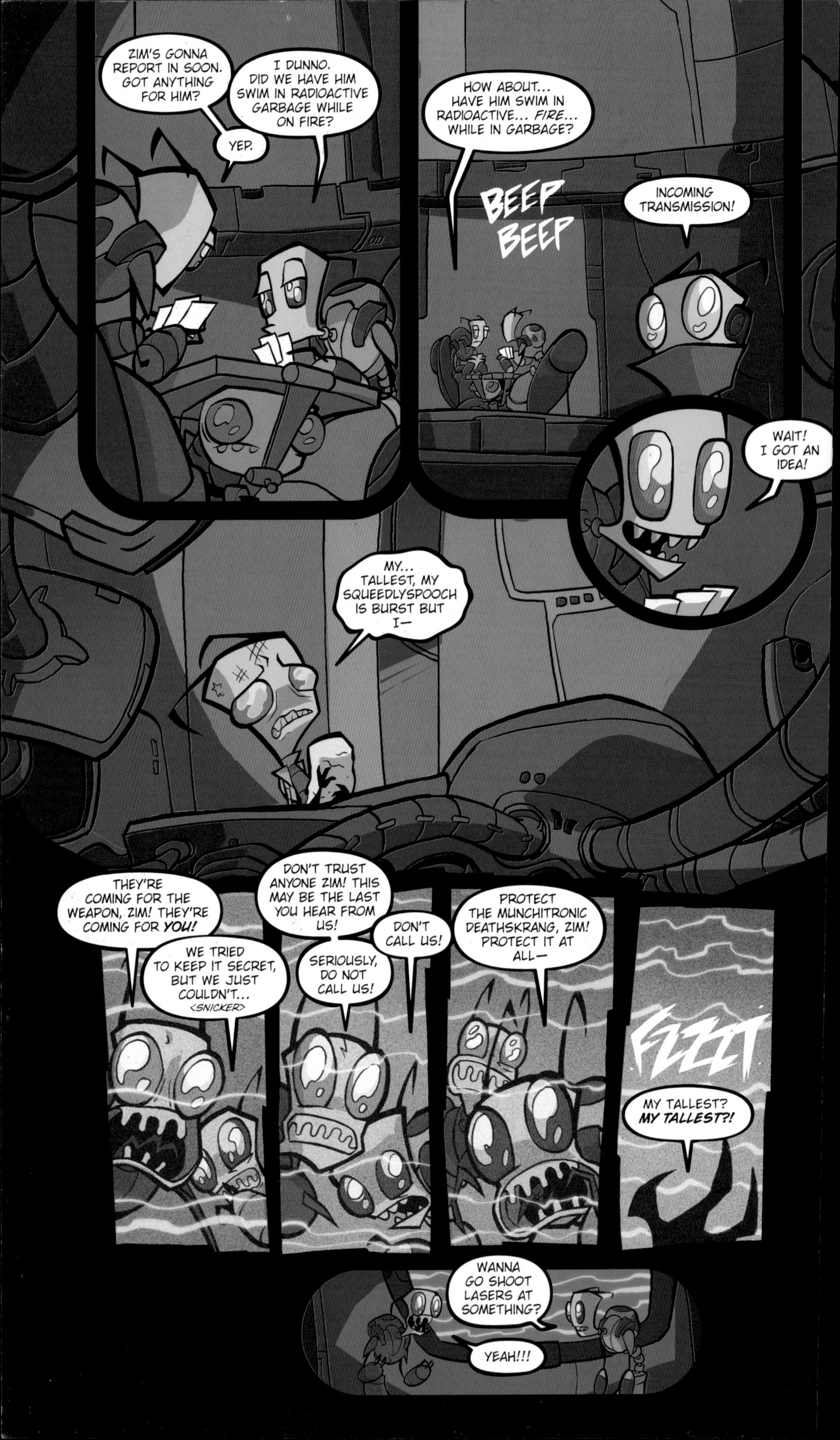
ZIM'S GONNA REPORT IN SOON. GOT ANYTHING FOR HIM?
I DUNNO. DID WE HAVE HIM SWIM IN RADIOACTIVE GARBAGE WHILE ON FIRE?
YEP.
HOW ABOUT... HAVE HIM SWIM IN RADIOACTIVE... *FIRE*... WHILE IN GARBAGE?
BEEP BEEP
INCOMING TRANSMISSION!
WAIT! I GOT AN IDEA!
MY... TALLEST, MY SQUEEDLYSPOOCH IS BURST BUT I—
THEY'RE COMING FOR THE WEAPON, ZIM! THEY'RE COMING FOR ***YOU!***
WE TRIED TO KEEP IT SECRET, BUT WE JUST COULDN'T...
<*SNICKER*>
DON'T TRUST ANYONE ZIM! THIS MAY BE THE LAST YOU HEAR FROM US!
DON'T CALL US!
SERIOUSLY, DO NOT CALL US!
PROTECT THE MUNCHITRONIC DEATHSKRANG, ZIM! PROTECT IT AT ALL—
FZZZT
MY TALLEST? ***MY TALLEST?!***
WANNA GO SHOOT LASERS AT SOMETHING?
YEAH!!!

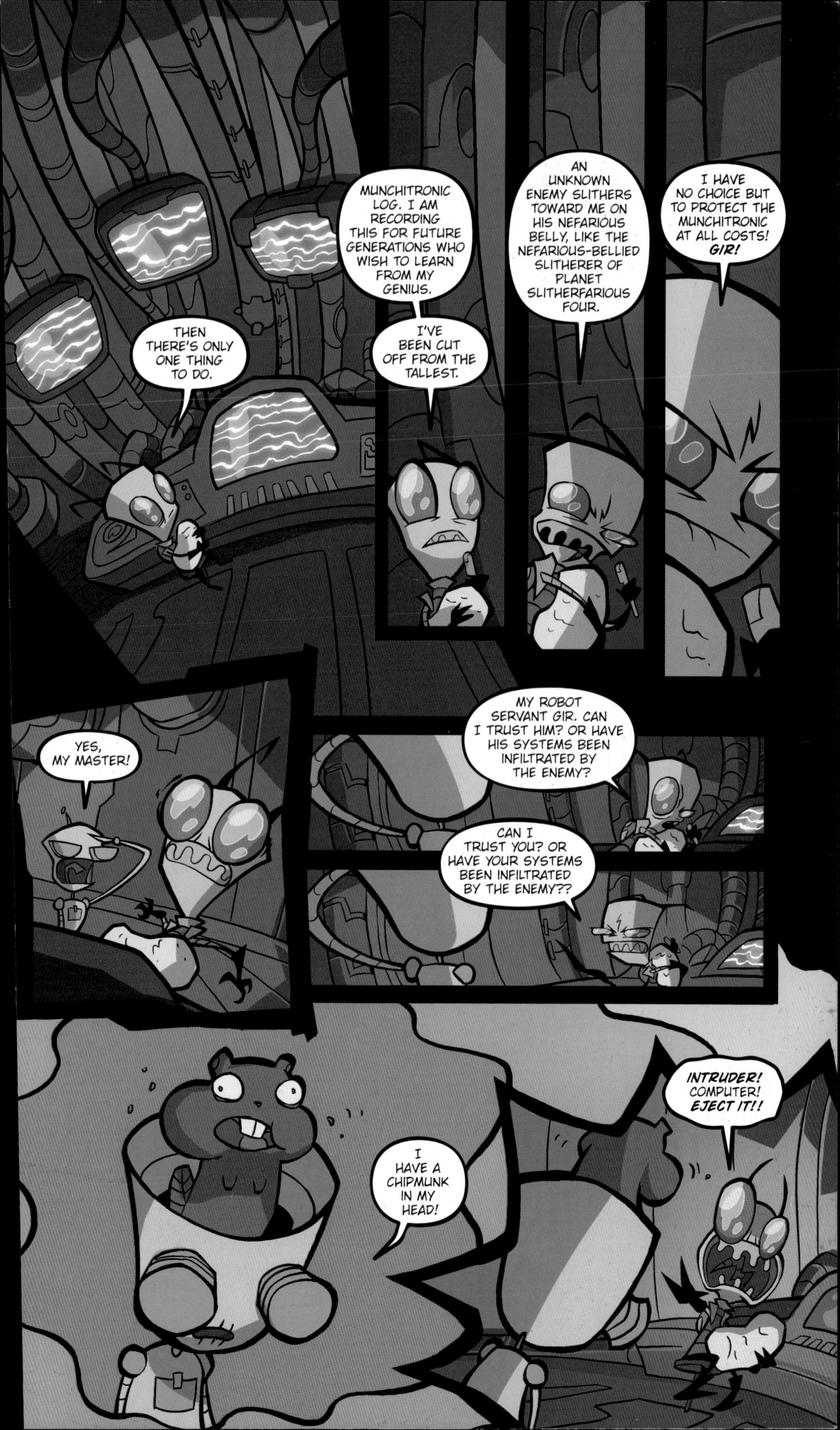
THEN THERE'S ONLY ONE THING TO DO.
MUNCHITRONIC LOG. I AM RECORDING THIS FOR FUTURE GENERATIONS WHO WISH TO LEARN FROM MY GENIUS.
I'VE BEEN CUT OFF FROM THE TALLEST.
AN UNKNOWN ENEMY SLITHERS TOWARD ME ON HIS NEFARIOUS BELLY, LIKE THE NEFARIOUS-BELLIED SLITHERER OF PLANET SLITHERFARIOUS FOUR.
I HAVE NO CHOICE BUT TO PROTECT THE MUNCHITRONIC AT ALL COSTS! GIR!
YES, MY MASTER!
MY ROBOT SERVANT GIR. CAN I TRUST HIM? OR HAVE HIS SYSTEMS BEEN INFILTRATED BY THE ENEMY?
CAN I TRUST YOU? OR HAVE YOUR SYSTEMS BEEN INFILTRATED BY THE ENEMY??
I HAVE A CHIPMUNK IN MY HEAD!
INTRUDER! COMPUTER! EJECT IT!!

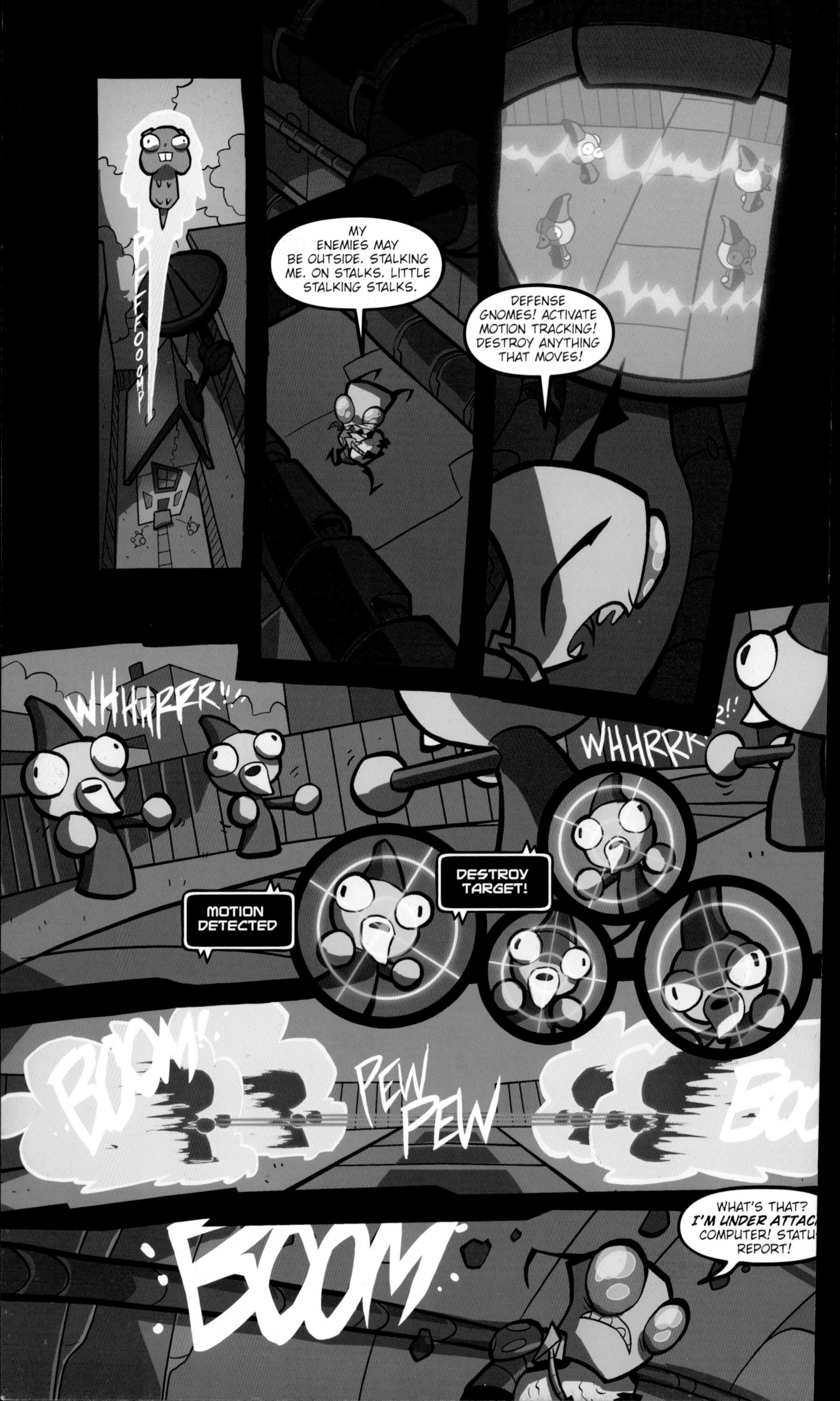
PFFFFOOOOMP
MY ENEMIES MAY BE OUTSIDE. STALKING ME. ON STALKS. LITTLE STALKING STALKS.
DEFENSE GNOMES! ACTIVATE MOTION TRACKING! DESTROY ANYTHING THAT MOVES!
WHHRRRR!!
WHHRRR!!
MOTION DETECTED
DESTROY TARGET!
BOOM!
PEW PEW
BOOM
WHAT'S THAT? I'M UNDER ATTACK! COMPUTER! STATUS REPORT!

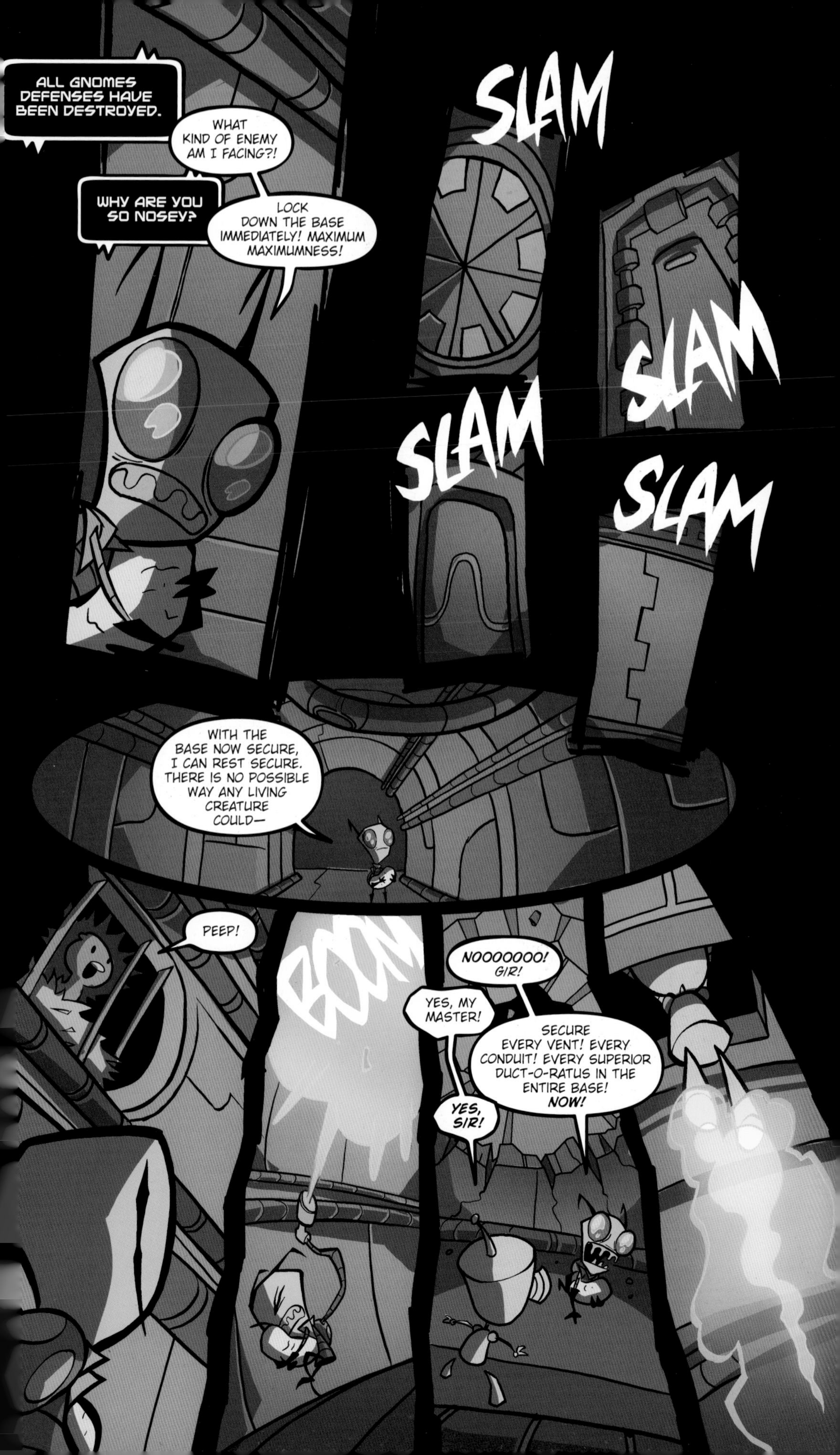
ALL GNOMES DEFENSES HAVE BEEN DESTROYED.
WHAT KIND OF ENEMY AM I FACING?!
WHY ARE YOU SO NOSEY?
LOCK DOWN THE BASE IMMEDIATELY! MAXIMUM MAXIMUMNESS!
SLAM
SLAM
SLAM
SLAM
WITH THE BASE NOW SECURE, I CAN REST SECURE. THERE IS NO POSSIBLE WAY ANY LIVING CREATURE COULD—
PEEP!
BOOM
NOOOOOOO! GIR!
YES, MY MASTER!
SECURE EVERY VENT! EVERY CONDUIT! EVERY SUPERIOR DUCT-O-RATUS IN THE ENTIRE BASE! NOW!
YES, SIR!

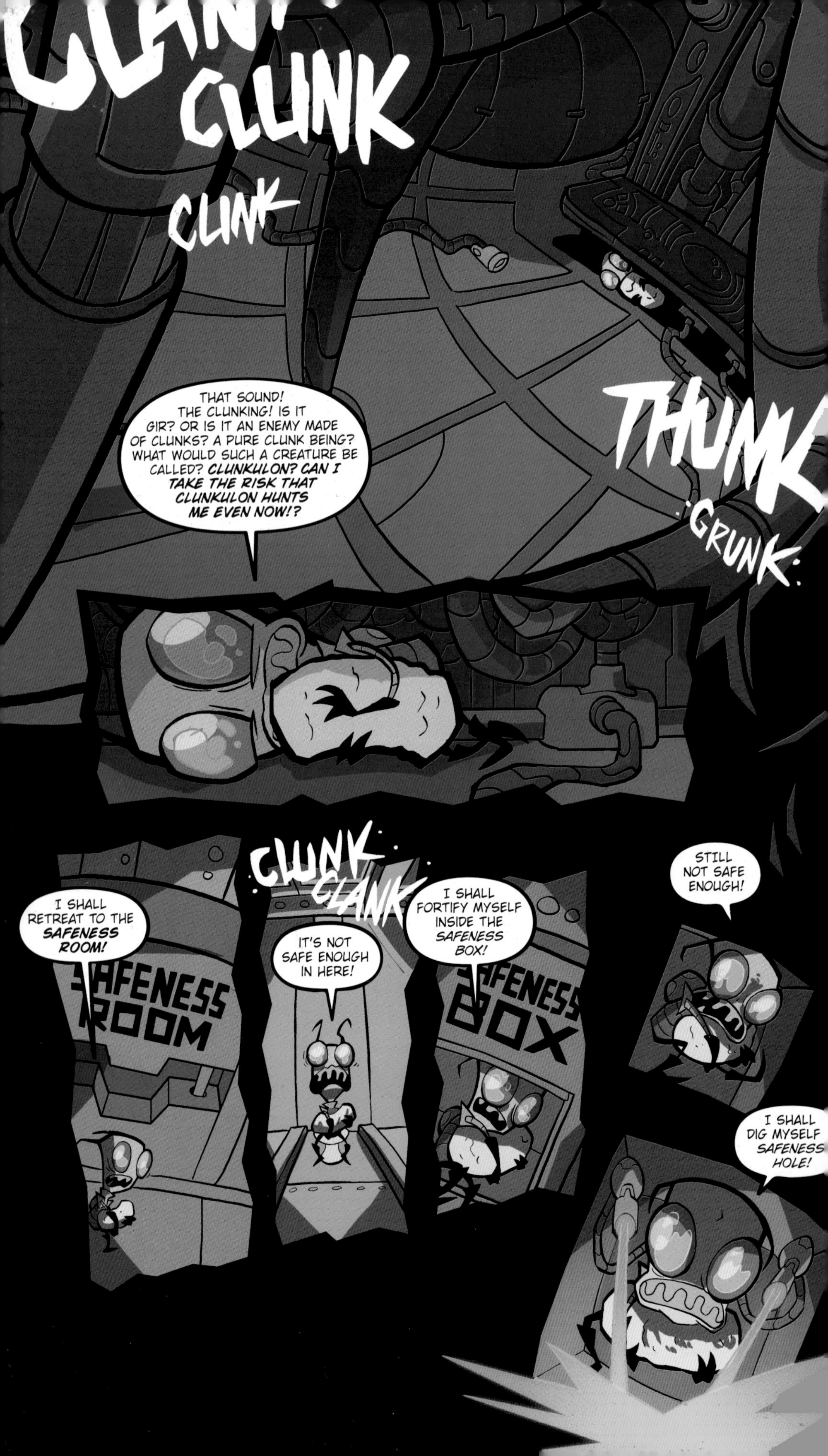
CLANK
CLUNK
CLUNK
THAT SOUND! THE CLUNKING! IS IT GIR? OR IS IT AN ENEMY MADE OF CLUNKS? A PURE CLUNK BEING? WHAT WOULD SUCH A CREATURE BE CALLED? CLUNKULON? CAN I TAKE THE RISK THAT CLUNKULON HUNTS ME EVEN NOW!?
THUNK
GRUNK
CLUNK
CLANK
I SHALL RETREAT TO THE SAFENESS ROOM!
SAFENESS ROOM
IT'S NOT SAFE ENOUGH IN HERE!
I SHALL FORTIFY MYSELF INSIDE THE SAFENESS BOX!
SAFENESS BOX
STILL NOT SAFE ENOUGH!
I SHALL DIG MYSELF SAFENESS HOLE!

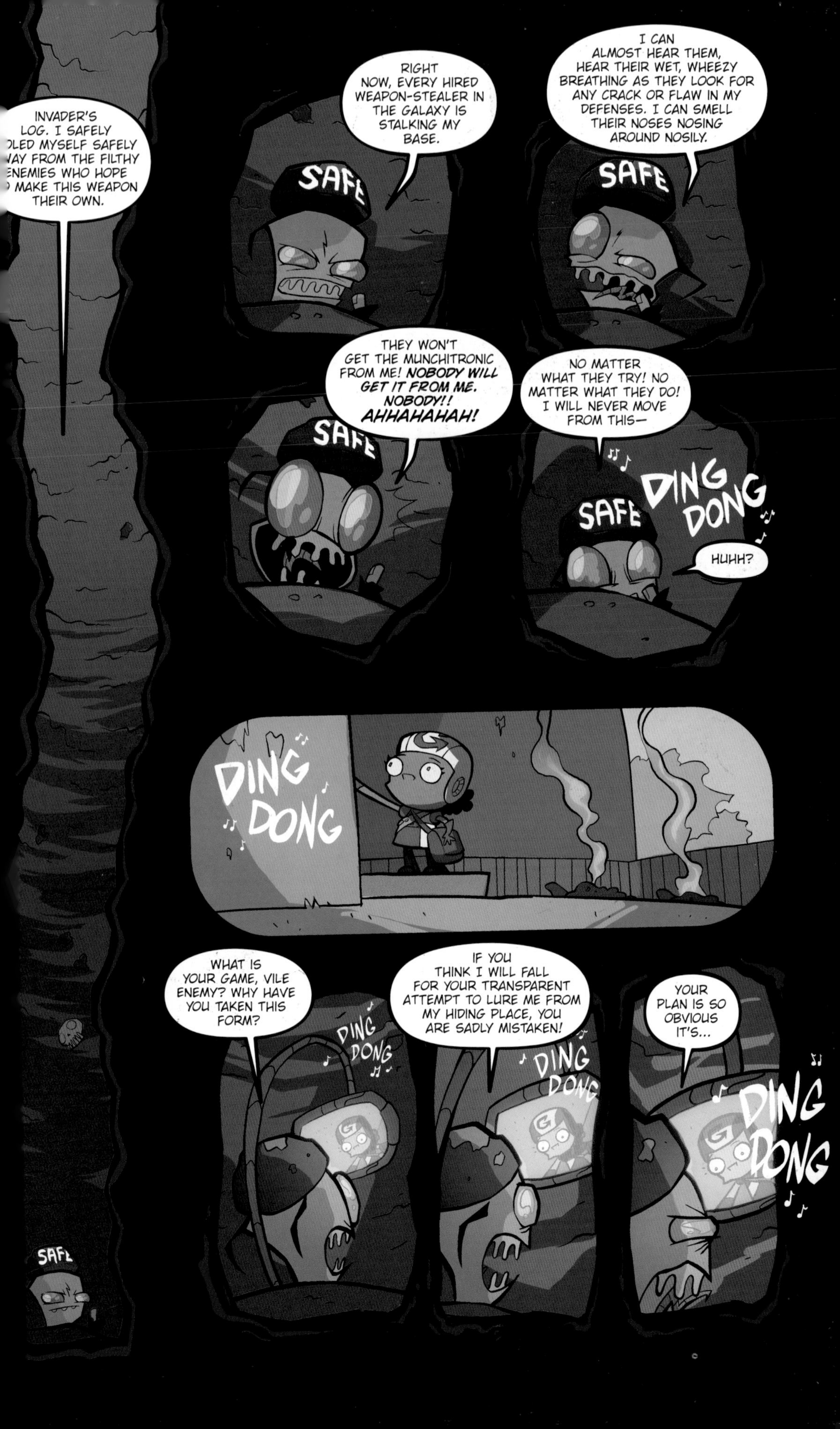

INVADER'S LOG. I SAFELY OLED MYSELF SAFELY VAY FROM THE FILTHY ENEMIES WHO HOPE MAKE THIS WEAPON THEIR OWN.
RIGHT NOW, EVERY HIRED WEAPON-STEALER IN THE GALAXY IS STALKING MY BASE.
SAFE
I CAN ALMOST HEAR THEM, HEAR THEIR WET, WHEEZY BREATHING AS THEY LOOK FOR ANY CRACK OR FLAW IN MY DEFENSES. I CAN SMELL THEIR NOSES NOSING AROUND NOSILY.
SAFE
THEY WON'T GET THE MUNCHITRONIC FROM ME! ***NOBODY WILL GET IT FROM ME. NOBODY!! AHHAHAHAH!***
SAFE
NO MATTER WHAT THEY TRY! NO MATTER WHAT THEY DO! I WILL NEVER MOVE FROM THIS—
SAFE
DING DONG
HUHH?
DING DONG
WHAT IS YOUR GAME, VILE ENEMY? WHY HAVE YOU TAKEN THIS FORM?
DING DONG
IF YOU THINK I WILL FALL FOR YOUR TRANSPARENT ATTEMPT TO LURE ME FROM MY HIDING PLACE, YOU ARE SADLY MISTAKEN!
DING DONG
YOUR PLAN IS SO OBVIOUS IT'S...
DING DONG
SAFE

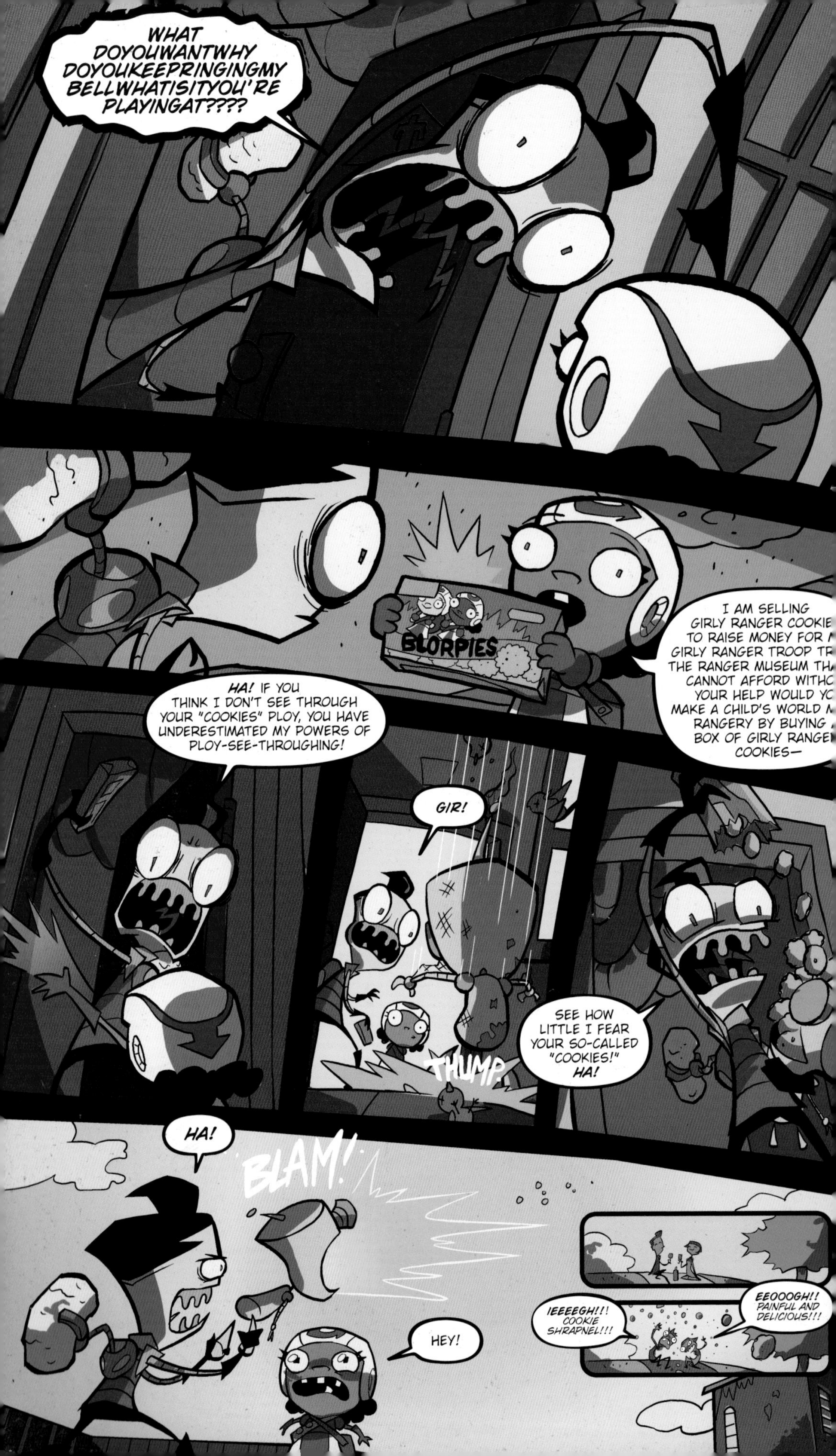

WHAT DOYOUWANTWHY DOYOUKEEPRINGINGMY BELLWHATISITYOU'RE PLAYINGAT????
BLORPIES
I AM SELLING GIRLY RANGER COOKIE TO RAISE MONEY FOR M GIRLY RANGER TROOP TR THE RANGER MUSEUM THA CANNOT AFFORD WITHO YOUR HELP WOULD YO MAKE A CHILD'S WORLD A RANGERY BY BUYING A BOX OF GIRLY RANGER COOKIES—
HA! IF YOU THINK I DON'T SEE THROUGH YOUR "COOKIES" PLOY, YOU HAVE UNDERESTIMATED MY POWERS OF PLOY-SEE-THROUGHING!
GIR!
SEE HOW LITTLE I FEAR YOUR SO-CALLED "COOKIES!" HA!
THUMP
HA!
BLAM!
HEY!
IEEEEGH!!! COOKIE SHRAPNEL!!!
EEOOOGH!! PAINFUL AND DELICIOUS!!!

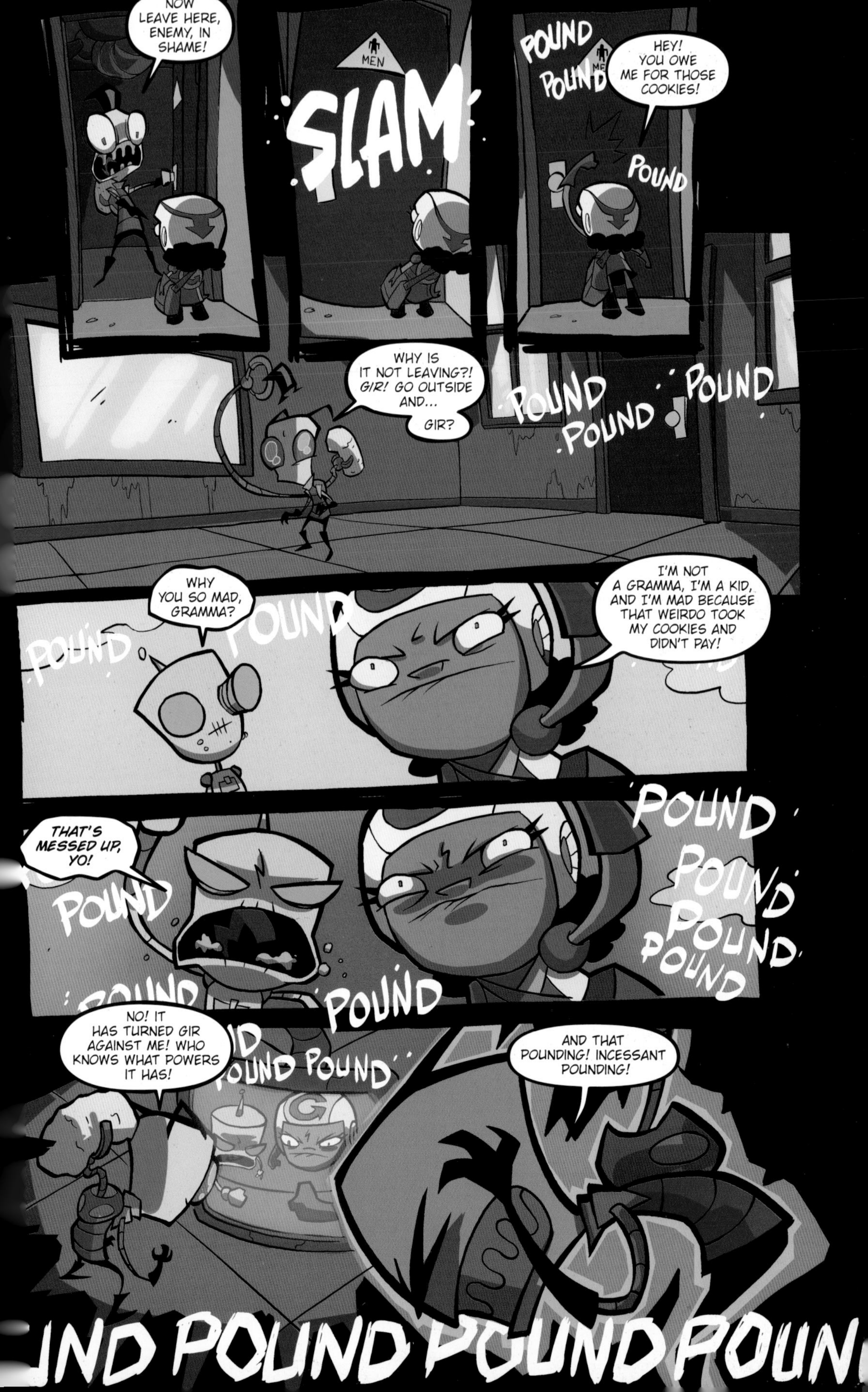
NOW LEAVE HERE, ENEMY, IN SHAME!
MEN
SLAM
POUND
POUND
HEY! YOU OWE ME FOR THOSE COOKIES!
POUND
WHY IS IT NOT LEAVING?! GIR! GO OUTSIDE AND...
GIR?
POUND
POUND
POUND
WHY YOU SO MAD, GRAMMA?
POUND
POUND
I'M NOT A GRAMMA, I'M A KID, AND I'M MAD BECAUSE THAT WEIRDO TOOK MY COOKIES AND DIDN'T PAY!
THAT'S MESSED UP, YO!
POUND
POUND
POUND
POUND
POUND
POUND
NO! IT HAS TURNED GIR AGAINST ME! WHO KNOWS WHAT POWERS IT HAS!
POUND POUND
AND THAT POUNDING! INCESSANT POUNDING!
POUND POUND

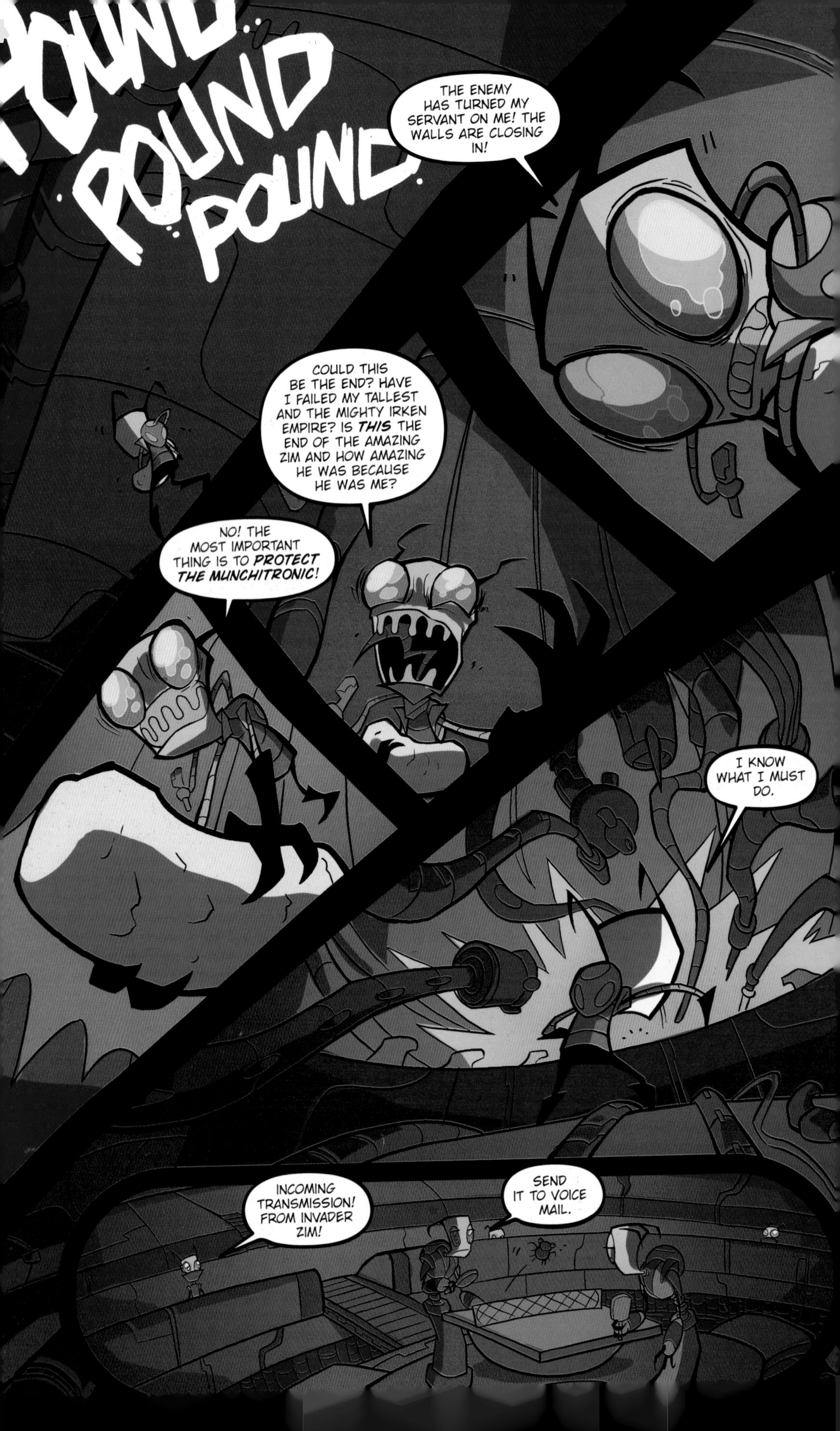
POUND POUND POUND POUND
THE ENEMY HAS TURNED MY SERVANT ON ME! THE WALLS ARE CLOSING IN!
COULD THIS BE THE END? HAVE I FAILED MY TALLEST AND THE MIGHTY IRKEN EMPIRE? IS THIS THE END OF THE AMAZING ZIM AND HOW AMAZING HE WAS BECAUSE HE WAS ME?
NO! THE MOST IMPORTANT THING IS TO PROTECT THE MUNCHITRONIC!
I KNOW WHAT I MUST DO.
INCOMING TRANSMISSION! FROM INVADER ZIM!
SEND IT TO VOICE MAIL.

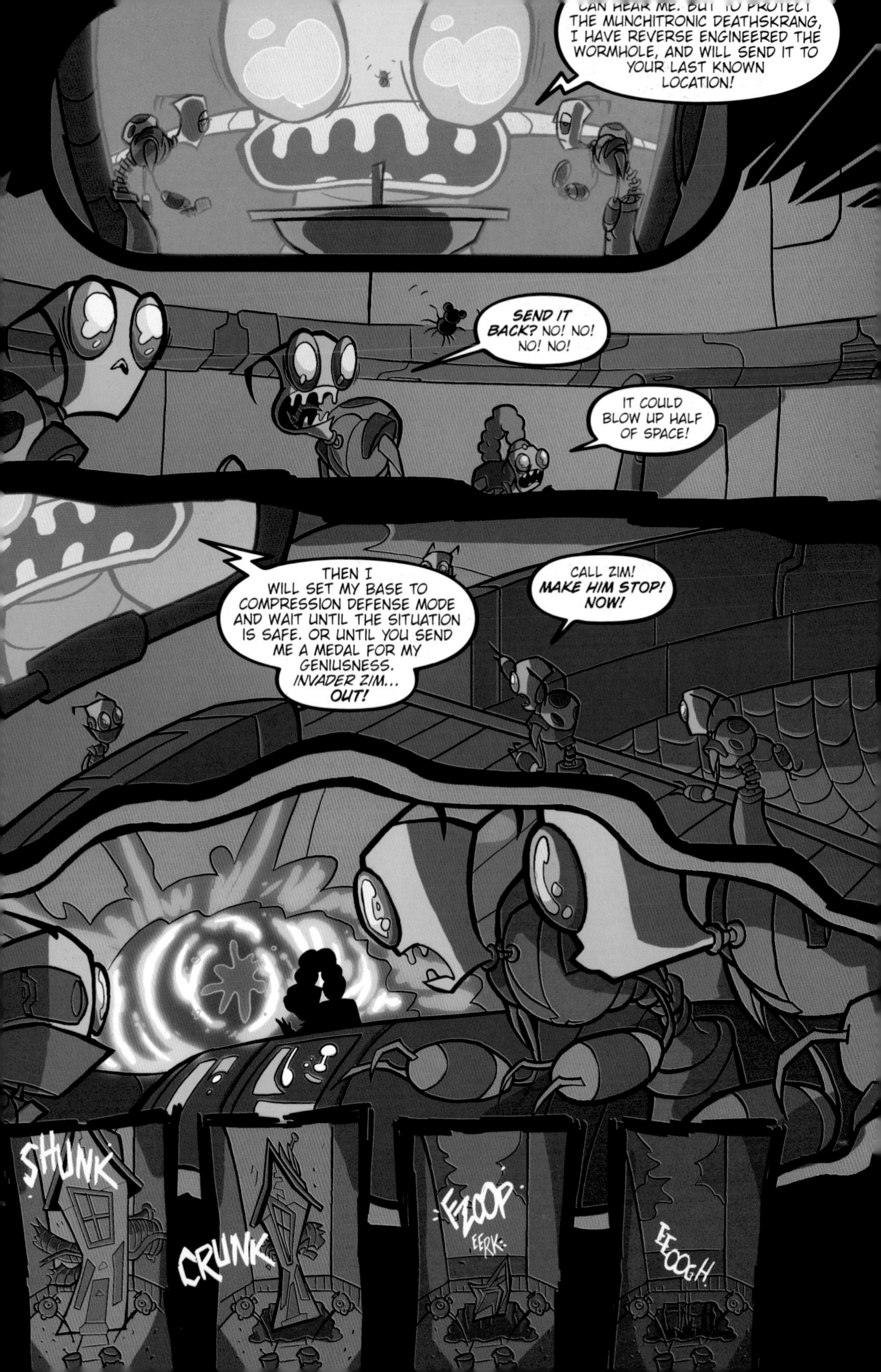
CAN HEAR ME. BUT TO PROTECT THE MUNCHITRONIC DEATHSKRANG, I HAVE REVERSE ENGINEERED THE WORMHOLE, AND WILL SEND IT TO YOUR LAST KNOWN LOCATION!
SEND IT BACK? NO! NO! NO! NO!
IT COULD BLOW UP HALF OF SPACE!
THEN I WILL SET MY BASE TO COMPRESSION DEFENSE MODE AND WAIT UNTIL THE SITUATION IS SAFE. OR UNTIL YOU SEND ME A MEDAL FOR MY GENIUSNESS. INVADER ZIM... OUT!
CALL ZIM! MAKE HIM STOP! NOW!
SHUNK
CRUNK
FZOOP
EERK
FLOOGH

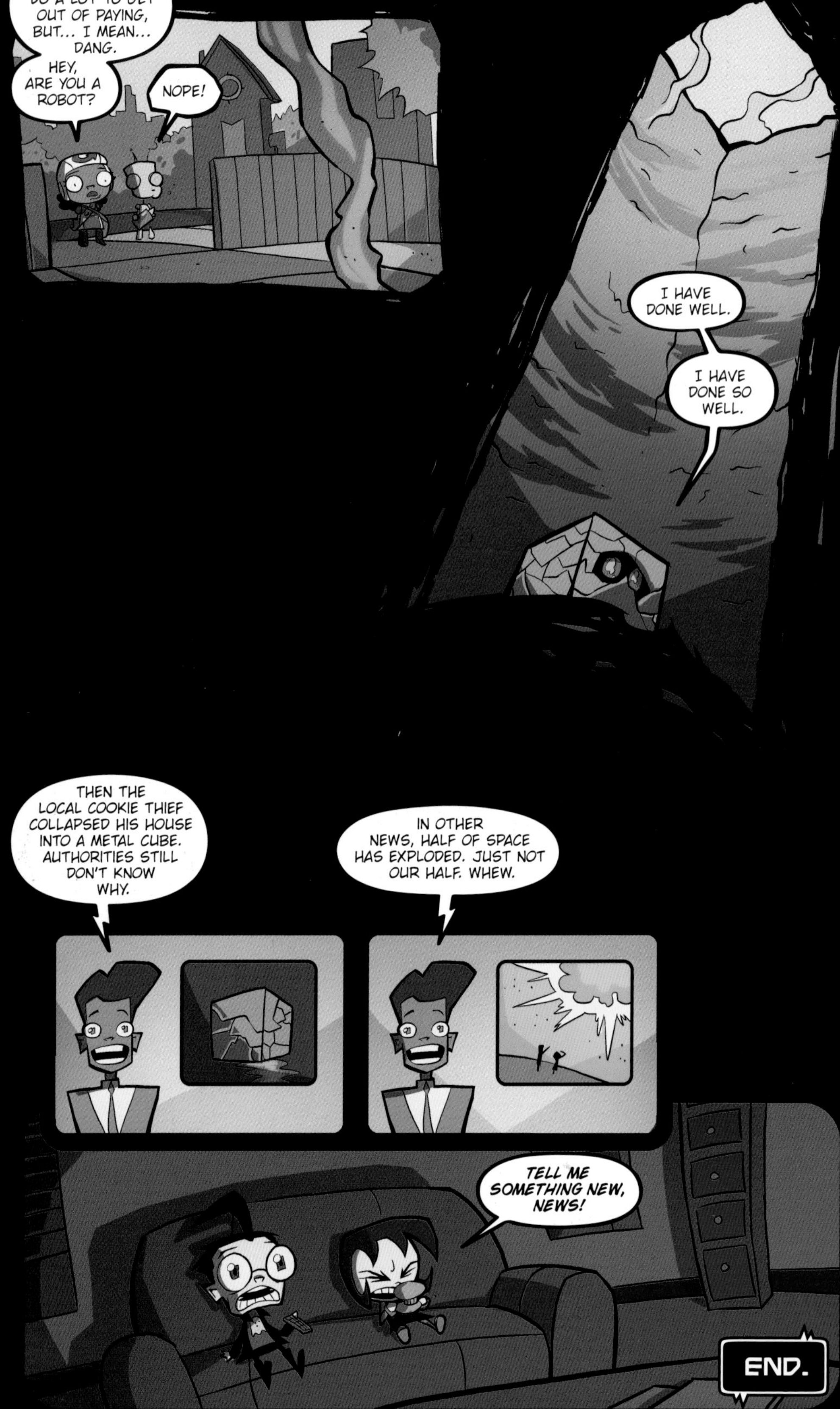

OUT OF PAYING, BUT... I MEAN... DANG.
HEY, ARE YOU A ROBOT?
NOPE!
I HAVE DONE WELL.
I HAVE DONE SO WELL.
THEN THE LOCAL COOKIE THIEF COLLAPSED HIS HOUSE INTO A METAL CUBE. AUTHORITIES STILL DON'T KNOW WHY.
IN OTHER NEWS, HALF OF SPACE HAS EXPLODED. JUST NOT OUR HALF. WHEW.
TELL ME SOMETHING NEW, NEWS!
END.

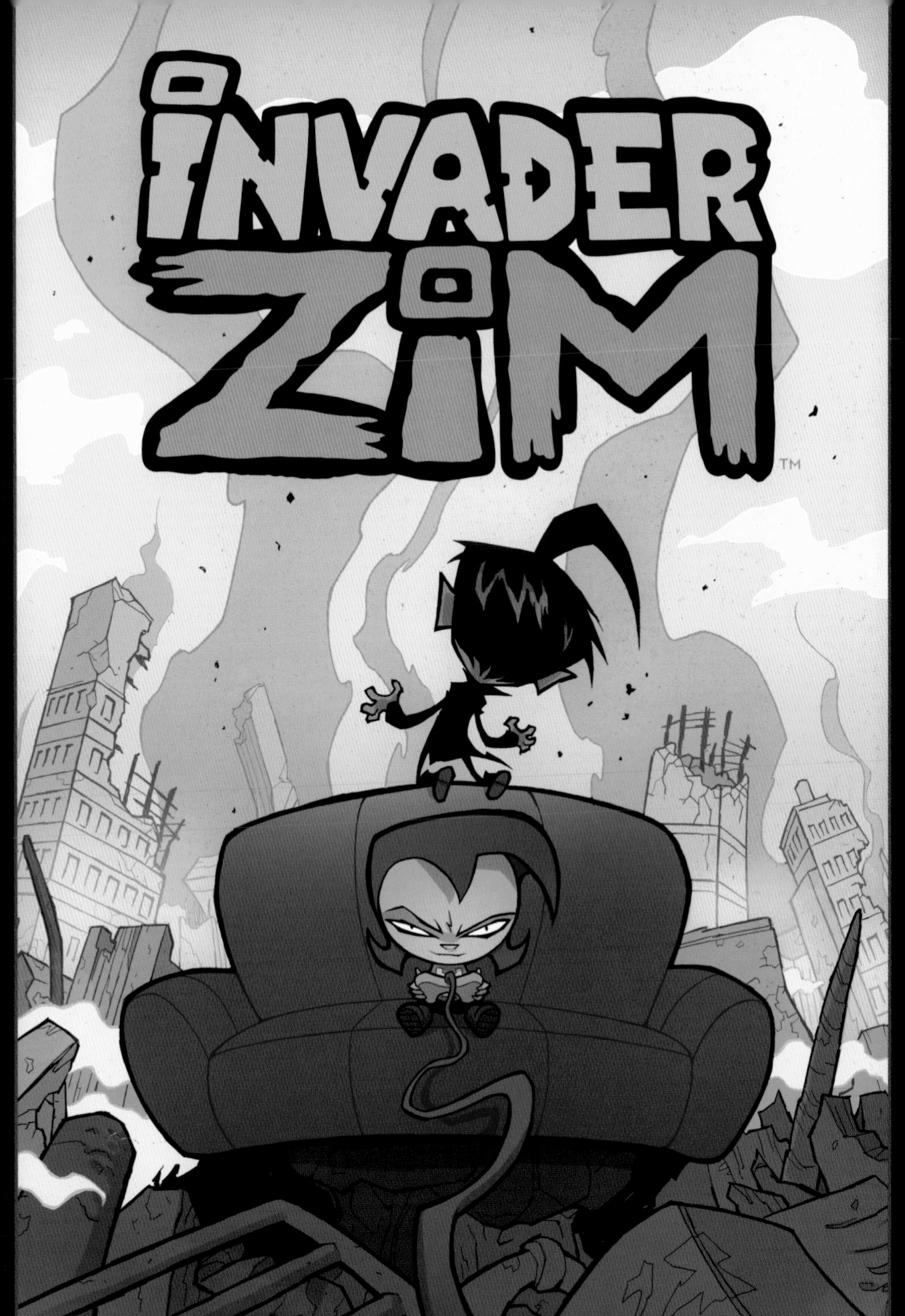
INVADER
ZIM™

CHAPTER: 5

illustration by AARON ALEXOVICH and SAVANNA GANUCHEAU

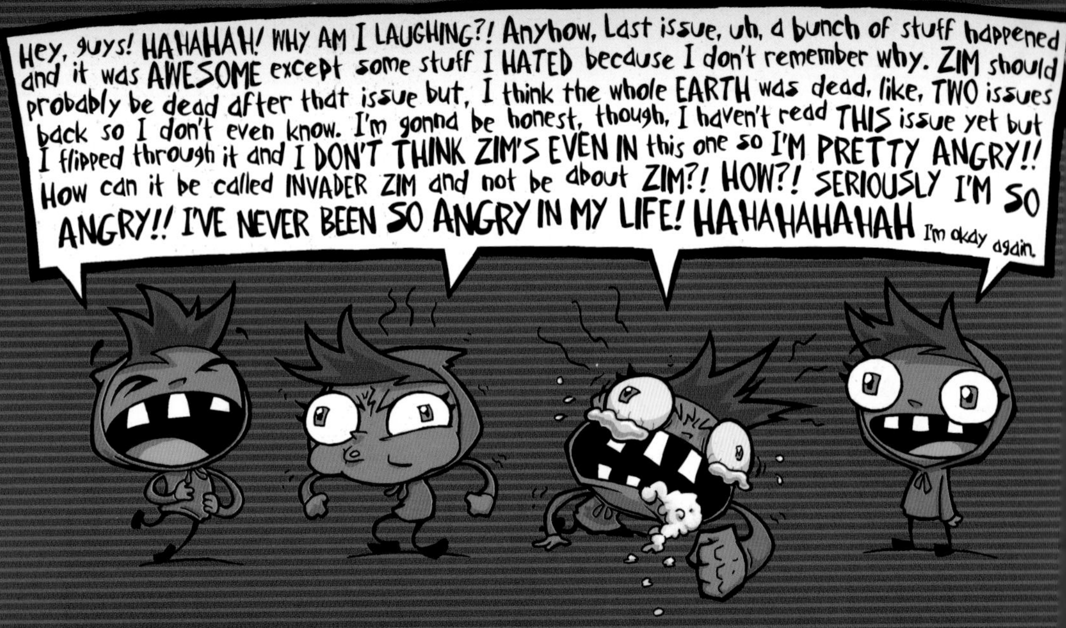
Hey, guys! HAHAHAH! WHY AM I LAUGHING?! Anyhow, Last issue, uh, a bunch of stuff happened and it was AWESOME except some stuff I HATED because I don't remember why. ZIM should probably be dead after that issue but, I think the whole EARTH was dead, like, TWO issues back so I don't even know. I'm gonna be honest, though, I haven't read THIS issue yet but I flipped through it and I DON'T THINK ZIM'S EVEN IN this one so I'M PRETTY ANGRY!! How can it be called INVADER ZIM and not be about ZIM?! HOW?! SERIOUSLY I'M SO ANGRY!! I'VE NEVER BEEN SO ANGRY IN MY LIFE! HAHAHAHAHAH I'm okay again.

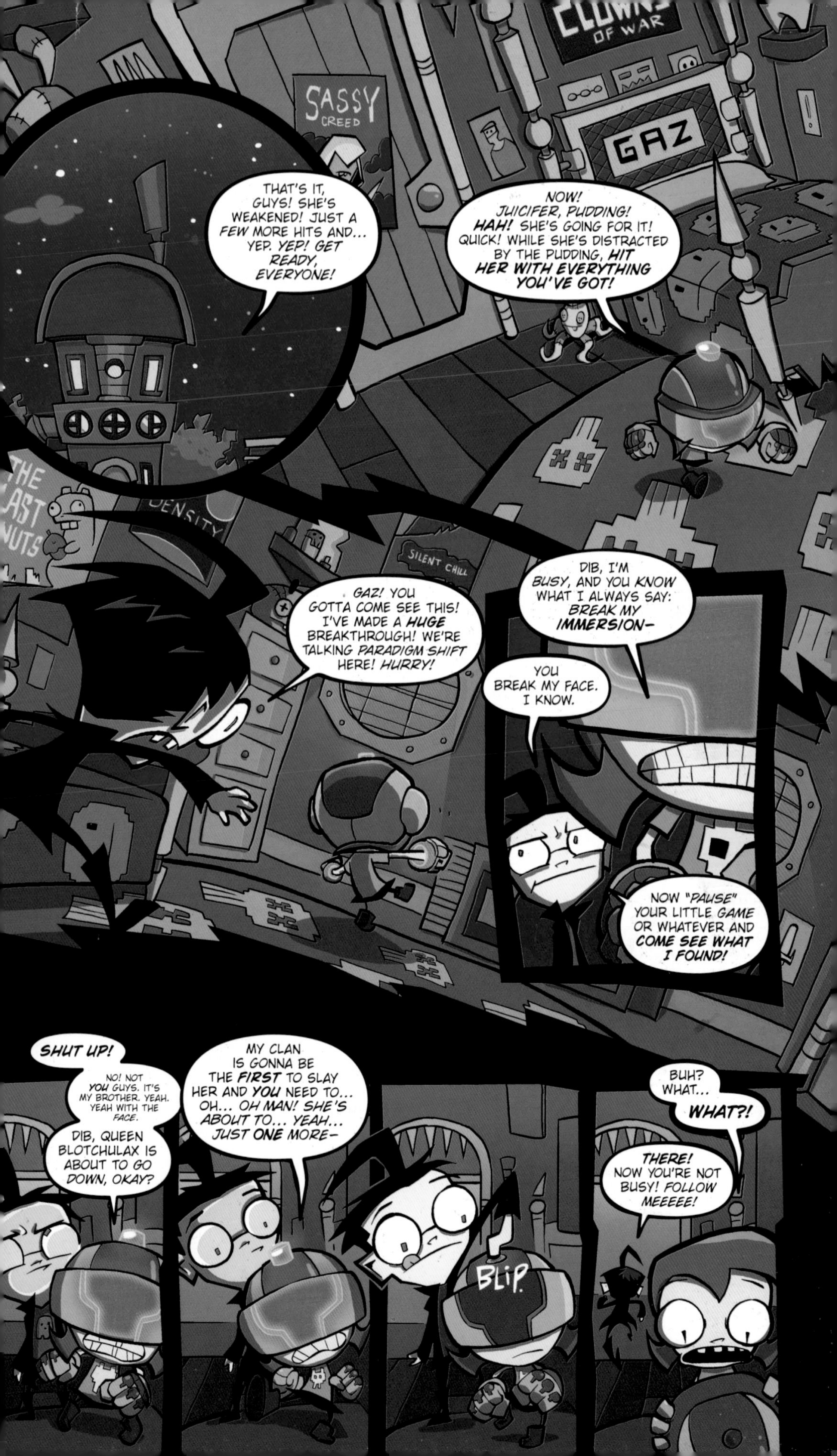

SASSY CREED
GAZ
THAT'S IT, GUYS! SHE'S WEAKENED! JUST A FEW MORE HITS AND... YEP. YEP! GET READY, EVERYONE!
NOW! JUICIFER, PUDDING! HAH! SHE'S GOING FOR IT! QUICK! WHILE SHE'S DISTRACTED BY THE PUDDING, HIT HER WITH EVERYTHING YOU'VE GOT!
SILENT CHILL
GAZ! YOU GOTTA COME SEE THIS! I'VE MADE A HUGE BREAKTHROUGH! WE'RE TALKING PARADIGM SHIFT HERE! HURRY!
DIB, I'M BUSY, AND YOU KNOW WHAT I ALWAYS SAY: BREAK MY IMMERSION–
YOU BREAK MY FACE. I KNOW.
NOW "PAUSE" YOUR LITTLE GAME OR WHATEVER AND COME SEE WHAT I FOUND!
SHUT UP!
NO! NOT YOU GUYS. IT'S MY BROTHER. YEAH. YEAH WITH THE FACE.
DIB, QUEEN BLOTCHULAX IS ABOUT TO GO DOWN, OKAY?
MY CLAN IS GONNA BE THE FIRST TO SLAY HER AND YOU NEED TO... OH... OH MAN! SHE'S ABOUT TO... YEAH... JUST ONE MORE–
BLIP.
BUH? WHAT... WHAT?!
THERE! NOW YOU'RE NOT BUSY! FOLLOW MEEEEE!

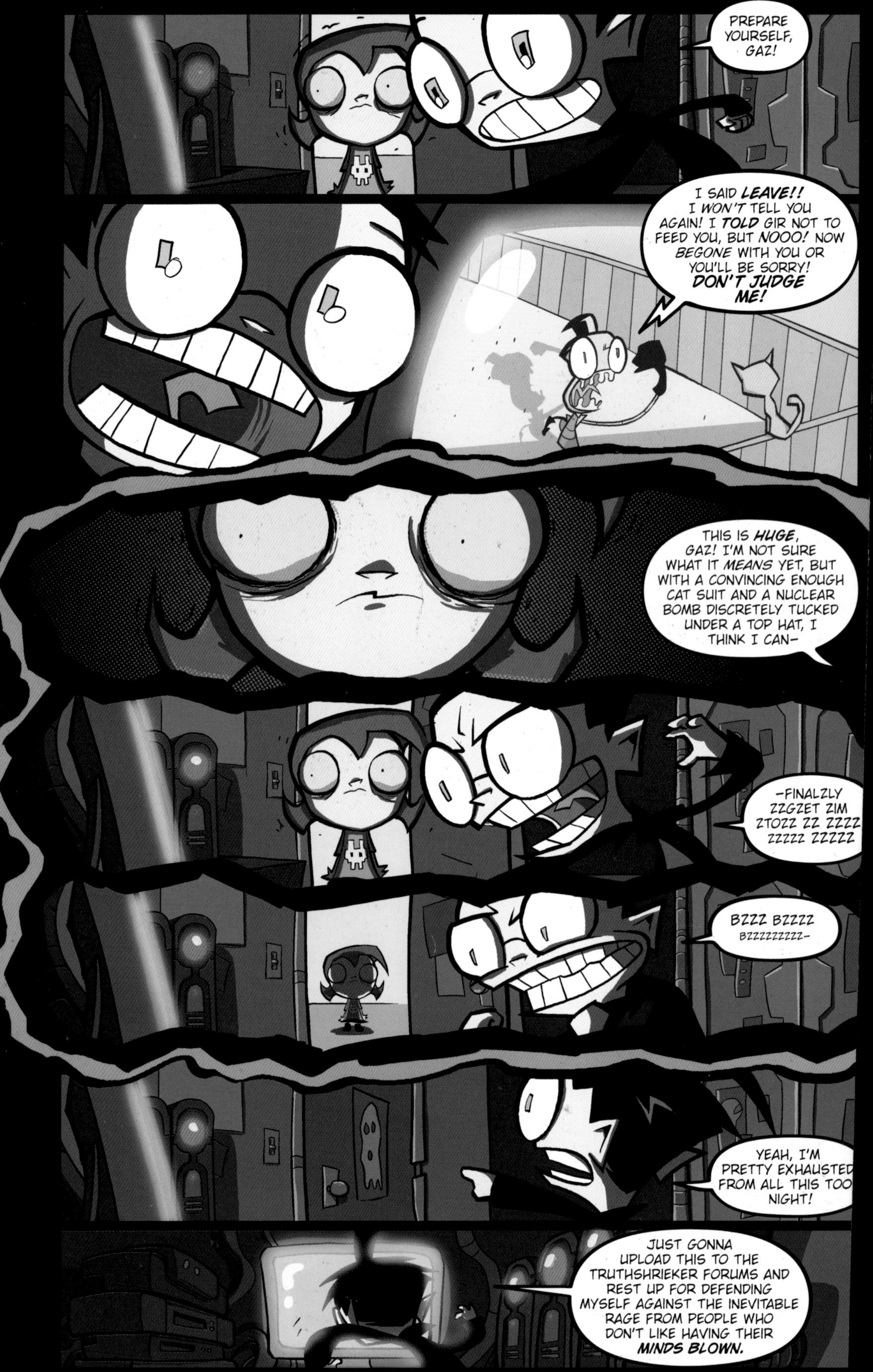
PREPARE YOURSELF, GAZ!
I SAID **LEAVE!!** I *WON'T* TELL YOU AGAIN! I **TOLD** GIR NOT TO FEED YOU, BUT *NOOO!* NOW *BEGONE* WITH YOU OR YOU'LL BE SORRY! **DON'T JUDGE ME!**
THIS IS **HUGE**, GAZ! I'M NOT SURE WHAT IT *MEANS* YET, BUT WITH A CONVINCING ENOUGH CAT SUIT AND A NUCLEAR BOMB DISCRETELY TUCKED UNDER A TOP HAT, I THINK I CAN–
–FINALZLY ZZGZET ZIM ZTOZZ ZZ ZZZZ ZZZZZ ZZZZZ
BZZZ BZZZZ BZZZZZZZZZ–
YEAH, I'M PRETTY EXHAUSTED FROM ALL THIS TOO NIGHT!
JUST GONNA UPLOAD THIS TO THE TRUTHSHRIEKER FORUMS AND REST UP FOR DEFENDING MYSELF AGAINST THE INEVITABLE RAGE FROM PEOPLE WHO DON'T LIKE HAVING THEIR **MINDS BLOWN.**

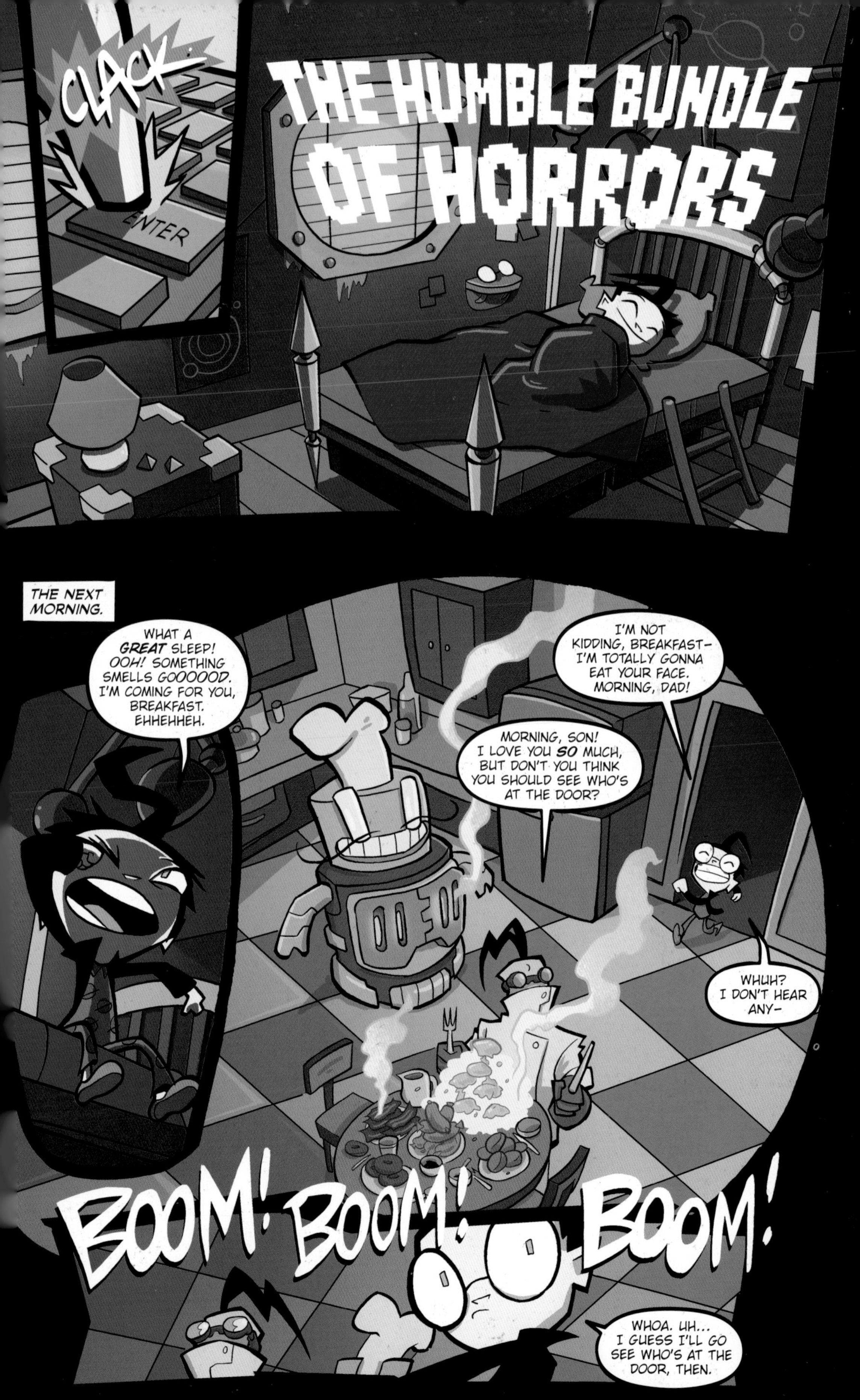
CLACK
ENTER
THE HUMBLE BUNDLE OF HORRORS
THE NEXT MORNING.
WHAT A GREAT SLEEP! OOH! SOMETHING SMELLS GOOOOOD. I'M COMING FOR YOU, BREAKFAST. EHHEHHEH.
I'M NOT KIDDING, BREAKFAST– I'M TOTALLY GONNA EAT YOUR FACE. MORNING, DAD!
MORNING, SON! I LOVE YOU SO MUCH, BUT DON'T YOU THINK YOU SHOULD SEE WHO'S AT THE DOOR?
WHUH? I DON'T HEAR ANY–
BOOM! BOOM! BOOM!
WHOA. UH... I GUESS I'LL GO SEE WHO'S AT THE DOOR, THEN.

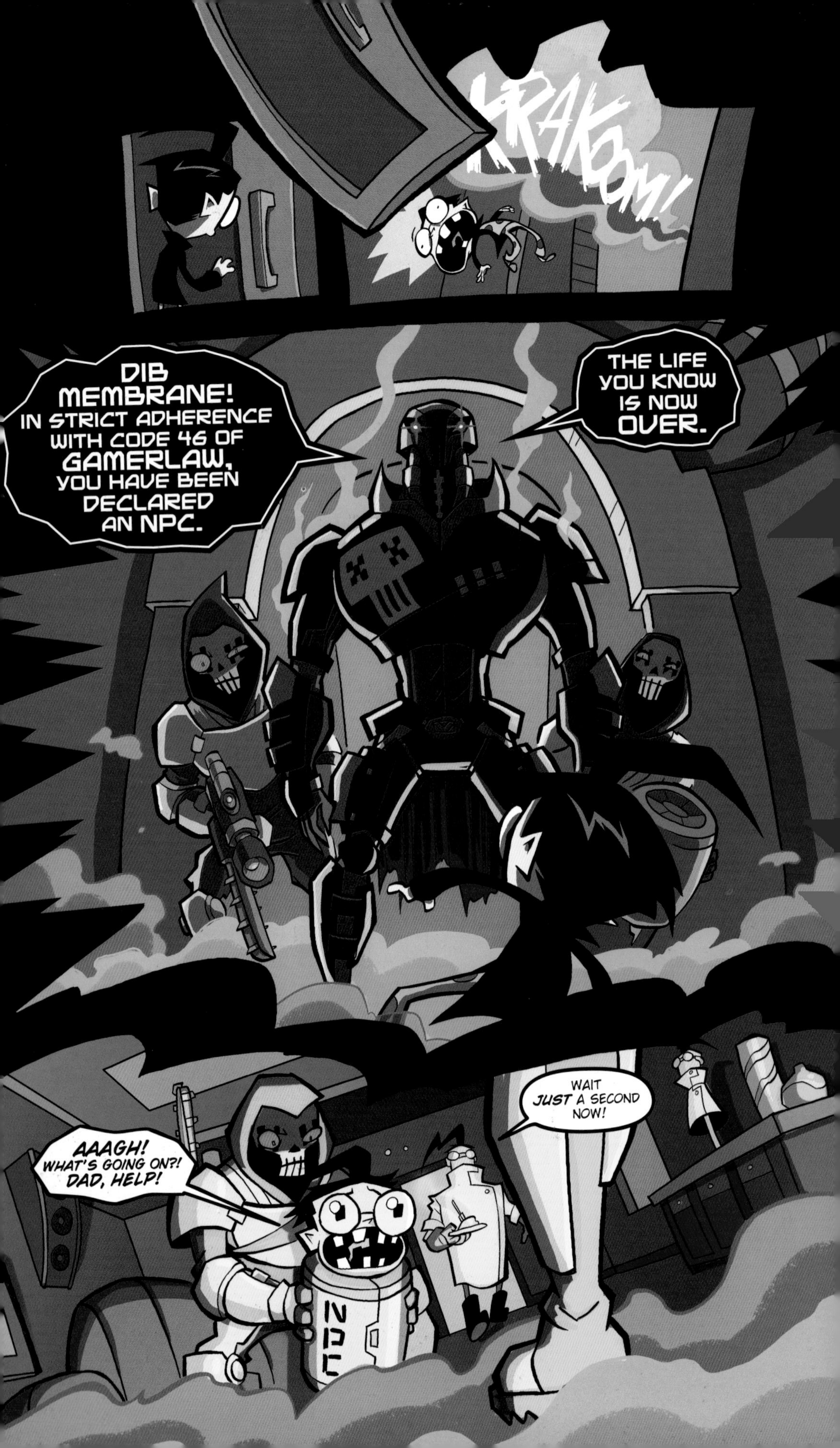
KRAKOOM!
DIB MEMBRANE! IN STRICT ADHERENCE WITH CODE 46 OF GAMERLAW, YOU HAVE BEEN DECLARED AN NPC.
THE LIFE YOU KNOW IS NOW OVER.
AAAGH! WHAT'S GOING ON?! DAD, HELP!
WAIT JUST A SECOND NOW!
NPC

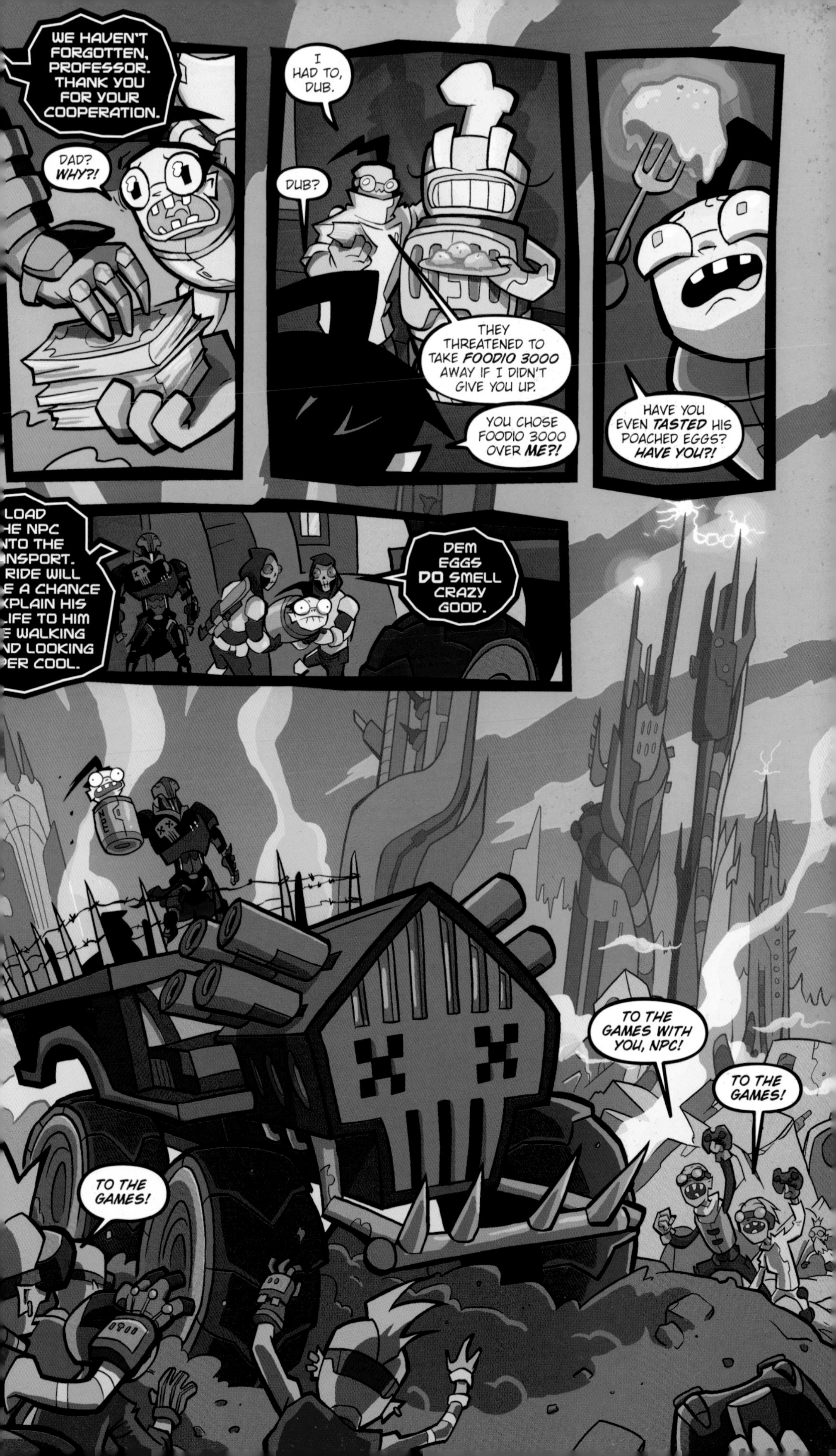
WE HAVEN'T FORGOTTEN, PROFESSOR. THANK YOU FOR YOUR COOPERATION.
DAD? WHY?!
I HAD TO, DUB.
DUB?
THEY THREATENED TO TAKE FOODIO 3000 AWAY IF I DIDN'T GIVE YOU UP.
YOU CHOSE FOODIO 3000 OVER ME?!
HAVE YOU EVEN TASTED HIS POACHED EGGS? HAVE YOU?!
LOAD
HE NPC
NTO THE
NSPORT.
RIDE WILL
E A CHANCE
XPLAIN HIS
LIFE TO HIM
E WALKING
ND LOOKING
PER COOL.
DEM EGGS DO SMELL CRAZY GOOD.
TO THE GAMES WITH YOU, NPC!
TO THE GAMES!
TO THE GAMES!

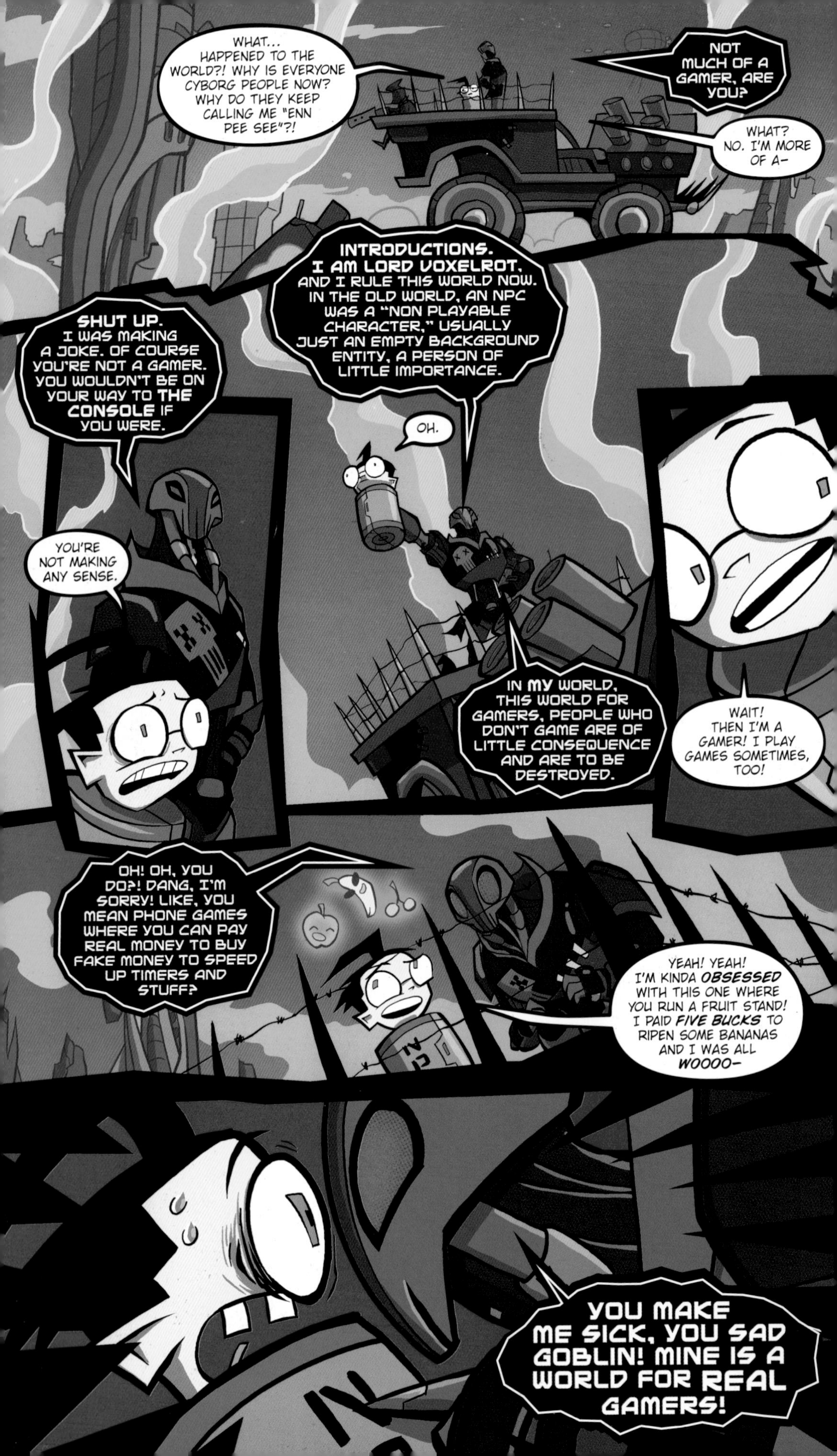
WHAT... HAPPENED TO THE WORLD?! WHY IS EVERYONE CYBORG PEOPLE NOW? WHY DO THEY KEEP CALLING ME "ENN PEE SEE"?!
NOT MUCH OF A GAMER, ARE YOU?
WHAT? NO. I'M MORE OF A-
SHUT UP. I WAS MAKING A JOKE. OF COURSE YOU'RE NOT A GAMER. YOU WOULDN'T BE ON YOUR WAY TO THE CONSOLE IF YOU WERE.
YOU'RE NOT MAKING ANY SENSE.
INTRODUCTIONS. I AM LORD VOXELROT, AND I RULE THIS WORLD NOW. IN THE OLD WORLD, AN NPC WAS A "NON PLAYABLE CHARACTER," USUALLY JUST AN EMPTY BACKGROUND ENTITY, A PERSON OF LITTLE IMPORTANCE.
OH.
IN MY WORLD, THIS WORLD FOR GAMERS, PEOPLE WHO DON'T GAME ARE OF LITTLE CONSEQUENCE AND ARE TO BE DESTROYED.
WAIT! THEN I'M A GAMER! I PLAY GAMES SOMETIMES, TOO!
OH! OH, YOU DO?! DANG, I'M SORRY! LIKE, YOU MEAN PHONE GAMES WHERE YOU CAN PAY REAL MONEY TO BUY FAKE MONEY TO SPEED UP TIMERS AND STUFF?
YEAH! YEAH! I'M KINDA OBSESSED WITH THIS ONE WHERE YOU RUN A FRUIT STAND! I PAID FIVE BUCKS TO RIPEN SOME BANANAS AND I WAS ALL WOOOO-
YOU MAKE ME SICK, YOU SAD GOBLIN! MINE IS A WORLD FOR REAL GAMERS!

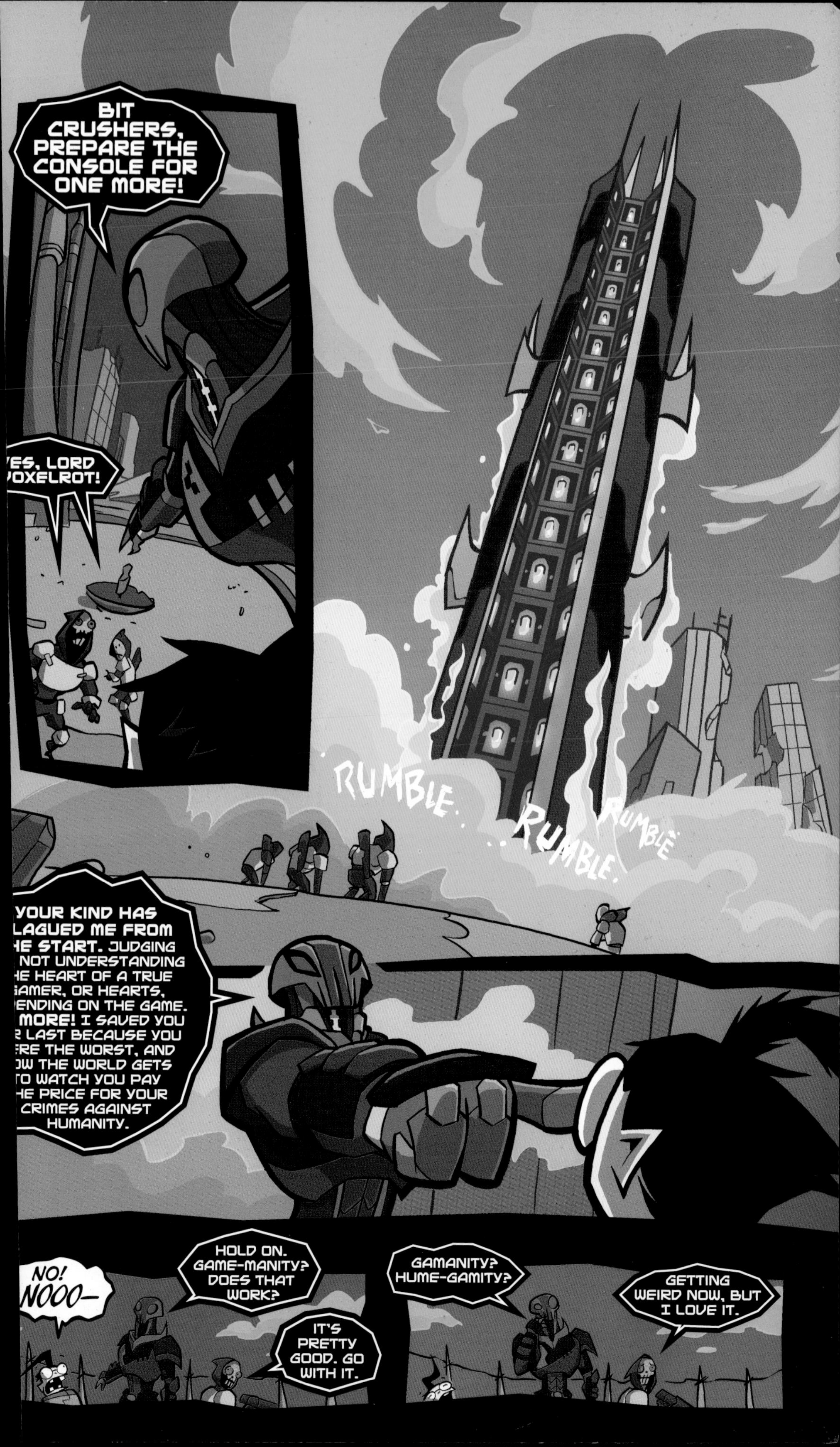
BIT CRUSHERS, PREPARE THE CONSOLE FOR ONE MORE!
ES, LORD OXELROT!
RUMBLE...
...RUMBLE.
RUMBLE
YOUR KIND HAS LAGUED ME FROM HE START. JUDGING NOT UNDERSTANDING HE HEART OF A TRUE AMER, OR HEARTS, ENDING ON THE GAME. MORE! I SAVED YOU R LAST BECAUSE YOU RE THE WORST, AND W THE WORLD GETS TO WATCH YOU PAY HE PRICE FOR YOUR CRIMES AGAINST HUMANITY.
NO! NOOO—
HOLD ON. GAME-MANITY? DOES THAT WORK?
IT'S PRETTY GOOD. GO WITH IT.
GAMANITY? HUME-GAMITY?
GETTING WEIRD NOW, BUT I LOVE IT.

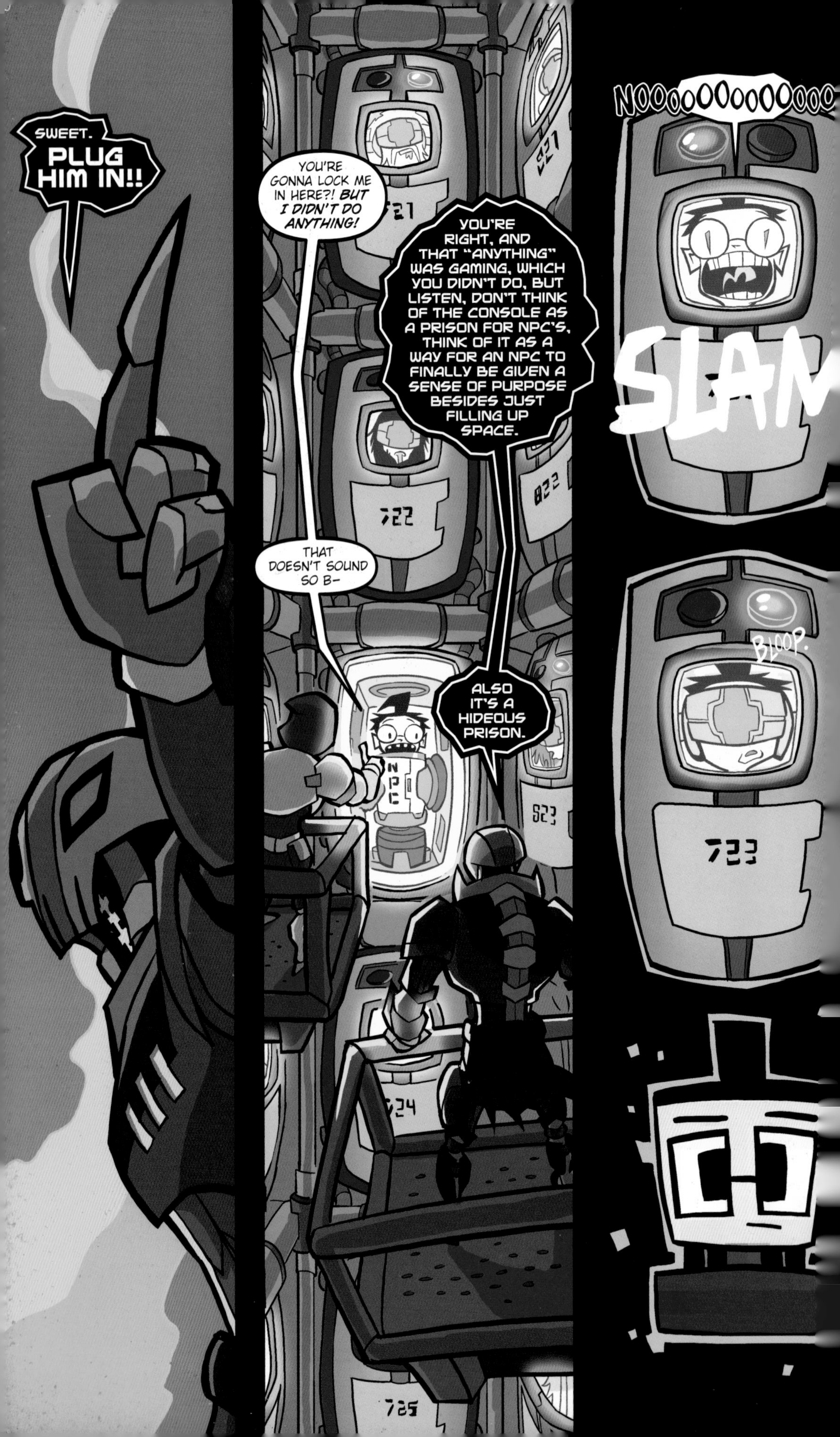
SWEET. PLUG HIM IN!!
YOU'RE GONNA LOCK ME IN HERE?! BUT I DIDN'T DO ANYTHING!
YOU'RE RIGHT, AND THAT "ANYTHING" WAS GAMING, WHICH YOU DIDN'T DO, BUT LISTEN, DON'T THINK OF THE CONSOLE AS A PRISON FOR NPC'S, THINK OF IT AS A WAY FOR AN NPC TO FINALLY BE GIVEN A SENSE OF PURPOSE BESIDES JUST FILLING UP SPACE.
THAT DOESN'T SOUND SO B-
ALSO IT'S A HIDEOUS PRISON.
NOOooOOooOOooo
SLAM
BLOOP.

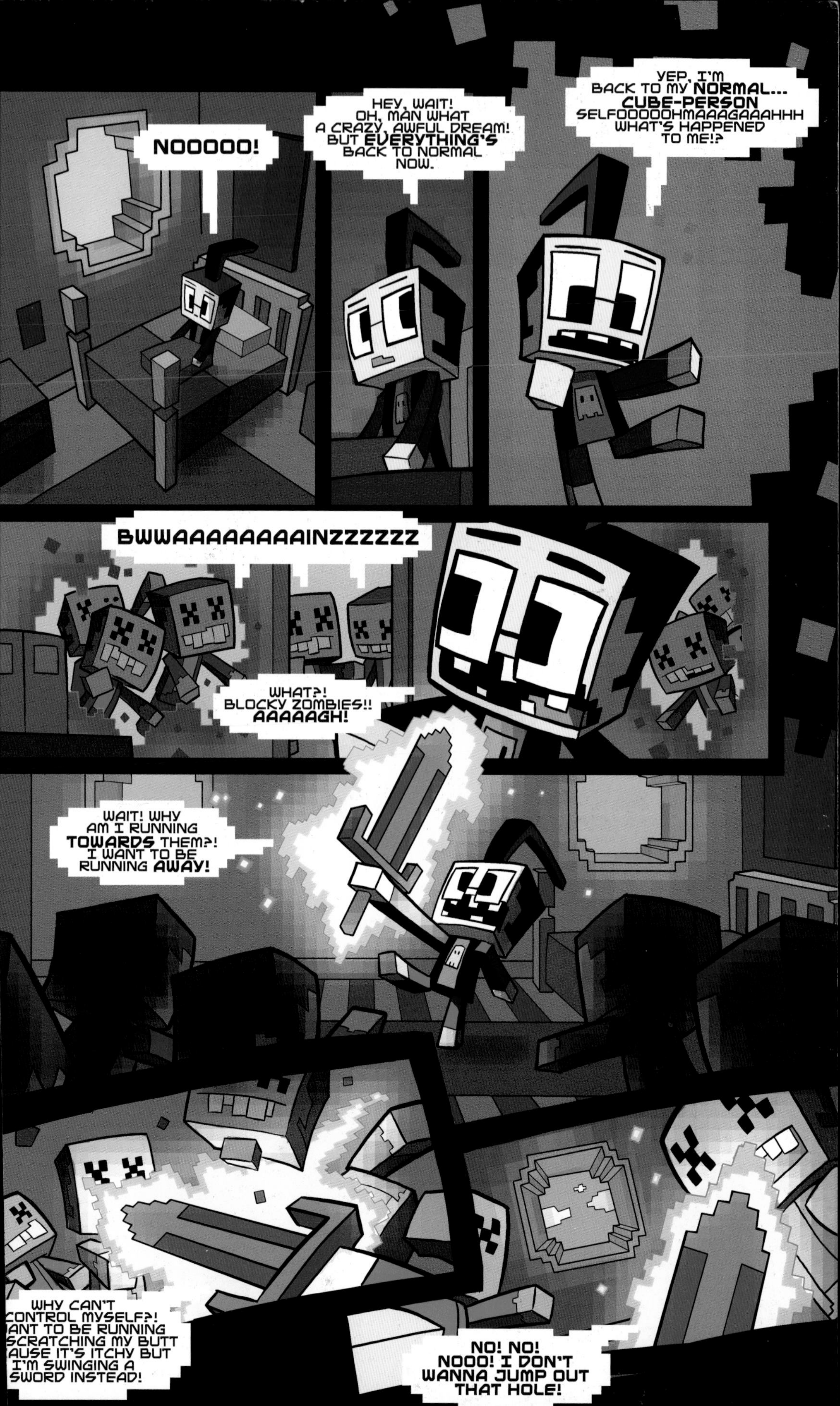

NOOOOO!
HEY, WAIT! OH, MAN WHAT A CRAZY, AWFUL DREAM! BUT EVERYTHING'S BACK TO NORMAL NOW.
YEP, I'M BACK TO MY NORMAL... CUBE-PERSON SELFOOOOOHMAAAGAAAHHH WHAT'S HAPPENED TO ME!?
BWWAAAAAAAAINZZZZZZ
WHAT?! BLOCKY ZOMBIES!! AAAAAGH!
WAIT! WHY AM I RUNNING TOWARDS THEM?! I WANT TO BE RUNNING AWAY!
WHY CAN'T
CONTROL MYSELF?!
ANT TO BE RUNNING
SCRATCHING MY BUTT
AUSE IT'S ITCHY BUT
I'M SWINGING A
SWORD INSTEAD!
NO! NO! NOOO! I DON'T WANNA JUMP OUT THAT HOLE!

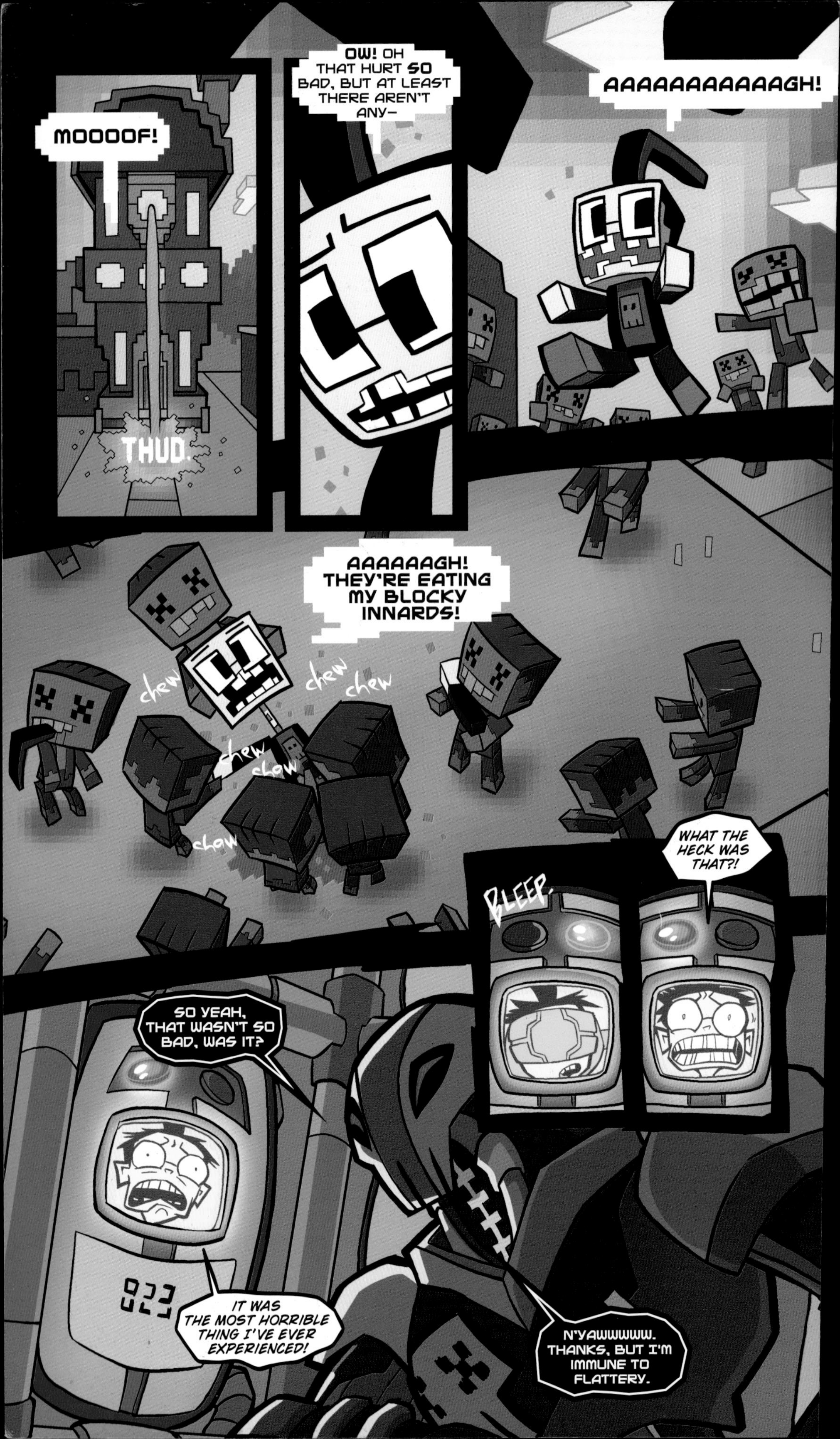

MOOOOF!
THUD.
OW! OH THAT HURT SO BAD, BUT AT LEAST THERE AREN'T ANY—
AAAAAAAAAAAGH!
AAAAAAGH! THEY'RE EATING MY BLOCKY INNARDS!
chew
chew
chew
chew
chaw
chaw
BLEEP.
WHAT THE HECK WAS THAT?!
SO YEAH, THAT WASN'T SO BAD, WAS IT?
IT WAS THE MOST HORRIBLE THING I'VE EVER EXPERIENCED!
N'YAWWWWW. THANKS, BUT I'M IMMUNE TO FLATTERY.

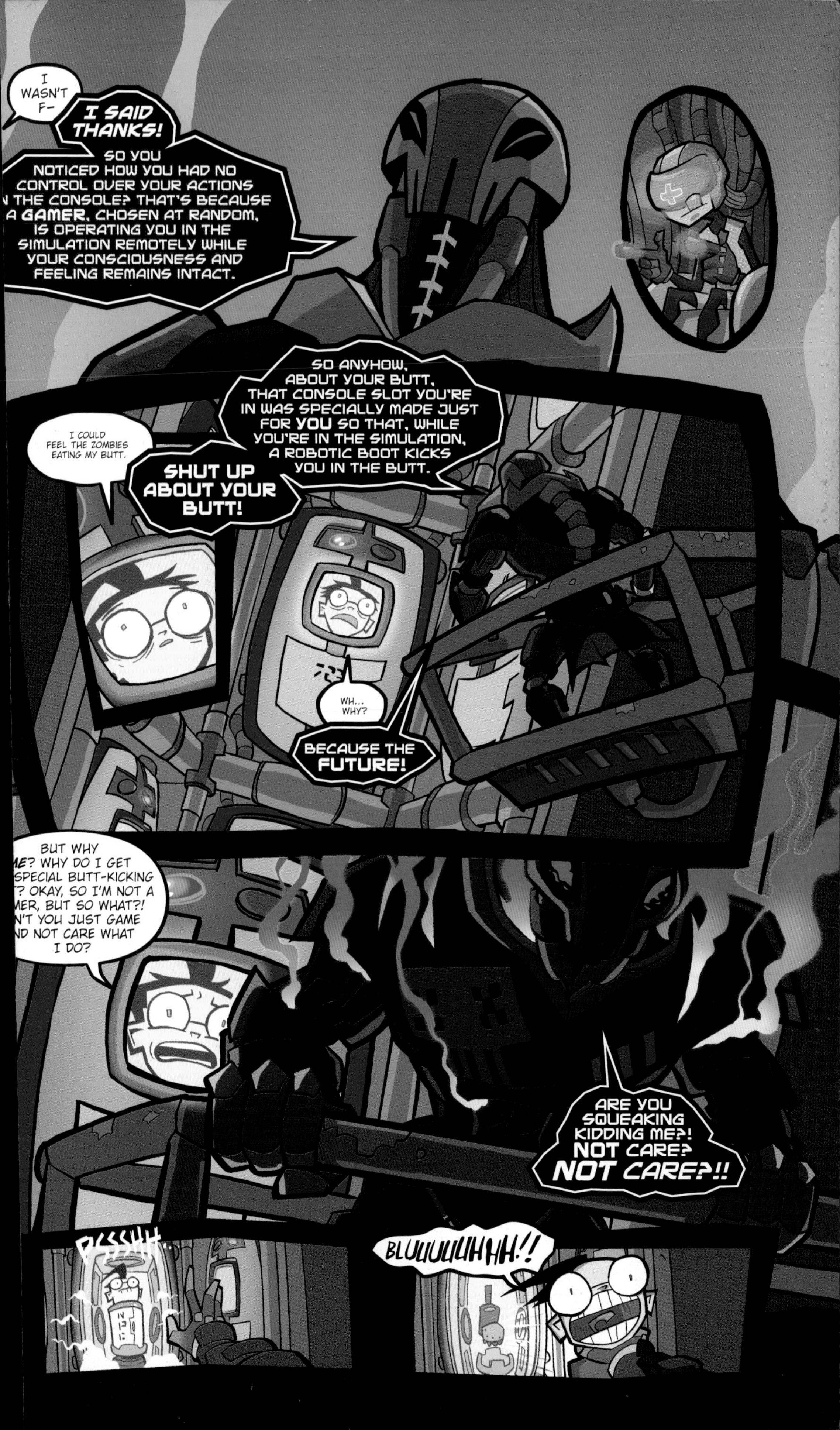
I WASN'T F–
I SAID THANKS!
SO YOU NOTICED HOW YOU HAD NO CONTROL OVER YOUR ACTIONS N THE CONSOLE? THAT'S BECAUSE A GAMER, CHOSEN AT RANDOM, IS OPERATING YOU IN THE SIMULATION REMOTELY WHILE YOUR CONSCIOUSNESS AND FEELING REMAINS INTACT.
SO ANYHOW, ABOUT YOUR BUTT, THAT CONSOLE SLOT YOU'RE IN WAS SPECIALLY MADE JUST FOR YOU SO THAT, WHILE YOU'RE IN THE SIMULATION, A ROBOTIC BOOT KICKS YOU IN THE BUTT.
I COULD FEEL THE ZOMBIES EATING MY BUTT.
SHUT UP ABOUT YOUR BUTT!
WH... WHY?
BECAUSE THE FUTURE!
BUT WHY ME? WHY DO I GET SPECIAL BUTT-KICKING T? OKAY, SO I'M NOT A MER, BUT SO WHAT?! N'T YOU JUST GAME ND NOT CARE WHAT I DO?
ARE YOU SQUEAKING KIDDING ME?! NOT CARE? NOT CARE?!!
PSSSHH
BLUUUUUHHH!!

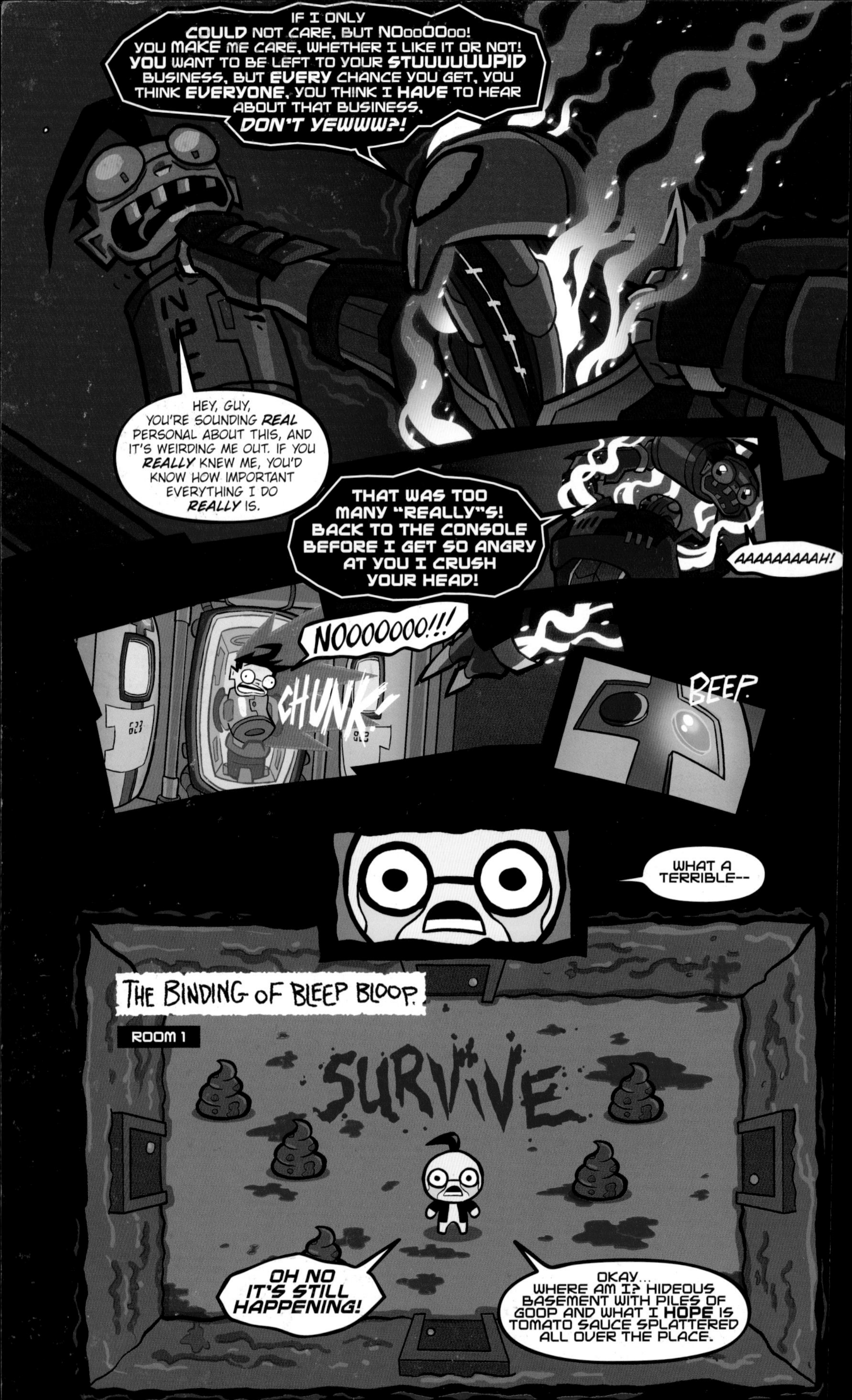
IF I ONLY COULD NOT CARE, BUT NOooOOoo! YOU MAKE ME CARE, WHETHER I LIKE IT OR NOT! YOU WANT TO BE LEFT TO YOUR STUUUUUUPID BUSINESS, BUT EVERY CHANCE YOU GET, YOU THINK EVERYONE, YOU THINK I HAVE TO HEAR ABOUT THAT BUSINESS, DON'T YEWWW?!
HEY, GUY, YOU'RE SOUNDING REAL PERSONAL ABOUT THIS, AND IT'S WEIRDING ME OUT. IF YOU REALLY KNEW ME, YOU'D KNOW HOW IMPORTANT EVERYTHING I DO REALLY IS.
THAT WAS TOO MANY "REALLY"S! BACK TO THE CONSOLE BEFORE I GET SO ANGRY AT YOU I CRUSH YOUR HEAD!
AAAAAAAAAH!
NOOOOOOO!!!
CHUNK!
BEEP
WHAT A TERRIBLE--
THE BINDING OF BLEEP BLOOP
ROOM 1
SURVIVE
OH NO IT'S STILL HAPPENING!
OKAY... WHERE AM I? HIDEOUS BASEMENT WITH PILES OF GOOP AND WHAT I HOPE IS TOMATO SAUCE SPLATTERED ALL OVER THE PLACE.

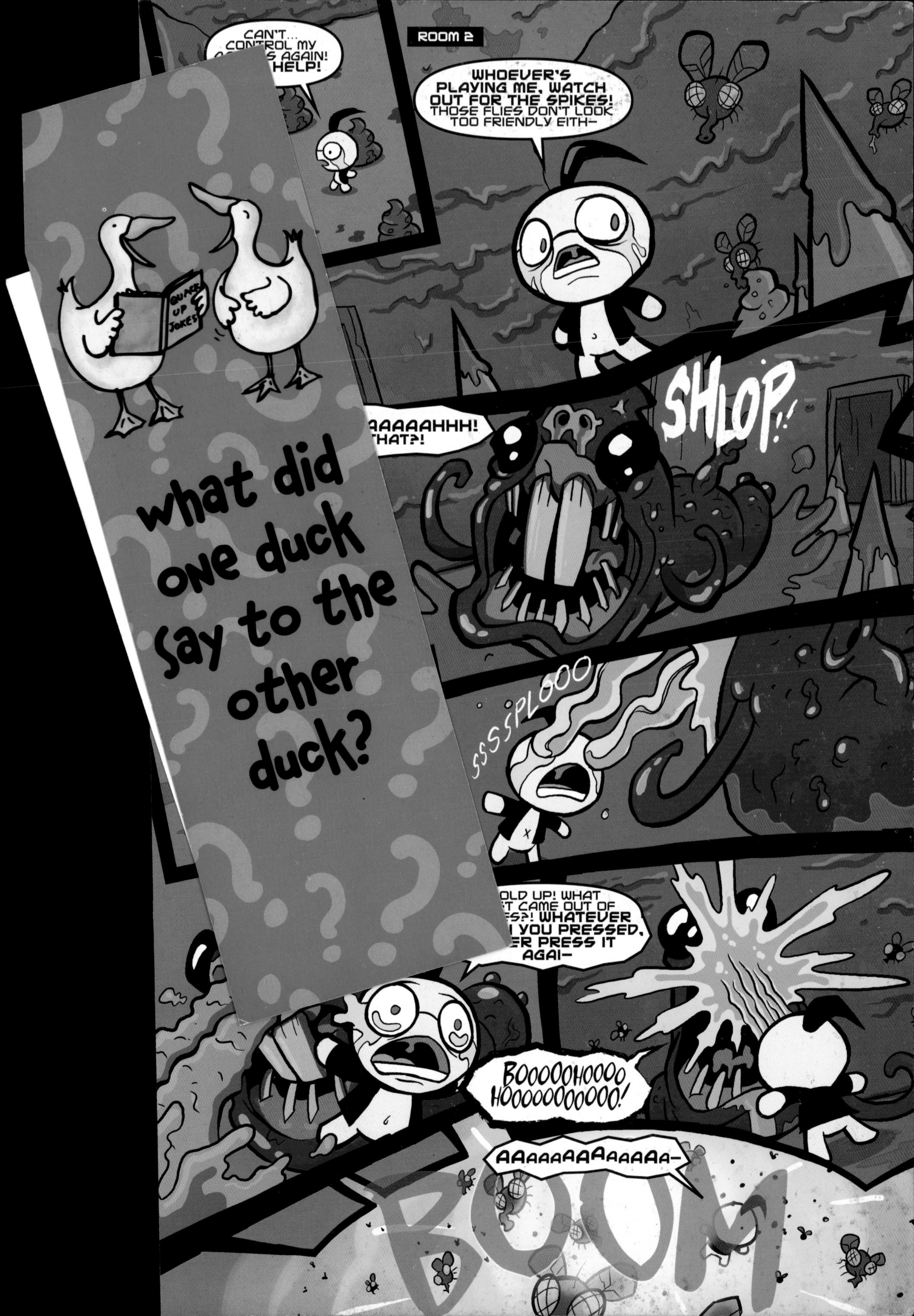

CAN'T... CONTROL MY
AGAIN! HELP!
ROOM 2
WHOEVER'S PLAYING ME, WATCH OUT FOR THE SPIKES! THOSE FLIES DON'T LOOK TOO FRIENDLY EITH–
QUACK UP JOKES
what did one duck say to the other duck?
AAAAAHHH! THAT?!
SHLOP!
SSSSPLOOO
OLD UP! WHAT
T CAME OUT OF
ES?! WHATEVER
YOU PRESSED,
ER PRESS IT AGAI–
BOOOOOHOOOO HOOOOOOOOOOO!
AAAAAAAAAAAAA–
BOOM

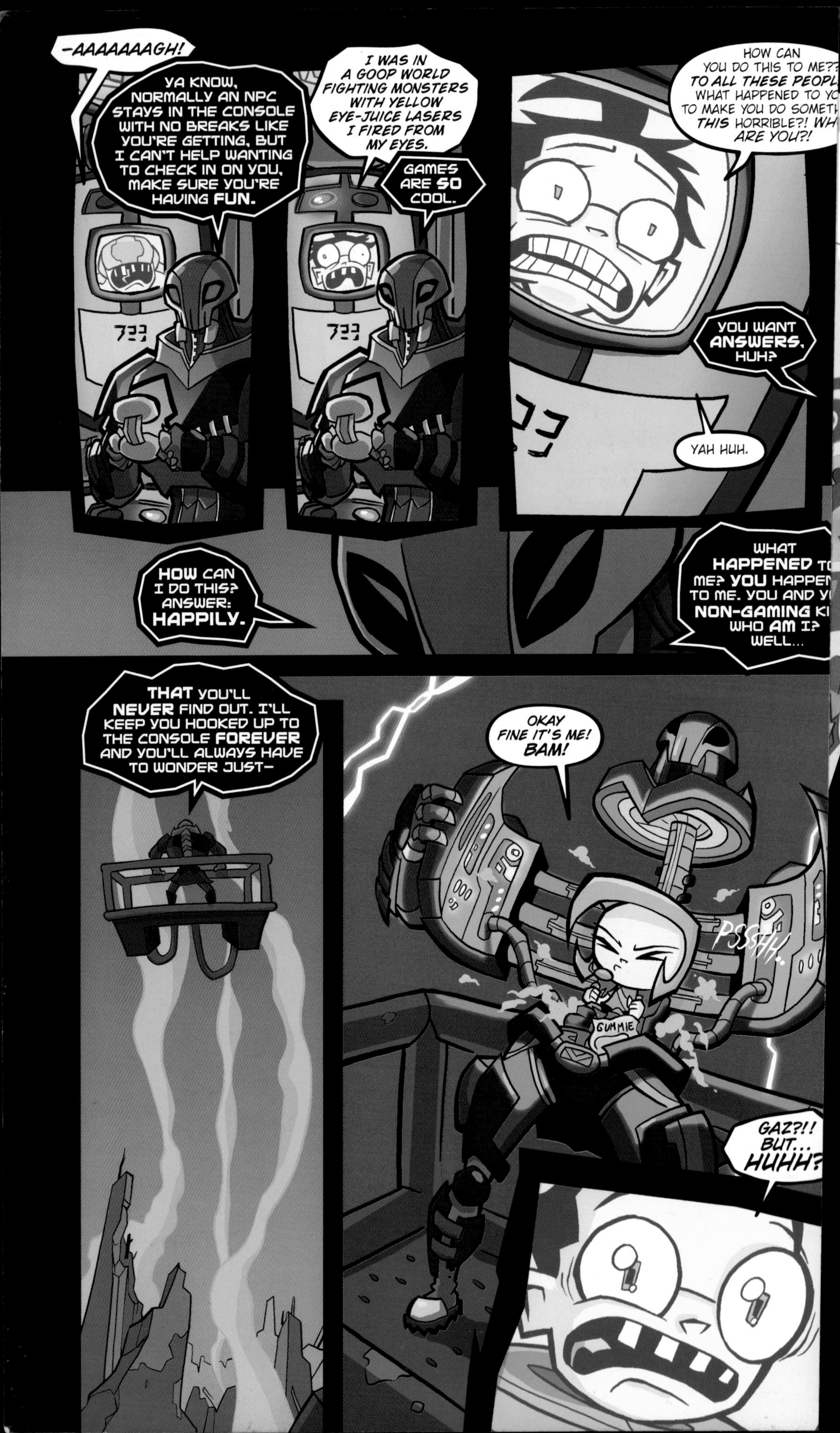

-AAAAAAAGH!
YA KNOW, NORMALLY AN NPC STAYS IN THE CONSOLE WITH NO BREAKS LIKE YOU'RE GETTING, BUT I CAN'T HELP WANTING TO CHECK IN ON YOU, MAKE SURE YOU'RE HAVING FUN.
I WAS IN A GOOP WORLD FIGHTING MONSTERS WITH YELLOW EYE-JUICE LASERS I FIRED FROM MY EYES.
GAMES ARE SO COOL.
HOW CAN YOU DO THIS TO ME?? TO ALL THESE PEOPL WHAT HAPPENED TO YO TO MAKE YOU DO SOMETH THIS HORRIBLE?! WH ARE YOU?!
YOU WANT ANSWERS, HUH?
YAH HUH.
HOW CAN I DO THIS? ANSWER: HAPPILY.
WHAT HAPPENED T ME? YOU HAPPEN TO ME. YOU AND Y NON-GAMING KI WHO AM I? WELL...
THAT YOU'LL NEVER FIND OUT. I'LL KEEP YOU HOOKED UP TO THE CONSOLE FOREVER AND YOU'LL ALWAYS HAVE TO WONDER JUST-
OKAY FINE IT'S ME! BAM!
PSSSHH
GUMMIE
GAZ?!! BUT... HUHH?

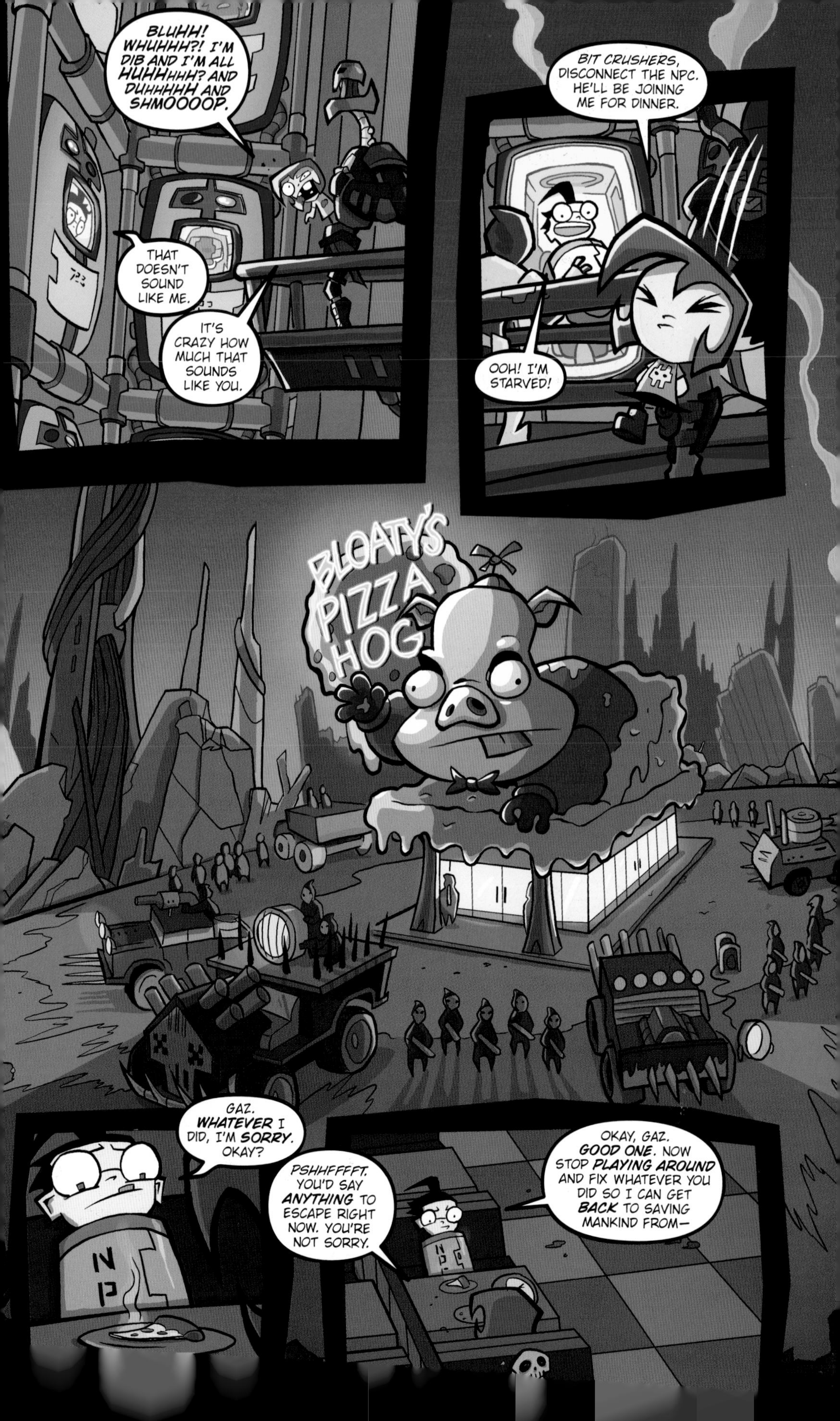
BLUHH! WHUHHH?! I'M DIB AND I'M ALL HUHHhhh? AND DUHHHHH AND SHMOOOOP.
THAT DOESN'T SOUND LIKE ME.
IT'S CRAZY HOW MUCH THAT SOUNDS LIKE YOU.
BIT CRUSHERS, DISCONNECT THE NPC. HE'LL BE JOINING ME FOR DINNER.
OOH! I'M STARVED!
BLOATY'S PIZZA HOG
GAZ. WHATEVER I DID, I'M SORRY. OKAY?
PSHHFFFFT. YOU'D SAY ANYTHING TO ESCAPE RIGHT NOW. YOU'RE NOT SORRY.
OKAY, GAZ. GOOD ONE. NOW STOP PLAYING AROUND AND FIX WHATEVER YOU DID SO I CAN GET BACK TO SAVING MANKIND FROM—

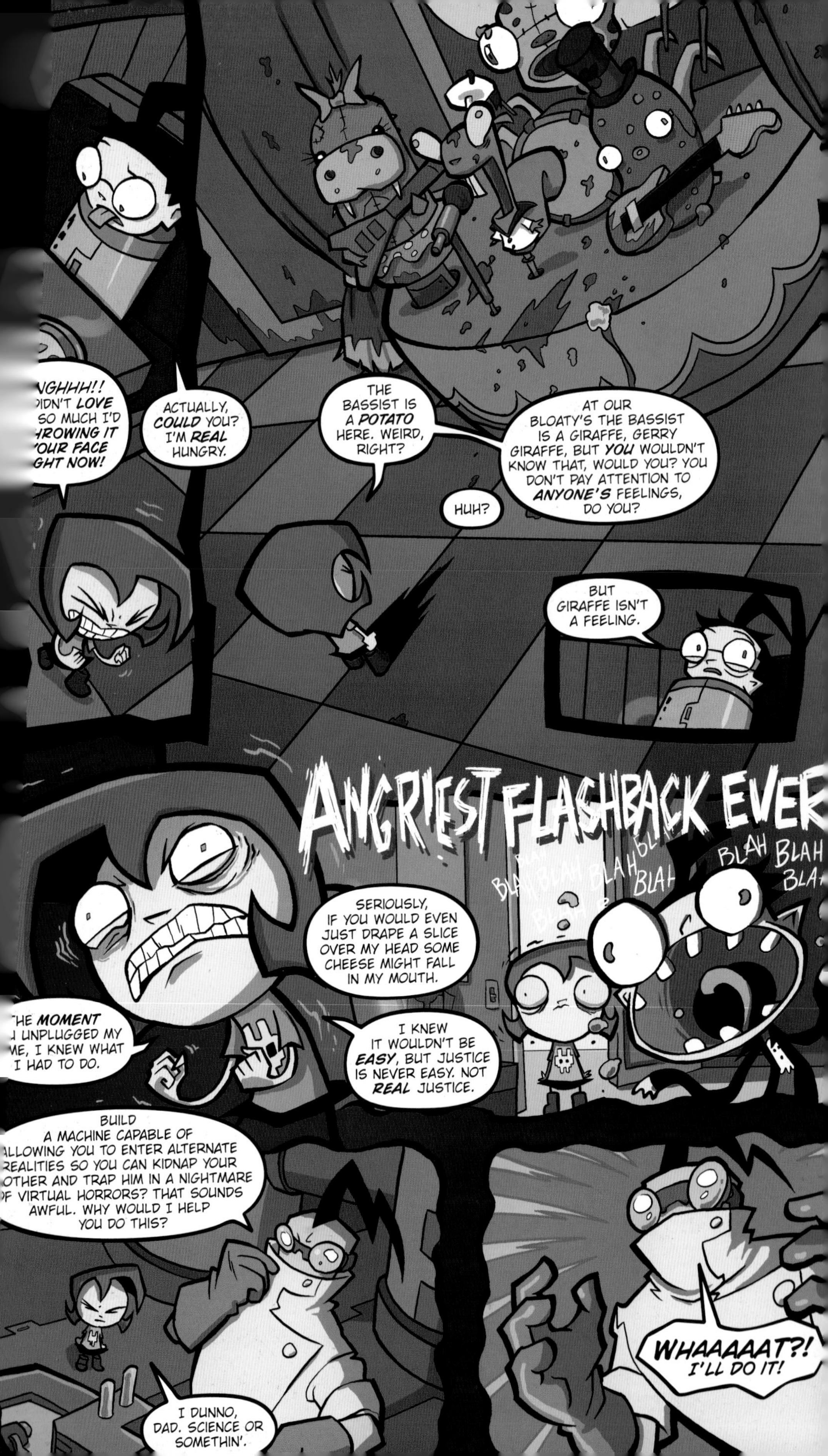

NGHHH!! DIDN'T LOVE SO MUCH I'D HROWING IT YOUR FACE GHT NOW!
ACTUALLY, COULD YOU? I'M REAL HUNGRY.
THE BASSIST IS A POTATO HERE. WEIRD, RIGHT?
HUH?
AT OUR BLOATY'S THE BASSIST IS A GIRAFFE, GERRY GIRAFFE, BUT YOU WOULDN'T KNOW THAT, WOULD YOU? YOU DON'T PAY ATTENTION TO ANYONE'S FEELINGS, DO YOU?
BUT GIRAFFE ISN'T A FEELING.
ANGRIEST FLASHBACK EVER
BLAH BLAH BLAH BLAH BLAH BLAH BLAH BLAH BLAH
SERIOUSLY, IF YOU WOULD EVEN JUST DRAPE A SLICE OVER MY HEAD SOME CHEESE MIGHT FALL IN MY MOUTH.
HE MOMENT UNPLUGGED MY ME, I KNEW WHAT I HAD TO DO.
I KNEW IT WOULDN'T BE EASY, BUT JUSTICE IS NEVER EASY. NOT REAL JUSTICE.
BUILD A MACHINE CAPABLE OF ALLOWING YOU TO ENTER ALTERNATE REALITIES SO YOU CAN KIDNAP YOUR OTHER AND TRAP HIM IN A NIGHTMARE F VIRTUAL HORRORS? THAT SOUNDS AWFUL. WHY WOULD I HELP YOU DO THIS?
I DUNNO, DAD. SCIENCE OR SOMETHIN'.
WHAAAAAT?! I'LL DO IT!

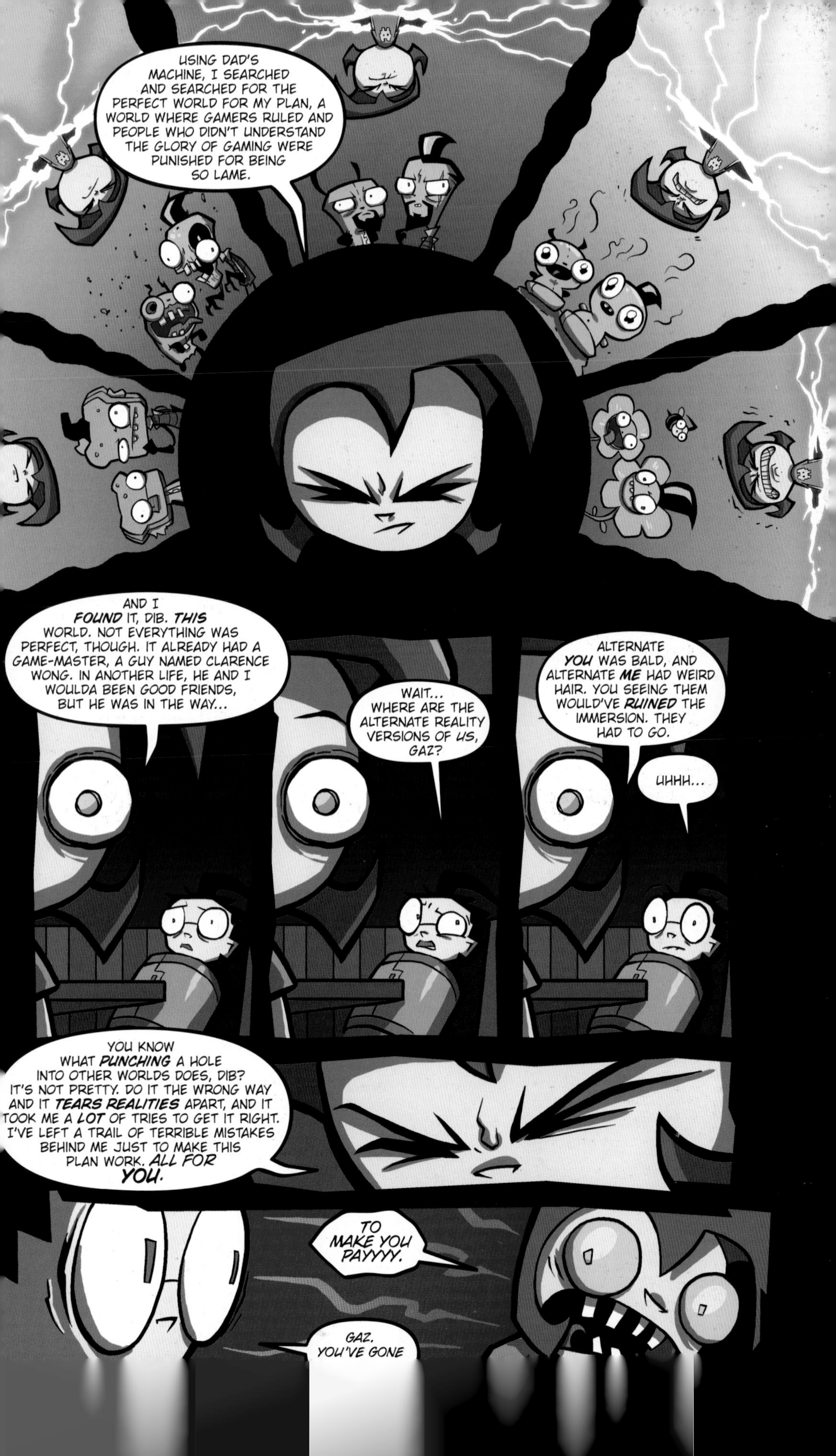
USING DAD'S MACHINE, I SEARCHED AND SEARCHED FOR THE PERFECT WORLD FOR MY PLAN, A WORLD WHERE GAMERS RULED AND PEOPLE WHO DIDN'T UNDERSTAND THE GLORY OF GAMING WERE PUNISHED FOR BEING SO LAME.
AND I FOUND IT, DIB. THIS WORLD. NOT EVERYTHING WAS PERFECT, THOUGH. IT ALREADY HAD A GAME-MASTER, A GUY NAMED CLARENCE WONG. IN ANOTHER LIFE, HE AND I WOULDA BEEN GOOD FRIENDS, BUT HE WAS IN THE WAY...
WAIT... WHERE ARE THE ALTERNATE REALITY VERSIONS OF US, GAZ?
ALTERNATE YOU WAS BALD, AND ALTERNATE ME HAD WEIRD HAIR. YOU SEEING THEM WOULD'VE RUINED THE IMMERSION. THEY HAD TO GO.
UHHH...
YOU KNOW WHAT PUNCHING A HOLE INTO OTHER WORLDS DOES, DIB? IT'S NOT PRETTY. DO IT THE WRONG WAY AND IT TEARS REALITIES APART, AND IT TOOK ME A LOT OF TRIES TO GET IT RIGHT. I'VE LEFT A TRAIL OF TERRIBLE MISTAKES BEHIND ME JUST TO MAKE THIS PLAN WORK. ALL FOR YOU.
TO MAKE YOU PAYYYY.
GAZ. YOU'VE GONE

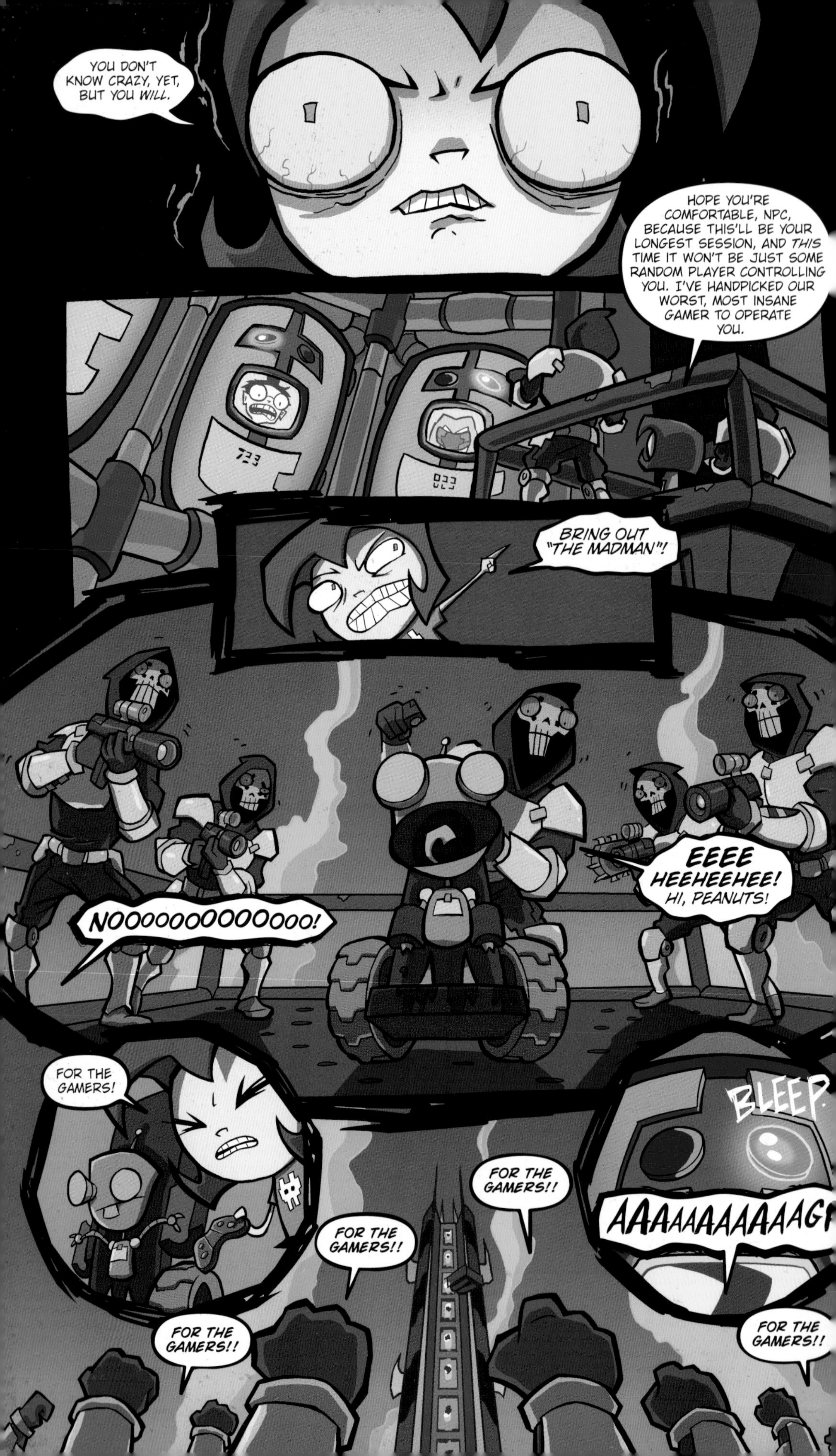

YOU DON'T KNOW CRAZY, YET, BUT YOU *WILL*.
HOPE YOU'RE COMFORTABLE, NPC, BECAUSE THIS'LL BE YOUR LONGEST SESSION, AND *THIS* TIME IT WON'T BE JUST SOME RANDOM PLAYER CONTROLLING YOU. I'VE HANDPICKED OUR WORST, MOST INSANE GAMER TO OPERATE YOU.
BRING OUT "THE MADMAN"!
EEEE HEEHEEHEE! HI, PEANUTS!
NOOOOOOOOOOOOO!
FOR THE GAMERS!
BLEEP
FOR THE GAMERS!!
FOR THE GAMERS!!
AAAAAAAAAAAG!
FOR THE GAMERS!!
FOR THE GAMERS!!

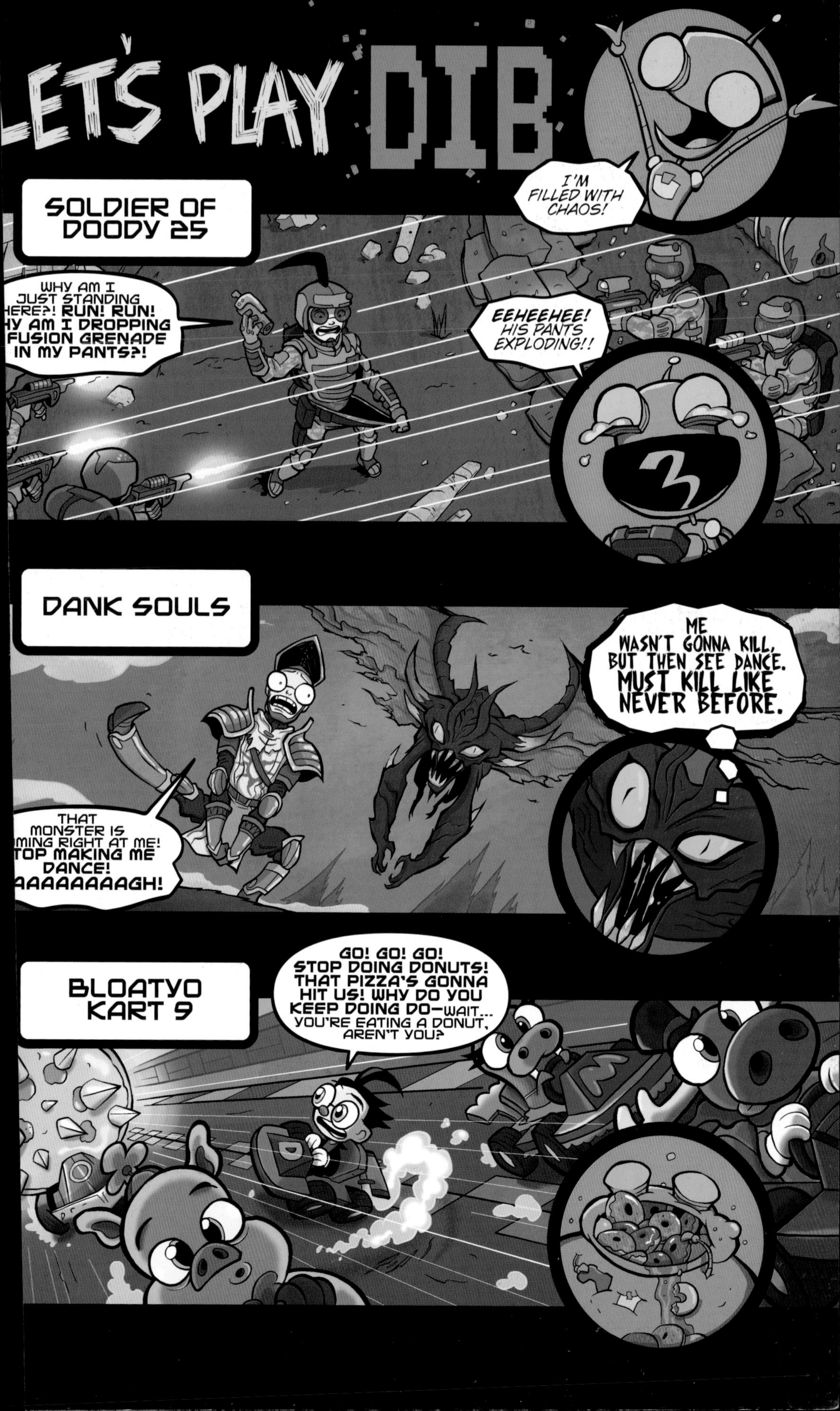
LET'S PLAY DIB
I'M FILLED WITH CHAOS!
SOLDIER OF DOODY 25
WHY AM I JUST STANDING HERE?! RUN! RUN! HY AM I DROPPING FUSION GRENADE IN MY PANTS?!
EEHEEHEE! HIS PANTS EXPLODING!!
DANK SOULS
ME WASN'T GONNA KILL, BUT THEN SEE DANCE. MUST KILL LIKE NEVER BEFORE.
THAT MONSTER IS MING RIGHT AT ME! TOP MAKING ME DANCE! AAAAAAAAGH!
BLOATYO KART 9
GO! GO! GO! STOP DOING DONUTS! THAT PIZZA'S GONNA HIT US! WHY DO YOU KEEP DOING DO—WAIT... YOU'RE EATING A DONUT, AREN'T YOU?

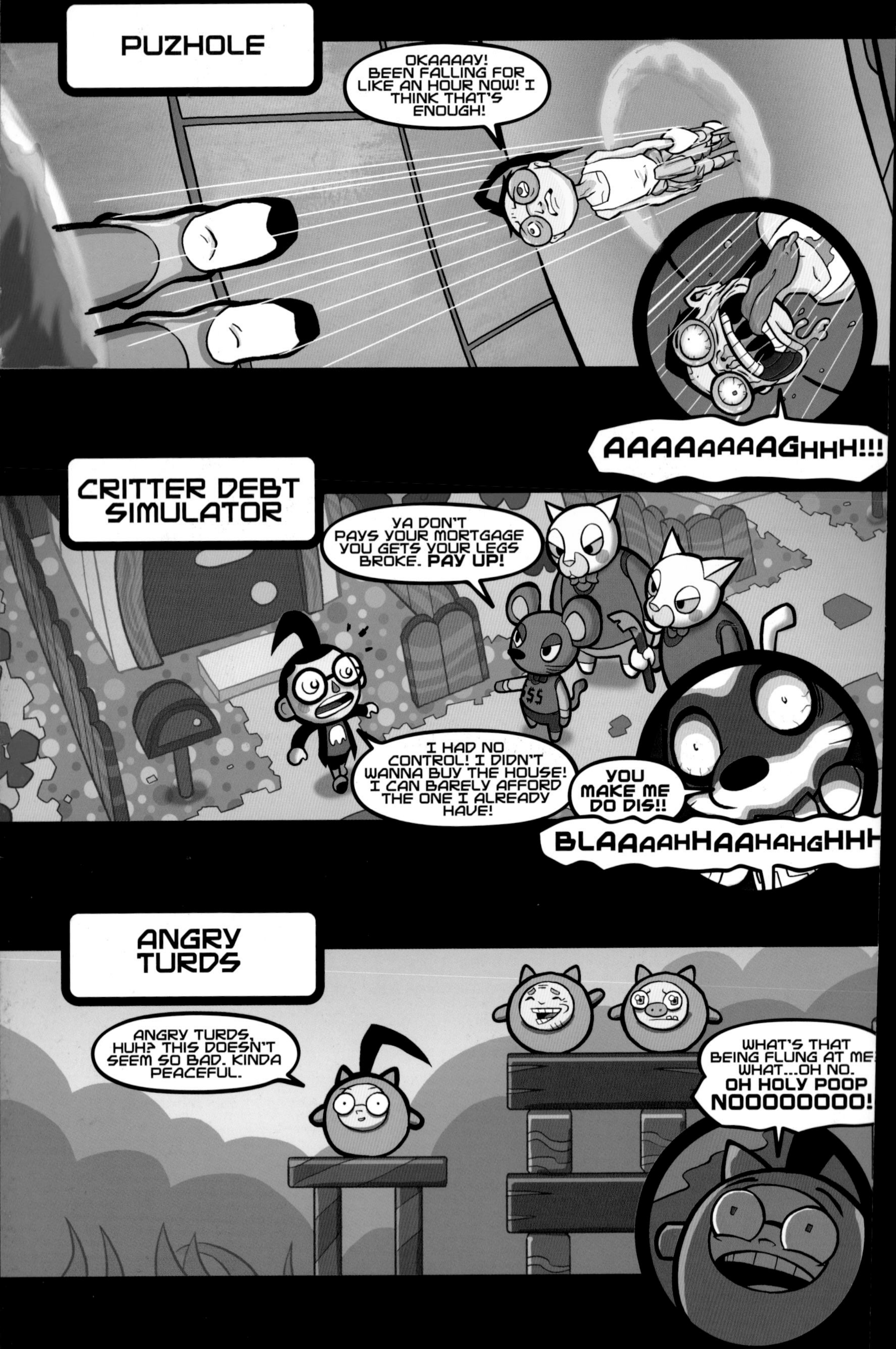
PUZHOLE
OKAAAAY! BEEN FALLING FOR LIKE AN HOUR NOW! I THINK THAT'S ENOUGH!
AAAAAAAAGHHH!!!
CRITTER DEBT SIMULATOR
YA DON'T PAYS YOUR MORTGAGE YOU GETS YOUR LEGS BROKE. PAY UP!
I HAD NO CONTROL! I DIDN'T WANNA BUY THE HOUSE! I CAN BARELY AFFORD THE ONE I ALREADY HAVE!
YOU MAKE ME DO DIS!!
BLAAAAHHAAHAHGHHH
ANGRY TURDS
ANGRY TURDS, HUH? THIS DOESN'T SEEM SO BAD. KINDA PEACEFUL.
WHAT'S THAT BEING FLUNG AT ME? WHAT...OH NO. OH HOLY POOP NOOOOOOOO!

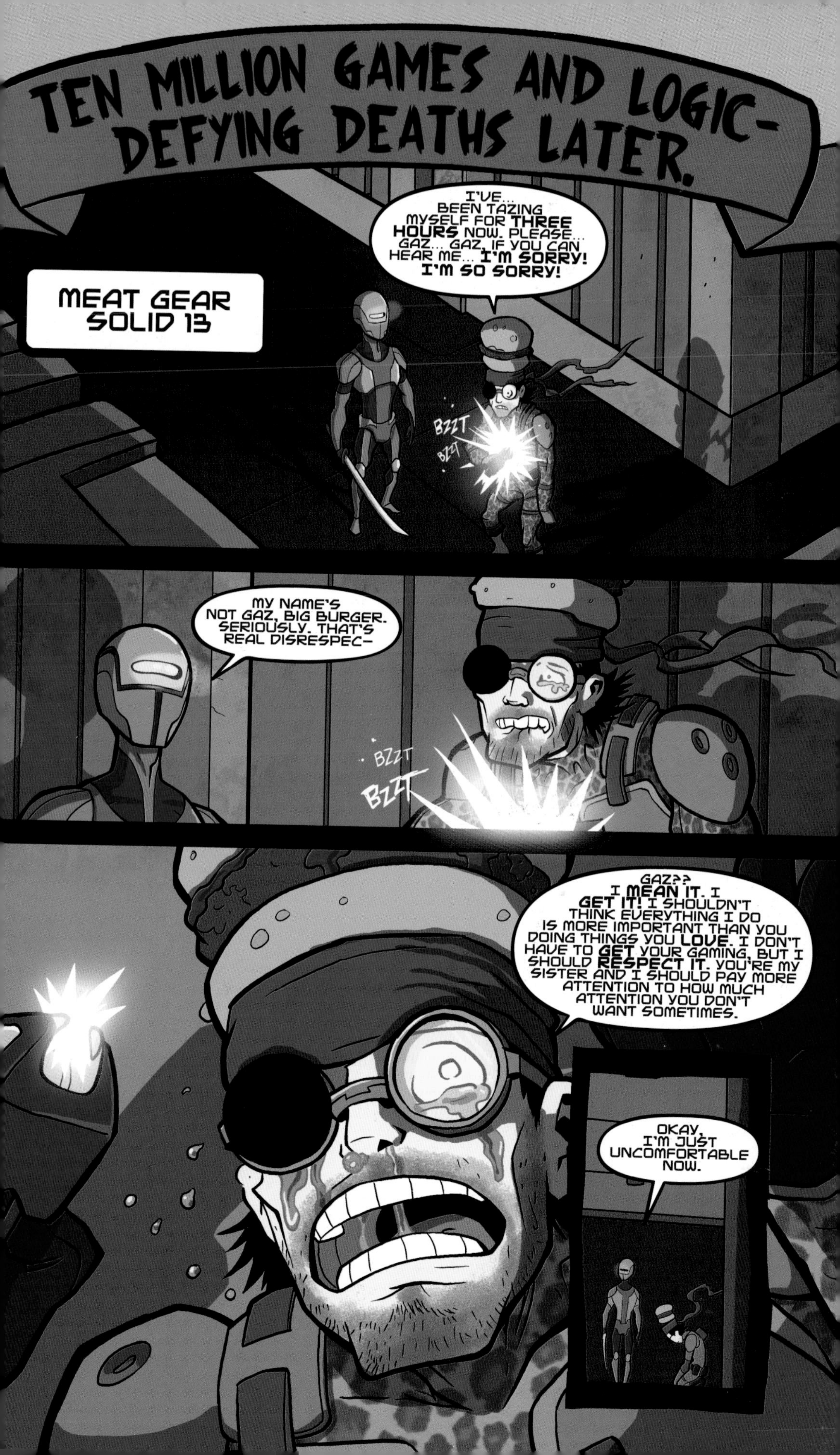
TEN MILLION GAMES AND LOGIC-DEFYING DEATHS LATER.
MEAT GEAR SOLID 13
I'VE... BEEN TAZING MYSELF FOR THREE HOURS NOW. PLEASE... GAZ... GAZ, IF YOU CAN HEAR ME... I'M SORRY! I'M SO SORRY!
BZZT
BZZT
MY NAME'S NOT GAZ, BIG BURGER. SERIOUSLY. THAT'S REAL DISRESPEC—
BZZT
BZZT
GAZ?? I MEAN IT. I GET IT! I SHOULDN'T THINK EVERYTHING I DO IS MORE IMPORTANT THAN YOU DOING THINGS YOU LOVE. I DON'T HAVE TO GET YOUR GAMING, BUT I SHOULD RESPECT IT. YOU'RE MY SISTER AND I SHOULD PAY MORE ATTENTION TO HOW MUCH ATTENTION YOU DON'T WANT SOMETIMES.
OKAY, I'M JUST UNCOMFORTABLE NOW.

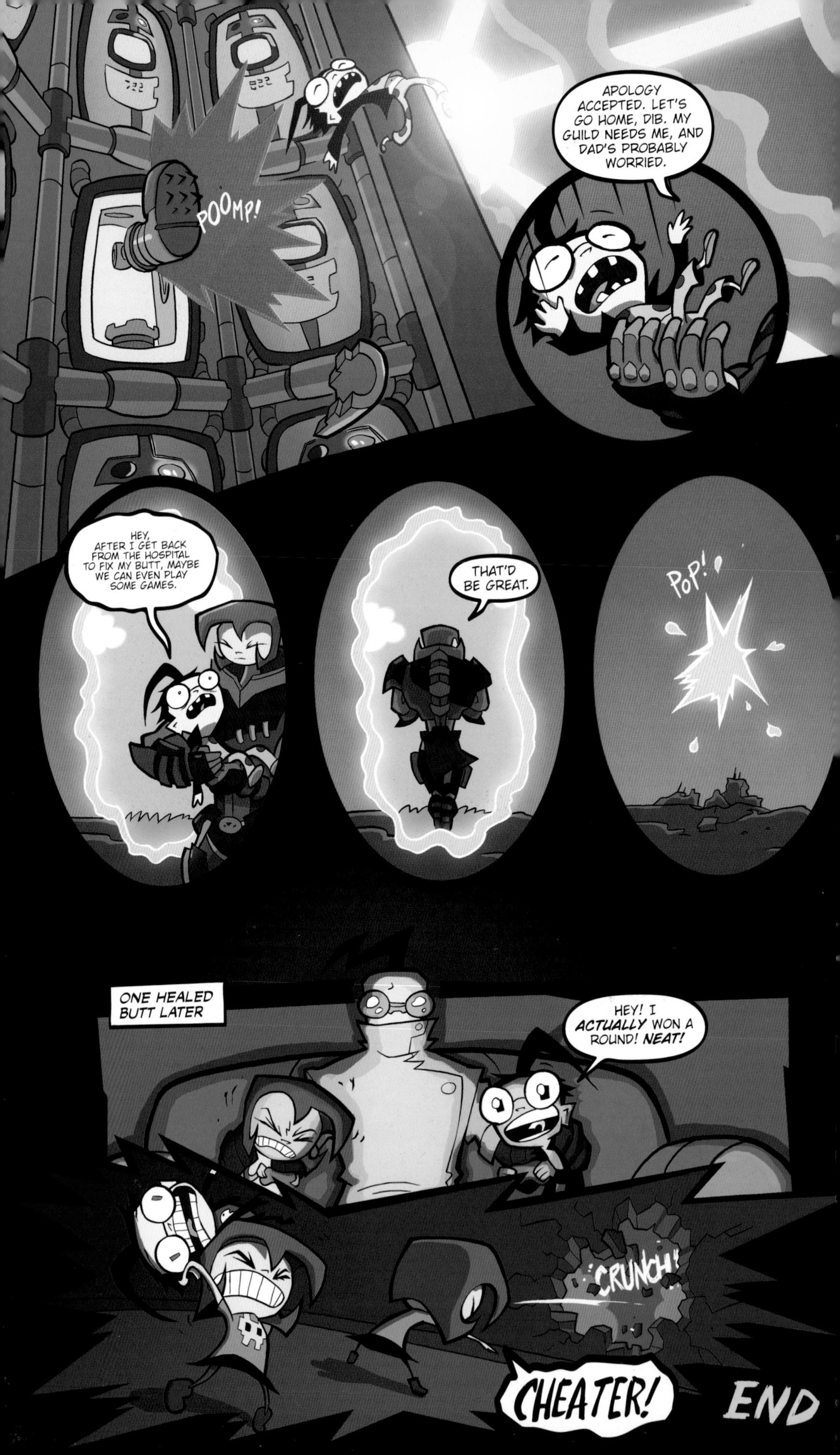
POOMP!
APOLOGY ACCEPTED. LET'S GO HOME, DIB. MY GUILD NEEDS ME, AND DAD'S PROBABLY WORRIED.
HEY, AFTER I GET BACK FROM THE HOSPITAL TO FIX MY BUTT, MAYBE WE CAN EVEN PLAY SOME GAMES.
THAT'D BE GREAT.
POP!
ONE HEALED BUTT LATER
HEY! I ACTUALLY WON A ROUND! NEAT!
CRUNCH!
CHEATER!
END

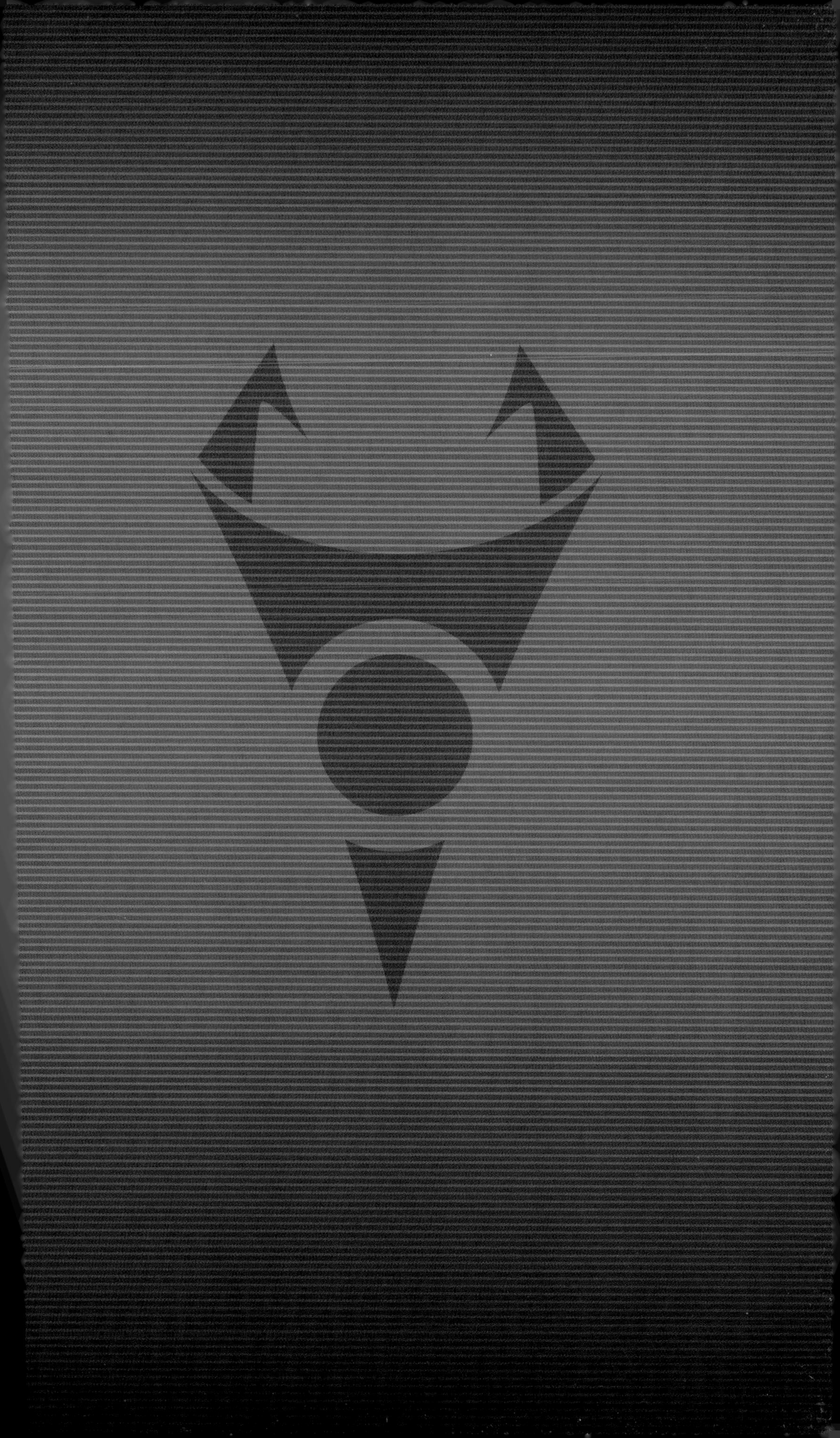

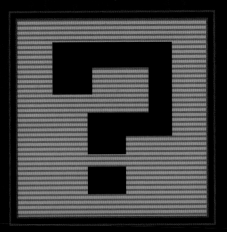

@JhonenV

JHONEN VASQUEZ

Jhonen Vasquez is a writer and artist who walks in many worlds, not unlike Blade, only without having to drink blood-serum to survive the curse that is also his greatest power (still talking about Blade here). He's worked in comics and animation and is the creator of *Invader ZIM*, a fact that haunts him to this day.

@erictrueheart

ERIC TRUEHEART

Eric Trueheart was one of the original writers on the *Invader ZIM* television series back when there was a thing called "television." Since then, he's made a living writing moderately-inappropriate things for people who make entertainment for children, including Dreamworks Animation, Cartoon Network, Disney TV, PBS, Hasbro and others. Upon reading this list, he now thinks he maybe should have become a dentist, and he hates teeth.

AARON ALEXOVICH

Aaron Alexovich's first professional art job was drawing deformed children for Nickelodeon's *Invader ZIM*. Since then he's been deforming children for various animation and comic projects, including *Avatar: The Last Airbender*, *Randy Cunningham: 9th Grade Ninja*, *Disney's Haunted Mansion, Fables, Kimmie66, ELDRITCH!* (with art by Drew Rausch) and three volumes of his own beloved horror/comedy witch comic dealie, *Serenity Rose*.

 @essrose

MEGAN LAWTON

Megan Lawton is a huge bro type trapped in the body of a small art school goth. She is also a storyboard and comic artist fresh out of college, ready to fight everyone and everything in the world with her bear hands. Following her BFA in Illustration from San Jose State, she went through story internships at both Pixar and Blue Sky Studios. She probably works too much, but she parties hard enough to make up for it. Megan likes sharks, monsters and making people uncomfortable with her relentless use of puns.

@dinolich

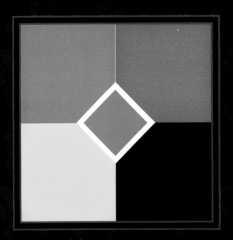

@cunch

J.R. GOLDBERG

J.R. is a visual designer and illustrator who has worked in comics and animation. Not only is she responsible for making sure your eyes love the colors on the *Invader ZIM* pages, but she is responsible for all color in reality. If you see in color, thank J.R. for allowing this. Thank you, J.R. Goldberg. Thank you. She currently works and lives inside the color turquoise.

@SimonHuttT

SIMON TROUSSELLIER

Well, I'm Simon Troussellier. I'm a French artist, usually working in video game industry. Putting colors on a comic is a first one for me! So when Jhonen bat-signaled me to work on *ZIM*, how could I say no? Aliens, robots, ice cream. Everything I love. I hope nobody's eyes has been hurt by all those marvelous colors we've put together for you. A-plus!

RIKKI SIMONS

@rikkisimons

Rikki Simons colored some bits of this comic you are holding. He colored a whole bunch of the *Invader ZIM* TV series too. He was also the voice of GIR and Bloaty the Pig. He makes his own comics too, like *Ranklechick* and *Rhumbaghost,* and with his wife Tavisha he makes *The Trinkkits, ShutterBox, Super Information Hijinks: Reality Check!* and *@Tavicat* (you can find all these at tavicat.com). Rikki's hobbies include passive aggressive gardening, smiling at ducks, writing love letters to *Monty Python,* and trying to start a new Surrealist movement by arguing with a potato.

MILDRED LOUIS

@Froregade

After studying animation at Sheridan College in Canada, Mildred Louis found herself falling in love with comics as a visual storytelling medium. Currently she's working on an ongoing Magical Girl-inspired webcomic series titled *Agents of the Realm,* as well as a queer high fantasy graphic novel titled *Bound Blades* with its first chapter al- ready released, and plans to continue in 2016. In her free time, she enjoys punching and kicking (in the appro- priate kickboxing environments), and perusing food blogs right before bed.

CASSIE KELLY

Cassie Kelly was born in the District of Columbia, in October of 1986. Originally starting her artistic career in product design and illustration, she only just started coloring comics in early 2015. She currently resides in Charlotte, NC, with her husband, Drew, and their children: Valentine, Rogue, Mozart, Garak, and Pickle.

@IM_CBAD

WARREN WUCINICH

Warren Wucinich an illustrator, colorist and part-time carny currently living in Durham, NC. When not making comics he can usually be found watching old *Twilight Zone* episodes and eating large amounts of pie.

@warrenwucinich

MORE BOOKS FROM ONI PRESS...

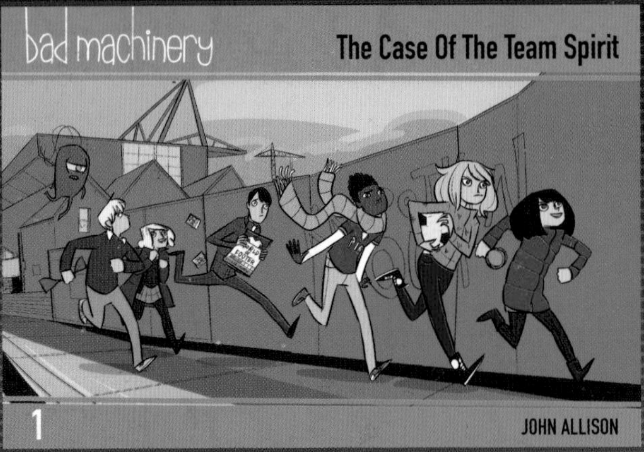
bad machinery
The Case Of The Team Spirit
1
JOHN ALLISON

BAD MACHINERY
VOLUME 1: THE CASE OF THE TEAM SPIRIT
By John Allison
136 pages, softcover, color
ISBN 978-1-62010-387-6

COURTNEY CRUMRIN
VOLUME 1: THE NIGHT THINGS
By Ted Naifeh
136 pages, softcover, color
ISBN 978-1-62010-419-4

JUNIOR BRAVES OF THE APOCALYPSE
VOLUME 1: A BRAVE IS BRAVE
By Greg Smith, Michael Tanner & Zach Le
216 pages, hardcover, two-color
ISBN 978-1-62010-144-5

BUZZ!
By Ananth Hirsh & Tessa Stone
176 pages, softcover, two-color
ISBN 978-1-62010-088-2

SCOTT PILGRIM COLOR HARDCOVER
VOLUME 1: PRECIOUS LITTLE LIFE
By Bryan Lee O'Malley
192 pages, hardcover, color
ISBN 978-1-62010-000-4

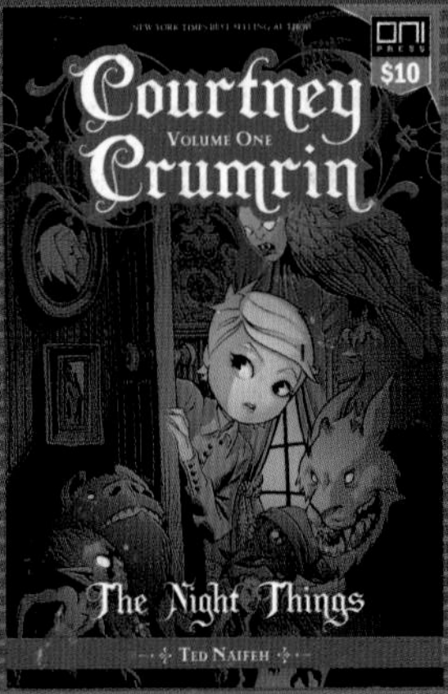
$10
Courtney
Volume One
Crumrin
The Night Things
Ted Naifeh

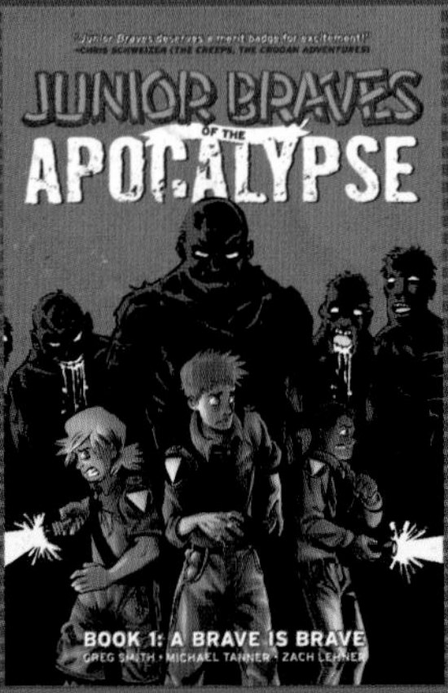
JUNIOR BRAVES
OF THE
APOCALYPSE
BOOK 1: A BRAVE IS BRAVE
GREG SMITH · MICHAEL TANNER · ZACH LEHNER

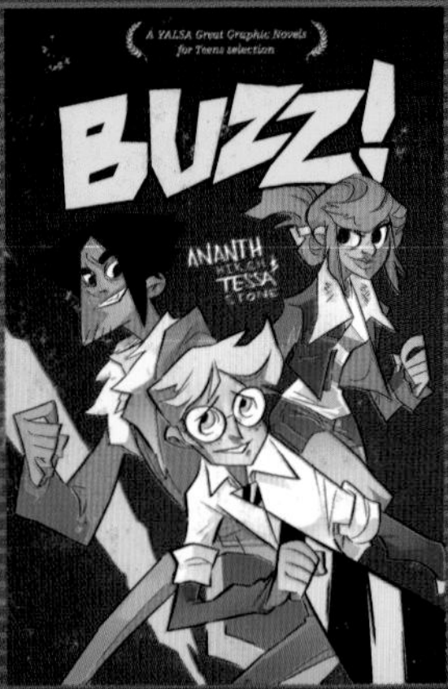
BUZZ!
ANANTH HIRSH
TESSA STONE

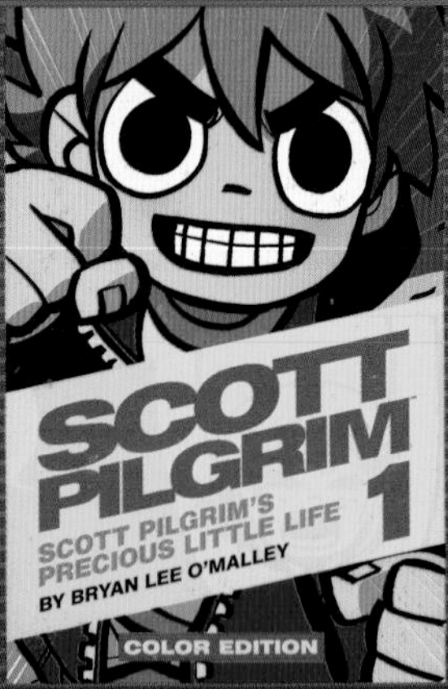
SCOTT PILGRIM 1
SCOTT PILGRIM'S PRECIOUS LITTLE LIFE
BY BRYAN LEE O'MALLEY
COLOR EDITION

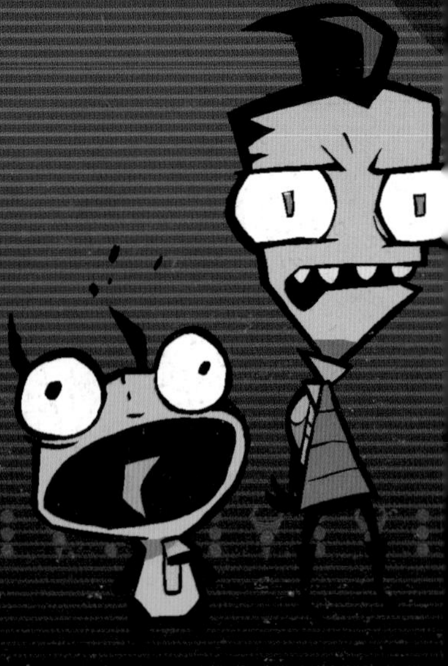